HAMMURABI'S DAGGER

JAY P. COOPER

Sea King
PRESS

This book is a work of fiction. Names, characters, places, and incidents are the product of the author's imagination or are used fictitiously. Any resemblance to actual events, locales, or persons, living or dead, is coincidental.

Published by Sea King Press, Corona del Mar, California
seakingpress@gmail.com

Sea King
PRESS

Cover Design: Eula Palmer

Printed in the United States of America

First Edition 2012

ISBN 978-0-615-70787-7

ACKNOWLEDGEMENTS

I began writing this book in the early 1990s, veered off to write a few short stories, and continually avoided finishing the book. Throughout this time, my dear friend Ruth Silver encouraged me to go back and do it. I am grateful for her persistent encouragement. I also want to thank my friends Barry Michaelson and Dennis Klarin for trying to tempt me to complete it by promising investments. With Barry it was 37 cents up front; with Dennis, a percentage after 100,000 are sold. Such optimism! I extend thanks to Judy Artunian who completed the first edit, providing all the punctuation I carelessly left out, and to Nancy Rayl for her constructive comments. My sincere gratitude goes to my wife, Judy, a writer herself, for her attempt at a final edit and for, after giving up, finding me the talented editor Anne Marie Welsh who did an excellent job when, by this time, my tired old eyes no longer permitted me to work the text. And finally, my thanks to my daughter Beth, son Bryan, family and friends who have waited patiently all these years for it to be published.

PROLOGUE

THREE WEEKS IN SEPTEMBER

In the early twentieth century, a German former patent clerk named Albert Einstein, using a concept called quantum physics, developed the universal theory of relativity. It forever changed human concepts of space and time. Until then, the popular premise was that present time was only NOW: The past existed in history, the future only in imagination. Einstein changed that.

Some scholars, many of them physicists, now liken time to a circular dimension in which past and future continue to flow like energy waves, but on different circular tracks and in a dimension separate from the present. They insist these energy waves bend and, at times, warp. They hint at a phenomenon called parallel universes, where similar but separate dimensions exist side by side.

A small minority of these scholars ardently believes that the fabric surrounding those separate dimensions can be penetrated and that time travel in either direction is possible. For some inexplicable reason there are a few people who can, for an infinitesimal breath of time, perceive the past as momentary reality or actually glimpse the future. These people, and we know not how or why, are somehow able to pierce the veil, and if only briefly, make the trip.

In Pittsburgh, Pennsylvania, in early fall of 1955, a series of strange events occurred which have never been satisfactorily explained. These events involved a number of people. Most of the individuals concerned deny to this day that anything out of the ordinary ever happened. They laugh at the popular myth that the old county jailhouse had spawned the phenomenon. The jailhouse was a forbidding, Victorian stone fortress, since torn down. This citadel of justice blocked the western exit to the downtown area and for decades inhibited commercial development.

A few old-time Pittsburghers claim that some of the black sandstone bricks in the northern wall of the jailhouse were imported from the Holy Land and were actually a part of the ancient wall of the Temple Mount in Jerusalem. They point as proof to the huge brass plate on the northern wall on which is inscribed the complete text of the Ten Commandments. Some of the more senior guards still talk of restless souls that roamed the old county prison: spirits of those, they say, who died in terrible agony and suffering during the great siege of Jerusalem in 70 C.E. Most realists chuckle at this kind of ridiculous talk.

But notwithstanding the skeptics and the irreligious scoffers, the fact remains that for three weeks in September 1955, time seemed to stand still and a mystery unfolded, many aspects of which, over half a century later, remain unsolved.

It began during the stifling heat of late August. The last gasp of what had been a particularly muggy summer held the city in a suffocating grip. On a Monday morning, Pittsburghers awoke to a *Post Gazette* headline that chilled even the most cold-blooded and heartless among them.

A dual murder had occurred at the Carnegie Museum. Two guards had died in what reporters were calling a ruthless sacrificial murder.

CHAPTER 1

THE FIRST WEEK, EARLY SEPTEMBER 1955
THE CARNEGIE MELLON MUSEUM, PITTSBURGH

On a pleasant Saturday afternoon in early September, a group of faithful parishioners from a nearby Catholic church attended an outing at the local Carnegie Museum. They were led by a priest whose forte was liturgical history. An assistant curator who was introduced as an archeologist, an expert on early Middle Eastern history, accompanied him. The group focused their attention on early Christian artifacts. Most of the items were on loan from the British Museum and had come from Mesopotamia, an area known in ancient history as the Fertile Crescent. This was where Western recorded history is deemed to have originated.

Among the visitors was Sal Dematteo, a young Italian-American lawyer. He wandered, completely bored, with the church group among the rows of glass cases. His mind jumped from football to his latest forays in the legal arena, to the marvelous sexual experience of the night before with his wife. He dutifully followed her, as she listened raptly to the priest and the curator who explained in copious detail the symbolic meanings of the many carved vessels and finely wrought jewelry they were viewing. At times, he watched her body. He thoroughly enjoyed the way it moved. Two-thousand-year-old pieces of junk failed to distract him. But Catherine's presence was enough to stimulate more immediate senses. The lawyer was totally unaware that he was being observed closely by a large, rather stout man wearing almost impenetrable glasses and a heavy plaid sweater—excess clothes for such a warm day.

The curator had paused at one of the glass exhibit cases. He began recounting the story of one of the artifacts. The case housed a gold dagger with a sapphire on the handle. "This is a ceremonial dagger, steeped in legend and mysticism, a priceless object," he said. "It is reputed to have originally belonged to the famous Babylonian lawgiver, Hammurabi, a gift of tribute from the King of Lydia." He leaned closer to the case. "It left a bloody trail across ancient history that ended with the fall of Jerusalem in the year 70 of the Common Era. For several centuries it had resided in the Holy of Holies sanctuary in the Hebrew temple in Jerusalem."

He went on to say that Cyrus, the great Persian emperor, gave it to the Jewish high priest when the Jewish tribes were permitted to return from exile in Babylonia.

"During the great Jewish war of the first century C.E.," he continued, glancing at his audience to determine interest, "after the Romans destroyed and sacked Herod's temple, it disappeared. It mysteriously turned up in 1850 in a shop in Damascus where it was purchased by a Lord Carrington for the British Museum. If anyone is interested in the tale of this bloody dagger, it is a part of my Ph.D. thesis," the curator closed with a smile. "Don't fail to read it, folks. It should be published within a few months."

As the lawyer absentmindedly gazed at the dagger it seemed to take on an inordinate bright gleam. For a few seconds he thought it actually flickered as if illuminated by some inner fire. He blinked his eyes. The brilliant light was gone. And just as quickly, the incident was completely lost to his conscious mind. To a person whose prime interests were criminal law, sports, his family and sex with his wife, ancient history had little if any connection with his life.

The stout man also stopped by the same case and stared at the dagger for several minutes, perhaps infatuated by its glow. His eyes followed the lawyer when he went outside on the balcony and lit a cigarette. The stout man continued to scrutinize the lawyer for some time through a large plate glass door. Then he wheeled around and left the area.

As the lawyer puffed on the cigarette his eyes fastened on a large statue of a marching soldier in the center of the spacious plaza below, a hero from a long-past war. For the wink of an eye he saw a long line of marching soldiers, clad in armor with gleaming spears and swords. This massive force covered the entire plaza. At the far end he saw a great victory arch. Behind it loomed the magnificent pillared Temple of Jupiter. Soldiers in the lines were shouting in unison, words that sounded like "Hail Titus." With a shrug of his head he idly dismissed this brief visual interlude.

Too damned much religion for one day, he thought. He was interrupted by a familiar voice. It was his wife. She advised him that the tour was over and it was time to leave. In less than an hour he would pop his first beer of the day.

CHAPTER 2

A FEW DAYS BEFORE, ON THE LAST MONDAY IN AUGUST
PITTSBURGH

The Pittsburgh Metropolitan combined law enforcement committee met on the last Monday in August. An executive member of each agency, a rank and file force member who had a current and important case, and a couple of lawyers from the county District Attorney's office attended.

The committee was the brainchild of Captain Andy Seiler who believed that if the various area law enforcement entities communicated and exchanged information on a regular basis, it might improve the quality and effectiveness of law enforcement in Allegheny County. It was a radical idea that Andy had implemented while a lieutenant in the military police in Germany in 1945. His idea had been strongly resisted by the old guard in the police force, but the new mayor—an anomaly in the political community who was not, to the surprise of the stultified hierarchy, immune to new ideas—had backed Andy's idea.

This morning they were meeting in the FBI office in the Federal Building. The windows in the small conference room were wide open. The air conditioning was broken and the August humidity was at its normal sweltering end of the summer high. Coats were hung on the back of chairs, guns were hung on hooks on the wall, ties were open at the collar and some of the more portly attendees were already beginning to sweat.

Bert Williams, FBI Special Agent in charge of the Pittsburgh office, had just made a presentation on the ten most wanted criminals and finished a short briefing on the local Communist party activities. Some of the group was nodding off and others smothered yawns.

Andy Seiler, chairing the meeting, gulped a glass of ice water and called on Ed Flaharty, a senior detective from the Oakland district. Ed looked like a cop. His blonde, closely cropped hair, slim spare body and face like the map of Ireland marked him as a minion of the law. Ed was about to wake up the authorities. He rose and strode listlessly up to the blackboard and pulled down a rolled up relief map of the county.

"We've had two murders in the last two weeks. Three days apart." His laconic pronouncement did little to stir any interest. Murder was not a stranger to this group. He pointed at a spot on the map. "Both homicides occurred here. Both were Carnegie Museum guards. Both bodies were found in the parking lot behind the museum."

"What was it, Ed?" Larry Carter, an assistant D.A. in the county was interested. "Robbery? Museum guards, they never have any valuables on them. These guys earn nothing."

"Not robbery. Their wallets were intact."

"Then what?" chimed in Marvin Marx, another county D.A. "Random murders, some nut have it in for museum guards?"

"I might agree with that premise except for one key point," said Flaharty.

"Okay, Ed, don't keep us in suspense." Jerome Becker, a sergeant from Andy Seiler's elite Metro force and the only black member of the group, had a quizzical look on his face. "What's peculiar about these killings? You got something odd going on here?"

Jerome was well known for his remarkable intuition. It had propelled him from a beat cop to a Metro sergeant in five short years.

"Both men were killed by a very sharp, thin knife, like an ice pick."

"Okay," nodded Marx. "So it's the same guy."

"Worse, both corpses had one wound in the back of the neck, in the exact same spot and both corpses were in the same position, flat on their backs, with their arms folded across their chest," said Flaharty.

"Jesus," muttered Jerome, "ritual murders."

"Ritual murders," echoed Marvin Marx.

After the meeting, Larry Carter and Marvin Marx walked out together. They stopped to chat with Mike Cormier, the Assistant Federal D.A.

"What's your take?" queried Cormier. "Murder cult?"

"Possibly," agreed Marx.

"Sounds like a fairy tale to me." Carter chuckled. "You guys are reading too many mystery stories. Some crazy with an ice pick. Not our problem till they find the guy."

The other two men shrugged.

Jerome Becker, his six-foot-three frame towering over Ed Flaharty, was most concerned about the incidents. He accompanied Flaharty down the stairs where they stopped at the small snack bar in the lobby and got coffee.

Jerome put two dashes of cream in his coffee. "I like it white," he quipped.

"I like mine black," Flaharty smiled. "Jerome, what the hell do you think?"

"Don't have to be a brain surgeon. It has to do with the museum."

"That's what I think."

"Let's put an undercover man out there." Becker blew on his coffee. "Harry Abrams is perfect. He could pose as anyone, from a plumber to a senior curator."

"I'd appreciate that," said Flaharty. "Best cover would be to make him a guard."

"Good idea. He'll be in place tomorrow."

The two men shook hands. Becker looked around for the parking elevator. He spotted it. An afterthought occurred to him. "Checked out the roster of former guards yet?"

"We're working it," Flaharty said. "Nothing yet."

Ed Flaharty headed for the front lobby door. Outside he ran into Marvin Marx. His face was tilted upward in a curious posture, gazing at the front façade of the Federal Building.

"Look at that statue of the eagle. Looks like it's ready to fly away." He glanced at Flaharty. "What are you guys doing about the museum thing?"

"We're putting an undercover guy out there." Flaharty tried to catch his words. If you told people you had someone undercover at a site, then chances are the guy's cover would be blown. "This is confidential, you understand."

"Sure, sure," agreed Marx. "Mum's the word."

As Flaharty walked slowly up Seventh Avenue toward the police parking lot, he was acutely aware of the humidity. He also felt uneasy. He had just violated cardinal police procedure. He told an outsider about an undercover operation. True, the guy was a D.A., but lawyers talked too much. Well, probably no harm done. As he rounded the corner Marx was still staring upward at the winged sculpture. What the hell, Flaharty thought, is so damn interesting about that bird?

CHAPTER 3

THE FIRST WEEK, EARLY SEPTEMBER 1955
PITTSBURGH OFFICE OF ANTONIO SALVATORE DEMATTEO

The Grant Building stood like a giant sentinel overlooking the Allegheny River. It defiantly faced Mount Washington and proclaimed proudly that it was the tallest building in the city of Pittsburgh. In 1955, with the Westinghouse KDKA antenna astride its pinnacle, it had no peer in the Golden Triangle.

Antonio Dematteo stared silently out the grimy window of his fifteenth-floor office. Rain splashed against the window, a steady staccato that hypnotized him as he watched the late afternoon commuters crawl along Grant Street toward the Boulevard of the Allies and the Liberty Bridge. Their headlights, moving at a barely perceptible pace in the gathering dusk, were like predatory monsters seeking helpless victims. The day was warm; the penetrating chill that perennially pervaded the city as winter approached was still absent. The inhabitants of the Steel City could look forward to at least a month of Indian Summer before gloom, dirt-covered slush and clumsy galoshes intruded on their lives.

Sal, as he was called by his friends, or Antonio Salvatore, as his diminutive, sainted mother had named him, should have been concentrating on the Feeney case, but he was clearly preoccupied. Tom Feeney, a guy from the neighborhood, had been charged with second-degree murder. A brawl in a bar, and somehow somebody died from a blow to the head; he'd been struck by a beer bottle that shattered his skull. Tom's brother, Jack, a good friend, had called him to take the case. He never liked Tom, too volatile and stupid, a prize asshole. But, there were some cases you had to take.

Father O'Malley had called, too. "You're not supposed to like your clients," he pontificated. "Just defend them to the best of your ability. He's from the neighborhood."

What the hell was so sacred about the neighborhood? A few square miles of substandard housing, where a motley assortment of human beings of diverse origin lived, worked, made love, bore babies, got sick, prayed, argued, laughed, cried, urinated and died. It was the six-foot-two frame of Father O'Malley towering over the neighborhood that made the difference. He was a giant guardian of the faith who converted the area into a special parish.

There were things he had to do. Get Abe Fulton to investigate. Get statements from the witnesses before the D.A. got to them. Call Cavanaugh at the clerk's office to see if he could get the right judge for the bail hearing. The cigarette in his left hand had a half-inch of ash on the end. He needed to turn on a light, but he couldn't rouse himself. It had just happened again. It was happening more and more frequently. At first, there were very brief flashes that crossed his conscious mind, only at night. He thought they were dreams, random without rhyme or reason. Then recently they were interrupting his thoughts, invading his conscious mind. Events that had no relationship to his life or to anything he had ever experienced. Troubling, violent scenes, shouting, screaming in strange languages that, to his shock, he understood.

What the hell was happening? Was he cracking up?

There was no insanity in his family. He had served in Korea but his unit, a signal corps company, had seen little action. He returned a first lieutenant. He suffered no ostensible trauma. He sat for the Pennsylvania bar exam and passed the first time. He married Catherine Kowalczyk, a nice Northside Polish-Catholic girl, and in two years had bred a daughter. He joined in a law partnership with two guys from school and built a fairly thriving law practice. He played softball, drank and smoked moderately, was in a Friday night poker club and went to church on Sundays. He loved his Polish wife. His sex life was good and his daughter was flourishing.

Sal's father, Frank Dematteo, a plumbing contractor, raised his two boys and a daughter as strict Catholics. Frank had city connections and got contracts. He was participating in the American dream. His mother, Angela Dematteo, was a decent woman who loved her religion and her children. She was a great cook. Initially she had doubts about Catherine, but she resolved them by assuring herself that Catherine, while not a nice Italian girl, was a nice Catholic girl. All totaled, Antonio S. Dematteo had a functional childhood and a normal, balanced family life.

The dreams, or delusions or whatever the hell they were, had begun a couple of weeks ago. At first, not very often. Last week, while on the courthouse steps, something strange, almost chilling, had occurred. He had argued a discovery motion before Judge Caplan. It had gone pretty well. He was leaving the courthouse and found himself in what appeared to be an open plaza of some sort. There were statues and stone columns at the front of the courthouse. There were people in strange clothing that draped over them like curtains. They were speaking a foreign language, which he recognized but couldn't place. He remembered there were horses and buggies—no they were chariots—driving along on Grant Street. But it wasn't Grant Street. The vision was fleeting and passed. He was sure he had imagined it. Maybe a flashback from a movie. He tried to shrug it off.

Then, twice more, something similar happened. The second incident was the most vivid and disturbing. It had happened this afternoon. Sal was sitting in his office reviewing some statements on an embezzlement matter. A well-known bank manager had systematically looted his bank. It was a tough case, but there was fancy Fox Chapel-area money for a retainer. Sal was alone. It was three o'clock in the afternoon. He had begun staring at the clock on his bookcase. It disappeared and the office was on fire. He was in a huge burning building. There were people screaming in agony. Other people were wielding swords and spears and killing indiscriminately. He was crouched over a dying man. An old man was dressed in an ornate gold costume soaked red with his own blood. He had piercing eyes. Like hot coals. Sal was in the iron grip of this dying man. The old man spoke to him in an unfamiliar language. But the voice was loud and commanding and he understood. He was being given an order, a direct command, to kill someone. It sounded as if the man had said, "You must kill your brother!" The vision faded.

Less than four minutes had passed. The clock read 3:04. Sal, dizzy, and damp with sweat, shook his head trying to clear his thoughts. He went outside the office. The waiting room was empty. Janet and Margie, their two secretaries, were both typing. Janet looked up. "Hi, Mr. Dematteo, you okay?"

"Yeah, sure, I must be getting the flu. I'm sweating. I don't know why."

"Take an aspirin, you will feel better." She smiled.

"Yeah," he muttered, shaking his head again.

Sal went to the water cooler and took a long drink. He resolved to talk to somebody. But who? Father O'Malley? It's not likely he would understand. A psychiatrist, maybe, but he'll think I'm nuts. Maybe I am. But I know this is happening. My brother? Fat chance that goof could suggest anything positive. Anyway, his brother was off somewhere flying jets for the Air Force. He settled on David Gold, his partner. But the time had to be right. Maybe it would go away or stop or something. Maybe he needed an exorcist! What made him think of an exorcist? He went back into his office and stood at the window.

Sal and David had been friends and neighbors for many years. They had gone to Pitt law school together and cemented their close friendship in their first year. With Ed Finneran, another classmate, they formed a study group that had survived three grueling years of law school. David was a good kid with a sense of humor and a sharp business mind. They nursed each other through school. All three passed the bar the first time. Sal's mother liked David. He was a nice Jewish boy and he loved her meatballs. "Mrs. Demattao," he would say, "your meatballs are from heaven, so you must be an angel." "Oh!" she would say, "if he was only Italian, he'd be a real catch for my daughter Josephine."

The insistent buzzing in his ear demanded his attention. It awoke him from his reverie. He flipped on the intercom. "Yes, what is it, Janet?"

"It's your wife."

"Thanks, uh, is Mr. Gold in the office?"

"Yes, he's here."

"Good, you about ready to leave?" He noticed it was five o'clock. The electric clock provided a beacon of light in what he now realized was a dark room. He had lost almost two hours in a deep and concentrated stream of consciousness. A whole afternoon and no recollection of any logical thoughts. Just a mass of confused disorder.

"Yes, sir," she answered. "I'm out of here. By the way, I buzzed you a couple of times and you didn't answer. I have a couple of messages for you. I figured you were busy. Nothing urgent. Need anything else?"

"No, thanks, Janet. See you tomorrow."

"Tomorrow's Saturday."

"Oh right, uh, see you Monday. Have a nice weekend."

"Thanks."

He flipped to Catherine. "Hi honey, how are you?" He listened and nodded. "Makes sense. Poker game has been called off. I'll see you in about an hour. Love ya, kid. Kiss the baby."

Sal hung up and looked at her picture. A smiling, well-endowed girl with blue eyes and short blonde hair. Three hard-ass beer drinking brothers, but she was their antithesis. A good mother and a loyal wife. What the hell was his problem? Why was this stuff happening? What if it manifested itself in court or in bed during sex? Was he possessed? Did he really need a priest? My God, where are these people from? Who are they?

He went through the deserted waiting room and knocked lightly on David's door. "Hey, David, you there?"

"I don't know," came the answer. "It's Friday night and I'm in the Oliver Grill drinking a martini. Come on in."

Sal pensively opened the door and stepped into David Gold's half-darkened office.

CHAPTER 4

THE FIRST WEEK
OFFICE OF DAVID GOLD, PITTSBURGH

In 1955, Pittsburgh was a typical Midwest industrial town. The city was perched at the confluence of the Allegheny and Monongahela Rivers, where the Ohio River began its long, weary journey, via the Mississippi River, to New Orleans and the sea. The river was lined with legions of smokestacks that daily belched choking fire and smoke, the product of giant sites that boasted names like Carnegie/Illinois and Jones & Laughlin.

During World War II, untold tons of steel had poured out of these factories to feed a war machine that needed tanks, airplanes, guns, ships, jeeps and weapons in quantities so vast that in 1940 the first American draftees, who drilled with broomsticks and dropped practice flour bombs on simulated tanks, could not in their most exaggerated dreams have imagined. Pittsburgh was a melting pot of eastern and western European culture. There were Eastern Orthodox Greeks, Slavs and Russians; Germans, Pollacks, Italians, Czechs and Irish Catholics, every manner and facet of the Protestant church, and Jewish synagogues and temples dotting the city. There were the white Baptists in Mt. Lebanon and the black Baptists in the Hill district.

The city was blessed with the Pittsburgh Pirates baseball team and the Pitt Panthers football team everybody loved. Then there was the new postwar professional team called the Steelers; everyone wanted to love them, too, but had their doubts.

The city had electric streetcars that charged up and down the main avenues. Noisy monsters that shook and clanked and carried tired workers to and from the downtown area. A couple of miles east of the University of Pittsburgh, Andrew Carnegie had generously endowed a small prestigious school called the Carnegie Institute of Technology. It adjoined the Carnegie Museum, which was housed in a sprawling, two-story, stone building, and had achieved world-class status. It boasted a well-stocked public library and a spectacular range of exhibits that carried visitors through a time tunnel that began with the Mesozoic dinosaur age and ended with the technological wonders of the twentieth century.

Into this historic city inhabited by a vibrant and varied mass of humanity, on June 23rd 1926, three years before the Great Depression wrecked the economy, a son, David Martin Gold, was born to Myra and Samuel Gold. He was named David after his paternal grandfather and Martin after his mother's dominant and imposing father.

While growing up David was an enigma to his family. A kid with an irrepressible urge to joke around, he was constantly being disciplined in school. In short, he was the class clown and neither Myra nor Samuel appreciated this role for their son. Both were serious people. David grew up in what was characterized as a Jewish neighborhood. Those "other people," as they were called by his grandmother, were regarded with suspicion and dread. It was a sad legacy from Eastern Europe. However, his viewpoint changed drastically in junior high school when he sat next to a kid named Coletta. They became close buddies. In 1942, an Italian family named Dematteo moved down the street. A boy, one year older than David, and two sisters—both of whom liked the little husky Jewish kid with his wacky humor—became his friend. David's friendship with Salvatore Dematteo was a close one. For several years he was invited to spend Christmas Eve with the Dematteo family. He ate ham and ravioli and drank "dago red" wine. Josephine, Sal's youngest sister, would embarrass him with kisses under the mistletoe. At fifteen, David had a definite longing for Josephine, which often manifested itself at home in bed. This also deeply embarrassed him. He liked Italians. They were like a second family to him and the girls were uninhibited, or so it seemed.

Becoming a lawyer had been an afterthought. In 1950, through luck, he had avoided a short and miserable career as a rifleman in Korea by joining an Air National Guard unit, the 112th, which was not called to Federal service. In 1951 he entered the University of Pittsburgh law school. A year later his friend Sal returned from Korea and also registered in the same class. Sal and David stumbled through two more years of agonizing study, both expecting to be washed out each semester. It never happened. They kept averting disaster by two or three percentage points. David and Sal graduated and sat for the Pennsylvania bar examination. While working as a clerk typist for his Air Guard unit, David was advised in a random telephone call from a friend that his name was in the local legal journal under a heading titled "Passed the 1954 Bar." Sal's name was also, mercifully, on the same list. A few months later, Sal and David formed a law firm with Ed Finneran. The three men addressed different areas of the law and proved to be a trio who complemented each other in a number of ways, including temperaments, contacts and clients.

Sal entered the office of David Gold. Short, at 5-foot-8-inches, with a stocky body and feet outstretched on the desk, he was smoking a rather large cigar. David was reading a newspaper, his face swathed in a swirl of smoke. He continued to stare at the paper.

"Did you know," he said, "that Skinny Reagan might get indicted? The crazy bastard has been kiting checks at his law firm. What is wrong with these guys? Are they losing it?"

"I hadn't heard," Sal retorted tersely.

"How's the Feeney case?" Nose still buried in the paper. "Walter's little brother was always a loser. You know some guys are just headed for—"

"David, I need to talk to you." Sal sounded a bit urgent. "Not about the Feeney case."

David quickly glanced up. "What's up, Sal?"

Sal was lighting a cigarette. "I need to counter that cigar. It's a foul piece of shit. It smells bad and it pollutes the air." Sal nervously fumbled with his matches.

David smiled. "It's the result of oral deprivation. My mother put me on the bottle too soon. Ask Dr. Freud, he agrees with me."

Then he noticed Sal's apprehensive demeanor. "Something on your mind, counselor? What is going on?"

"Look," Sal blurted out, "do you believe in past lives? Do you think that we may have lived before? Do you think it's possible to get flashbacks or visions or…" Sal was almost frantic in his speech.

David stopped him. "Sure, Sal, I also believe Dorothy went over the rainbow, Ike Eisenhower will convert to the Democratic party and Irish leprechauns are really green."

"David, I'm serious. Please just shut up and listen," Sal shot back.

David Gold put his feet on the floor, dropped the newspaper on his desk, placed his cigar carefully on a large ashtray and concentrated on the agitated face of his friend. "Okay, Sal," he said evenly. "Just calm down. Tell me what's bothering you."

"I don't know. I have been experiencing some kind of visions or hallucinations. They just happen and I don't understand why or what is going on."

"Dreams?"

"No, they happen during the day sometimes. I had one this afternoon. They last for a few minutes. It's like I get transported to another place."

"Jesus," muttered David, "are you serious? Any trouble at home?"

"No! Catherine's an angel."

"I agree, you got the best looking and best wife in the office."

"You're not married, David, neither is Finneran."

"I know, Sal, but if we were, you would still have the best looking wife in the office."

David kept looking at Sal intently, trying to snap him back to reality.

Sal slumped into a chair. "David, for several weeks I have been having glimpses into God knows where. It's beginning to happen more often. I had an incident this afternoon at three o'clock. It lasted four minutes. Then I stared out the window for two hours. I don't know what's going on!"

"Have you discussed this with anyone else?"

"No, no one. I've thought about a psychiatrist or Father O'Malley."

"Can you describe one of these incidents to me?"

"Well, this afternoon ... for Christ's sake don't laugh or I'll punch your lights out!"

David was not smiling. "I assure you I will give you my undivided attention."

David was concerned. He knew his friend well enough to recognize some grave symptoms. Sal Dematteo was not yanking his chain. Something was disturbing him. Maybe more than disturbing, frightening was a more accurate description. My God, he thought, Sal is really scared.

"Well, I believed I was in a burning building. A huge structure with great stone pillars. There was a lot of killing going on, a terrible massacre."

"What kind of weapons?" David asked. The cross-examiner was taking over.

"Spears, swords, daggers, some of the soldiers carried shields. I was crouched over a dying old man dressed in a flowing ornate costume. But it was soaked in his blood."

"How do you know he was dying?"

"I could see it in his eyes. They were angry, blazing with fury. Like a light bulb about to burn out." Sal was getting caught up. "He was shouting a command at me. He had my arm in a vise grip. I couldn't break loose. I tried."

"You mean you could actually feel him?"

"Yes."

"How about the fire?"

Sal's voice cracked. "I could feel the fire. It was like a torch on my skin."

"Tell me what he said." David felt his flesh tingle. Sal was back in the burning building. He had better get him out.

Sal was staring into space. "He spoke in a foreign language but I understood him. He said my brother was a traitor. He ordered me to avenge his terrible act. God wills it. I have to kill him with a dagger. He gave me a dagger, recited a prayer in the same strange language and then he died."

"Can you describe the dagger?"

Sal didn't hesitate even to contemplate the question. "Yes, it was unusual—gold, with an intricate design and a blue jewel on the handle where you grip it."

"Do you remember the prayer?"

"Not completely, but the first two words were… Let's see. They were something like 'Muh isrol'."

David Gold suddenly felt very cold. "Sal, are you sure?"

"Yes, God dammit, I am sure. You know something, David, don't you?" Sal was gazing directly at David's face. "What is it? Tell me!"

David sighed. "Were the words *shamah yisroel adonoy elohenu adonoy echod*?"

"Yeah!" shouted Sal. "That's it, David. My God, how did you know? What language is that? What does it mean?"

David rose and slowly went to the window. Far below the late afternoon gloom had become early evening darkness. The rain had become a soft patter. He gazed at the street, fifteen floors below, where hundreds of late shoppers and office workers congregated at the streetcar stops. There was a sea of umbrellas. In the lights of the city these moving forms were creeping shadows. They were ordinary people who led mundane lives. They would go home and eat Friday night dinner, grateful that tomorrow was not a work-day. The young girls would get dressed and wait for their dates or their girlfriends. They would look forward to an evening at the movies or smoking cigarettes and drinking highballs at a nearby bar. The young guys would do what young guys do: drink beer, play poker or try to get screwed. Their parents would relax by the radio or their new toy, a television set. Their concerns were simple: jobs, romance, having fun, paying bills, sickness, health or crying babies. That was the sum total of life, wasn't it? Not visions or hallucinations. He felt certain theirs was the real world. A few feet away, behind him, Sal waited.

David Gold rubbed his chin. For the first time in his life he had heard something that truly startled him, no, more than startled him. He felt the compelling draw of an ancient force that echoed through the ages. How could this man have heard this prayer? How could he describe this knife in such profuse detail? The product of an Italian Catholic family, a hardheaded kid who grew up brawling on the streets. The son of a building contractor with suspected mob connections. He couldn't grasp the scenario. It was just too bizarre, plain impossible.

"Sal, do you know or have you ever studied Hebrew?"

"No," Sal answered emphatically, "never. I never heard a Hebrew word spoken let alone studied it. I was never in a Jewish synagogue. I don't know a word of Hebrew."

"Sal, what you just repeated was the holiest of the holy prayers of the ancient Hebrews. Translated it means 'Hear O Israel, The Lord Is God, The Lord Is One'."

"I knew that," rasped Sal. "I knew it before you said it."

CHAPTER 5

THE FIRST WEEK, SATURDAY
PITT STADIUM

Pitt Stadium was a huge concrete bowl, perched on a hill, overlooking the city of Pittsburgh. It was at the end of a steep street, almost vertical, called Chesterfield Road. In the fall, during football season, thousands of fans who wouldn't pay the parking fee of three dollars or didn't want to get trapped in the after-the-game traffic jam trooped up the hill to watch their beloved Panthers engage in a slam bang, gladiatorial contest with a team from another Big Ten university. Today, the game of games was being unveiled. The University of Pittsburgh's famed Panthers vs. the vaunted Pennsylvania State Nittany Lions, an ancient rivalry of two football giants.

Catherine Dematteo was an avid football fan. It was one of the traits that Sal loved about his wife. This usually gentle girl would get so involved that certain ordinarily prohibited, graphically descriptive words would unabashedly flow forth from her. Her eyes would get slightly wild and, when the home team scored a touchdown, she would rise to her feet and excitedly beat on Sal's head. Her conduct was probably the result of being raised with three brothers, two of whom played football in both high school and college. Her older brother, Stan, had guarded left tackle for the University of Pittsburgh for three bruising years.

On this clear, brisk fall afternoon, Catherine was in a particularly hyper state. The Pitt marching band, with military precision, made its usual stirring entrance. French horns, trumpets, tubas and drums blasted the air. The "Star Spangled Banner" was broadcasting its moving patriotic message. The kickoff was about to take place. Catherine was so intent on the game that she failed to notice Sal's extremely restrained state. He had been distant and aloof the night before, but she attributed it to the fatigue of a busy week, a caseload that included the difficult Feeney murder case in which Father O'Malley had taken a personal interest.

Penn State won the toss and elected to kick off. The whistle blew, the ball sailed into the air and eleven human Penn State tanks rolled down the field toward the Pitt team, hoping to catch the receiver of the ball and nail him permanently to the earth, with as much violence as the referees would allow.

* * * *

Sal stared intently at the field, but he wasn't seeing a football game.

The twenty-two men on the field were assaulting each other with an assortment of weapons that included spears, nets, pitchforks and swords. One huge dark man drove a spear completely through the upper torso of another large, bearded man. The man screamed in pain and fell to the ground, a lifeless bloody body. Another heavy-set man in a leopard skin hovered over a fat older man with a large broadsword over his head, poised to strike the other, who cowered in fear and shielded his face with his hands. The executioner paused and looked to the audience for guidance. The exultant onlookers in the vast stone coliseum, wild with the smell of blood, cried "Death," almost in unison, thumbs on both hands clearly pointing downward. It was a gesture of vengeance for this warrior's cowardly performance.

A hand touched him. He glanced to his right. A beautiful young woman with long flowing black hair implored him with her dark eyes to stop the slaughter. She knew he couldn't. She whispered his name. He grasped her hand tightly and felt great empathy for her gentle, tortured soul.

****

"P, I, OVER HERE! T, T, OVER HERE." Five girls, dressed in short blue skirts, waving golden pompoms enthusiastically organized a cheer. "P I T T!" the crowd responded in unison with equal fervor.

The first quarter had ended and the teams were changing goals. The score was tied: Pitt, six; Penn State, six. Both teams had scored and aborted the extra point conversion.

Sal was aware that he had somehow missed an entire quarter. Over thirty or more minutes of his life had been somehow lost. The dark-haired girl with the straight classic features and haunting expressive eyes had turned into Catherine. Her azure blue eyes were looking at Sal with genuine concern. He was gripping her hand.

"What is it, Sal? What's wrong?"

"I don't know. I feel a little funny." He rose. "I'm going to get a drink. I'll be right back."

"Are you all right?"

"Yeah, yeah, I'm fine. I just need to go to the latrine."

"Maybe Stush should go with you." She nudged her brother who was busy arguing with his Buddy Charley Krantz over the merits of calling a center plunge rather than an off-tackle play. Catherine nudged him again. On the third and significantly harder nudge, he turned.

"Yeah, can't you see Charley and I are having an important discussion here?"

"It's Sal, he doesn't feel well and he's going to the bathroom alone. Maybe you better go along."

Stan looked disgusted. "Fine, I'll hold his hand. Cathy, give him an enema and a beer when you get home and he'll be fine."

When she turned, Sal had already left and was hurrying up the steps toward the exit ramp. About twenty rows up, immediately above the exit ramp, smoking his characteristic cigar, he saw a comforting sight. It was David. He was laughing heartily at something Irv Greene had just said. Irv was also grinning widely. Sal climbed a couple more rows, circled the ramp and paused next to David.

"Hey, Sal," said David, acknowledging his partner, "great game so far."

"David," Sal said softly in David's ear, "it happened again."

"Oh Christ, when?"

"A few minutes ago. I missed the entire first quarter." Sal's face was grim, his eyes dark, disturbed.

David Gold gripped his friend's arm. "Hey, Sal, take it easy. I'm playing racquetball tomorrow with Max Vogel. He will help us get to the bottom of what's going on here. But Sal, you got to promise to cooperate. Meantime, calm down, buddy. Have a beer and relax."

The crowd was cheering wildly. Sal and David turned to watch the game. Penn State's quarterback, Lon Chernowski, threw a long pass. Jack Felzer, Pitt's defensive left halfback, jumped high in the air and intercepted it on the Pittsburgh ten-yard line. Feltzer made it to the twenty-five before three Nittany Lions dumped him to the turf. The ref's whistle was blowing a shrill message that piling on had occurred and a penalty was in order. The Penn State fans had risen to their feet and were booing loudly. But their feeble protests were drowned out by the cacophony of Pitt fans who also were also on their feet, supporting both the interception and the call.

"I'll cooperate," promised Sal. "Whatever Max thinks I need to do."

"Don't worry," called David, "help is on the way." David watched his friend wend his way downward toward his seat.

As Sal returned to his seat, he calmed himself. Seeing and talking to David had restored him to the reality of a raucous football game.

"What's with Sal?" asked Irv. "He looks a little shook up."

"I wish I knew, Irving my boy. I wish I knew." He looked forward to his racquetball game and breakfast with Dr. Vogel the following day. I hope, he reflected, Max has some good ideas. If he doesn't, I'm damn well out of court.

Sal sat down next to Cathy and kissed her on the cheek. She smiled. His color was better. But still, something was definitely wrong. For the past week he just had not been himself. She had given it a lot of thought. There was only one person who she could talk to about this matter. Was it another woman? She had heard about things like this happening. But not so soon in the marriage. His indifference, his strange silences, his restlessness at night in bed. Perhaps she was failing as a wife. Tomorrow she would make an appointment with Father O'Malley. She knew he could help. She loved Sal so much. She was trying so hard to please him. She felt empty and frightened, as if she were peering at her husband over a deep, ominous chasm and she could not reach him.

CHAPTER 6

THE SECOND WEEK, SUNDAY

Every Sunday morning, rain, shine, snow, ice, blood or mud, Dr. Max Vogel and David Gold played racquetball at the local Y Athletic Club (provided they were both in town). After they sweated off a few calories they brunched across the street at the Webster Hall Hotel and added far more calories than they had shed. It was David's concession to luxury dining after years of twenty-five cent White Castle hamburgers and canned soups. That excluded, of course, the meals his mother fed him which, he conceded, were also fatty, tasty and filling. The Y was located in the Oakland area, almost directly across the street from the University of Pittsburgh with its thirty-four story Cathedral of Learning, a massive Gothic edifice, that loomed like a phallic symbol in the cultural center of the city.

H.J. Heinz, the ketchup and pickles magnate, had erected a non-sectarian chapel next to the cathedral. Across the road loomed Carnegie Library and Museum, another notch in old Andrew Carnegie's record give-away program, almost an apology for the dirt and smoke his steel mills had visited on the city.

Max Vogel finished drying himself and slipped into his colorful underwear. "So what is so urgent? I was planning on leaving early to have an early dinner with my mother."

"Max, you can have dinner with your mother. She loves to cook for you. A Sunday brisket, what could be more tasty?" David was smiling broadly. "Furthermore, Dr. Vogel, I'm buying brunch. How can you pass that up?"

"I can't," said Vogel. "But why, Mr. Lawyer, are you spending some of your ill-gotten gains on me? I won two games today and you didn't moan. I'm a little concerned."

"I'll explain," David said soothingly. "After our first cup of coffee."

Max shrugged. He was a patient man with a copious mind, a five-foot-six frame and a barrel chest. Four years of medical school, a year interning at the Presbyterian Hospital as the token Jew, a year as a resident trainee at the Western State Psychiatric Institute, and a widowed mother who still had the first nickel his father Morris Vogel had deposited in the bank in 1938 after he opened Morry's Department Store. All of this had conditioned him to the eccentricities of the human temperament.

That morning Max was slightly more than hungry. His short stack of pancakes became a large stack, his usual one fried egg became two, and he ordered a side of bacon which was very unusual since he rarely ate pork.

David ordered grapefruit juice, two poached eggs, dry rye toast and a pot of coffee. He silently sipped the coffee and considered whether he should actually broach the subject to Max Vogel. "Max," he said, making a decision that, if not Max, then who? And if not now, when?

"David, spit it out already. You are like a boiling pot about to explode. You have been like this all morning. Your racquetball game is indifferent, you're not concentrating, you are clearly distracted, and you bought breakfast. Did you impregnate a young lady? I don't perform abortions," he explained. "They are illegal."

"No, no, hell no. Max, it's about my law partner."

"Sal or Finneran? Who is stealing from whom? Lawyers, eh!"

"Max, this has to be in the strictest confidence."

"Okay, Mr. Lawyer, but I don't enjoy the same immunities as you. You're not the patient. What is so important?"

David considered carefully how to approach a subject that was not only delicate but would sound more than a little wacky.

"Tell me, Max, do you believe in an afterlife?"

Dr. Max Vogel, a brilliant, dedicated student of Sigmund Freud and Fredrick Engel, who thoroughly believed in the science of psychotherapy, the physics of Albert Einstein and the presence of graphic sexual symbols everywhere, opened his eyes wide in surprise. Not at the substance of the question but at the fact that his penchant for reading people conveyed the message that David actually appeared sincere.

"More specifically, do you believe in past life?"

A plump waitress interrupted. "More coffee, guys?" she asked. Max nodded yes. David shook his head no. David waited until she poured, took a deep breath, sighed and continued.

"Let me give you a summary."

David told him what Sal had said. He proceeded to recount the tale of the burning building and the dying old man. He described all the circumstances, including the jeweled dagger. He did not mention the prayer. He was saving that anecdote for later, to wait for Max's reaction.

"Well, what do you think, Max? Visions? Some strange spirit? The onset of mental illness? Any ideas?"

Max was staring incredulously. "What is this, Gold? A big put on? Let's yank the doctor's chain and then we will all have a good laugh. Is it worth a four-dollar breakfast and the loss of two racquetball games?"

David shrugged. "I knew you would react like that. Max, we have known each other for twenty years. We went to grade school together. I swear on a stack of Bibles this really happened."

"David, if Sal really told you a story like that, he is suffering from a serious delusional syndrome. Past lives and afterlife are sheer bullshit. We have a hospital full of people who think they are everyone from Napoleon to Eisenhower. Some of them get messages from the devil or God. One guy is convinced he single-handedly invented the atomic bomb and is going to blow up the world. Another woman is Joan of Arc. Some have dual or triple personalities. David, Sal may be very sick or he may be retreating from the world for some subliminal reason. It sounds like he needs help."

"Okay, Max, let me give you the bottom line. At the tail end of the incident Sal restated part of a prayer he claimed the old man in the vision had recited."

"So what, the Catholics have lots of prayers."

"This is one prayer the Catholics don't recite."

"All right, David," Max was getting slightly exasperated. This joke, if it was a prank, was being stretched too far. "I'll bite; this must be the punch line. What was the prayer?"

"It was the *SH'MA*. 'Hear O Israel, The Lord Is God, The Lord Is One'."

Dr. Max Vogel wore a very strained look. He closely examined every aspect of David's demeanor.

"You are serious? Sal claims he heard an ancient Hebrew Old Testament prayer?"

"Right, and he has never been exposed to a word of Hebrew. He was never inside a temple or a synagogue. He said he knew what it meant before I translated it." David's voice had become very quiet.

"More coffee?" the plump waitress asked. She was smiling broadly, looking for a good tip.

"No," growled Max Vogel, "I've had enough."

"Sorry, mister." She wandered off in a huff.

"So, Max, what do I tell Sal? Go talk to your priest? See a psychiatrist? Forget it, this too will pass? Maybe you have the name of a good shrink I can give him. What do I do?"

Max pondered for a moment. "Can you get him to come up to the Institute?"

"Sure, I think so. When?"

Max thumbed through a mini appointment book that he retrieved from his coat pocket. "Let's see, we have patient rounds at nine and an hour staff meeting at ten. How about tomorrow morning at eleven? I'll buy you both lunch in the cafeteria."

"If you don't hear from me by ten, we will be there."

David paid the bill to the once cheery waitress, who was now not so cheery, and the two friends left the restaurant. David left a decent tip as if to apologize for Max's gruff response to the coffee query.

Outside in the cool September air, David paused at the corner and watched Max carefully cross Fifth Avenue and move down the street toward his parked his car. Traffic whizzed by, people, always in a hurry, going somewhere, some place. Rushing toward certain eternity. David was not in a hurry. He had no plans for the afternoon. He thought about some girls he might call but no one of real interest popped into his mind. But he had other options. Drop by to see his parents. Listen to Dad complain about politics and Mother complain about Dad and his habits. Call a couple of his buddies and maybe go to a movie. The latter seemed like the best idea.

He zipped open his jacket. The soft breeze sent a warm sensation through his body, still heated after the racquetball workout and the subsequent steam bath. It was two o'clock on a Sunday afternoon. The world was probably as normal as could be expected. There was no war, at least not one in which his country was involved. The University of Pittsburgh had won a big football game the day before. His Saturday night date with Vida Steinman had gone okay. He even kissed her goodnight. But not a very passionate kiss. Not a hell of a lot of chemistry there.

The Sal incident nagged at his subconscious. Either his partner, whom he had known for years, a cheerful, dark-haired Italian kid with a growing mustache and a damn good looking wife, was sinking into some sort of potentially psychotic state, or something even more incomprehensible was taking place. Either possibility seemed to forebode a dreary, depressing and perplexing future.

CHAPTER 7

THE SECOND WEEK, MONDAY
MAGGIE SEILER

The Western State Psychiatric Institute was located on a hill, next to the medical school and three blocks from Fifth Avenue, a busy main artery leading to downtown Pittsburgh. It was nestled in a hospital complex, almost in the center of the General Hospital, The Montifiore and the local Children's Hospital. The large red brick building had an austere and forbidding look, as if it held obscure secrets that could or should not be revealed.

At 10:45 on a mild Monday morning, with a hint of fall fragrance in the air, the two lawyers, neither carrying briefcases and files, the weapons of their trade, climbed up the long stone steps leading to the main entrance. Once inside, it became immediately apparent to both Sal and David that this hospital was very different from others. There was a hushed, almost reverent silence about the place. No busy doctors, nurses and orderlies charging through the antiseptic halls. No voices urgently paging doctors to surgery or other duties. No candy stripers and no persons waiting to be summoned to the side of their loved ones. The lounge was empty and so were the halls.

David approached a middle-aged woman in a white uniform who sat behind a desk with a sign that read Information.

Sal was in a state of complete denial. He had a vague notion as to why he was in a mental hospital on a Monday morning when he should be at the office working his cases. It wasn't making much sense. He felt jittery and uncomfortable.

"What the hell am I doing here, David," he muttered. "I'm too busy for this. Let's get out of here. I need to get to the office. This is ridiculous!"

"Listen, Sal." David's tone was strident. "I canceled an important business meeting because you promised me you would meet with Max. You are not backing out now. We are going upstairs."

David turned to the lone woman at the desk. "We have an eleven o'clock appointment with Dr. Vogel."

She took out what apparently was a hospital directory and answered in a very subdued voice, as if speaking in a normal tone might disturb some long-sleeping corpse. "Second floor, Room 211. Take the elevator on the right."

Sal and David found the elevator and buzzed the Up button. A nurse in a spotless white uniform, with black hair pulled up tightly in a large bun at the top of her head, carried her white cap and a file in her left hand as she joined them at the elevator.

"Good morning," she greeted them quietly, smiling.

"Morning," replied David. He couldn't help but notice her piercing dark eyes and her aquiline nose. She was a thin girl, but there was a regal, almost timeless beauty about her. He would like to know her better. She also exited on the second floor and turned to go down the hall. She glanced back at David and Sal. "Have a nice morning," she said.

"Thanks," David answered. He resolved to find out more about her from Max. David turned to Sal. His friend's gaze was riveted on the slim retreating figure of the girl.

"David, I know her. I have met her."

"Where?"

"I don't know, but I tell you, I know that girl."

"Okay, Romeo, I hear you. Let's go see Max." David was skeptical but Sal had sure been having some strange experiences. "We need to see Max."

David suddenly felt like he was being swept into a web of curious circumstances. He didn't particularly like the feeling. He sensed a certain almost morbid excitement combined with the uneasy realization that he might be entering areas that transcended anything he had ever before encountered.

Max Vogel's office had a small anteroom where patients would wait for their therapist to render august decisions on the future of their mental state. His office was relatively spare but there were two chairs, a small two-seat couch and a cheap wooden desk. The window looked out upon the surrounding city. The thirty-four-story Cathedral of Learning was in full view to the left. Max rose and shook Sal's hand. "Good to see you, Sal. Did your partner tell you I beat him twice at racquetball? It's a record for me."

Sal shook his head. "He never mentions his defeats. It's a wonderful quality that keeps his life ever a rose-colored dream."

"Sit down, guys," said Max. "Let's talk. Lunch is in about an hour and it's on me. The food here is exquisite. So is the company. Most patients eat separately but a few are allowed in the cafeteria. Nobody dangerous."

Dr. Max Vogel, a psychiatrist at the start of his career, had a soothing but deliberate voice. It was deep but not threatening. David observed that Max in his own work environment seemed comfortable and eminently professional. He reminded David of Gregory Peck in *Spellbound*. Unfortunately, there was no Ingrid Bergman to add glamour to the landscape.

To David's surprise, there was a knock at the door and glamour did arrive in the form of the nurse they had met earlier.

Max beamed. "Maggie, please come in and meet Sal Dematteo and David Gold, two of the most brilliant lawyers in the city of Pittsburgh. Mary Margaret Seiler, gentlemen, psychiatric nurse extraordinaire."

"We shared the same elevator," she said. "Nice to meet you both. Dr. Vogel, I'm sorry to intrude. But I need an okay on this medicine for Mr. Kepler. He's been very upset. He thinks there are two Communist assassins in the building out to kill him."

Max scrutinized the prescription and signed it.

"Maggie, why don't you have lunch with us? Check with me in about an hour. I'll see Mr. Kepler after lunch."

"Thank you," she agreed. "I'd love to have lunch with two barristers. Do you guys give free legal advice?"

"Only to beautiful dark-haired women," smiled David. "You qualify."

"My, my, a silver-tongued attorney. On a Monday morning, how unique."

"Excuse me, Miss Seiler." Sal joined the conversation. "Haven't we met before?"

"My goodness, another silver tongue."

"Look guys," laughed Max. "We got work to do. Save your flirting for lunch."

Maggie left the room.

"I love that girl," explained Max. "She is an oasis in this desert of a hospital. All the good-looking nurses go to the general hospitals."

"Have you dated her?" queried David.

"Three times, it's like dating a vestal virgin. But I'll testify on a stack of Bibles she is one smart cookie and great company. But enough about Maggie."

"David, would you mind waiting? Why don't you go into the anteroom and read a magazine. Sal and I need to talk."

"Yes, sir." David saluted and left the room. He hoped Maggie would return so he could get in a few words and a little information, like a phone number or a little encouragement.

Sal was visibly nervous. "Max, er, Dr. Vogel..."

"Max is okay, Sal. We have known each other long enough. Now relax and tell me what is or what you think is going on."

Max extracted a large pad from the desk drawer and wrote Sal's name at the top.

"First, Max, I know that girl," insisted Sal.

"Why is that so important, Sal?"

"Well, frankly, I believe she or someone who looked like her was in one of my visions."

Max wasn't prepared for that.

"Sal, let's start at the beginning. Let's not draw any medical conclusions, like visions, delusions or hallucinations. Let's get at the facts. Let us refer to whatever is happening as an episode. Now, to the best of your recollection when did these episodes start?"

Sal paused to gather his thoughts. "Well, about a week ago I was leaving the courthouse and..." Sal recounted the three episodes, two of which had taken place the previous weekend. He gave Max graphic, detailed descriptions of both occurrences.

Max took notes. He only interrupted a couple of times.

"So you believe Maggie or someone who looked like Maggie was sitting next to you in the arena?"

"Yes, except her hair was long and flowing. She was incredibly beautiful, dressed in a long white gown. She was terrified. It was almost unreal; in fact, come to think of it, there was an aura of unreality about each episode." Sal had a faraway detached look in his eyes. "Nothing was clear."

"What do you mean? The picture or what you were observing was shrouded in a mist?"

"Yes, that's it. But I could see and hear everything."

"And the language was English?"

"No, I initially thought it was Latin. But I know a little Latin. It wasn't, it was another language."

"Can you write any of the words down? First, I'll need you to concentrate. Put everything else out of your mind." Max's voice took the tone of a firm but not threatening order. "This is important, Sal."

There were several moments of complete silence. Max noticed Sal had begun to sweat. To Sal, the pad of paper in front of him had taken on a secondary form. It became a piece of parchment and then changed to a stone tablet. He hesitantly scrawled some words. The characters were completely unrecognizable. Max watched him carefully, doubting what he saw. He knew that Sal appeared to be in a trancelike state. Sal slowly handed Max the paper. He said nothing.

Max looked at the writing. He really expected to see Hebrew. To his surprise it was neither Hebrew nor English. He studied the writing carefully. During his undergraduate studies, Max had taken a year of classical languages. He wasn't completely sure, but he believed he recognized the origin.

"Sal," he asked firmly, rousing him quickly from his reverie. "Are you familiar with Greek?"

"No." Sal nodded laconically. "I was never in Greece. Never studied it. Read the *Iliad* in English. It was required."

"Well, that's very interesting. I'm not entirely sure but I believe what you have written here is classical Greek."

* * * *

For Sal, lunch was reserved for answering a few questions. He picked at a bologna sandwich and played at eating some canned vegetable soup.

Maggie and David engaged in a constant patter. Small talk, feeling each other out. They listened to Max's questions, but in between checking their mutual chemistry.

Max looked perplexed. He continued his interrogation of Sal about the writings. "You never read any Greek? Don't know anything about the Greek language?"

"Nothing. Ate in a few Greek restaurants. I like onions."

Sal was beginning to re-enter the current world. "How could I write in Greek? How could I know Hebrew words? Am I cracking up?"

"I don't know," admitted Max. "But we are going to find out. Sal, this can be dangerous if you are involved in some activity like driving."

"Or," continued Sal, "like sex, or like a trial, or like making a speech, or like just plain conducting my daily life."

"I know one thing," assured Max, "I don't believe you are psychotic."

Maggie and David, deep into a subject about a recent movie, paused. They waited for a further pronouncement. None came.

"I need to consider this syndrome further," said Max, who had already planned to bounce it off his colleague Bernie Adler. He needed consultation. He needed another perspective. Dr. Adler was his mentor and one of the foremost psychiatrists in the country. He would call him after lunch. This was complicated stuff.

"Sal," he continued "I will ring you tomorrow morning. We will set up some more sessions. Do not panic. There are explanations and we will find the answers."

David glanced at his watch. "We have to get to the office." He was almost sorry the lunch was over. He decided there would be other lunches with this lovely, fascinating young lady.

* * * *

At 5:10 that afternoon, David's phone rang. He picked it up. The staff had already departed. He was very pleased. It was Maggie Seiler.

"Hi, David. I enjoyed lunch. What are you doing for dinner?"

"Nothing. Can I view your etchings?"

"Sure," she answered. "But first I need to know something. Are you interested in my body or in my helping your friend?"

"Both," replied David. That was pretty straight talk. Didn't sound much like a vestal virgin.

"What is your priority?"

David considered the question and the person asking the question. "Helping my friend, of course," he replied.

"Good, meet me at Paoli's spaghetti joint. Can you be there at seven? Max let me read today's notes. Pretty spectacular stuff. Please don't tell Sal. I'm Max's chief nurse. It's a little unethical, but he thought I could help. I want you to meet somebody. I think he might throw some light on this matter. Max asked me to see him and show him the writing."

"Who is this guy?" asked David.

"Well, he's kind of a time detective. Do you know where Paoli's is located?"

"Sure, on Murray Avenue. A time detective? What the hell is a time detective?"

"He's an archaeologist/historian, a kind of Sherlock Holmes. His specialty is to unlock the secrets of the past. He reviews the evidence and then makes some educated guesses as to what era certain objects are from and when certain events took place. Max and I think we need to know a lot more about the time period into which Sal is apparently escaping."

"Escaping! You think Sal is actually going back into the past?" David's voice rose in disbelief.

"Well, counselor, something is going on. Will I see you at seven?"

"Absolutely, Nurse Seiler. I will be there."

David hung up the phone. The franchise agreement he was reviewing suddenly seemed boring and mundane. He shook his head. The premise Maggie had advanced was too improbable, too inconceivable, too ridiculous to contemplate. He scratched his head, took off his glasses and lit up a cigar. Or was it?

CHAPTER 8

THE SECOND WEEK, MONDAY
BENSON P. THROCKMORTON

"Meet Benson P. Throckmorton." Maggie gestured at a spare, young man with a light, almost ghostly skin pallor illuminated in the restaurant's lighting. He beamed out of a round face that sported large horn-rimmed glasses. He wore a rumpled, frayed green sweater and ancient gray pants that resembled a pair of pajamas.

David reflected. If he had been asked how he thought somebody named Benson P. Throckmorton should look, this guy would fill the bill exactly. David smiled and warmly shook Benson's hand. He was greatly relieved. He had pictured the time detective as some suave, pipe-smoking hero who would be a potent rival for Maggie's affection.

"Mr. Throckmorton, a pleasure."

"Please call me Ben or Benson," requested the time detective.

David sat down at the table. Maggie was in slacks. Her luxuriant hair was no longer in a bun but hung loosely about her shoulders. David studied her regal features. If nothing positive came out of Sal's problem, the time and effort he expended had already netted him an enormous benefit. He placed this girl in a certain unique class. He had only met her that morning, yet he felt totally relaxed in her presence, as if he had known her for years.

Paoli's was a brightly lit, traditional Italian restaurant, complete with red-checkered tablecloths, Chianti bottles on the table and an abundant selection of Italian specialties. A smiling waitress in a crimson blouse and a short, checkered skirt that resembled a tablecloth, bounced up to the table prepared to take their order. The blouse was supported by a rather ample chest from which, try as he might, David was unable to shift his gaze. As he ordered ravioli with meat sauce he noticed Maggie's sardonic smirk.

"I prefer cheese lasagna," she said. "How about a bottle of Riesling?"

David agreed with a silent nod.

Maggie looked up at the waitress. "A bottle of Johannesburg Riesling please. Make sure it's chilled." She smiled. "My friend needs a cold drink."

"You don't miss much, do you, lady?"

"No," she agreed. "It's part of my medical training."

Benson, oblivious to the exchange, chose spaghetti with large meatballs. David watched Benson put on a napkin to guard his precious green sweater from the vagaries of meat sauce. I hope, observed David to himself, nothing happens to soil that valuable garment.

Maggie began by reciting Benson's qualifications.

"Benson is a third-year doctoral candidate in ancient history, specializing in the classification of archaeological antiquities. He is literate in several dead languages, including Hieroglyphics, Aramaic, Cuneiform, classical Greek and Latin. He is on a grant project at the Carnegie Museum investigating some Babylonian artifacts, which are currently on loan from the British Museum. I met Benson when I dated his brother Arnie. He is at medical school in Boston. Oh and by the way, Ben is also a student of the paranormal."

"It's kind of my hobby," he chuckled. "You ought to see the faces of my colleagues when I tell them a 3,500-year-old statue can actually affect events in the present. You know, it's all inherent in the latent psychic energy. It can be both positive and negative. As Dr. Jung has stated on more than one occasion, the barrier between physics and metaphysics is often blurred."

"I haven't read Dr. Jung in any detail. I've heard of him. I'm sure he believed his premises were valid."

"Oh, they are valid. You don't subscribe to his theories?"

"Maybe I don't understand them. Is there a simple example?" David was sure the question would stump the time detective. He was wrong.

"Certainly. In 1923 Howard Carter found the tomb of the boy king, Tutankhamen. Within a few months several members of the expedition died of mysterious causes."

"Sure, but what has that to do with Carl Jung's theories?"

"We are now sure there was a deadly psychic energy enshrined in one or more of the many artifacts found in that dig. This toxic force was unloosed during the excavation. That gave rise to the legend of the curse that now surrounds the short life of this obscure Egyptian pharaoh.

"Curse?" echoed David. "You can't be serious."

"I am serious, Mr. Gold." Benson's boyish face assumed a stern expression. "Very serious," he repeated.

"Then what happens to this so-called energy? Does it just kind of float around and circulate in the air picking out victims at random?" David waved both hands in the air nervously, knocking over a half-filled glass of water. Some of it trickled onto Maggie's lap before she could catch it with a napkin.

"Hey, guys," Maggie interrupted. "We are off track here. We have a number of issues to discuss. Can we save this topic till later?" She carefully wiped the table and looked in the direction of the waitress who, having seen the incident, rushed over to the table with a large towel.

"Accidents happen," the waitress bubbled. "No harm done." She leaned over David and proceeded to absorb the remaining water with the towel. Her left breast was less than four inches from David's nose. The proximity of her bosom shut down David's conversation completely. His eyes were wide open and his head was completely inert. The occurrence didn't phase Benson. He was determined to reply.

"Like all energy," Benson said, "it eventually dissipates until some event or activity happens that causes it to reactivate."

When the waitress completed her task, she smiled. "Would you like another tablecloth?"

"No," replied Maggie. "This will do just fine." She turned her attention back to the two men. "Now guys, can we continue? It's getting late."

David noticed Maggie was struggling to conceal her irritation. He felt embarrassed. The evening was not going at all as he planned. Why was he always so clumsy with women he was trying to impress?

"Miss Seiler," he said, "please, continue."

"Thank you, Mr. Gold. You should know that with Dr. Vogel's agreement I showed Ben a copy of the words Mr. Dematteo had written down and also discussed the narrative that he had transcribed during their interview."

Suddenly Benson interposed. He was surprisingly articulate. His speech didn't match the absent-minded professor image that emerged at first impression.

"Mr. Gold, David, Mr. Dematteo's episodes seem to evolve around a golden dagger. His descriptions of the surroundings, the forum, the arena, suggest a period related to the ancient Romans. As to the incident in the burning building, well, I'm not entirely sure where that fits. As for the dagger, I believe I know what dagger he is referring to and the exact location of the object at this time."

"Is that possible, Mr. Throckmorton? How could you?"

"First, let me track some history and you can draw your own conclusions. What do you know about the Babylonians?"

"The Babylonians?" David repeated. "Not much. The usual stuff, cradle of civilization, located between the Tigris and Euphrates Rivers near what is now Baghdad.

"Let me relate a short chronicle from ancient history. I think it may help to explain my theory. Any objections?"

"Of course not. Explain away."

"The Babylonians and their neighbors to the south, the Assyrians, were the superstars of the ancient world. They developed a well-ordered, advanced civilization. Their architectural skills were spectacular and their sense of art superb. For example, the Hanging Gardens is now one of the Seven Wonders of the World. The temple to their principal god, Marduk, is a great edifice even by our modern standards. Their legal code, developed about 1750 B.C. by the great lawgiver, Hammurabi, was a more advanced system of jurisprudence than any code of law or ethics forthcoming for the next 3,000 years. Some scholars claim that the Law of Moses emanated from Hammurabi's code. It's plausible there are marked similarities. Witness the fact that sexual abusers of women and children were punished severely, especially when incest was an issue. In any event, their sanitation practices, writing skills and mathematical advances were responsible for a quantum leap in civilization."

Benson was absorbed in the tale. He put down his fork and spoke, gesturing with his hands. He didn't seem to care that his spaghetti was getting cold.

David nibbled at his food. This funny looking little man was a rapt storyteller. "Well, this is very interesting," David said, "but how does it tie in with Sal's issues?"

Benson ignored the interruption. "Three weeks ago the museum got a shipment of artifacts on loan from the British Museum. It is a treasure trove from the early Mesopotamian world. A fascinating collection of pottery, jewelry, weapons and tablets with depictions of long-forgotten deities such as the goddess of fertility and war, Ishtar, and the sun god, Shumash. There are even a few objects from the tombs of Ur, the city where Abraham was reputedly born."

"That," interjected David, "does not sound like the era that Sal describes when he recounts these visions or whatever he seems to be experiencing."

"True, except for one cogent detail," said Benson. "There is in this collection an exquisite gold dagger. This object has a deep blue sapphire jewel encrusted on its handle. It is a remarkably intact piece. The dagger has an inscription embedded on the handle beneath the jewel. The symbols seem to indicate it was a gift to King Hammurabi from Croesus, a minor but very rich Lydian king who was paying tribute to Babylon."

"Okay, Hammurabi had a dagger. The ancient world must have been rife with daggers. What has all this got to do with—"

"Patience, Mr. Gold," cautioned Maggie.

"Well," said Benson quietly, "this dagger bears a definite likeness to the dagger your friend Sal describes in his so-called visions or episodes. I think it is the same dagger."

"But, how could it be?" David took a deep draught of wine, deeper than he intended, causing him to cough. He gasped. "This is pretty far-fetched." He turned to Maggie with a pleading look.

"David," chided Maggie, "take a drink of water and listen."

David needed some coffee. This was getting complicated and the table had run out of wine. "Okay," he apologized. "I stand reprimanded. Sorry. Let's get some coffee."

Summoned by Maggie, the waitress, in her bountiful, top-heavy presence, appeared at the table. She asked Benson if he was finished with his dinner. He nodded yes, but requested that she wrap up the balance so he could take it home. All three asked for coffee.

Benson continued. "There were two significant events in Babylonian history that lead me to believe we are dealing with the same artifact. The dagger, because of its origin during Hammurabi's reign, became a sacred treasure. It was carefully preserved and passed down through the royal dynasties of Babylon. It became a symbol of Babylonian strength and resiliency. In fact, it was trotted out during the annual feast of Ishtar and laid at her feet as a sign of homage."

"You can actually pinpoint the location of this specific dagger from tablets and writings that are over 3,000 years old?" David asked.

"Yes," confirmed Benson, "we can. In 1934 the French archaeologist, Andre Parrot, unearthed an almost intact statue of Ishtar plus some basalt tablets. Ishtar looked like a bathing beauty with wings. The tablets were a perfectly preserved set of Hammurabi's legal code. They were restored and can now be viewed in the Louvre. Other tablets discovered at the same dig referenced a sacred golden dagger that was a legacy from the now fabled King Hammurabi."

"Amazing! However, if I am not mistaken, we are still several hundred years from the Roman Empire. You know, you speak about this like it happened yesterday."

"It did happen yesterday. The annals of recorded history are only a minor blip when we consider that man's knowledge stretches back millions of years."

"You're right. Sorry for the interruption."

"In 605 B.C., a warrior king named Nebuchadnezzar embarked on a campaign of expansion. In the process he moved south and conquered the Jewish states of Judea and Israel. He deported most of the Hebrew tribes to Babylon."

The waitress arrived with a pot of coffee and some chocolate cake that Maggie had ordered to share. Throughout Benson's recitation Maggie had remained silent, carefully observing David's reactions. First, boredom, followed by rank skepticism, and then curious interest tinged with a rising fascination. David began picking idly at a piece of chocolate cake. He scraped off some icing with a fork and tasted it. He grimaced. It was too sweet. He began sipping coffee. He was clearly somewhere else, waiting for the next chapter.

"Now," resumed Benson, "the story really heats up. About seventy years later, the Persians overrun Babylon. They launch the halcyon days of the mighty Persian Empire. One land that stretches from India to the Mediterranean. From the Caucasus Mountains to the Persian Gulf, a single nation, ruled by one man, Emperor Cyrus the Great.

"Sometime during the reign of Cyrus a certain secret society, a murder cult, came into possession of the dagger. It was probably stolen for them by a cult member, a minion of Cyrus, name of Haman. It was actually sanctified by this group as a holy object. They believed it had mystical qualities that gave them supernatural powers. This sect, while following Ishtar, actually worshipped an evil male harpy, a servant of Ishtar. A peculiar demon called Humbaba."

"Humbaba. That's a real name?"

"Real as the 3,000-year-old statues depicting this demon. He was the god of pestilence."

"Pestilence, huh. Lousy assignment."

"Hush," whispered Maggie. "You lawyers are certainly a chatty bunch."

"Well, Humbaba seemed to enjoy his work," Benson continued. "There was plenty of pestilence in the ancient world. In any event, this cult was as cruel and ruthless a gang of brigands as ever gathered under one roof. They murdered without mercy. They used very thin stiletto-like knives and generally dispatched their victims by piercing them once in the nape of the neck, execution style."

David glanced at Maggie. "Not nice people at all."

She agreed with a somewhat disdainful nod.

"Now comes the juicy part. Cyrus took a beautiful Jewish virgin named Esther as one of his many wives. At the time, Esther chose not to reveal her ancestry. Perhaps you have heard of Esther? She is listed by the encyclopedia Judaica as one of the four most beautiful women in the world."

"Yes, I've heard of her," quipped David. "I wonder who the other three were?"

Benson smiled. "Sorry, don't know who ran the beauty contest."

"Of course Esther the Queen, her beauty was legendary," said David. "It's a venerable story, even the New Testament recognizes the character. Wasn't the name of the King, Ahasuerus?"

"Yes, in the Hebrew version. But we are now sure it was Cyrus the Great. Esther's story is a real tale of modesty, courage and self-sacrifice. Or," Benson grinned, "there is a more seamy side, which involves sex, sin and sacrifice. Cyrus was captivated by her. The quote from the book is 'All who beheld Esther were struck by her beauty.' Cyrus was more than struck. He was stupefied. He got rid of his number one wife, named Vashti, and made Esther chief keeper of the bedroom. Vashti, by the way, was Haman's niece. This stooge of Cyrus, positive he was about to lose his job, blamed the Jews. He concocted a conspiracy with the murder gang to completely eliminate them."

"*Entrez la femme*," offered Maggie. "Esther intervenes."

"Right! A magnificent counter move. Esther to the rescue. Well, we know in a weak moment that Haman persuaded Cyrus to sign a decree to execute all the female children of the Jews. Thus, he said, would their seed wither and die. Haman contracted with the cult to act as his agent. They would carry out the genocide, and he would reward them with great riches and honor.

"Esther and Mordecai, her uncle, a minor tax official in Cyrus's retinue, somehow uncovered the plot. In a conference that probably took place in Cyrus's bedchamber, Esther disclosed she was a Jew and pointed out the decree would require that she be put to death. Cyrus was appalled. The thought of losing Esther to the executioner was more than he could stand. He repealed the decree. Esther wasn't finished. She cleverly inferred that Haman had tried to seduce her. She even arranged a compromising situation that convinced Cyrus her accusations were true. That ended the ball game for Haman. He was sentenced to be hanged. Hence the famous statement: 'He was hanged higher than Haman.'

"Cyrus next sends a platoon of Persian shock troops to stamp out the murder cult. Most of the gangs are killed in the resulting battle. Unfortunately, a few escaped. By the way, Haman's name is the origin of the term 'Hamas,' which in Arabic means to resolve a problem by total destruction at its source. The troops did find the golden dagger and retrieved it for Cyrus."

"Okay," said David, "Esther was a paragon of virtue. But I ask you, was this story of Esther a detour or part of the five-hundred-year road to Rome?"

"It is the heart of the story," Benson replied with a sigh. "In antiquity 500 years was a drop in the well. A year later Cyrus, entreated by Esther, was convinced to allow the Hebrew tribes to return to Judea. Of course, Esther was to remain with the king, which she willingly did. That was her self-sacrifice.

"In 534 B.C., a large segment of the Persian Jewish community migrated back to their homeland and began to rebuild it. They carried with them gold and silver vessels plundered from Solomon's original temple. They also carried the sacred dagger of Hammurabi. It was presented as a gift to the Jews prior to their departure. Cyrus gave it directly to the Jewish high priest. We believe that the dagger became part of the trove ultimately deposited in the Holy of Holies. The sanctified heart of the Hebrew temple.

When the second temple was constructed on the Temple Mount in Jerusalem, it became the personal property of each successive high priest. It remained there until destruction of that temple by the Romans in 70 A.D."

"Interesting," commented David. "I learned about Esther in religious school. I've never heard this part of the story."

David poured himself another cup of coffee. Finding the cream, he tipped the pitcher over too far and watched it run over into the saucer. "What about the dagger?" he asked. He was beginning to see a possible connection to Sal's episodes but hesitant to even speculate on what had occurred to him.

"As I said, the description of that dagger is similar to the description given to Dr. Vogel this morning by your friend Sal. The dagger is now less than two miles from here on the second floor of the Carnegie Museum."

David raised the back of his hand to his mouth. "You are sure it's the same dagger?"

"Same dagger," echoed Benson. "I translated the words that Mr. Dematteo had written on the paper. It was classical Greek, a common language used throughout the ancient world after the conquests of Alexander in 323 B.C. Many Hebrews spoke classical Greek."

"Okay, I'm all ears. What did the words mean?"

"It stated, 'I give thee the weapon which will avenge the terrible perfidy of the traitor Josephus'!"

"Josephus? Who in hell is Josephus?"

"Josephus was a Jew, a reputed turncoat. During the battle for Jerusalem he allegedly revealed the secret water cisterns underneath the Temple to Titus the Roman commander. This enabled Titus to finally breach the walls of Jerusalem, ultimately capture and sack the city. The story of the six-month siege is told by Josephus, an eyewitness, in his book *The Jewish War*.

"Oh, and by the way," added Benson, "Josephus became a famous historian and a citizen of Rome. He also assumed a Roman name, Flavius Josephus. He was awarded Roman citizenship by his mentor, the Emperor Vespasian, and permitted to assume the Flavius family name."

"Benson, I'm still lost," said a weary David. "How does all this dovetail with Sal's accounts of his so-called glimpses of the ancient world?"

"Josephus had a brother," continued Benson, "Aaron Ben Mattathias. The family was descendants of the Maccabees who had ruled Judea in the previous century. David, I believe that Aaron was present in the second temple when it was destroyed by Titus. He was known to be a close friend of the high priest Ananias. The dagger was a part of the trove kept in the Holy of Holies. It was in the sole custody of Ananias."

David leaned back in his chair and turned to Maggie. "Then you believe," he said deliberately, "wait a second. How could you learn all this in one day?" David looked quizzically at Maggie.

"I didn't," replied Benson. "Been studying this dagger for the last two weeks. Tracked it in old treatises. Made phone calls to other antiquity buffs, ancient scholars, dealers and archeology departments at major universities. Even contacted the Hebrew University in Israel. They confirm the possible existence of such a weapon. I had a hunch this particular sacrament was special."

David spoke carefully. "You know, folks, lawyers are skeptics and cynics by nature. We tell stories to juries that are outrageous. Sometimes we are surprised when we sell our snake oil. The human mind can only absorb so much, then it either snaps or registers grave doubt. You know that, Maggie."

"There is a third alternative," suggested Benson before Maggie could answer.

"And that is?"

"We accept that there are dimensions that we don't yet understand. We exploit the one aspect of human behavior that has propelled man from primeval mud to the edge of a scientific age that defies imagination."

"And that is?"

"Why, curiosity, Mr. Gold. What else? We have an opportunity here to probe the unknown. Let's take full advantage of it." Now Benson dropped the bombshell.

"You see, I believe these visions may be real. They might be messages from another dimension or more likely another time, or both. It is possible they are being generated by the energy of the dagger."

The last statement was too much. David was exasperated. He was out of his depth with these paranormal musings. His voice rose in frustrated anger.

"My cup runneth over. Surely goodness and mercy shall follow me for the rest of my days. Message! What message? From who? From what? From where?"

"That, Mr. Gold, is what we must find out."

Several people from adjoining tables were tossing curious glances their way.

"Shh, David, you're shouting," cautioned Maggie. "Can't you stay calm for a few minutes?"

David tried to bridge his natural inclination to disbelieve. He adjusted his mind to reason, like a lawyer attempting to arrange a set of totally illogical facts.

"Okay, folks, I'll play. Let's explore the premises here. Sal Dematteo is apparently experiencing portraits or flashbacks from some era in the ancient classical world. They possibly involve a priest and an ancient dagger that were in the second temple in Jerusalem. The dagger, an inanimate object, is somehow connected with or is generating Sal's negative visions."

"Episodes," corrected Maggie.

"Episodes," repeated David. "Sorry, folks, if you believe this fairy tale, I got a bridge for you. It goes from Manhattan Island to Brooklyn."

David suddenly held up his hand. "Wait a minute, hold it. Sal and Catherine were on a museum tour last Saturday. Sal told me he was totally bored."

"Did he mention a dagger?" asked Benson.

"No, he didn't want to discuss the outing. But he certainly could have seen the dagger."

"Correction, he did see the dagger. I conducted the tour."

David was shaking his head. "Assuming there is a scintilla of truth here, what are you suggesting we do next?" He looked straight at Benson. "How can you prove it's the same dagger? What the hell is the message you claim is being transmitted?"

Benson ignored the underlying edge of sarcasm in David's voice. A grin spread across his face.

"I can understand your skepticism, Mr. Gold."

"Skepticism is the understatement of the century."

"Okay," said Benson, "tell me, does Mr. Dematteo have a brother and if so, where is he?"

"He does," confirmed David. "His brother, Art, is in the Air Force. I think he is somewhere in Texas."

"Aha," exclaimed Benson, "a warrior."

David looked straight into Benson P. Throckmorton's huge glasses. "Tell me, Mr. Time Detective, do you, a scientist, believe all this? And you, Miss Nurse, with your education and medical background, do you believe it?"

"I don't know, David." Maggie answered softly. "Like I told you this morning, something way out of the ordinary is happening."

"We need a viewing next," Benson added. It was a matter-of-fact statement. Like when you are ordering breakfast or requesting a phone number from the operator.

"A viewing?" asked David. "What do you mean?"

"Yes, and soon. To prove my theory. We need to confront Mr. Dematteo with the dagger. I will place bets that he will identify it. When can you get him to the exhibit? We are open Wednesday till 9:00 P.M."

"I don't know," said David. "Let's see, this is Monday. Let's shoot for Wednesday evening after work, say about seven."

"Perfect, I believe this is most urgent, Mr. Gold, uh David, most urgent," Benson repeated. "Something is brewing. I feel it. I think these visions are tied to the two murders at the museum this weekend. We need to put a time fence around Mr. Dematteo's episodes and soon."

"David, Benson has a sense about these things." Maggie had her finger pressed against her lips. "You must try hard, please."

David sighed deeply. "Murders," he muttered. "I am zoned-out now for sure. Please tell me you are not referring to the story in the papers this morning?"

"I am," confirmed Benson.

"You would advise the police of your suspicions?"

"Of course not. Would they believe me?"

"Why not? It's a great story." David shook his head. "I can't believe I am agreeing to this. What the hell is going on here?"

"I don't know, Mr. Gold, but maybe, just maybe, we can find out."

Benson rose from the table. He retrieved his leftover spaghetti, grabbed some Italian bread as an added benefit, stuffed it into the paper carton and abruptly said "Good night."

"Hold it, Benson. I have another question."

Benson halted and turned. "Okay."

"You said this psychic energy would gradually disappear. When do you believe it will go away?"

"You still don't understand?"

"What exactly, Benson, don't I understand?"

"This negative energy is being generated by a curse. The energy will dissipate when the curse is satisfied."

"Then what the hell will satisfy the curse?" David couldn't control the upward roll of his eyes.

"That, Mr. Gold, is exactly what we have to find out."

This time Benson didn't wait for another question. He hustled out the door, leaving Maggie and David staring at each other.

"David, you're angry?"

"No, not really, just confused, Maggie. That was a lot of crap to swallow. I feel like I'm on a Let's Pretend Show."

"I know. I apologize for subjecting you to this ordeal without any prior explanation. I'd like to take care of the check."

"Oh no, Doctor Seiler. For all of the entertainment I received this evening, dinner is on me. I insist!"

CHAPTER 9

THE SECOND WEEK, TUESDAY
BERNARD P. ADLER, M.D.
MEMBER OF THE AMERICAN BOARD OF PSYCHIATRISTS

Max was seated in a comfortable, overstuffed chair in Bernie Adler's plush, oak-paneled office. He faced the large double window that overlooked the expanse of Schenley Park. Bright sunlight filtered through fall's oranges and yellows in the trees, and caressed the luxuriant green shrubbery that seemed to stretch for endless miles across the park.

Max had many memories of this office. All medical students specializing in psychiatry were required to undergo two years of analysis. He had spent much time on the leather couch, hiding behind the myth that his mother had ruined his life. In the process he learned it was merely a defense mechanism to disguise his own perceived inadequacies. He now also knew how fortunate he was to have Adler, the old master himself, as his analyst. Adler had mentored Max Vogel like an errant son. It was an ego-shattering two years, but Max had honed his skills, swallowed the experience and emerged as a competent embryo psychiatrist.

"Max," Bernie Adler said, snapping Max out of his daydream, "life is matter and energy. When the matter dies, the energy dies. The story you just told me is impossible. Consider a dagger with malignant properties, and a nurse that the patient recognizes and claims he met before in a dream. You believe this fantasy?"

Dr. Bernard P. Adler, eminent psychiatrist and Chairman of the Mental Hygiene Department at the University of Pittsburgh Medical School, looked puzzled. "Max, what have you learned? How many times have I emphasized that in your practice you will hear many bizarre tales. That you must resist the temptation to let your imagination rule. These are very sick people. They hear voices, see things, have visions. They must be treated."

"I know. I know," agreed Max. "But if you could have observed this man. The only explanation is that he was drawing data from his subconscious. He recites a Hebrew prayer. He writes in classical Greek. Both languages he claims never to have studied or even heard of before. Bernie, consider this: The subject is a thirty-three-year-old Italian-American lawyer with an undergraduate degree in business. He was an Army officer in Korea with no history of combat trauma. He is ostensibly a well-balanced, well-adjusted human being, happily married. He has a younger brother and a sister whom he professes to care for very much. Both parents are alive. They neither beat nor abused him, but in fact they are the personification of a close, loving Italian family. He claims there is no history of mental illness in the family, at least with which he has any knowledge. I am baffled. What do I do next? Turn him over to a more experienced therapist?"

"No, not yet. How about hypnosis? You were very proficient at clinical hypnotherapy in school. Perhaps if you put him under, you could elicit some facts from his past life that he has totally submerged or failed to reveal. One short session hardly scratches the surface. We need to know a lot more about this man and his background."

"Good idea. I will try that." Max Vogel decided not to tell Adler about Maggie's time detective. That would sound too ludicrous.

"I'll set something up this week. You want to attend?"

"No, this is your case, Max. But I definitely want to review the results. I will stay in touch. If we get sufficient data, we can draw some preliminary conclusions. Perhaps we can even present a case study at the spring National Psychiatric Association Diplomate Convention." Bernie looked excited by the prospect. "It's in New York at the Waldorf this year."

"I'm not yet a diplomate."

"So what? I'll invite you as my guest. This is an opportunity and a challenge for you. I believe you're up to it. Good luck."

Max rose and they shook hands. "I know how busy you are. Thanks for your time."

The slightly graying psychiatrist, acclaimed for his published works, his vast knowledge in his field and for his ability to empirically diagnose and treat the most difficult of cases, closely watched the young man leave his office. He was convinced that Max would someday be an outstanding doctor. Adler knew Max was downcast. He had given his pupil totally unsatisfactory answers. The case was extremely interesting, but Max would work his own way through it. Adler had some ideas, but it was time for Max to fly solo.

* * * *

Max stood in front of the elevator and pressed the button. Two medical students were standing next to him arguing about the results of a blood test. He could hear their discussion, but it was not registering. Max's thoughts were elsewhere, on the initial report of one Benson P. Throckmorton. Max had received a briefing from Maggie Seiler, who was waiting in his office at eight when he had arrived at the hospital that morning. He had great confidence in this young lady. She had suggested the intervention of Throckmorton. The so-called time detective had come up with some startling, albeit implausible, possibilities.

Tomorrow evening, with David's help, they were to have what was termed as a viewing. He could not bring himself to discuss the next step with Adler. It violated every recommended procedure in a prescribed treatment program. Allowing a patient to have a confrontation with some sort of an artifact at this early stage of therapy and then try to draw some valid conclusions from the event was most unorthodox.

He had to hurry back to the hospital. He had a full afternoon. As the elevator crawled toward the ground floor, the thought crossed his mind that perhaps he was allowing his admiration for Maggie to cloud his judgment and force a premature or, at best, an unwise decision.

He trusted this young lady. She somehow possessed a wisdom and poise far beyond her twenty-eight years. You felt it when you were with her. It must have been that way when the ancient Greeks consulted the Delphi oracle or when the Old Testament Jewish prophets foretold future events with disquieting accuracy.

The elevator had reached the ground floor. Max woke up. He roused himself. What crap! These are not credible, scientific thoughts. But well, what will it hurt? He needed a lot more information on Sal Dematteo. This incident would only be a building block in developing a file. It might be revealing. His patient, viewing a dagger from somewhere in antiquity that he believed he had seen in a vision. He would observe the patient's reactions when he saw the dagger. It would make a fascinating item to include in the case study.

However, Max Vogel's attempt at pragmatism could not quell a growing uneasiness that he was being drawn into the eye of a deadly whirlpool that was engulfing more and more innocent people.

CHAPTER 10

THE SECOND WEEK, TUESDAY
FATHER O'MALLEY

Father Sean O'Malley sipped his morning cup of coffee and munched absent-mindedly at his toast. He had a busy Tuesday scheduled. He had to attend a meeting with the high school coach on the future of the football program at St. Mary of the Sacred Heart, an afternoon session with Tom Sheehan, the building contractor, on expanding the middle school facility, and a discussion with the Feeney family on their son's trouble. That reminded him that he had to call Sal Dematteo and check on the legal progress of the Feeney case. He sighed. It was a sad day when a parish family had to face the specter of one of their sons being accused of murder. He preferred the football meeting. He had played first string, left end, at Notre Dame for two years. Football was his first love, next to the Lord Jesus, of course.

The phone jangled loudly. Mrs. O'Rourke, his housekeeper, answered and advised him that Catherine Dematteo was on the line. He liked Catherine. Who didn't? A beautiful child, a gracious daughter of the Church.

He picked up the phone. "Good morning, Catherine. You want to meet this morning? Well, let me look at my schedule."

He knew in advance how busy he was. He was about to refuse and reset the time, but he detected what was obviously a frantic note in her voice.

"Something wrong, Catherine?" he asked.

"Yes," she answered softly.

"Okay, how soon can you be here? A half-hour. That will be fine." That still left him an hour before his meeting at the high school, a few minutes' walk from the Parish house.

Catherine was prompt. She arrived dressed in a brown skirt, a beige blouse, stockings, high heels, always well groomed. She stood before him, moving her hand slowly over her face, forehead to chin, first sitting then standing, as she struggled to decide how to approach the subject.

"Sit down, Catherine," he gestured with a friendly smile. "How is the little girl?"

"Oh, just fine, Father. She recognizes all of us. She has her father's sense of humor." A glimmer of concern crossed her face.

"Something's on your mind, Catherine. Please, let's lay it on the table."

"It's Sal, Father," she forced the words out. "He has been, I don't know, he's so distant. He's restless at night. Not sleeping well. He seems… oh, I don't know…far away much of the time. Sometimes I can't reach him." She looked down at her lap. "At first I thought it was another woman. But I don't think so." She searched his face, pleadingly. "Wouldn't I know if there was another woman?"

"Of course," agreed Father O'Malley. "This doesn't sound like the general symptoms of a failed marriage. Are you two getting along? Is he loving to you and the little girl? When did you notice this change?"

She reflected. "Maybe two weeks ago." She then recounted the incident on Saturday at the football game.

"He was staring at me. But I swear, Father, he wasn't looking at me. He finally left his seat and went to the bathroom. When he returned he seemed better. He had stopped and talked to his partner."

"Have you asked him about all this?" Father O'Malley felt a rising concern. This was the best young attorney in the parish. He did not want to hear that Sal Dematteo was having something like a nervous breakdown. Especially with the Feeney case on the horizon.

"Yes, I've tried to discuss it. He won't answer me, Father. He just says it's nothing. It isn't nothing. It's taking my husband from me." There was a slight break in her voice and then she sobbed.

"Catherine," he said, "I will talk to him. Perhaps he is working too hard. Not to worry. I'm sure it will work itself out. I'll call Sal today. We will talk again very soon."

Catherine felt relieved. She had unburdened herself to someone she trusted. She felt confident the massive presence of Father O'Malley would fix whatever was wrong.

The priest glanced at his watch. "I have to go, Catherine." He patted her hand. "Trust in God," he said.

I trust Father O'Malley, she thought.

* * * *

When Catherine left, he reached for the phone. He realized he had fifteen minutes to get to his next meeting. He would postpone the call till later. This would give him more time to consider the situation. Contacting Sal late in the afternoon would be better. You could usually find him in the office then, after court. Sal was a good and decent man. Father O'Malley believed that whatever issue was troubling him he could help him solve.

CHAPTER 11

THE SECOND WEEK, WEDNESDAY
DR. IBRAHIM RASHEED

David brought his battered 1949 Chevrolet two-door sedan to a sudden stop. He had almost passed the ordinary-looking two-story brick duplex with 610 above the door. The numbers were small and difficult to see in the gathering twilight. Maggie had described the building, explaining that if he passed the third street light, he had missed the house.

He had forgotten to count the street lights but at the last moment he had spotted the number. He glanced at the paper in his hand. That was it, he confirmed the address: 610 Greenfield Road. Most of the houses on the street had the same commonplace look. All built in the twenties. They housed working class families, were boxlike and austere but livable. The Seilers lived upstairs in the two-story duplex. David climbed the stairs and knocked on the door. A small faceplate on the door announced that this was the Seiler home and also said God Bless You. David knocked again, lightly.

A woman he assumed was Maggie's mother answered the door on the second knock. "Come in, please," she said.

The living room was decorated in what you might call old country style. A sign reading God Bless Our Home graced the fireplace. God was everywhere, thought David. The furniture and the lamps were cheap, 1930s-style items, the wallpaper was flowered green but showing signs of age. The room was neat, clean and comfortable. Its appearance quickly countered any negative impressions of the austere building. That and the kindly Irish lady who gestured for David to have a seat.

"Mary Margaret will be right with you, Mr. Gold. She was a little late coming from the hospital. Always something going on there, you know."

Mrs. Seiler didn't seem to mind that he was Jewish or maybe she didn't realize.

Contrary treatment came from a tall blonde kid in his late teens. When the kid came into the room, he didn't smile or change his blank expression. He nodded to David but didn't introduce himself. "I hear you're a mouthpiece," he said.

"Right," agreed David. "Have a need for one?"

"Na, my Uncle Andy is a police captain. I got all the connections I need."

"Connections are good," agreed David. "Don't hesitate to call though if you need help."

"My Uncle says Jewish lawyers are smart. How come?"

"They are," agreed David. "It's because our mothers fed us Wheaties every morning."

The kid laughed. David knew the boy was playing dumb. Just testing, he guessed.

Maggie breezed into the living room from somewhere in the back.

"Hi, David, I see you've met the pride of Greenfield Road. God's gift to women. That's my kid brother, Bart, and you have met my mother, I assume."

"Don't interrupt, Sis. I'm talkin' to the lawyer. Guy talk."

Bart had decided that maybe David was okay. "Thanks for the offer," he said. "You never know when a lawyer can come in handy."

"Yeah, you never know."

David smiled at Maggie. He was almost startled by the change in her appearance. At dinner on Monday evening she was casual, black hair loose and flowing, very light makeup, tan slacks and a dark nylon blouse. Tonight she had on a chic blue dress, silver earrings and a small silver necklace adorned with a tiny silver cross. Her hair was pulled up in a ponytail. Her makeup was modest. Not too much but enough to accent her bright dark eyes and slightly angular features. What a knockout, David thought. No wonder Max was ready to convert.

"We better go," she said. "We have to meet Benson at seven."

"Yeah, we also need to pick up Sal and Catherine."

"Good idea to get his wife involved," said Maggie. "That's often more therapeutic than anything we medics can do."

Maggie gave her mother a good-night kiss on the cheek. "I won't be late, Mom. I have an early day tomorrow."

When they left and bundled themselves into the car, David apologized for the ragged state of the automobile. He was mesmerized by her appearance. He was stammering. "I should of had it washed."

Maggie chuckled. "Try riding the street car at rush hour. This car is a chariot. It could be a Cadillac or a limousine as far as I'm concerned. I bet I won't get pinched once. Unless I invite it."

"You got a deal, Miss Seiler. Just let me know the invitation. Give me a sign and I'll comply."

"I'll cross my eyes and you can pinch away. Drive on," she said. "We've got work to do, Mr. Counselor, and little time to do it."

After a few minutes of silence she said, "I noticed you staring at the cross. Does it bother you?"

"Not at all, Miss Seiler. I'm afraid it is you that bothers me but in a very positive way."

"Oh Lord, a Jewish Irishman. Save me."

* * * *

Sal and Catherine were in the front room waiting when the Chevrolet ground to a stop. Catherine's mother was holding the baby. The baby was crying, and Catherine was hesitant to leave. Sal was on the phone trying to return Father O'Malley's call. He was having no success. The priest was attending a DeMolay dinner at a local restaurant. Sal hung up. I'll get him later, he decided. He figured it was about Feeney. Nothing new in that quarter anyway.

"Go, Cathy," insisted her mother. "Baby's tired and hungry. When she has her bottle she will go right to sleep. Have a good time."

Sal and Catherine crawled into the more-than-cozy back seat. After the introductions Catherine got very quiet. She was clearly apprehensive.

"We are going to the museum first," David said. "We are going to meet Mr. Benson Throckmorton. Then we are going out to dinner. It's on me."

"Why," quipped Sal, "you get a new client today?"

"Yeah, I also got a five-dollar fee and two small ones."

"Someone want to tell me why we are going to the museum?" queried Catherine, clearly puzzled.

"Well, there is a Babylonian exhibit," Sal began.

"Listen," Maggie broke in bluntly, "you guys have to quit this blarney. Catherine, I know this is our first meeting. But I have to be frank with you. I think you should know Sal has been having a few problems. Nothing serious, we think. I work for his consulting doctor. I'm a psychiatric nurse. We believe we can help. We are going to meet with a scholar who can possibly give us some important information and perhaps steer us down a path toward the proper therapy."

"I know about Sal's problems," she said. "I live with this guy. But I didn't know he was going to a doctor."

"You know?" exclaimed Sal. "How long have you suspected?"

"About a week. The way you spaced out at the football game last Saturday. I notice everything you do. I love you. That's how wives operate."

Maggie liked this girl. Not a lot of nonsense. "Catherine," she said, "when we meet with Benson you will hear the full story. Please, keep an open mind and don't get frightened."

"I'll try not to panic but understand, Miss Seiler, this is my guy."

"I understand. Please call me Maggie."

They turned the corner at Forbes Street, near the park, and pulled into the museum parking lot. Aside from a few student cars, the area was empty. David pulled up next to a shiny new two-door Buick.

"Max is here," David said. "Never known him to get to a meeting early. Max is notorious for last-minute entrances. There must be a good reason for his beating us here."

"Max always has a reason," said Maggie.

* * * *

The Andrew Carnegie Museum and Library was an icon of culture in the Pittsburgh Civic Center of Oakland. Corinthian columns, now gray with soot, adorned the entrance. Fierce stone lions of Judah guarded the door. The sprawling stone building covered a large city block, and had been constructed in the early twenties when the old industrial tycoon was still alive. Some writers lumped Andrew Carnegie in the robber baron category. But most grudgingly admitted he had given the city that spawned his steel mills a highly respected technical university and a well-endowed museum and library, both free to the public.

Max had indeed arrived early, by design. The antiquities exhibit was on the second floor in a spacious well-lit room aptly named The Classical World. The segment of most interest to him was the visiting exhibit of Babylonian relics from the British Museum. He wandered among several glass cases filled with artifacts and paused at a case titled The Persian Era. In the center of the exhibit, lying neatly in a leather, velvet-lined case was a golden dagger with a deep blue sapphire on the grip. The blade was a rich gold alloy. The note explaining the item read "Ceremonial Dagger presented to Hammurabi, King of Babylon, 1792 to 1750 B.C.E. by King Croesus, of Lydia, an ancient civilization believed to have been located on the island of Crete and totally destroyed in 1450 B.C. by a volcanic eruption."

Max Vogel studied the object. It certainly resembled the dagger that Sal Dematteo had described during his interview. Bernie Adler would call it coincidence. Is such a coincidence even statistically possible? Perhaps Sal might have seen a picture of such a knife in a book or a movie. A competent statistician would have eliminated that possibility almost immediately. The truth was, the dagger Sal said he saw was almost identical, down to the blue sapphire on the handle. But Sal had, in fact, recently visited the museum. Even if the description had been filed away somewhere in his subconscious, what about the rest of the incident? How to explain that?

"Beautiful piece, isn't it, Doctor?"

Max turned, startled. He found himself next to a scholarly looking young man with large glasses, casually dressed in corduroy trousers and an open plaid shirt. The young man was smiling broadly.

"I knew who you were immediately," he explained, "from Maggie's description." He extended his hand. "Welcome to the museum. I'm Benson Throckmorton."

Max shook hands and proceeded to inspect the time detective, grateful that he had come early. He needed to chat with this man in private.

Max had never been one for small talk. He got right to the point. "What do you think is happening here, Dr. Throckmorton? Can you explain these events?"

"Please call me Ben." He shrugged. "I don't quite have my doctorate yet."

Benson paused, then stated with some authority, "Well, there is a remote possibility of time travel or perhaps reincarnation."

Goddamn remote, Max thought to himself, but said, "Got any other explanations? That's pretty difficult to swallow."

"All speculation. A good detective, a la Hercule Poirot, needs more data. That is why we are here tonight. However, I am surprised you think my rationale is so far out. Evidently, while you have studied Freud, perhaps you haven't spent much time with Carl Jung. He validates a number of my theories in his writings, especially in his book *Synchronicity*."

"Mr. Throckmorton, Dr. Jung's writings have been pretty well discredited."

Max breathed deeply. This is becoming more and more convoluted, he thought. Adler may have to commit me before I'm through. It takes upwards of two to four years to do a valid psychoanalysis and after a one-hour session with a patient, I'm in a museum talking to a loony who believes in reincarnation and time travel and thinks he's Sherlock Holmes and Carl Jung rolled into one. I'm going to get sued for malpractice!

"Listen, Mr. Throckmorton, I really didn't come here to argue the merits of Freud versus Jung. I have an idea I may want to try out tonight. Will you cooperate?"

"Be happy to help, Doctor, but please call me Ben. What is your idea?" Benson switched roles without effort.

"I may try," said Max, "to conduct a hypnotherapy session if the situation seems right."

"Sounds like fun, Doc. Just give a signal of some sort, and you get the floor. What a great idea." Benson could not contain his ebullience.

A tall, heavy-set black man, impeccably dressed, joined them. He seemed to be the only other person on the floor. He had appeared out of nowhere and had silently moved in close enough to overhear their conversation.

"Mr. Throckmorton?" he asked in a clipped English accent.

"Yes," said Benson. "You are?"

"Dr. Ibrahim Rasheed. I was told you were on the floor."

"Of course, Dr. Rasheed, I'm so delighted you could come."

Dr. Rasheed extended his hand.

"Dr. Vogel, this is Dr. Ibrahim Rasheed. I invited him. He is Director of Antiquities at the American University in Beirut. What an honor and a pleasure. We are most fortunate. Dr. Rasheed is attending a conference here at the museum on early Mesopotamian civilization. Perhaps he can help us. This is Dr. Max Vogel."

Max quickly offered his hand, which Dr. Rasheed returned. Max was gracious but his expression remained fixed, almost impassive.

"A pleasure, Doctor." Rasheed's voice was deep and rich, his tone cultured and well modulated.

"My pleasure," said Max. If this guy wasn't an actor he should be. He looked like a cross between Paul Robeson and Sidney Poitier. What the hell was he doing here?

"Your field, Doctor?" asked Rasheed.

"Medicine," replied Max. "Psychiatry to be exact."

"Then not an archaeologist. Here on pleasure or business?"

"Not much pleasure," answered Max, "but I studied classical languages in undergraduate school."

That was all Dr. Ibrahim Rasheed needed to know. In any event, he showed no further interest in Max Vogel. He turned to Throckmorton.

"Thank you for asking me here tonight. I have heard of this dagger." He gestured at the case. "I wondered if it was indeed Hammurabi's dagger. I am leaving for New York early tomorrow morning. I must be in Beirut on Sunday. I certainly wanted to examine it before I left."

"I believe it is the real thing," said Benson. "I've run all the standard tests. Translated the language and checked with a number of authorities. It appears to be genuine. I am delighted you know of this item. Its origin is relatively obscure."

"Well, as you know, Mr. Throckmorton, obscure objects are often the stuff that ends up explaining the past to us."

At that moment, David, Maggie, Sal and Catherine rounded the corner and joined the group. Their appearance seemed to jolt Dr. Rasheed. Benson made the introductions. Everyone shook hands.

Dr. Rasheed studied Maggie. His first reaction had changed to curiosity. He could not take his eyes off of her, an obvious fact that rattled David. Who the hell was this guy? What was this guy's problem? As Sal saw the entourage of three people, he wasn't so sure bringing Cathy was a good idea.

When he glanced at Sal, Rasheed's eyes opened wide in surprise. But he remained silent.

"Dr. Rasheed," said Benson, "is a world-renowned expert on classical civilization. I asked him to join us because I believe he may be able to help us in our history lesson. It concerns the dagger, Dr. Rasheed."

Rasheed nodded. "Glad to assist if I can."

Neither Max nor David objected. But neither cared much for the idea.

Sal shrugged and Catherine looked perplexed.

"Dr. Rasheed was about to tell us of his knowledge of the dagger."

Sal had fixed his gaze on the dagger. "I think that's it," he muttered. He began to wish he hadn't involved Catherine in this mess. But it looked as if there was no way to avoid it.

Rasheed blinked. He realized he had been rude in fixing his attention on Maggie. "I am most sorry if I appeared discourteous, Miss Seiler. But I don't know if you have been told this before. There is a lovely mural in the Cairo museum. It is a picture of a beautiful Egyptian princess with her retinue. Her visage bears a striking resemblance to yours. The mural dates around the beginning of the first millennium of the Common Era, long before the Memeluks, probably sometime during the last Ptolemy Dynasty."

"Well, thank you, Dr. Rasheed. That was indeed a lovely compliment for a humble Scotch-Irish girl from County Derry." Maggie remained cool and unflustered. "The Ptolemys," she repeated, "wonder if they were beer drinkers."

Somehow the city of Cairo struck a spark with Sal but he'd never been to Cairo, or had he? He shook his head quietly as if trying to recall some lost facts.

Catherine was watching Sal. She was bewildered, and turned to David. "I want to leave," she said. "I thought we were going to dinner. What's going on here? Why are we all meeting here?"

"We are going to dinner, Cath," assured David.

Maggie quickly moved over next to Catherine. "Please don't get upset, Catherine. We are really trying to help Sal." She patted her arm. But Catherine was far from mollified.

"What's wrong with him?"

"May I suggest," interposed Benson, "that we hear out Dr. Rasheed. I'm sure his time is limited."

"Well, thank you, Mr. Throckmorton. Let me tell you what I know about the dagger of Hammurabi." He looked directly at Benson. "Have you ever heard of the Sicarians?"

"Yes, of course. They were a band of Assyrian assassins who lived at the time of the Roman/Jewish wars. Belligerent bunch, if I recall. Helped to foment that war. They are, I assume, extinct."

"Correction, they still exist," said Rasheed. "The Sicarians are a secret organization called the Brotherhood of the Dagger. They use thin, razor-sharp knives to dispatch their unfortunate victims. They were fanatics, similar to the worshippers of Kali in India. They used knives instead of strangler's scarves. Even the Romans feared them. They actually have a five-hundred-year history."

Maggie's left hand encased David's arm. Her eyes met his and she shook her head.

Rasheed continued. "They considered a certain dagger to have supernatural powers. In fact they worshipped it almost as a deity. It disappeared after the destruction of Herod's temple. This dagger is sacred to these men. They seek it, almost with the same zeal as the Christian knights sought…What was it?"

"The Holy Grail," said Benson quietly.

"Yes, that's it. I believe this may possibly be that very sacred dagger of the Brotherhood," Rasheed gestured toward the case, "that was in the safekeeping of the Jewish high priest Ananias. This was when the second temple was destroyed by the Roman General Titus. The Brotherhood still seeks the return of their holy dagger. They believe it gathers its power from the ancient Babylonian God Ishtar and the demon Humbaba."

"The same dagger," added Benson, "that Cyrus gave to the Jewish high priest when the Hebrews migrated back to Judea? Of course, just as I suspected. They were the secret murder cult referred to in the Book of Esther."

"But it was in the British Museum," said Max. "Why couldn't they find it there?"

"It was not on display," said Benson. "It was buried away in a vast collection of Babylonian artifacts shipped to the museum in the 1860s. The dagger was never shown at the British Museum. It was in storage. This is its first public exhibition in centuries."

Benson looked pleased. In listening to Rasheed, he had made a truly amazing discovery. He believed he may have just confirmed the historic era of Sal's so-called episodes.

"May I ask the doctor?" said David, ever the consummate cross-examiner. "You say the Sicarian Brotherhood is still in existence. In what part of the world do they operate?"

"We believe their headquarters to be in Syria. They enter Lebanon at will. The border is like a sieve."

"But," said David, "they don't spend full time looking for an old dagger."

"No, of course not. They are brigands and thieves. They sow terror. They extort money and kidnap for ransom. They assassinate for pay. They believe if they can recover the dagger, their sect will become all powerful again."

David felt like this whole scene was a rehearsed script. They were all characters in a chilling, preordained drama in which they were destined to participate. Perhaps the outcome was already written somewhere. Perhaps nothing could change it.

Benson suggested the group adjourn to a conference room where they could sit down, have a cup of coffee, and continue the conversation.

There was an undercurrent of foreboding in the room. Each person was reacting differently.

Catherine was visibly nervous. Sal seemed detached, but had ostensibly remained in reality. He was not having an episode. David turned to Sal, concerned that something weird might happen to frighten Catherine. David knew nothing would impact the imperturbable Maggie. This was psychodrama to her. She was into all this stuff.

Max was overtly skeptical, but looked determined to participate in the game. He took a clinical approach; he had a plan. He was waiting impatiently for further developments and for the right time to put his plan into operation.

Dr. Rasheed was more than mildly inquisitive. He sensed hidden agendas in the room. There was more involved here than mere curiosity about this relic from the remote past.

Benson, elated, was clearly having fun.

"Well, Mr. Dematteo, did you see anything remotely familiar in that exhibit?" Benson asked.

"Yes, I think so," answered Sal. "That knife, I think I may have seen it before."

"Do you remember where?"

"I believe during the episode that I had in my office last Friday." Max had called his visions episodes. Sal had adopted the term.

Catherine turned to David. "Would you or somebody," she asked angrily, "care to tell me what is going on?"

Max knew it was time to intervene. If David tried to explain, he might have two patients on his hands.

"Catherine, Sal has been having some, eh, remarkable episodes. As you know I'm a psychiatrist."

"Dammit," said Sal. "I didn't want her this involved."

David spoke next. "Sal, she is involved. She has to be able to understand or the shock may be too much. She lives with you. She is your wife. You cannot continue to shield her. Stop denying this thing. Maybe she can help us!"

Sal put his face in his hands in a sign of despair.

"Am I cracking up, Dr. Vogel?"

"I don't believe so," Max said quietly. "But you must take an honest approach and face what I believe to be your deepest repressed fears. You have friends here who want to help, and your wife who cares for you and needs you."

"Sal," Catherine had tears in her eyes. "Just be honest with me. No matter what is happening, I love you and I will stand by you." She began to sob.

Benson tried to inject calm into the proceeding. "Listen, folks. Perhaps if Catherine would just listen to a story she may better—"

Maggie Seiler raised both hands in a calming posture.

"Hold it, guys. We are asking this woman to accept a premise that we ourselves don't begin to comprehend. We are discussing this woman's husband like he's in a test tube."

Maggie rose from her seat and went over to Catherine. She looked at her full in the face. Their eyes met. "Catherine, I want you trust us. We have assembled a first-class team. We are going to help Sal get through this trauma and you are going to help too. But you must stay calm and work with us."

Catherine Dematteo peered deep into those dark, intense eyes and saw what she needed—a strong, reassuring sincerity that spoke of trust and friendship. She collected her emotions. "I will listen. I will help. I apologize."

Maggie hugged her silently. She sat down. "Continue with your story, Benson." It was almost a command.

A truly amazing woman, David thought.

Benson cleared his throat; his story-telling voice began to spin its magic. "This tale begins and ends with one Joseph Ben Mattathias, aka Flavius Josephus. He was a charismatic man from a family of Jewish priests whose lineage could be traced to the Hasmonean dynasty. The Jews were a sorely divided people, obsessively protective of their beliefs and customs.

"The Romans ruled Judea through a succession of incompetent and corrupt Procurators and Legatees. It was a turbulent era in Roman history when, through treachery and murder, the ruling line passed from Julius Caesar to Marc Antony to Octavian, who took the name Augustus Caesar. His line ruled Rome as emperors during much of the early life of Josephus.

"In 64 C.E., at age twenty-seven, Josephus visited Rome. He was impressed, in fact overawed by its majesty and power. While his training was as a priest, his intellect and acumen was such that when he studied Roman military tactics, he not only understood them, but also was able to formulate strategic methods to counteract and oppose them. Two years later, Josephus was appointed Commander of Jewish troops in Galilee. His mission was to organize the defenses of the various cities. The Jews rose in revolt; they had had enough of Gessius Florus, the idiot procurator that Nero had appointed. They soundly defeated the Roman General Cestius, and prepared for a Roman onslaught. It came a year later in the person of Vespasian, a most able and determined Roman General."

David looked over at Sal, who was idly thumbing through a large volume titled *Classical Archeology*. Benson had deliberately placed the book in a strategic position to catch Sal's attention. Sal paused and pointed at a picture of what appeared to be ruins of a Roman city.

"Ephesus, Ephesus," mumbled Sal.

"Who? Where?" Benson started to say.

Everyone else in the room except Ibrahim Rasheed responded in some way.

Max put the first finger of his left hand quickly to his mouth signaling for silence. This was the opening for which he had been waiting. Sal was clearly off having an episode.

"Sal, this is Dr. Vogel. Can you hear me?"

No reaction.

"Sal, this is Dr. Vogel. Why don't you tell me where you are and what is happening."

"It's my brother. I can't carry out the command of Ananias." Sal was close to a frenzy but he was speaking in another voice. It was low and sepulchral. *"I searched but I couldn't find him. Now he is dying,"* Sal continued.

"What is your name?" Max asked. "Who is dying?"

"I am Aaron."

David silently slipped up behind Sal and looked over his shoulder. He studied the picture in the book. It was a large black and white photograph of the ruins of an old Roman city. The caption read, "Ephesus: Well-preserved ruins of a classical Graeco-Roman city on the Anatolian coast. Ephesus was a prominent commercial and vacation resort of the ancient Roman world."

"Ephesus, that's in Turkey!" said David. "What is Sal during in Turkey? Why in hell is he in Ephesus?"

CHAPTER 12

FRIDAY
EPHESUS 102 C.E.

He was dying in Ephesus. He looked through red-rimmed, fever-wracked eyes and entreated Clonarus, his Greek slave. "I want a rebbe! I must have a rebbe!"

The slave, who had faithfully served him for fifteen years, nodded knowingly to the Greek doctor.

"He claims to be Jewish. I will go to the old quarter and find a rabbi. Will he survive long enough?"

"I don't know," replied the physician. "Go now. Hurry."

The slave ran into the street. He passed the large library and the brothel. It was dusk and women not busy at the moment lounged in the front of the building. One young woman cried out, "Clonarus, come and see me later. I will be free for you."

He paid no attention. He moved quickly. He was a handsome, well-muscled, blonde youth, with fine-chiseled features, a slave since age seven. His master had purchased him at the market in Salonika after the Roman legions had quelled a minor uprising in his home city of Mycenae. His mother, a fragile girl of nineteen, had been sold to an itinerant merchant who used her himself for a time and then resold her to a pottery maker. She survived five more years, and then died of a terrible disease that stole her mind and wracked her body. She acquired the disease after the pottery maker had rented her out on a regular basis.

Clonarus fared considerably better. His master was a generous man of stature in the Roman community. Clonarus was taken to the capitol where he was taught to read, educated and lived in relative luxury. He performed sex, but only for his master, and then only on rare occasions. These contacts ceased when he reached the age of eight and began traveling with his master to far off places like Judea where his master had a spacious estate given to him by a previous emperor, Titus. There the old caretaker, a grizzled Jew named Eleazar, had taken a liking to him. He was allowed to fraternize with Eleazor's daughter, Miriam. His master promised him freedom when he died. Clonarus promised Miriam he would return when he was free and marry her.

Once, after the death of Titus, when they were in Rome, he met the Emperor Domitian at the grand palace near the great Temple of Jupiter. Clonarus's athletic prowess served him well. He was allowed to practice for, and participate in, the Greek games held in the grand Coliseum. For his showing in the racing and javelin competition, the emperor had awarded him a silver wreath. His master had treated him well. Now suddenly, at early dusk on a fall evening, he was faced with freedom and an uncertain future.

He jogged down Marble Road to Harbor Street, past the huge multi-layered arena. It was empty and silent. The Temple of Artemis was deserted and sheathed in evening shadows. Later, by torchlight the priests would begin their nightly rituals. When he reached the quarter at the other end of town, he was aware of a pronounced change. There were no chariots and few people about. Homes were smaller, in some cases only one-roomed huts. The pungent smell of food cooking was everywhere. Fires burned in stoves and smoke poured from chimneys. He stopped a bearded, older man in a dark cloak. He was wearing a small black cap in the center of his head. "I must find a rabbi," he said.

The man pointed toward a larger squat stone building at the end of the street. "It is the Sabbath. The rabbi will be in prayer."

The youth was not to be discouraged. He entered the building. Several men were scattered about the room. They were chanting loudly in a strange language. They all faced a plain wooden cabinet in the front of the room. A large six-pointed star adorned the cabinet.

Clonarus noted there were no statues or images of gods. What a strange way to pray.

A young man with quizzical eyes stopped him. "What do you want here?" he whispered.

"I must find a rabbi. My master is dying and begs for one."

"It is the Sabbath," said the man, irritation in his voice.

"He dies now. He cannot wait. He cries out for a rabbi."

The young man appeared to understand. He walked to the front. He leaned over and whispered something to another young man who was cloaked in what Clonarus assumed to be some sort of a multi-colored prayer shawl. The shawl had fine cloth fringes on each end.

The second man rose and studied the tall, blonde youth who stood impatiently at the rear of the room. He then carefully folded the shawl. He strode up to the youth and beckoned him to come outside.

"I am only a rabbi in training. The chief rabbi will not leave his congregation on the Sabbath. Who is your master?"

"His name is Josephus, Flavius Josephus, the writer and historian." The blonde youth carefully watched the rabbi in training. He was prepared to use force if necessary.

The rabbi patted the youth's arm and smiled. "You are sure he is dying?"

Clonarus revised his initial idea for a tough tactic. "Yes," he said softly, adding, "you will be amply rewarded."

Again the rabbi studied the young man and the response. "I will come. It is a mitzvah," he said. "Let us go."

When they arrived, the life force of Flavius Josephus had noticeably lessened. He breathed only with great effort. The doctor knew the end was near.

The rabbi entered the room and looked into the dying man's tortured eyes.

"Are you a rebbe?" the dying man rasped.

"I am," the rabbi assured him quietly. He unwrapped the soft cloth shawl, kissed it and started to recite a prayer.

"Wait, Rebbe." The dying man interrupted the prayer. "I have an important message. You must listen and believe me." He summoned all his strength and grasped the rabbi's arm. His hoarse voice suddenly cleared and he spoke in a calm, even tone.

"I am Joseph Ben Mattathias. I led the Jewish forces in Galilee in the great Roman war." He sat up and could not be made to lie down.

"I did not show the Roman forces the hidden passages beneath the temple. I only wanted to save my people. That is why I begged them to surrender. I knew they would be destroyed. As I go to meet my Lord Jehovah, I swear it was so. The slaughter in Jerusalem was not on my head. I only wanted to save my people I…" His voice faltered. "I did not show Titus the secret passages. There was another—"

His voice failed. He fell back on his bed. His breathing became shallow again before he exhaled once, a deep, wracking whisper of a sound from within his chest. He had breathed his last.

"Hear O Israel," sang the rabbi. "The Lord is God. The Lord is One. Take in peace the soul of your servant Joseph Ben Mattathias." He turned to the youth. "Does he have kin?"

The youth shrugged. "None here in Ephesus. He has family in Alexandria. Can we give him a religious burial? He has ample resources."

"We can and we will." The rabbi began to chant the Kaddish, the Hebrew prayer for the dead. "Yit'gadal v'yit'kadash sh'mei raba b'al'ma di v'ra khir'utei …"

* * * *

There was a loud crash of glass outside the conference room. Benson threw open the door and moved toward the exhibit. A short, dark man wearing a facemask was poised over the case that housed the dagger. He wheeled around in surprise at Benson's sudden appearance. He carried a hammer and a sharp, thin knife in his right hand. He edged toward Benson in a hostile gesture as if he meant to attack. Then he hesitated. The six-foot-three frame of Ibrahim Rasheed had come between Benson and the burglar. Rasheed glared at the masked intruder in unconcealed anger. The man turned and raced for the exit. He dashed down the stairs, out the door and tossed his mask into nearby bushes. Then he threw himself into a waiting car. With a screech of tires, he and a driver sped off into the autumn twilight.

"Did you retrieve the dagger?"

"No, I was stopped. There were too many people. He was there! This giant black man. I don't understand why or how."

"Then we will have to go with another plan."

"A hostage. Who then?"

"The woman. The dark-haired one. She is the one in the prophesy. Surely they will pay dearly for her."

* * * *

On the second floor of the museum, the severely shaken group was close to panic. Sal had roused himself and was asking for an explanation of what happened. Benson was unnerved. This last incident had unraveled his normal composure. Catherine had her arm tightly around Sal, and even Maggie showed overt signs of fear.

Three guards had converged on the glass case and the central security office had put a call into the police.

Hammurabi's dagger was safe. Benson removed it from the shattered case. He placed it in a locked box. "This goes into my office until tomorrow morning. This situation is even more urgent than I thought."

Max stood by in a kind of shock. His usual unperturbed demeanor showed signs of more than a slight crack.

David watched Dr. Rasheed. "Well, sir," he said, "that guy sure beat it quick when he saw you. Who was he?"

Ignoring David, Dr. Rasheed did not respond. He kept a vigil on the stairs as if he were expecting the man to return.

Finally he spoke. "I'm afraid, Mr. Gold, it has begun. It is the Brotherhood. You know, Mr. Gold, you and I spring from the same loins." He put a huge hand on David's shoulder. "You from Abraham, Isaac and Sara, and I from Abraham, Hagar and Ishmael. We are often opposed to each other. I think maybe we are on the same side this time. Be most careful, you and your friend, Mr. Dematteo. There are strange forces at work."

Dr. Rasheed's gaze shifted to Maggie. "Guard the beautiful dark-haired woman well, Mr. Gold."

David was startled. Rasheed's eyes were aglow with a strange penetrating light. "I think you and I will meet again."

David felt a cold chill creep slowly along his spine. This incident was more than he, perhaps any of them, even Benson, had expected. Rasheed's speech to him was more than odd; it felt like a dire warning. He shivered.

Maggie came over and crooked her arm over David's left shoulder as if to shield him. "Dr. Rasheed, would you join us for dinner?"

"Afraid not," he replied while looking at his watch. "But thank you for the invitation. I must catch an early airplane." He leaned close to Maggie. "Please take care, Miss Seiler."

"I will, thank you. But why me, Dr. Rasheed? How am I involved with this dagger?"

"Frankly, I don't know, Miss Seiler. But I do know that you are somehow a part of this. Benson!" Rasheed rapidly changed the subject. "We must talk now, quickly, before I am required to leave."

The unlikely pair vanished into the conference room and closed the door, leaving an astonished group.

Two policemen, one a spare, light-haired plainclothes man in his late thirties, who introduced himself as Detective Ed Flaharty, examined the crime scene and took everyone's name.

"Nothing actually taken." He seemed relieved. "I'll be contacting each one of you. I understand Mr. Throckmorton and the big black guy, Dr. Rasheed, were the only ones who actually got a good look at the thief. I'll talk to them now. The rest of you can leave, if you like. Be sure we have your addresses and stay in town. This knife valuable?" He addressed the question to David.

"I guess so. It's over three thousand years old, irreplaceable. By the way," added David, "I got a brief glimpse, but I couldn't tell you what the guy looked like. He had on a mask.

"Okay," said Flaharty. "If you think of anything, call me. Here's my card."

* * * *

It was close to eleven before the group, now reduced to five people, had finished eating. They had settled on seafood at the Craig Tavern, a shrimp and chips restaurant with bright lights, a juke box that alternatively played Frank Sinatra or Doris Day, and served good Pennsylvania beer. After the second bottle of beer, everyone was more relaxed but clearly tired. Sal had drunk three bottles of Fort Pitt. He was one up on the rest of the group.

Max kept his eyes on Sal who seemed to be with them, but his conversation was delivered in brief sentences and without much expression or humor. Max calculated that Sal had lost twenty minutes during his episode in the conference room. But for the attempted robbery, the episode might have lasted longer. Max had taken notes. He would have his secretary type them in the morning and maybe call Bernie. Maybe. He hadn't yet made up his mind. He had grave doubts as to whether Bernie Adler was ready for his own version of what had occurred.

Maggie and Catherine were having an animated discussion. The two had struck up an immediate friendship. Catherine needed the support. She was badly shaken. Her jagged nerves displayed themselves in exaggerated demonstrations of nervous laughter, contrary to her normally shy, withdrawn personality.

Sal spoke. "Cath, I'm sorry, but I've got a hearing at ten on the Feeney case. I need about an hour of preparation time. We better get going."

Max insisted on paying the bill. He liked to spend bits of his mother's ample fortune. Furthermore, the outline of an outstanding case study that would certainly make the books was beginning to take shape. Nobody argued. Doctors with wealthy parents didn't need to impress anybody. Lawyers with embryo practices were delighted to have dinner bought for them, especially by doctors with wealthy parents.

After proper good nights and thank you's to Max, everyone piled into the Chevrolet and drove in silence to Sal's house.

Before Sal and Catherine got out of the car, Maggie reached over into the back seat and pressed Catherine's hand. "How about if I call you tomorrow?"

"Please, I would appreciate that very much. Thank you for everything."

Sal muttered his good night and said something about "I'll see you in the morning."

* * * *

David pulled to a stop in front of Maggie's house. He shut off the motor and prepared to get out of the car.

"Hey, you want to talk about Max's observations tomorrow night?"

"Sure, where and what time?"

"My house, about eight. No beer, just coffee. Do you think I'm too forward? Do you like Irish girls?"

This time David couldn't resist. He leaned over, looked into those enigmatic eyes and kissed Maggie full on the lips. The contact lasted several seconds longer than either of them planned. She responded far more amorously than he expected.

"Well, counselor, you have passion," she said whimsically. "But it ain't bad." She kissed him again, but this time lightly. "See you tomorrow night. It's late and we have both had a long night. Don't bother, I'll make it to the door safely."

David waited until she had found her key and unlatched the door. She turned, smiled and waved. As David drove home, he contemplated the evening. Another eerie encounter had occurred. This, added to events that were already beyond explanation. The drama had taken a macabre turn with the appearance of the intruder. Dr. Rasheed had inserted a factor into the equation that brought a further air of mystery to the whole evening. Who the hell was he anyway?

David pulled to a stop in front of his apartment. He sat in the car, inert, frozen in time. Suddenly David felt that he was peering through a cracked mirror. His life as he knew it was all there. Friends, family, law practice, Max Vogel, his partner Sal, Cathy, the city of Pittsburgh where he had been born and raised. All normal, all as it should have been. A few new characters had arrived, Benson and, of course, Maggie, this gem of a woman he had just met. People come and go in your life, that's not uncommon. But the view was distorted. Something was badly out of focus. Instead of the mirror, he was looking through a cracked prism. On the other side, the world was spinning wildly; space and time were jumbled. There was an immense jigsaw puzzle with too many pieces. The pieces not only didn't fit, but didn't seem to belong in his life, maybe in anyone's life. For one brief instant he wondered if this whole thing was happening at all.

CHAPTER 13

THE SECOND WEEK, THURSDAY
ED FINNERAN

"Hear Ye, Hear Ye, all rise, the Federal Court of the western district of Pennsylvania, Judge Ronald Hanes presiding, is now in session."

Judge Hanes, bald as a cueball, looking like a cross between a melon and a white pumpkin, strode up to the bench. He banged his gavel once and sat his two-hundred-and-ten-pound body down heavily behind the bench. The judge appeared awake. He was well known for sleeping occasionally through boring hearings or even trials. Most lawyers who spent time in Federal Court recognized that if you wanted to make a point with Hanes, it had to be accomplished in the first hour of the hearing. The onlookers, all of whom had stood up, rejoined their chairs and waited for the procedure to begin.

David was running late. He dashed up the stairs and entered the courtroom slightly breathless. He dropped into a seat near the front of the room where most of the lawyers were waiting for their matters to be called. This was motion calendar morning. No trials were scheduled.

Hanes looked up from reading the calendar and scowled. "Well, Mr. Gold, late as usual. What poor, persecuted client do we represent today?"

David, desensitized to Judge Hanes and his customary sarcasm, rose and grinned. "The Great State of Pennsylvania, Your Honor, in the person of the 112th Fighter Interceptor Group of the Pennsylvania Air National Guard."

Hanes looked disappointed. "Well, I see you are first on the calendar. Who represents the plaintiff here?"

"Martin Kalb, Your Honor, and we are ready."

Marty Kalb was in his late forties and beginning to go to fat. He wore bifocals, sported a graying mustache and was dressed in a threadbare gray suit. Marty was a well-known activist lawyer who perennially represented lost causes and specialized in tweaking the noses of those in power. There were many who whispered that Marty was a menace and most likely a Communist. David felt if this was the best the Communists could muster in Allegheny County, there couldn't be much of a local threat.

"This is a motion for a preliminary restraining order," announced the bailiff.

"Proceed, Counsel," said Judge Hanes, nodding at Marty.

Two Jewish lawyers, he observed silently, not much of a choice here. This plainly irritated him. He would have to decide the issue on the merits.

"Your Honor, the plaintiff, Mr. Watts, a poor, hard-working local farmer, seeks a preliminary restraining order against the defendant's low-flying airplanes. They fly at all hours of the night, seven days a week, directly over his property. His livestock and poultry have been emotionally disturbed and are unable to procreate. In addition, he and his wife are on the edge of a nervous breakdown due to lack of sleep. We believe the low flying is deliberate and done with intent to cause severe distress. Unless this court grants an immediate order, the plaintiff will suffer irreparable damage."

"Mr. Gold," said the Judge, "your view."

"If the Court please, Your Honor, we have investigated the matter. We are willing to meet and try to adjust our schedules to a reasonable extent. The plaintiff has never invited us to sit down and amicably discuss the matter. We have received several written ultimatums from my learned opponent, Mr. Kalb, but never once has he agreed to meet with us and mediate. The Air Guard is trying to be a good neighbor. I would remind you that we are engaged in the defense of this nation, a vital pursuit that is a twenty-four-hour-a-day mission. An order against conducting salient national defense activities would set a most dangerous precedent and in our view is patently illegal."

"David, your hotshots are just trying to aggravate Mr. Watts because he keeps petitioning General Martin," Marty Kalb countered. "That's why they fly in the middle of the night, low over his property. This bull about protecting the nation is hogwash."

"Now, now, Mr. Kalb, let's keep it civil," cautioned Judge Hanes.

"Under the Sovereign Immunity theory, Your Honor, if this plaintiff complains of an injury to property, he can bring an administrative action under the Federal Tort Claims Act. At this point that is the extent of his remedies. There is no basis in law or equity for the issuance of a restraining order against the federal or the state government conducting activities in its sovereign capacity," David replied.

Kalb jumped up in mock anger. "Another example of big government oppressing its citizens. This is shameless!"

"That is quite enough, Mr. Kalb," cautioned the Judge. "Motion for temporary restraining order denied," barked Hanes.

"With prejudice, Your Honor?" David asked.

"Without prejudice." Hanes looked disgusted. "Further, I order briefs submitted with supporting authorities in thirty days. If the matter gets settled, briefs are unnecessary. Mr. Gold, why don't you and those high-octane flyboys get together with Mr. Watts and work out some deal."

The judge turned. "Mr. Kalb, you know I can't move the airport, let alone halt defense activities. Why don't you and Mr. Watts meet with the folks out there and make an honest effort to compromise."

Hanes banged the gavel, entirely satisfied that he had acted in an eminently judicial manner.

"Next matter," called the bailiff.

Disgusted, Marty Kalb looked at David. "You stooge farts are all alike. You're part of the tyranny. You know, Gold, I am sick of you." He leaned his angry face close to David's. "I will get you, Gold."

David was taken aback by Kalb's venom. "Marty, why don't you do yourself a favor and zip up that uncanny knack you have for irritating everybody in sight."

David startled. Marty had a broadsword in his right hand. He wore a black chain mail tunic. His bare legs were knobby and hairless. His skinny arms showed a noticeable lack of muscle. When David blinked and looked again, Marty was back in his gray suit and was at least twenty feet away. David turned to Mr. Watts who angrily watched the exchange. "Mr. Watts, call me anytime. I'll set up a meeting with General Martin. I will personally help you get some peace and quiet."

Watts's attitude changed. "Yes, sir. I would appreciate that."

Marty Kalb glowered. David was well aware that Marty hated above all what he termed the damn military machine. He didn't want to compromise. He had heard Marty say many times, "I will unmask and reveal the corrupt, decayed and rotten hierarchy of fascists that runs the military."

Marty stomped out of the courtroom. His manner indicated he wasn't finished. David was sure there would be other days and other issues. He wondered just exactly how Marty was going to get him.

The Federal Courthouse was on the north end of Grant Street next to the Pennsylvania Station. You could hear the trains as they pulled out to various parts of the country. David paused and watched the station in the distance out of the second-floor courthouse window. He chuckled. Poor old Marty, always jousting with windmills. But why the hell was he so angry? It seemed out of proportion. The troops probably were buzzing old Watts's property. But not because they were angry with him. Watts had a nineteen-year-old daughter who was the object of considerable interest at the 112th.

And, what about that flick of time, there in the courtroom, when he thought he saw Marty as some kind of an ancient warrior? This Sal thing was really beginning to get to him.

David slowly ascended the wide staircase. The courthouse was almost empty. He liked the quiet at the north end of Grant Street. The environs of the Federal Courthouse were a sedate escape from the noisy bustle of the street.

* * * *

About a mile away, on the south end of Grant Street, stood the County Courthouse, a forbidding, gray stone, Romanesque building complete with a bridge that connected the courthouse to the adjacent Victorian jailhouse. The prison, like a medieval fortress, solemnly guarded the approaches to downtown Pittsburgh. The bridge was aptly named the Bridge of Sighs, a tribute to the many miscreants who made journeys from the courtroom to the harsh cells beyond.

This Thursday in September, courtroom ten of that Allegheny County center of justice and jurisprudence was witness to a hearing far more rancorous, spirited and lively than the one in which David had appeared. Sal Dematteo had his hands full trying to control the Feeney boys and their supporters. The hearing was basically to determine if there was sufficient evidence to hold Tom Feeney over for trial in Common Pleas Court, to set bail if feasible and to hear a plea to the charge of second-degree murder.

They had drawn Judge Homer Washington. He was the sole black judge in the county. A token black who didn't act like a token. Two of the Feeney brothers didn't like having a black judge. In fact, these sons of Eire didn't like having a judge at all. Their noisy antics weren't doing much to help their brothers' cause. Mrs. Feeney sat, hands clasped in silent resignation. She had long ago, since her sainted husband had passed on, given up trying to control her four boys. Her only comfort, her daughter Elizabeth, was working and couldn't attend until late in the morning. She hadn't yet arrived.

Judge Homer Washington was a fair man with a sense of humor that was slightly ribald. But he was not one to put up with any nonsense. He generally had a jocular attitude in court but at this moment he was boiling mad. "If there is one more outburst from this side of the room, I will clear the courtroom and hold a couple of you characters in contempt. That means fine and/or jail. Damn it," he said. "This is a courtroom, not a circus. Mr. Dematteo, got anything more to say?"

Sal requested the judge to pause for a minute. He leaned over to Walt, his friend and the oldest and most mature of the Feeney brothers. "Walt, can you get these wiseasses to shut up? We have a great judge here but we're losing him fast. He'll lock your brother up and throw away the key."

Sal was suddenly conscious of large figure of a man in a black suit with a white collar standing at the back of the room. "I want absolute quiet!" he boomed at the crowd. "This court will have respect and decorum from all of you or you will have to answer to me."

Father O'Malley was very angry and the audience knew it. A restless silence settled over the room. You could hear a feather drop and the bailiff breathing hoarsely through tobacco-varnished lungs. The judge acknowledged this irregular assistance. "Your divine intervention is most welcome, Father. The boys are a little unruly today. I was about to put a couple of them in the pokey." He banged the gavel. "Continue, Mr. Dematteo."

There was an underlying murmur from the other side of the room, where the family and friends of the deceased had gathered. They were from another nearby neighborhood with the unlikely name of Hazelwood. An unlikely name since the neighborhood was populated mostly by mills and mill workers and there were few trees and certainly none were hazel. This group had made the two-mile trip downtown to assure justice, from their viewpoint, prevailed.

The gavel banged again with even more force. Sal rose and faced the court. "Your Honor, Mr. Feeney is a reputable citizen with roots in this community. He has no past record of any arrests or convictions for serious crimes. He would never flee the jurisdiction. We ask the court set bail at five hundred dollars."

Again, a murmur of objection from the opposite side of a highly charged courtroom. Again the gavel slammed down on the bench. The prosecutor, Danny Carter, objected strenuously. "Your Honor, this is a murder case. A man is dead under violent circumstances.

The People feel required to call for bail of at least . . . ," Carter considered for a second, then continued, "two hundred and fifty thousand dollars." That was a good round number. Enough to satisfy those members of the gallery who were the most vocal supporters of the deceased.

"This was a barroom brawl," argued Sal. "The District Attorney knows it. He also knows Mr. Feeney is not a risk and will appear for trial if and when ordered."

"Alright, alright." Judge Washington decided to put a stop to any further wrangling. "Let's get the formalities over with. Mr. Feeney, how do you plead, guilty or not guilty?"

"Not guilty," mumbled Tom Feeney. He was slouching in his chair.

"Speak up, Mr. Feeney. This court can't hear you."

Sal nudged Tom and whispered, "Act respectful, damn it. Stand up!"

Walter leaned over and popped Tom on the back of his head. Tom came to an immediate brace. "Not guilty, Your Honor."

At that moment David entered the courtroom and slipped into a seat in the rear, next to his partner Ed Finneran.

"How's it going?" he asked.

"Sal's doing okay. Sufficient evidence to bind Feeney over for trial. I think the best the D.A. can prove is negligent manslaughter. Some character testified he saw Tom Feeney throw a beer bottle. It's still a felony."

The judge made a quick decision. "Mrs. Feeney, will your son show up for trial?"

"Yes, Your Honor. Father O'Malley and I will make sure of that."

Father O'Malley nodded in the affirmative.

The judge banged his gavel. "Trial is set for November twenty-third, 1955, in the criminal division of the Common Pleas Court of Allegheny County. Bail is set at fifteen thousand dollars. Any objections?"

Both counsels signified approval. Judge Washington banged his gavel for at least the tenth time that morning. "So ordered. Let's take a fifteen-minute recess so everyone can cool down."

The court reporter was busily recording the order. The room was slowly clearing. Sal remained behind and chatted with the Assistant District Attorney and Ernie Burke, the bail bondsman.

"Ed, you free for lunch?" David asked his partner.

"Sure, I have a workman's comp hearing at three."

"We need to talk. Let's go to Casey's. We can catch up with Sal later."

As David rose to leave, a hand touched his shoulder. He wheeled around and looked up into Father O'Malley's stern countenance.

"David, how are you?"

"Well, I'm fine, Father."

Father O'Malley nodded at Ed Finneran.

"Ed, all well with you?"

"Yes, sir. Can't complain."

"Good. I wonder if I can have a few minutes of both your time."

"Of course, Father. Say when."

Ed Finneran also agreed.

"Now, if possible."

"Ed and I are about to get a sandwich. Care to join us?" David glanced at Ed.

Ed assented with a nod. "Goin' to Casey's, Father. Best hot corned beef in Pittsburgh."

"Except for Hebrew National," quipped David.

A belligerent crowd had gathered on the courthouse steps. A lone cop was anxiously surveying the situation. Two groups had formed. They eyed each other. They were clearly in a hostile mood. They blocked the steps causing neutrals to circumvent the crowd. Jack Feeney and a tall, husky, blonde kid in his early twenties with mean eyes and a hard scowl on his face were standing eye to eye, toe to toe and were about to get into a pushing match.

A diminutive reporter from the *Pittsburgh Gazette* was trying to incite the Hazelwood group. "How do you guys feel about your buddy being killed?"

A good riot would sell papers. The cop was getting really nervous and was about to call for reinforcements. A cross word could easily ignite this powder keg. Father O'Malley had apparently anticipated trouble. He had made a phone call. He breathed easier when an old vintage two-door Plymouth pulled up and another priest got out.

Father Patrick Dunn, a pugnacious priest who had boxed middleweight at Holy Cross, knew the leaders from Hazelwood. He was at least a foot shorter than the tall, blonde kid, but he marched up to him and said angrily, "Well, Elwell, are the Catholics goin' to fight the Catholics this morning? Is it one town against another? Get your boys together and go on home. You think a battle and maybe some more mothers cryin' over more dead or injured sons is goin' to help your dead friend? Have you lost all reason? You want a war? There is one mother already grieving for her lost son."

Father O'Malley conferred with Walter Feeney. "Walter, a riot is going to hurt Tom's case. Help me get this gang out of here."

The elder Feeney, the only beacon of reason in the group, had been uncomfortable with the turn of events. "Please, everyone," he spoke loudly, "let's go home. Tom will be out on bail tonight. Any disturbance will hurt his case."

At that moment Elizabeth Feeney, who had finally gotten away from her job at the bank, arrived. "Get out of here, all of ya," she shouted at both groups. She put her arms tenderly around her mother. "C'mon, Mom, let's go get a cup of tea." She glared at her two younger brothers. "Damn hooligans. Haven't you caused your mother enough trouble?"

The boys' sheepish looks were an adequate reply.

A squad car pulled up and disgorged four burly policemen with nightsticks. Two more cops came around the corner. The original cop on the scene sighed deeply in relief. The thought of wading into that crowd as a lone keeper of law and order had not been very inviting.

David couldn't help but admire Elizabeth. She got right to the core. Even Walter had been hesitant to stop the pending altercation. For one second David had considered stepping in to help, but he wisely stayed clear of the crowd. A Jewish lawyer in this mob would have been as popular as Lucretia Borgia in a room full of poison victims.

The milling groups began to slowly disperse in opposite directions. Tension lessened noticeably. Father O'Malley shook hands with Father Dunn. "Patrick, thank you so much for coming down. You really helped."

"Glad you called me, Sean," said Father Dunn. "I have to run. I think we need a joint mass this Sunday. We can't let this thing get out of hand."

"Good idea. I'll call you later today. Will you be at the rectory?"

Father Dunn thought for a moment. "Call me after four, Sean, I'll be there."

Father O'Malley's lanky body and long legs double-timed down Fifth Avenue and braked to a stop in front of Casey's Bar and Grill. The sign in large script on the window announced that Casey's had been in business since 1926. Both Ed Finneran and David had to shift into high gear to keep pace with the good Father.

They entered Casey's where the lunch hour was almost over. Male waiters in black bow ties and white aprons were busy clearing the tables. Dirty glasses and dishes soiled with gravy stains were clinking while the boys busily hustled under Casey's jaundiced eye.

"Why, Father O'Malley," Casey's face lit up with a hospitable grin. "This is a real honor." It wasn't his current station as a priest that stimulated the welcome. Father O' Malley's autographed picture, in full regalia and carrying a football, hung in a conspicuous place on the left wall, not far from an aging, grainy snapshot of Knute Rockne. Autographed black-and-white pictures of many other vintage athletes also graced the brown, paneled wall.

The three were seated quickly and proceeded to order large roast beef sandwiches. David passed on beer for coffee. But both Finneran and Father O'Malley opted for a bottle of local Fort Pitt lager.

"Close one, huh, Father?" commented David.

"Too close. There's a lot of bad blood out there. Were goin' to have a joint mass next Sunday. I hope we can settle things down."

The sandwiches arrived complete with horseradish, hot mustard and sauerkraut. David took a huge bite and nearly choked at the Priest's next words.

"I know you guys are busy so I'll get right to the point. What's wrong with Sal Dematteo?"

"Well, Father," said Ed Finneran, "he's fine. He did well gettin' Feeney out on fifteen thousand dollar bail. What with a potential murder charge and—"

"I don't mean that. What's wrong with him?"

"Father," stammered David. "Ed is not familiar with Sal's problem. We were going to discuss it today at lunch."

"Oh, sorry, Ed. Catherine's been to see me and called me twice on the phone. I've tried to talk to Sal, but he won't discuss it. He assures me that Tom Feeney will probably get off either with probation and a fine or be acquitted.

"That's not the issue. What's wrong with Sal?" Father O'Malley repeated the question for the third time. He addressed it directly to David. It was clear he wasn't going to go down that road a fourth time.

David sighed. Boy, this Sal thing was getting more and more complicated. "Father, Sal is seeing a psychiatrist. A very good one at Western State who I know personally. He believes Sal is suffering from a mild traumatic syndrome. I'm sorry I can't discuss it in any detail. It is strictly a confidential doctor-patient relationship, and I'm not privy to their sessions." Using the old parable that many things were better off left unsaid, David skipped details of the recent episodes.

"What's goin' on?" interrupted Finneran.

"If he gets sick, who will represent Feeney?" asked the Father.

"Feeney will get excellent representation," assured David. "But, Father, we may need your help. Can we count on you?"

"Of course. But can't you at least tell me what the doctor thinks is happening?"

"What's goin' on?" interrupted Ed again. This time more forcefully. The conversation was beginning to sound like a twenty-question game.

Casey wandered over. "Everything okay, boys?"

"Food's great as usual, Casey," David said. Casey waited for more accolades. When none came he ambled off toward the bar.

"Alright," David rubbed his head ruefully. "But this must be kept in the strictest confidence. If this gets out, there will be hell to pay." He glanced around. There were no other patrons nearby. "Sal has been having some strange episodes," he blurted out in a low voice. "Mind flashbacks, hallucinations, or…," he stopped to clear his throat, "or visions."

Ed Finneran had a very literal mind. He didn't believe in elves, fairies, witches or visions. Ed's philosophy was that reality was what you could see, feel and hear. He even had trouble with some of the more mystical aspects of religion. He was flabbergasted. His buddy and partner Sal was experiencing something that his other partner called "episodes."

"What the hell kind of episodes?" snapped Ed.

David refused to answer. He had taken the silent equivalent of the Fifth Amendment. "Ed, let's table that question for a moment. Father, does Catherine know and understand?"

"Yes, she does. She's met the doctor and talked to him. How can I help?" asked the priest.

"For now, keep the family calm. I will talk to the doctor and have him brief you."

That was all David could think to say. But somehow he knew the priest had a further, more compelling function to perform in the drama that was rapidly unfolding. He had no clue as to what that role would be or what further contribution the priest would make. He only knew that this man would become an important actor and in the very near future. Anyway, Father O'Malley was satisfied for the moment.

Ed Finneran was not satisfied. "I've known Sal for fifteen years. We went to high school together. There was no more put-together guy. If he's having episodes, he's got a brain tumor or brain fever or something."

"The doctor is testing now for organic causes," David assured him. "We don't know any more. But Ed, if he needs help, you and I have got to be there for him. We may have to appear in court or assist on a case, whatever needs to be done."

"Father, don't worry about Feeney," said Ed. "I'll get Paul Kelly to represent him if we need a substitute criminal lawyer. He owes me one. As for Sal, you and I will pull him through, David. If there is any way I can help. But I need to be informed." Jesus, he murmured to himself, visions.

David agreed. "To be sure, Ed. You will know what I know when I know it."

Father O'Malley had an extremely concerned look on his face. "May the good Lord Jesus and all his angels and saints protect that fine boy and his family."

David heartily concurred. They might need the Lord before they were through. In fact, he felt sure they were going to need all the help they could get. Angels and saints weren't a bad idea, and a little assist from the Big Boss would certainly be welcome.

CHAPTER 14

THE SECOND WEEK, THURSDAY
MAGGIE'S HOME

Benson sipped tea and spoke in his usual professorial tone. "I believe the episodes that Mr. Dematteo is experiencing are time messages." As usual, Benson would toss out an absurd premise and wait for a reaction. Maggie didn't flinch. David responded and quickly.

"That little dagger thief in the museum wasn't a time message. I was right behind you and Rasheed. He had a nasty looking shiv, and he was ready to use it. You saw it, Benson. What the hell was the message?"

"Of course, that wasn't a time byte. The man was real enough. But before we debate, I suggest we listen to Dr. Vogel's notes." Maggie had recorded them on a wire tape. She had brought the machine home so they could listen to what transpired. The voice they heard was Dr. Max Vogel relating what had occurred that afternoon.

David and Maggie, even Benson, were transfixed by what emanated from the tape:

Under hypnosis at 4:30 p.m., Thursday September 24th, the patient, Sal Dematteo, related a very troubling incident. He believed he was in a deep cistern, a cave somewhere underneath an unnamed city with several other men. They apparently were hiding. They had food and water and some weapons. A friend of Sal's or whoever Sal is or was, let's assume for discussion Josephus or his brother, found his way to their place of concealment. He brought terms of surrender from the Romans. Josephus was prone to accept, but the others strongly objected. They threatened his life if he agreed.

The notes were puzzling after that point.

The group then entered into a suicide pact. Sal argued against it. Suicide was a sin against God. He was unanimously overruled. The group decided suicide was the only honorable course of action. Life in the Egyptian mines, crucifixion or death by beast or man in the arena was unthinkable. Resigned to his fate, the patient stated that he helped to develop a system of drawing lots to determine who would kill whom and who would be the sole survivor and be forced to kill himself.

At 5:05 p.m. Sal became very agitated. He described in vivid detail the grisly scene as one by one these men killed each other by slashing each other's throats. By some miracle or by clever design, the patient was the only survivor.

He made his way out of the tunnel and, it appears, turned himself over to the Romans.

At 5:30 p.m. the session ceased. The patient was exhausted but seemed to be fully restored to reality. He smoked a cigarette, shook hands, thanked me and left. I had given him a post-hypnotic suggestion that he would wake up refreshed and remember nothing of the encounter. Note: Must have Maggie check this incident with Benson Throckmorton ASAP. This syndrome is most puzzling. The narratives that the patient recounts are most logical and are in graphic detail.

Benson slapped the table, spilling the remainder of his coffee on the floor along with the cup. "That happened!" he exclaimed. "That actually happened. It's recorded in his first and most famous book, *The Jewish Wars*."

Maggie excused herself, went to the kitchen and procured a large towel. She wiped up the coffee and then scrubbed briefly at the rug with some soapy looking cleaner.

"Please continue, Ben," she said casually. "I think you are on to something."

Benson was unaware of his own actions. He plunged back into his discourse, and in a few seconds became completely immersed in his tale.

"In the summer of 67 C.E., the Roman General Vespasian, after quickly dispersing the army that Josephus had formed to oppose him in the Galilee, bottled up a large contingent of Jewish insurgents in the fortress city of Jotapata. For six weeks the Jewish defenders, directed by an inspired Josephus, conducted a brilliant tactical defense.

"Jotapata could only be attacked from one direction. It stood on the edge of a cliff with deep ravines on three sides." Benson's hands were moving rapidly as he described the city. "On the northern side a hill sloped up to the city gate where Josephus had constructed a high wall of earth and stone.

"When Vespasian's artillery hurled huge long-range missiles at the town, Josephus led his troops outside the gates. They fought back the Roman legions with great losses to both sides.

"The Romans then began to construct a large platform with which to continue the assault on the city wall. To protect his men from missiles and arrows, Vespasian erected wooden and stone barriers so the men could work unharmed. Jewish shock troops made continuous assaults almost shutting down platform work.

"Josephus knew this was merely a delaying tactic and sooner or later the Roman platform would be built. He decided to raise the height of the existing wall. After a Roman barrage Josephus had a railing built over which he stretched wet raw ox hides to deflect the rocks, hurtling weapons and firebrands and raised the wall another thirty feet.

"Vespasian, amazed at the incredible defense, cut off food and supplies. But with characteristic resourcefulness, the Jews found a south gully where men could sneak out clothed in sheepskins to fool the Romans and return with needed supplies.

"In angry desperation, Vespasian launched another attack. This time his men were met at the walls with boiling oil and a melted clover plant, called fenugreek, which caused the attackers to slip and fall off their siege engines. The ropes they had slung to the parapets became slick and impossible to scale and once more they were repulsed at the ramparts with great loss.

"Imagine this remarkable guy." Benson was excited to the point of exhilaration. "Josephus was raised and trained as a scholar and priest. In 64 C.E., he journeys to Rome to negotiate the freedom of some captive priests and while there studies Roman military tactics. Two years later, without any formal military training, he is able to counter the best Roman attempts to capture Jotapata with a grab bag of ingenious strategies.

"You know what war was in ancient times. It was sheer brute force. Body against body, most wounded bled to death. At the end of a battle, it was not uncommon to see scores of headless bodies strewn all over—"

"Benson! What about the cistern incident? We know the battles were not fun and games." David was not entertained. He'd had a long, tiring day and this whole mess was beginning to rag at his nerves.

David and Maggie's eyes met almost simultaneously. She looked amused. Her eyes begged for patience. "Benson sometimes gets carried away," she said.

"Sorry," apologized Benson. He then proceeded to continue almost without a hiccup to tell his tale.

"On the forty-seventh day of the siege Roman power overwhelmed the defenders. The Roman platform now topped the city wall. In a thick, early morning mist Titus, Vespasian's son, stole into the citadel with a troop of handpicked legionnaires and stabbed all the sentries. They opened the gates. The resulting slaughter was terrible to behold. The defenders were too exhausted to put up much resistance.

"Josephus, realizing all was lost, retreated with forty citizens to an underground cistern deep beneath the fortress from which there was no escape.

"On the second day, a Jew, actually a friend to Josephus, found them. He brought terms, promising to spare their lives, from the Roman commander. Josephus, ever the pragmatist, praised the group's conduct on the battlefield but to die an ignominious death either by their own hand or on a Roman cross seemed a useless gesture. Suicide, he reminded them, was a sin under the law of Moses. He recommended they accept the generous terms. To a man they disagreed with their commander and forced him to agree to join a suicide pact. The Roman terms were refused. Josephus, as their leader, was then asked to develop a system whereby lots would be drawn and each man would receive an assignment to cut another man's throat. He did and (surprise, surprise) he ended up as the last man alive. He then left the underground cave, walked out, surrendered to the Romans, was put in chains and brought before Vespasian.

"That, my friends, is the story behind the incident in Sal's episode," said Benson.

"You know," commented Maggie, "there's a certain pattern unfolding here. Can you guys see it?"

"Pattern," echoed David wearily, "I can't see a pattern."

Benson closed his eyes. He rubbed his hands together in a gesture peculiar to college professors who are contemplating some weighty problem. "I think I see it," agreed Benson. "Of course, the time messages, even though not sequenced chronologically, are conveying a proposition or trying to establish a position."

"Exactly," confirmed Maggie. "Let's analyze it for a moment. Episode one: A quick glance at a Roman city, an incomplete message. Episode two: In a burning building, possibly in Jotapata. Message: Your brother betrayed us. You must kill him."

"Not Jotapata," interjected Benson. "Jerusalem, Herod's temple in Jerusalem is in the process of being sacked and burned. The dying man is probably the high priest Ananias."

Maggie continued. "Episode three: An arena where captive Jews are being slaughtered. Josephus is there with a woman. He appears indifferent to the slaughter of his own people. She is very upset, but knows he is powerless to prevent this horribly savage carnival. Message: Josephus is a traitor to his people. He attends a gladiator show to watch Jews being brutally executed.

"Episode four: Ephesus, Josephus is dying, is looking for absolution, makes a dying declaration that he didn't betray the temple or the Jews. Frantically asks for a rabbi to hear his statement and then expires, denying any complicity in the resulting carnage.

Message: I was always a Jew. I only tried to help and prevent my people from being destroyed as a nation. Josephus, trapped in an underground cistern, is forced to participate in a suicide pact with his fellow defenders. The men kill each other as per plan but somehow Josephus, the survivor, is the last person alive. He chooses not to commit suicide, leaves the sanctuary and surrenders to the Romans. Message: His deceit and cowardice are monumental. He aborts a sacred pact with his comrades to save his own body. However, there is a P.S. here that Benson has supplied. The man directed a valiant defense of the city during the course of which he demonstrated impeccable courage."

"Hold it," cautioned David, now into Maggie's analysis. "If this is an attempt to indict Josephus, it is a mixed message. How about the dying declaration? Your premise doesn't hold up."

"But, counselor, it is valid." Benson jumped back into the fray. "Do you get all your messages from one source? Isn't your whole world built on the adversarial submission of facts and law by two or more parties?"

David was incredulous. "Wait, this is too far-fetched. You're telling me that Sal Dematteo is receiving submissions of evidence, flashes of testimony from the past to establish the guilt or innocence of some character from the first century? Some sort of a cosmic tribunal has been convened? Maggie, help me here. This is pure 'Twilight Zone' stuff."

"David," said Maggie, "we've been in the equivalent of the Twilight Zone since Sal had his first interview with Max Vogel."

David lowered his head and stared at the floor. "Okay, I have two questions. One: Is there any rational explanation for any of this? Two: Why, with all the human life on this huge planet in this vast solar system in an infinite universe, has Sal Dematteo been chosen as a judge for this trial or proceeding or whatever it is?"

Benson chose to answer. "Are you familiar with the past life concept?"

"No, well, yes," David corrected himself. "I have been reading science fiction since I was a kid. Ray Bradbury, Isaac Asimov, Kurt Vonnegut, you name it. I read it. I also saw movies like *The Day the Earth Stood Still* and *The War of the Worlds*. Some of the stories talk about reincarnation and past lives. But they are stories, fiction, fantasy."

"What if," postulated Benson, "we returned from time to time with always the same people around us but in different capacities? Human beings are really energy. It is the energy that survives. Suppose then that Sal was some sort of an important judge in a past life, and they are now asking for a verdict to set aside or sustain some terrible historical right or wrong. After all, Einstein said time is circular, not linear. What if the energy doesn't vanish but continues and returns from another dimension?"

"If I supposed that, I would check in with Max as a resident, certify myself and beg for treatment," said David. He buried his face in his hands. "You don't have any answers," he almost shouted.

"David," Maggie said again, in her subdued tone, "we don't have the answers to your questions. But look at the progress we have made in just three days. We have got to stay calm." She put her hand on his shoulder. "I know how wacky this all sounds, but I intend to report this conversation to Max with our ideas in the morning. I believe that to help Sal we need more answers."

"You are absolutely correct," Benson said. "We need to find out if someone else, not Josephus, actually did reveal the secret tunnels under the temple to the Romans. We need to get some idea as to why Sal is the focus of this spate of time messages. Finally, we need to transmit these conclusions to Sal while he is under hypnosis. Perhaps if he renders a verdict, the ordeal will end."

"We need a drink," Maggie said. "I'll get a little booze for a nightcap. We've stretched the envelope enough for tonight. Meeting adjourned. Scotch okay?"

Bart Seiler entered through the front door. He noticed David immediately. "Hey, counselor," he quipped, "how's business?"

"Oh, hi, Bart. Business stinks. We're out of Wheaties and can't afford more."

"We have some Post Toasties. Hey, Sis, can we spare some cereal for this guy? He looks like he needs it."

"We can spare your comedy, Mr. Funnyman," said Maggie. "You're in early. Go to bed. The rest will do you good."

"Nuts," Bart said. "Wrestling's on." He went into the kitchen, opened the refrigerator, popped a beer bottle and turned on the TV.

Maggie poured three stiff shots from a quart of Black Label. "Okay, you guys, down it, go home and have sweet dreams." The three swallowed their drinks almost simultaneously in one gulp.

"Sweet nightmares," muttered David. "Listen, folks, I'm out of court for a couple of days. Tomorrow night is the start of the Jewish New Year. These are high holy days, and I have to go to temple with my parents. Sunday I'll be out at the airport with the Air Guard unit all day. Can I call you Sunday evening, Maggie?"

Benson didn't hear Maggie's reply. Something he considered relevant had occurred to him. "You know, yesterday morning I saw the darnedest ad in the *Wall Street Journal.* It was under the heading 'Miscellaneous for Sale.' It said 'For sale: four Dead Sea Scrolls. Biblical manuscripts dating back at least 2,000 years.' I've answered the ad for the museum. I have the damndest feeling that we may get some answers there if those manuscripts are authentic, and I can get a look at them. Well, got to go folks. It's been fun. Good night, all."

The time detective vanished though the door without another word, leaving both his friends duly astonished.

"The Dead Sea Scrolls. I'm too bushed to speculate on that one. I got an early morning." David looked at Maggie. She was, he thought, a sea of sanity. "You are an amazing lady," he said. "I'm glad you're in on this. I'd be a wreck without you. I may already be a wreck."

She suddenly switched the subject. "David, I hate to burden you with this but I need to tell someone. I think I'm being stalked."

"Stalked! Are you sure? Have you seen anyone?"

"No, I haven't seen anyone. But I have this odd feeling. It's like I sense a presence. When I turn to look there's no one there."

"Maybe, Miss Tough Lady, your nerves are a little jangled. We are all human and something pretty difficult to explain is happening."

"I thought about that angle. But I can't get rid of this feeling."

"Maggie, isn't your uncle a cop?"

"Yes, Uncle Andy is a captain. He's stationed downtown. He supervises Metro for the whole city."

"Call him. Let him put the office on alert. That way if you see anyone suspicious and report in, they will respond quickly."

At first she resisted the idea. But why not? She frequented too many dark parking lots in the evening at the hospital.

"Maybe you're right. I'll call and chat with him tomorrow."

"Maggie, if you need me, call anytime, and I mean anytime." David leaned over and kissed her. She put her arms around his shoulders and kissed him back. "You better leave," she said. "The thought of danger makes me passionate."

"We will resume Sunday, Miss Seiler, where we left off, and you won't get rid of me this easily."

Bart ambled in from the kitchen. He noticed the intimate scene. "Post Toasties anyone?"

"I'll post your toasties," laughed David. "I better go."

David sauntered down the stairs, exhausted. He got into his car, started the motor and sat for a moment. Tonight had been revealing. Were they really getting insight into Sal's episodes or was this all some sort of convoluted joke? He reviewed the week's events. Only six days ago his law partner had wandered into his office and related a tale that was right out of an Alfred Hitchcock movie. Since then the tempo of events had increased to the point where he himself felt inextricably enmeshed, watching a surreal portrait of ancient Rome and first century history unfold against a real twentieth century background. Where would and how could it possibly end? No screenplay writers could have dreamed this one up.

He drove away. He just wanted to take a hot shower and rest. He completely failed to notice the small, thin man in the dark suit lodged behind a tree directly across from Maggie's apartment.

* * * *

The man extinguished a cigarette. He studied the second-floor apartment. The lights were out. The occupants were in bed. He felt chilled and weary. For the past two days he had followed the rules he was taught in training. He had shadowed the dark-haired girl, observed her habits and the patterns of her life. She was consistent. She went to the hospital at 7:00 A.M. She stayed in the hospital the entire day. She left for home at 6:00 P.M. She did not usually leave the house. She lived with her mother and another man who was probably her brother. She was visited tonight by another man. He left at 11:00 P.M. The hospital parking lot was where she was most vulnerable. That was where they would have to take her. He wanted to get this thing over with. He hated this foreign country. The food was terrible, the language difficult. He and Ali had to pray in the little room they rented. He was concerned about where and how they would hide the girl until they obtained the sacred dagger. Ali had told him not to worry. He would take care of it.

He walked slowly down the street toward the little coupe they had rented. To get the car, Ali had spent a goodly portion of the money they'd been given to carry out this undertaking. He had no idea how they would leave the country. They had Lebanese passports and forged visas. He wished he were back in the old city of Beirut where he knew all the streets and alleys. Where, when they killed or kidnapped someone, they could safely vanish within minutes. He'd had a bad feeling about this mission, as if Ishtar, their blessed God, was not smiling on them. He felt the outline of the thin, deadly knife strapped tightly to his left hip. It gave him comfort. He was on a holy quest. The return of the consecrated dagger to the Brotherhood would restore them to the great power they had lost when the cursed Persian, Cyrus, had given their sanctified weapon to the Jewish heretics.

CHAPTER 15

THE SECOND WEEK, FRIDAY
BENSON THROCKMORTON, A TRIP TO NEW YORK

The Trans World Airline DC-8 chugged to life and slowly wheeled around to face the runway. The weather was clear and sunny, and flights were leaving on schedule. The traffic at Greater Pittsburgh Airport had been fairly light for a Friday, at least for the afternoon flights.

Benson Throckmorton settled himself comfortably into a window seat in the coach section and munched on a candy bar. An early morning call to a close colleague at Columbia University had confirmed that a trip to investigate the *Wall Street Journal* ad was in order. By tomorrow morning, the Columbia people would have discovered the source of the ad and hopefully set up a meeting with the salesman. It was a crazy, long-shot hunch, but the word in the archeological pipeline was that someone had smuggled four Dead Sea Scrolls out of Jordan and that these might actually be genuine. The Metropolitan Museum was also interested, as was the antiquities department at the University of Pennsylvania.

The aircraft had become airborne and was clawing its way upward to cruising altitude. Benson produced a book and began to read about the exploits of an obscure Hittite King whose capitol city Hattusha, in southern Turkey, was excavated by the famous English soldier adventurer T.E. Lawrence in 1912.

A stewardess interrupted his foray into the Hittite world. "Would you care for lunch, sir? Our flight is about three hours."

"Just coffee, please," said Benson. "Thank you."

Benson closed the book and focused on the fleecy cloud formations to his right. His mind skipped to the Dead Sea Scrolls and the improbable events that had led to their discovery. In 1947, while searching for a lost goat in remote limestone cliffs, a Bedouin boy, Muhammad of the Tamirch tribe, happened upon some large pieces of pottery concealed in a cave. This cave was located on the edge of the Wadi Qumran, a riverbed that winds its way into the Dead Sea. He investigated the articles and found inside them some moldering leather parchments. Totally unaware of the significance of his find, he returned the following day with a friend. They carted away the leather parchments and sold some of them for a pittance to a Muslim sheik. Other scrolls found their way into history through a trail of seedy antique shops and clandestine encounters worthy of the best Hollywood plots. Until 1952, the Tamirch tribe had made a business of selling their trove of findings from the caves until they reached a Syrian Orthodox antique dealer who contacted St. Marks, in Jerusalem, a repository of ancient rare manuscripts.

Events moved quickly as St. Mark's took custody, recognized their value and proceeded to convene a group of scholars to study them. The Dead Sea Scrolls represented a remarkable saga of Jewish and early Christian history, transcending the Old Testament and reaching well into the second century of the Christian Era. However, some of the scrolls were rumored to have been smuggled to New York because of the belief they would fetch a better price. Hence, the incredible *Wall Street Journal* ad. Obviously the major issue was their authenticity, the prime reason why the museum agreed to finance a New York trip for their time detective.

Coffee arrived with a sweet roll. The stewardess, who until two months ago had been a registered nurse at a Pittsburgh hospital, smiled and proceeded to chat with Benson. The aircraft was half empty and she had plenty of time.

"On business?" she asked.

"Oh, yes, I'm an archaeologist. I'm going to view some artifacts in New York."

"We are overnighting in New York," said the young lady, hoping perhaps Benson might need a dinner companion.

Benson failed to get the message. He was lost in contemplating the meaning of scrolls and what he could possibly learn from their texts. "Well," he said, "I hope you enjoy New York."

The young lady soon lost interest and went to attend to the other passengers.

Benson felt it was improbable, but possible that these scrolls might cover that portion of the first century when the Judeans had risen like a phoenix to challenge the might of Rome. But there were other considerations. To obtain these items for the Carnegie Museum would be a real coup. To study them and report on their meaning and content would be the opportunity of a lifetime.

The flight, an uneventful two hours and fifty-three minutes, circled LaGuardia Field and prepared for landing. Benson, now well into the story of the Hittite dig, absentmindedly buckled his seat belt. The DC-8 bounced twice on the runway and then settled down to a smooth landing.

The time detective prepared for the next move. If things went according to plan, his friend, Professor Boris Gurevich, would be waiting at the terminal. From then on he would have to play the game by ear. With luck, by Saturday afternoon he would be examining a portion of what, to date, had proved to be the most significant archaeological discovery since Napoleon, during his ill-fated Egyptian campaign, had found the Rosetta Stone.

CHAPTER 16

THE SECOND WEEK, SATURDAY
THE DEAD SEA SCROLLS

Professor Boris Gurevich was a bear of a man. A Russian émigré who, in 1948, was forced to leave the country by way of Siberia, he had assumed the identity of a jewelry salesman. With forged papers and a few well-placed bribes, he had made his way to Hong Kong where he proceeded to dispose of a number of the illegally exported jewels that he had sewn into the lining of his greatcoat.

The route to the U.S. was long and arduous by way of Vancouver, Canada. Finally, when his identity as the former Director of Antiquities at the Leningrad University was revealed, he was offered an appointment at Columbia University School of History and Archaeology. The school procured a temporary work visa for Boris. Later, through the good offices of their former President, Dwight D. Eisenhower, the work visa was converted to resident alien status.

Boris was accustomed to clandestine activities. He enjoyed intrigue. During World War II he had worked in the Ukraine, behind German lines, as a NKVD operative. His penchant for survival was legendary. His exit from the Soviet Union to escape one of Stalin's paranoiac purges had been even more spectacular. His only regret was that he had been forced to leave his wife Irina in Russia.

It had taken Professor Gurevich a few hours to determine the source of the *Wall Street Journal* ad. He traced it to an obscure Lebanese antique and rare book dealer on 23rd Street. A phone call and a check by the dealer on his current identity had enabled Gurevich to obtain a late Saturday afternoon appointment with the dealer for himself and a colleague.

The bookstore was located a block from the 23rd Street subway stop in a rundown industrial area on the east side. At precisely 3:00 P.M., as directed, the two men paused outside the store window. Benson studied the name inscribed on the window. It read in flowing script Aram Katoubian, Rare Books and Antiques. The shop itself was bathed in the stale air of decay, as if its contents were part of a burial chamber or some long-abandoned crypt.

Gurevich led the way through a door that jangled when opened. To describe a person as having a Middle Eastern appearance is perhaps trite. What occurred to Benson was the early middle-aged man who approached them was the epitome of an educated individual, with both the resemblance and manner of the many races that had left their stamp on the history of the Middle East. He was not an Arab but he had swarthy skin. His features bore no trace of Semitic ancestry. He was handsome in a western European context, with relatively tall stature. His English was precise and impeccable. He wore a two-piece suit with a tie that Gurevich observed as fairly tasteful.

"I am Katoubian," he said, greeting his visitors, "the proprietor here."

Boris Gurevich extended his right hand and introduced himself, and Benson presented a card, which Katoubian examined and placed in his upper shirt pocket. He had scrutinized Benson's card.

"You are not a professor?" he asked. "May I inquire as to your interest in this endeavor?"

"Certainly, I am a staff archaeologist at the Carnegie Museum. I conduct seminars at the University of Pittsburgh. I research and verify the authenticity of ancient manuscripts and objects. That is why I am here. To examine the items that you have advertised as a segment of the Dead Sea Scrolls and determine, if I can, their origin and their genuineness."

While he was speaking, Benson noticed two men lurking in the rear of the shop. While they did not appear menacing, it was obvious from their concentrated manner that Mr. Katoubian was taking no risks of being robbed or hijacked.

"Fair enough," replied the shopkeeper. Or was he a shopkeeper? Benson sensed that he was too suave and too articulate to be an ordinary bookstore proprietor. This was not the kind of man who spent his life in a poorly lighted shop, on an out-of-the-way street, on the lower east side of Manhattan.

"Fine, gentlemen." Katoubian seemed satisfied. "How can we proceed?"

"I would like to examine the manuscripts," said Benson

"Under what ground rules and for how long?" asked Katoubian.

Benson turned to Boris. "Your interest."

Boris glanced at the two men in the back. "I will work with Mr. Throckmorton. It will take several hours."

Katoubian contemplated the scenario. "I hope you won't consider me mercenary, gentlemen, but I would appreciate a show of good faith. Say, five hundred dollars when I produce the scrolls. For that paltry amount you can take whatever time you need. I will avail you of my office upstairs. It is warm and comfortable and well lighted."

Boris raised his eyes toward the second-floor landing. They would be ensconced in an office without egress to the street. He took quick stock of the situation. They were carrying little cash money. What possible reason would these men have for attacking them? Placing them in the secluded office as a workplace seemed like purely a defensive maneuver. He patted his overcoat lightly. He could handle those two men in the rear even if they had guns.

"Agreed," said Benson eagerly without consulting Boris. "But you will have to take a museum check." He produced a blank check.

Katoubian hesitated. He wanted cash.

"I'm sorry, I can't get cash this quickly. I must be back in Pittsburgh by Tuesday," Benson said.

Katoubian examined the check. He shrugged his shoulders. "Come upstairs. I will trust you."

To their surprise they were ushered into a plush office. It was furnished with exotic but comfortable Middle Eastern furniture. There were brightly colored silk cushions strewn about, several strategically placed Aladdin-like lamps and an overstuffed couch that could have seated four people without crowding. The floor was adorned with a beautifully designed blue and white Turkish rug. A flat, empty wooden desk sat in the corner. This room presented a striking contrast to the stark, drab appearance of the shop below.

"Our clients," explained Katoubian, "like the mysterious aura of the shop. It adds to our credibility. Please be seated. Can we get you coffee or tea?"

"Coffee, please," said Benson.

Gurevich asked for tea.

Katoubian smiled, "You westerners and your coffee and the Russians and their tea. Will the twain ever meet?"

A few minutes later, one of the two men in the rear entered with a large brass tray loaded with a pot of tea, a carafe of coffee and several sweet cakes. He nodded, unsmiling, and left the tray. Benson poured some coffee and surveyed the surroundings. He would most likely be here several hours. It was 3:30 P.M.

Five minutes later Katoubian reappeared. He carried several heavy goatskin tubes. He opened one of them and carefully spread out a parchment made of some sort of animal skin—goat, calf or lamb. The scrolls had a brittle look to them. They were protected by thin sheets of cellophane.

"I assure you," said Katoubian, "these are four of the original scrolls."

Benson was concerned. Would handling them cause them to be damaged?

"Please take great care with these parchments," cautioned Katoubian. "We will leave you alone for two hours. Then we will return to check on your progress. The bathroom is in there." Katoubian gestured toward an adjoining room. "If you need anything, my men will be close by. I will be gone for a short time."

With great trepidation, working to control the anxiety tearing at his emotions, Benson sat down, extracted a large magnifying glass from a case in his pocket and began to study these extraordinary objects.

For two hours, in nearly unbroken silence, Benson and Boris studied sections of the scroll. Benson gingerly lifted the cellophane and shined a tiny pocket flashlight against the parchment. He felt the texture and studied the shape and style of the letters. Finally, as if their respective minds had communicated, they raised their heads and their eyes met in a startling acknowledgment.

"I believe they are real," said Benson, subdued and awed by the presence of this archeological treasure. "This is amazing," he continued. "The later scrolls are in Aramaic. These tablets appear to chronicle the first century during and after Christ. If they are not real, they are masterful forgeries. We can't be sure until we conduct Carbon 14 tests."

"I agree," responded Boris. "Even the goatskin parchment feels authentic."

"I need two more hours," said Benson. He consulted his watch. It was 5:30 P.M.

Katoubian entered the room. He was prompt. "Well?" he queried.

"They appear genuine, Mr. Katoubian. How did they get here?"

"Not important. They are here. They are the real thing. By the way, so is your check. Thank you."

"I need two additional hours," said Benson.

"Fine. I will return at 7:30. I trust we can talk business at that time. My men will remain outside." Katoubian was still not taking any risk that he could be swindled.

Precisely at 7:00 P.M., after ninety minutes of virtually soundless, concentrated study, Benson punched the desk in one his inimitable gestures. "There it is," he announced. "I know who was responsible and, as I suspected, it wasn't Josephus." He pointed out a passage and asked, "Boris, can you read that?"

Boris carefully scrutinized the faded words. His Aramaic was not nearly as proficient as Benson's. He read it several times trying to digest its meaning.

"Something about the sewers underneath the temple. Assisting the Romans to find the passages. Of course, Herod's temple. The siege of Jerusalem." He studied further. "Astounding, I never would have guessed."

Benson looked furtively at the door. He extracted a small camera from his jacket and rapidly shot a series of pictures. He had acted not a moment too soon. Katoubian returned. "Can we replenish your coffee?"

"We are fine, Mr. Katoubian. Thank you for your hospitality. I think I've seen enough. What is your price?"

Without hesitation Katoubian answered. "One million dollars."

"Significant," commented Benson.

"What about title?" interjected Boris. "How do we know these are not stolen artifacts? We don't need an international incident."

"The Israelis are really interested. Yagael Yadin has already contacted us," said Katoubian. "Why worry about title? This is a once-in-a-lifetime opportunity." Katoubian exhibited slight signs of agitation. He had obviously been previously cross-examined on the question of possession and title.

"I'll convey your offer to the Carnegie Foundation," agreed Benson. "I think a million dollars is a little high."

"Make me an offer," countered Katoubian.

"I'm not authorized to commit the foundation," said Benson. "You will hear from me in a few days."

After Katoubian carefully examined the scrolls to assure they were intact, the three men shook hands and the two archaeologists left. It was, as Benson observed later that evening, in many ways a shattering, deeply religious experience.

Benson remained in New York for two more days. He visited the Columbia University School of Antiquities. He had lunch with his close friend at the Metropolitan Museum. Unfortunately, he forgot to mention to the staff at the Carnegie Museum the name of the hotel where he was staying. It was Monday evening before an urgent phone call caught up with him.

The phone message, received at 1:00 A.M., was about Sal and some sort of incursion at the museum. Benson was upset but he felt the damage was probably manageable. He decided it was time to go home. He caught the early 7:30 A.M. flight from LaGuardia and landed in Greater Pittsburgh Airport at 10:00 A.M. He retrieved his car from a nearby lot and immediately went back to his apartment. There, he found a second message. It was from the Psychiatric Institute, and the substance of the message unnerved him.

CHAPTER 17

THE THIRD WEEK, SUNDAY
TEMPLE OF JUPITER

A usual Sunday consisted of a prayer meeting and a light meal at the home of his parents. This was not to be a usual Sunday.

When he awoke, it was early. The dark-haired girl lay next to him, her elegant hair spread out on the matted pillow. He marveled at her splendid beauty, which never ceased to stir his desire. Her body, its sensuous curves outlined beneath the sheets, moved slightly. He wanted to touch it, to caress it, to blend it with his body as they had the previous night, but he had a mission.

He donned his toga, put on his sandals, buckled on his short sword and noiselessly left the room. He called for his chariot. A Lydian slave procured the two magnificent black horses and harnessed them to the vehicle.

He made his way carefully across the city to Alexander's library. The morning air was cold, and he could smell the sea. The streets of the city were empty. The building was located near the harbor next to the magnificent Temple of Jupiter. He placed the chariot in the safekeeping of a lone caretaker who sleepily tethered the horses. The caretaker wondered what the man was doing out so early. But he was so tired from his late night carousing that he barely gave him a glance.

He entered the library, which was hushed and vacant. It had just opened its huge iron doors. He had a reasonably good notion as to where the dagger was kept. He crossed the main library room, past the rows of stone benches and the disapproving eyes of Neptune's statue, to a small alcove. Without hesitation he entered the alcove and began to ransack a large wooden cabinet. He broke the lock by hacking off the wooden hasp with his sword. It collapsed open on the second blow. He was oblivious to the noise the shock had created. He sought the dagger, but unable to find it, he panicked while frantically looking through the many drawers.

A guard burst into the alcove. "Stop," he cried, then shouted for assistance. He tried to seize the intruder but a crushing blow to the chin sent the guard sprawling across the room. Two other guards entered and grasped his arms. He struggled and broke loose. He grappled with another guard and sent him crashing into a wall. A third guard entered carrying a torch. Quickly sizing up the situation, he lashed out and struck him with a glancing blow across the forehead. The world went black and he collapsed to the floor.

* * * *

When he awoke he was staring into the puzzled face of a man dressed in a dark blue suit. A cop.

The policeman surveyed the burglar. The man wore gray sweat pants and a dark blue sweatshirt that had 106th Signal Battalion emblazoned on the front. He had a gash in his forehead that was bleeding profusely.

The man had no idea where he was or how he had gotten there. He was acutely aware, however, that he was handcuffed.

"Want to tell us who you are and what you were looking for?" asked the cop.

The guard stirred. He was badly shaken. "Guy has a punch like an elephant," he murmured. His jaw hurt a lot. He hoped it wasn't broken.

"I'm Antonio Dematteo," the intruder muttered. "I don't know how I got here, or why I'm here."

Immediately behind the cop a plainclothesman wearing an open shirt and a pair of khaki pants had entered. The man looked vaguely familiar. He kept looking at Sal.

"Get a towel and stop that bleeding," he barked. "Get that guard to Emergency! Now. Afterward, take his statement."

Ed Flaharty normally was off duty on Sunday but he was substituting for another colleague who was attending a wedding.

Someone furnished a large white towel to Sal. "Get the burglar to Emergency also." Flaharty did a quick double take. He never forgot a face. That was one of his strengths that he had finely honed as a cop.

"I do know you. You are one of the guys I questioned the other night after that character tried to steal that old knife. Were you looking for that knife? Are you drunk?"

"I honest to God don't know, officer. Please call my partner. His name is David Gold. He's an attorney. He's in the book."

"I have to arrest you on suspicion of burglary and assault with intent to cause bodily harm. I warn you that anything you say may be used against you. When we get to the station house and after we patch you up, you can call your partner.

"Wrap that towel around his head and get him into the wagon."

On the way out the back door of the Carnegie Museum, Flaharty stopped to talk to the head supervisor of the guards.

"Whose office is that, do you know?"

"Sure, Detective Flaharty," answered the supervisor. "That is Mr. Benson Throckmorton's office. He left for New York on Friday. He never remembers to lock his office. He's a staff archeologist."

"Throckmorton. He was another one of the guys I interviewed the other evening on that knife incident, along with that big black guy. What the hell is going on around here?"

The supervisor of guards shrugged his shoulders. "Well, Detective Flaharty, you know how it is. Museum's are just all violence and intrigue."

CHAPTER 18

THE THIRD WEEK, MONDAY
DR. BERNARD ADLER

In the early afternoon, as ordered, David checked Sal into the hospital. Max was able to procure a private room for Sal. He counseled the family to let Sal rest and he would call Catherine in a couple of hours. Max and David then went to the cafeteria for a long-delayed lunch. A few minutes later Maggie joined them.

"I've been trying to contact Benson," she said. "But he's out of town and unavailable. Obviously, if Sal was trying to get the dagger, he failed. But nobody seems to know where Benson concealed the damned thing."

"Maybe that's fortuitous," commented David. "At least they can't charge him with burglary, only assault and breaking and entering. Since it's a public building that had just opened, these charges might be difficult to sustain. I don't know. I need to do a little research."

David gulped his coffee. "I have to go to the office, some pressing client matters. Still need to pay Margie, Janet and the rent. What about tonight with Liebman, Max? How about 6:45 at Liebman's office? I'll bring Maggie."

"Thanks, fellas," said Maggie. "Now would somebody like to tell me who Liebman is and why we are going to his office?"

Max hesitated. "Maggie, Liebman is a rabbi. He also a very knowledgeable about early Judean history. If you would rather not come along—"

"I would rather come along." She cut Max off in the middle of a sentence. "You two guys are not getting rid of me this easy."

"God knows," assured David, grasping her hand tightly, "nobody wants to get rid of you, Maggie. You may be the best head in this whole puzzle. See you all tonight. Please watch out for my buddy and call Catherine."

Maggie nodded. "I'll call Catherine."

When Max finished what passed for lunch, he walked slowly toward the elevator. A germ of another idea crossed his mind. He was beginning to plot a new treatment strategy. When he reached his office he sat down and began fiddling with his files. His fingers drummed idly on the desktop.

He had several other patients to deal with, but first he must contact Bernie Adler. He rang Adler's office. A nurse answered almost immediately. Within ten seconds Dr. Bernard Adler, who to most people was literally inaccessible, picked up the line.

"Hello, Max, Happy New Year. What's the latest?"

"It's the Dematteo case, Bernie. I promised the judge I would bring you in on it. Sal's in custody here. What do you say? I hate to ask."

"Okay, Max, for you, I'll be a consulting therapist. I have a few minutes this afternoon. I'll be down in about an hour."

Adler hung up the phone and paused to finish an article by a respected British psychiatrist. The treatise was on shock treatment, its effects and outcomes. He had mixed feelings about the benefits. But this Italian lawyer sounded like an excellent test case. He was obviously meandering into a totally unreal world. Visions were the fruits of superstition and the figments of imagination. They often sprang from long forgotten, seemingly unrelated childhood experiences that lodged in some remote crevice in the brain. Sal's wanderings were becoming more frequent and more graphic and detailed in their description. Perhaps a series of shocks could restore the patient to reality. They would have to try. It would fit in well with his plans for a case study to be presented at the annual spring meeting.

Max had two appointments that required his time. He disposed of the first one in ten minutes. The second was a young college girl who at nineteen was becoming schizophrenic. He always believed there was some chemical reaction in the brain or body that caused an otherwise normal, seemingly well-adjusted human being to experience psychotic episodes. It was difficult syndrome to treat. His theory was pretty well debunked by the psychiatric establishment. The accepted treatment was a prolonged period of psychoanalysis. He completed his session with the young lady and rang the fourth floor to have Sal sent down to coincide with Adler's visit.

Adler breezed in before Sal arrived. "Max," he postulated, "I've been giving this Dematteo case a lot of thought. I think he's a candidate for shock treatments."

Max felt a sudden sense of alarm. In five years, in school and during his internship and subsequent residency, he had never questioned a decision or conclusion of his mentor. Maybe this was the time.

"But Bernie, shock treatment can have a devastating side effect. Besides, his family would never approve."

"They would if you recommended it. This may be our only chance to restore this patient to reality prior to the spring diplomat meeting. I believe it's worth a try."

"I'm sorry, Bernie, I'm not prepared to undertake anything as drastic as electroshock therapy with the limited observation we've had of this patient. I brought you here to witness a hypnotherapy session. It may or may not change your mind."

Adler was about to continue the argument when it occurred to him that this was the independent spirit he's been seeking from Max Vogel for the last year. "Okay," he agreed. "Let's conduct the session, then we will further review the treatment options."

Sal was brought into the office. He appeared relaxed. He was dressed in street clothes and well groomed. He had taken a brief nap and been given a sedative. He felt rested.

Max made the introduction. "Sal, this is Dr. Adler. He is going to work with us."

Adler smiled. He began the interview with questions. His tone was deliberate and soft spoken, his words concise. He was, thought Max with envy, the consummate professional.

"Mr. Dematteo, do you know where you are?"

"Certainly, Doctor, I'm in the Western State Psychiatric Institute. I'm here in custody because I allegedly assaulted a guard at the Carnegie Museum on Sunday morning. This is Monday afternoon." Sal glanced at his watch. It was 3:30 P.M.

"Allegedly? You didn't attack the guard?"

"Until you're convicted, Doctor, everything is an allegation."

"I see. Do you know why you attacked the guard?"

"I'm not sure. I think I was looking for the golden dagger, and he surprised me."

"What happens to you, Mr. Dematteo? You are an intelligent man. A professional, well educated. You know this conduct is not appropriate."

"Yes, Doctor, I know. I experience what Dr. Vogel calls episodes. I am somehow transported to another place. I know it sounds crazy, but I always see the same kind of people dressed in ancient costumes. They are like pictures from a Hollywood movie about old Rome. In some cases I see the same people. They talk to me. Some of scenes are violent and bloody. I've never been to Europe or the Middle East. At least not in this life."

"Do you believe you were in a past life when these episodes occur? Do you know why this is happening?"

"I don't know. I don't know about past lives or any of this crap." Sal was getting a bit irritated and uncomfortable.

"Are you frightened of the present? Do you fear losing your trials?"

"No."

"Are you fearful of losing your wife, your child? Is there some incident that happened to you in your life that has caused you to want to retreat from the world?"

"Not that I am aware of."

"Did you ever hurt your brother or have something happen to you when you were a child that frightened you?"

"No, sir, not that I can recall."

"Perhaps there is something you can't recall but that may have happened. Please concentrate."

Sal tried, but came up with nothing. "Doctor, there's nothing like that I can recall."

"Are you aware that you have discussed killing your brother?"

"Yes, I am."

"Do you hate your brother? Do you believe he is sexually more powerful than you?"

Sal snickered as if the premise was ridiculous. "Hate Artie? Why would I hate Artie? He's my kid brother. I care for him a lot." Sal completely ignored the allusion to sex.

"Why do you want to kill him?"

"I don't want to kill him." Sal was adamant, and getting angrier.

"Then, Sal, if not you, who wants to kill Artie?" That, Adler felt positive, was the crux of this entire case.

"I'm not sure. I believe his name is Aaron."

"Sal, how can we stop Aaron? How do we get rid of him? Do we have to kill him?"

"Frankly, Dr. Adler, I don't know. I know you guys think I'm nuts. Maybe I am. But I would certainly like to get this character out of my mind and out of my life."

"Sal, we don't use the term 'nuts.' As a lawyer you know that."

Max interceded. "Dr. Adler, please permit me to place Mr. Dematteo under hypnosis."

Max turned to Sal. "Do you object to being placed under hypnosis, Mr. Dematteo?"

"No, I don't."

Adler scrawled a note and handed it to Max. Max scanned it quickly. "A classic multiple personality case. Somebody named Aaron wants to kill his brother. Sibling rivalry also involved. We may need to shock the patient back to reality. Nothing very difficult here."

Max didn't reply. He proceeded to prepare Sal for the session. His routine was simple. He spoke slowly in a soothing, quiet voice, pausing only for a few seconds between sentences.

"Sal, please close your eyes. I want you to completely relax. All your tensions, all your concerns, all your fears and worries are draining away. You are day-dreaming. Concentrate on gentle ocean waves lapping at a distant shore. Your eyelids are heavy. You feel lazy. You can't open your eyes. Your body up to your head and down to your toes is floating. You are drifting deeper and deeper with each breath. I'm going to count backwards from fifteen and when I reach one you will be completely asleep but you will hear every word I say: 15, 14, 13, 12, 11, 10, 9, 8, 7, 6, 5, 4, 3, 2, 1."

Sal's breathing was regular. His eyes were lightly closed. His arms draped loosely at his side.

"Can you hear me?"

"Yes, I can. I feel great. I can see my wife and my daughter. God bless her."

"He's under," observed Adler.

"Sal, you have been having some experiences with strangers."

Max got no further. Sal's demeanor had changed. He was no longer at rest. He looked uncomfortable, as if he was lifting or carrying some sort of heavy load. Something drastic had impinged on his euphoric state.

"Sal, where are you? I want you to tell me everything that happens in as much detail as possible." Max checked the recorder. It was on and working.

"I'm in a dark room," said Sal. "There are bars on the window. It smells stale and it's cold." He looked down at his feet. "I have chains on my legs. There's a guard coming into the cell."

"Bring him out," said Adler.

"No, Bernie, not at this point. Stay cool. You are now in for the strangest experience of your illustrious career."

He had lost track of how long he had been a captive. He knew it had been many months. Although they kept him in chains, they had not brutalized him or even denied him food. After the surrender he had been taken before General Vespasian.

Titus, the general's oldest son, also a powerfully built and imposing figure, sat next to the General. They questioned him, whoever he was, on his knowledge of Roman tactics and his military background. Vespasian had called his defense of Jotapata inspired. The one attribute the Romans respected was military prowess.

Sal was now deeply into Aaron's life story.

I studied the General closely. A strong and intelligent face with eyes that saw and knew. He was a man destined for great things. Then the vision appeared to me. A gift from God. "General," I said forcefully, "within a year you will be the Emperor of Rome."

Vespasian brightened up. This pronouncement pleased him. He had heard of the Jewish prophets and their powers to foresee the future. Perhaps he thought I was a prophet of their strange God whom no one could see or touch. If this came to pass, he would richly reward me.

Vespasian was a careful man. He said I would be held but well treated. He would keep me for a year to test the efficacy of my prophecy, but I would not be harmed. They would take me to Caesura, the capitol city in the North that had been built many years before to honor the great General Julius Caesar and the son of Caesar by Cleopatra where King Agrippa ruled the Roman legate and administered the eastern provinces of the empire.

After a while I was summoned. The guard was gentle. "The general wants to see you. I know not why."

Vespasian is seated on a throne at the rear of the large hall decorated on both sides with colorful tapestries and life-size statues. King Agrippa and Miriamme, his queen, are there too and so is his eldest son, Titus. An honor guard of at least forty men is standing at strict attention around the general. When Vespasian saw me, he beamed. He gestured for me to present myself before the throne.

The guard brought me forward and I bowed my head to the general. This was clearly not a tribunal planning to order my execution.

"Release his chains," Vespasian commanded the guard. The guard hacked off my shackles with a broadsword. When they rattled loosely to the floor, I felt my spirits lift. Somehow, God had seen my trial and decreed my rescue.

"You are as an oracle," said Vespasian. "From this day forward you are counselor to the emperor. For as long as I live and as long as

my family shall continue to rule the empire, you are a special minion to Rome. You are henceforth under the protection of the Flavius family. You may go anywhere but to Jerusalem. For I have received the summons. The senate and the Pretorian Guard have chosen me to assume the imperial crown. I leave in a week with the tenth legion. When I am anointed you shall become a citizen of Rome. Titus will stay and command the legions in Judea. His mission is to take Jerusalem and quell the rebellion once and for all. Do you have any special requests?"

I was temporarily speechless. I could not believe my good fortune. To be set free, become a citizen of Rome and a confidant of the emperor, this far exceeded any dream of greatness I had ever entertained. "I would, if it please the mighty Vespasian, like to accompany your son to Jerusalem. I might help to convince my people to surrender and save many lives and much suffering."

Vespasian looked at Titus. His son immediately assented. It sounded like a good idea. This astute man could be a great asset in his search for glory. "Done," pronounced Vespasian.

He turned to Agrippa. "This man shall have the best apartment and servants at his disposal. He shall be treated well or I shall be much displeased."

King Agrippa understood. "He shall be, General. He shall want for nothing."

I felt the exhilaration of freedom and the majesty of power course through my veins. I was in my thirtieth year. Once again, God had intervened to deliver me from possible slavery and a life of terrible drudgery. I had been brought to the very councils of the most powerful man in the world.

Max checked the time. It had been almost thirty minutes since the session had started. Sal was stirring as if he needed to awaken. Bernie Adler had remained silent. He was clearly puzzled. He was not at all sure what had happened, but he understood that some unique phenomena had occurred. How, he thought, could this man have related such a logical tale in such amazing detail? He was reprocessing his original diagnosis.

"Sal, you are going to return to the conscious world when I count to ten. When you are roused you will feel refreshed. Nothing you have seen or heard will frighten or startle you. 1, 2, 3, 4, 5, 6, 7, 8, 9, 10. You are now fully awake and in the conscious world."

Sal opened his eyes. He was almost tranquil. "Some crazy trip, huh, Doctor?" He addressed his statement to Max.

"Sal, no more discussion. I think we have had enough for this afternoon. I want you to rest. You can call Catherine and let her know you're fine."

Sal nodded. He was calm but pensive. The attendant led Sal back to his room. A few minutes later Maggie came to visit him. "How is it going?" she asked.

"I don't know. I was just under hypnosis. I'm okay but I can't get rid of an uneasy feeling that something is very wrong."

Maggie patted him on the arm. "It will be okay. I just spoke to your mother. Your brother Art is on his way home."

"My brother, huh." Unfortunately, Sal wasn't picturing Art. He saw another man, his brother, whom the high priest Ananias had ordered him to kill.

* * * *

When the door to the office closed, Bernie Adler spoke. "You are sure he knows nothing about classical history. You know, many Catholics spend a great deal of time studying the first century—early Christian martyrs, the apostles, the crucifixion, in Catholic school they—"

"Bernie, he didn't go to Catholic school," said Max. "He went to public school and to the same secular university you and I did. According to both his wife and mother, he disliked history. David Gold, his partner and my friend, wholly agrees. The patient has never written Latin, Greek or Hebrew. Yet at times he can write and understand the languages. I'll bet a month's pay that Rabbi Liebman will confirm the validity and time frame of this incident as Benson did."

"Well," said the good Dr. Adler, "how the hell do I present this case at the spring meeting? I'll get laughed off the podium."

He continued, "Alright, Max, for now I withdraw my recommendation for shock treatment. We need to understand this whole syndrome better. But I don't want to hear any garbage about visions from the past or any other paranormal explanations for this behavior. I don't believe it."

"Fine, Bernie. David Gold and I will be chatting with Joshua Liebman tonight. At Hebrew seminary he was a history major with emphasis on antiquity. He is a rabbi with both feet in reality."

Once again Max made no allusion to the time detective. He was justifiably concerned that Dr. Bernard Adler would strenuously object to an eccentric student, not yet a Ph.D., being a consultant on a major psychiatric case.

When Adler departed, Max reflected for some time on the events of the past few days. He made a decision. He dialed Liebman with a view toward giving him a heads-up on the subject to cover at their meeting that evening. And he would consult with Benson on the period Sal was describing so he could better understand the history unfolding.

* * * *

The next day he met with Benson and let him listen to the tape. He was fascinated. This was a pivotal time, he said, and launched into another of his historical disquisitions.

"It had been a turbulent year for the city of Rome. Nero had burned a great part of the capitol. All sections were laid waste except the Palatine. He had tried to blame the Christian sect but one of his generals knew better. His guilt was revealed. When confronted by the Roman mob and the senate, Nero had committed suicide. Three generals had attempted to ascend the throne. All died or were assassinated within months. In desperation the senate and the Pretorian Guard had turned to their famed eastern general who had conquered all of Judea except Jerusalem."

Benson was fascinated by Sal's detailed description of events.

The guard bade him stand. His clothes were in tatters and his beard had grown long. At times being a prisoner had weighed so heavily upon him that he wished himself dead. He had dreamed of his wife and his family in Jerusalem. The Romans were not cruel toward him. They allowed him to walk in the sun but always with a guard. They did not beat him or threaten to sell him into slavery. But the isolation was a crushing burden. He craved company, and the solace of a woman. But most of all he aspired to shed the chains.

The news was sparse and not good. The Galilee had been subdued. All fortress cities had been captured. Those that had surrendered without a battle were treated well. The cities that resisted were destroyed and many men, women and children put to the sword. His people had suffered much.

The Jews didn't understand. They huddled behind walls, divided among themselves, and waited for the Romans who reduced their cities one by one. Roman power was omnipotent. They had God on their side, or so it seemed.

CHAPTER 19

THE THIRD WEEK, TUESDAY
PITTSBURGH COUNTY COURT

It was unseasonably cold for September. The rain that had dampened the city for two days the previous week had returned. It continued its steady assault on buildings, streets and people who huddled beneath their umbrellas and raincoats. Most were rushing to work or seeking shelter in a dry department store or coffee shop. They scurried across wet streets to their respective havens.

David felt dejected as he crossed Grant Street to the courthouse. Perhaps it was the sullen skies and chill air, not the normal weather that prevailed during Indian Summer. He pulled his raincoat collar tight around his neck. He hunched up his shoulders to guard against the trickles of water that were seeping into the coat. He knew it wasn't the rain that had depressed his spirits. It was what awaited him in courtroom ten.

He mounted the wide stone steps where only four days ago Father O'Malley and Father Duffy had prevented a violent free for all. He felt a growing apprehension. This was not going to be a good Monday. Probably it would not even be a good week. He entered the large, well-lighted room, glancing around to seek a familiar face. He shed his coat and made his way to the front row. The old wooden benches were crowded with spectators, witnesses, attorneys and crime reporters exchanging pleasantries, quips and observations involving the day's events, or something less profound like the result of the Pittsburgh-Temple game which had ended in a sorry six-to-six tie.

Max was already there. Seated alone in the front row, he was absorbed in reading a book, oblivious to the buzzing crowd and dull roar that pervaded the courtroom.

David approached the bailiff. "Morning, I'm Antonio Salvatore Dematteo's counsel. Can you tell where we are on the calendar?"

The bailiff, a sizeable fat man who had been on the county payroll for twenty-two years, looked up with a bored expression and an imperious tilt of his huge head. He slowly ran his eyes down the list.

"People vs. Dematteo. You're fourth. Say, is that Sal?" He suddenly sounded interested.

"Yes, it is," agreed David. "Can you move us up?"

"Sure, no problem." The bailiff reflected on the many five-dollar bills he had received from Sal for small favors. "Jeez, what happened?"

"We are not exactly sure. But I think the judge will probably want to do this hearing in chambers."

With a quick flourish of his pencil the bailiff announced, "You're first, counselor. Sal Dematteo, a defendant." He couldn't believe the smooth, young, competent trial attorney that he had watched work for the last two years was actually a defendant. What could he have done?

"Thanks," acknowledged David. "I appreciate your help."

David turned to Max who was still absorbed in his book. Out of the corner of his eye he saw Catherine and her oldest brother Stan enter the courtroom.

Max noticed David and closed his book. "Damn it, I should have seen this coming. I permitted a confrontation the other night that violated every basic tenet of proper psychiatric treatment."

"Max, stop flailing yourself. None of us could have foreseen this incident."

David was wrestling with himself. Responsibility was not a role he enjoyed. The truth is that Max was right. He should have seen it coming. But what could he have done? Committing Sal prior to the latest occurrence would have been impossible. Sal would never have voluntarily placed himself in a residential treatment situation.

Catherine, her eyes red both from crying and lack of sleep, caught his arm from behind. "David, what are we going to do?"

David embraced Catherine and shook hands with Stan." We will ask to have Sal placed in protective custody until we can sort this thing out. Max will testify. Judge Washington and the prosecutor will probably go along with the motion." He hoped.

Homer Washington, his usual jovial attitude undimmed by the dismal morning and the fact that it was Monday, stepped up to the bench as the bailiff, in his usual singsong voice, heralded the commencement of court.

"Oyez! Oyez! The County Court of Allegheny County, Judge Washington presiding, is now in session. All be seated; first matter, People versus Dematteo."

A skinny deputy sheriff ushered a disheveled and exhausted Sal Dematteo in front of the judge. Sal was handcuffed and refused to lift his head. He stared silently at the floor showing no emotion until he heard Catherine call out his name.

Judge Washington peered over his large, round spectacles in unconcealed surprise. "Sal," he muttered. "Will the People and defense counsel please approach the bench?"

The People were represented by Marvin Marx who was not a fan of Sal Dematteo's. He was an older, large gruff man who always looked unshaven. Sal had beaten him a couple of times when cases went to jury trials. Marvin was enjoying the fact that his nemesis had been grievously humbled.

"Mr. Gold," said the judge, "we don't see you over here very often. What's going on?"

"This is a sad day for all of us, Your Honor. Mr. Dematteo is ill, Judge. He clearly requires treatment. I have asked Dr. Vogel, who has been his attending physician, to appear in his defense."

"He can get treatment from the county," jumped in Marvin. "No special treatment for this guy. He belongs in a cell until trial. He's dangerous. He assaulted a guard at the Carnegie Museum, almost killed him." Marvin glared a bit too gleefully at Sal.

"Listen, Marvin, button up your hostility because the guy beat you a couple of times and try being a lawyer. You know he's not dangerous. And stop interrupting me. I believe His Honor is addressing me, not you."

"Your Honor, can we do this in chambers?" asked David addressing the judge.

"Alright, Gold, you want to play rough, we'll take Vogel's testimony in open court, right now. This scumbag will never practice law again."

"That will do it," intervened the Judge. "Mr. Marx, the People will speak when spoken to. One more personal outburst and I'll hold you in contempt. I will also instruct the district attorney to replace you. Court is recessed for one-half hour. Let's go back to my chambers and try to settle this matter."

Twenty minutes later, Judge Washington completed his review of the incident report and his examination of Max Vogel. Max had carefully chosen the words of the narrative leaving out some of the more bizarre aspects of the case.

"Let me summarize, Dr. Vogel," requested the judge. "You plan to associate Dr. Bernard Adler."

"Yes, I do. He is an outstanding expert on abnormal behavior problems."

"The defendant will be in protective custody?"

"Yes, Your Honor," said Max. "He will be in the restraint ward at the Institute under observation twenty-four hours a day."

"Put him in a strait jacket. Maybe he can defend some of the inmates." Marvin giggled. "He must have been pretty drunk."

David wisely kept his peace.

"That's fifty dollars, Mr. Marx, payable immediately. Have you anything else funny to say?"

"This is not open court, Your Honor," objected Marvin.

"True, but we are in session, Mr. Marx, and you are in contempt."

"I'll appeal, Your Honor," threatened Marvin.

"Why don't you do that," smiled the judge. "Meantime, are you going to pay your fine or do you want to join some of your friends in the jailhouse?"

Marvin grudgingly produced a checkbook and scrawled out an almost illegible check for the court.

"Bailiff, please collect the fine from Mr. Marx," instructed the judge.

It had become clear to David that there was a dynamic going on here that transcended the usual judge/lawyer relationship. Marx didn't like the black judge any more than he liked Sal, and His Honor felt the blatant disrespect and disdain that Marvin exhibited toward the court. Homer Washington was not about to let it shake his usual dignified demeanor or let Marvin get in the last word.

"Mr. Gold, would you write an order remanding Mr. Dematteo to the Western State Psychiatric Institute for observation and possible treatment? Dr. Vogel, I'd like a comprehensive report in three weeks. I'd also like a separate county psychologist's report. Any suggestions, Doctor?"

"Marcia Miller, Your Honor. She works closely with the Institute." Also, reflected Max silently, she has nice legs.

"So ordered," barked the judge. "Deputy, release the prisoner from his handcuffs into Mr. Gold's custody. Mr. Gold, it is ten o'clock. Please deliver Mr. Dematteo to the hospital no later than one o'clock this afternoon. You accept the responsibility?"

"I do, Your Honor. Thank you."

"What about it, Mr. Dematteo, this arrangement meet with your approval?" Sal sat silently and nodded a yes.

"By the way, an afterthought. What's the condition of the guard?"

"Stable, Your Honor," assured David.

"He was badly beaten," Marvin interjected.

"Mr. Marx, I'd like a full report on his condition by tomorrow."

The judge turned to the bailiff. "Reconvene the court," he said.

"Mr. Marx, would you care to join us and continue the calendar?"

A surly Marvin Marx agreed. He started to retort, but the remark was not worth another fifty dollars. He nodded affirmatively.

Sal had remained speechless throughout the entire proceeding. He had not uttered a word in his own defense. The deputy unlocked the handcuffs. David led Sal through the backdoor of the judge's chambers. Cathy and Stan were waiting in the hall. Frank and Angela Dematteo were also there. Both appeared deeply concerned.

"We gotta get the best lawyer in town," said Frank. "What do you think, David?"

"Sure, Frank."

Sal looked at his mother and at his wife with pleading eyes. "Honey, I don't remember why or what I was trying to do."

David shook his head as he watched his partner embrace his wife. He was sure it was going to be a very long and not very good week. He was right.

At that moment, Marvin Marx exited the courtroom and walked straight over to David. He thrust his face almost into David's line of vision. David could smell his bad breath.

"Listen, Gold," he said. "You ever embarrass me in front of a judge again, I will get your ass."

David was taken aback by the extremely high level of Marvin's irritation. It was the second time in a week that a lawyer had threatened him.

"Listen, Marvin," he snapped back. "You embarrassed yourself. Why don't you try for an attitude change? Don't threaten me or I'll haul you in front of the bar conduct committee."

Marvin Marx was furious. David couldn't believe his eyes. Marvin wasn't Marvin. David was looking at him through a cracked prism. Marvin's face was contorted and scarred. He was wearing an eye patch. He wore a toga and a chain around his left arm. His arm was raised in a threatening gesture. Evil. He was shrouded in a kind of mist. Something was interfering with the picture. David started to lift his hand in a defensive posture when the haze suddenly cleared.

Marvin's back was toward him and he was striding toward the courtroom door. Oh my God, he thought, now it's happening to me.

CHAPTER 20

THE THIRD WEEK
THE FIRST DAY OF THE JEWISH NEW YEAR

Max Vogel waited impatiently on the steps of Temple Beth Sholem for David to appear. He checked his watch. It was ten minutes after ten. High Holiday services started at ten o'clock. By now his mother would be wearing that mute look of angry frustrated condemnation that so typified his relationship with her. He was a psychiatrist with an irritated mother syndrome. It was like a case study come true. No wonder he chose psychiatry rather than some other avenue of medicine. It was to preserve his own mental well-being.

Max studied the façade of the temple building: the colorful dome, the large stained glass windows and the ancient stone architecture with its Hebrew letters that spelled House of Peace. It sheltered old people who had witnessed the dawn of recorded history, had survived many pogroms and persecution in many different countries and in many different places. It wasn't easy being Jewish. The holocausts of World War II were still fresh in his mind.

David came charging around the corner and stopped, surprised to find Max at the top of the steps.

"You're late, David," chided Max.

"For what?" queried David. "Do I have an appointment?"

"For services, what else?"

"Did my father send you?" David was bewildered.

Max laughed. "No, I want you to hang around after services. You and I are going to meet with Joshua Liebman."

"With the rabbi? What for?"

"We need another perspective. Liebman is a top scholar on Judean history. It's not that I don't trust Benson, but maybe we can find some better answers to some difficult questions."

"Fine, but I have a lunch appointment with my parents. How long do you think this will take?"

"A few minutes, we'll just arrange a time to confer with Liebman."

David agreed with a wave. "See you later."

He opened the great steel door of the temple and was greeted with the singing choir of fifty voices. He slipped quietly down the aisle and parked himself next to his father, who glowered at him. "Late as usual," he scolded.

David, who knew well that discretion was the better part of valor, didn't answer.

* * * *

After the services, Rabbi Liebman, a small, stout man in his early fifties, shook Max Vogel's hand and nodded amiably at David. Sarah Vogel was an important donor. David's parents, while members for many years, were not as generous as Sarah.

"Well, David, are you better behaved now that you are a lawyer?" teased the rabbi.

"At times, Rabbi." David recalled the many times he had been reprimanded and disciplined while a pupil in the religious school. "Hey, I was a kid. I was pretty young."

"We all were," said the rabbi. He turned to Max. "Well, Dr. Vogel, what is so important that we have to meet on a high holiday?"

"David and I wanted to schedule a couple of conference hours with you early next week if possible."

Liebman's eyebrows rose. "You want religious instruction."

"History instruction and maybe some of your thoughts on a particularly puzzling case in which we are both involved."

"Sounds mysterious." The prospect of getting into something a little more interesting than the next fund-raising event or the repair of the deteriorating school building piqued his interest.

"Certainly, how about Monday evening at 7:00 in my office?"

Max looked at David. "Suits me," agreed David. "Can I bring a non-Jewish friend?"

"Not a problem," said Liebman.

"Refresh yourself on first century history," said Max. "In particular one Flavius Josephus. He will be the subject of our discussion."

"Josephus, the traitor?"

"The same, Rabbi. Flavius Josephus AKA Joseph Ben Mattathias, the commander of the Jewish forces in Galilee during the Roman wars, and later a historian and citizen of Rome."

The two friends left the rabbi's study, parting at the door each to have lunch with their respective parents.

Rabbi Joshua Liebman was left staring at the door and pondering as to why a psychiatrist and a lawyer were so interested in events surrounding a man who nearly two thousand years before had betrayed Jerusalem and his people by leading the Roman legions through the underground cisterns beneath the temple. In the course of that betrayal, he showed them how to penetrate the defenses of the city that had so valiantly resisted capture for nearly two years. The result had been the destruction and burning of the temple and the merciless slaughter of untold thousands of Jews.

CHAPTER 21

THE THIRD WEEK, MONDAY
THE KABBALIST RABBI

"I don't get it," objected David. "We come for a history lesson, we're getting dragged to someone called a Kabbalist rabbi."

Maggie wore an amused smile. "Patience, Mr. Gold," she said.

"I'm trying hard."

David opened the front passenger door and escorted Maggie into the car. There was a sort of pall between them. Sal's episode and his subsequent placement in the restraint ward had a disturbing effect on both of them "I don't get it," he repeated. "Rabbi Liebman is a realist. He listened for about ten minutes to Max's story, and then glanced at the time and decided we had to pay a visit to this rabbi."

"Do you have any idea what doctrine a Kabbalist rabbi teaches?" asked Maggie.

"I'm not sure. My education never included their viewpoints. I believe, however, it has something to do with Jewish mysticism, belief in the supernatural. Their dogma includes Dybbuks, or devils, and something called a Golem, a Frankenstein monster raised from the dead. It isn't mainstream religion. I'm sure of that."

They had agreed to meet Rabbi Liebman and Max at the Chabad Orthodox Synagogue, located in an old house about a mile away, near the downtown shopping center of this area. On the way David looked over at Maggie and spied the small silver cross that hung conspicuously around her neck. "Maggie," he asked, "are you comfortable with all this?"

"I am, David. Are you?"

"No, orthodoxy makes me uncomfortable. It highlights our differences. It emphasizes the gulf between us. It's like from another planet."

"Wrong, David. It makes us all understand better the universal nature of religion. It highlights our similarities. The differences are cultural, not religious."

David didn't answer. This woman, a product of a Scotch-Irish home, constantly surprised him with her astute responses to complex situations.

He stopped the car in front of a huge, old combination brick and wooden home, built in the early twenties following the post-World War I real estate boom. The house had a dim light on the porch. A battered wooden sign in Hebrew and English perched on the front of the building announced that this was the site of a Jewish synagogue. The building had an ageless quality about it, as if it could have been set down anywhere, in any land, at any time and still belonged.

Max and Joshua Liebman were on the front porch, waiting for them.

"Now listen," instructed the rabbi, "this man is one of few Kabbalist rabbis left in the country. They espouse a mystic connection between God and man. They delve into what passes for the Jewish version of the occult. They have a comprehension of God and creation that is beyond the grasp and intellect of man. He doesn't speak much English. He may treat you like heretics, but I know him. He is actually a kindly man. I will talk to him in Hebrew and Yiddish. All questions will go through me."

"Why are we here, Rabbi?" David asked. "I don't get it."

"We are here, David, because Dr. Vogel has described a phenomenon to me that I don't understand and do not feel qualified to address."

Liebman turned to Maggie. At their initial meeting he had accepted her almost immediately. "Are you alright with this, Miss Seiler?"

"I am, Rabbi. There is no problem. I assure you."

"Good." With that, Liebman pushed the door open and they entered a shabby hallway void of decoration. There were no pictures, no rugs, only a hardwood floor and a small, gold-plated, nine-branched candelabra resting on a rickety wooden table. The wallpaper was faded and the one light fixture in the ceiling was covered by an aging shade-projected kaleidoscope of flickering shadows.

"These people live like monks," observed David.

"These people live just fine," said Liebman.

"Cool it, David," whispered Max.

They were greeted by a diminutive, gray-bearded man who wore a black fedora and a prayer shawl. The small congregation had just finished their evening service.

Solemn bearded men in black hats, all wearing black suits and some with long curls, were slowly filing out through the narrow hallway. They were a regiment, dressed the same, appearing the same. They hardly noticed the three men, but a glimpse of the dark-haired girl with a silver cross adorning her neck was enough to raise a number of eyebrows.

David smiled to himself. This will be one to tell their wives. The vision of a beautiful *shiksa* floating through this modest house of worship was a sight to startle the most secular among them.

Rabbi Moses Ben Veloshen was seated in the bowels of a brown overstuffed chair. He looked up when they entered. He was old, or appeared very old. His eyes were red rimmed and magnified by a huge pair of spectacles. His beard was a dirty gray and the lines in his timeless face were deep, rugged and extended into his beard. It was, David observed, the face of many rigorous journeys, of a people who had lost their lands and wandered the earth, but had not lost their souls.

The Kabbalist rabbi surveyed the group. He nodded at Joshua Liebman, looked completely through Max, stopped at David for a moment and shook his head affirmatively, then paused at Maggie.

David thought he saw a glint of recognition cross the old man's eyes. Then recognition turned to sadness. He gently grasped Maggie's hand. She was surprised but didn't object.

"*Shayna Maidel*," he muttered. He followed with what sounded to David like a blessing in Hebrew. When he dropped her hand, he patted it almost lovingly. There were tears in his eyes.

Even Liebman was puzzled by this act. However, he commenced to speak in Hebrew to the old man. His speech lasted nearly ten minutes and was interrupted by a couple of short questions. When he finished, he turned to the group and explained he had stated the problem to Rabbi Veloshen.

The Kabbalist was sunk deep in thought. For several minutes, left hand digging into the top of his beard, he silently cogitated. All he needs is a crystal ball or a magic wand, David noted restlessly to himself.

Suddenly, the aged theologian of Israel looked up and, eyes blazing, fastened his gaze on David. It was if he had received a revelation. He pointed his finger, not in an accusatory manner, but more as a gesture of identification. "The Kohane," he said aloud. The rest of the speech was in Hebrew and quite unintelligible to David. His pronouncement however brought an image of Isaiah, the dean of the Old Testament prophets, giving Abraham or somebody important one of his compelling messages.

Max, who had studied Hebrew, understood and was astonished.

Rabbi Liebman turned to David. With great hesitation he began to translate. Liebman, the orator, who on Friday nights and on High Holidays filled the synagogue with his ringing voice, was at loss for words. He pondered for a moment and then began.

"Rabbi Veloshen says you are a Kohane, of the priestly class, a descendent of the Maccabees, a member of the Mattathias family, and to save your friend from a tragic end you must go to the wall on the eve of the Day of Atonement (the Kol Nidre) and at sundown recite the sacred prayers and beg for forgiveness. He gives you his prayer shawl as a symbol of his belief in you and your submission to God."

"The wall," David said, incredulously. "The wall, what wall, where?"

"The western wall of the temple in Jerusalem," said Maggie softly, "that wall which the righteous refer to as the Wailing Wall."

"That trip is impossible," said Max emphatically. "The wall is in East Jerusalem. It is in Jordanian territory."

"The Kabbalist rabbi," repeated Liebman in an odd barely perceptible voice, "believes that is the only way, otherwise events, perhaps already written, will bring terrible sorrow and tragic loss to the Roman legate."

"Oh hell," reflected David, "that's just swell."

The audience was over. The response of each person differed considerably. But as they departed, all were silent, lost in their own personal interpretation of what they had heard. The interview obviously raised more questions than it answered.

David did notice that Rabbi Veloshen's gaze continued to follow Maggie. His expressive eyes spoke neither of admiration or lust, but of a great and mournful sadness.

Outside, the conversation began, and sounded more like a confused Babel than the comments of four intelligent and literate persons. Maggie remained mute. David was unnerved, the strain of the past few days becoming evident. "This whole damn thing is absurd," he said. "What the hell was that rabbi babbling about?"

Max chimed in. "Calm down, David, please."

At the same time, Liebman tried to speak, but David kept ranting. He was near hysterical.

"Go to the wall. Why doesn't he go to the wall? I have responsibilities. I have a law practice. Of all the damn wild goose chases. Who the hell is the Roman legate anyway?"

"David," Maggie had seized him by the shoulders. "David," she said quietly, "stop it. Can't you see it? Sal is the Roman legate."

Liebman had regained his composure. "Let us go back to my office," he suggested, "for some sensible discussion."

"A good idea," Max said. "Can you drive, David?"

"Of course."

Maggie's intervention had restored his equilibrium. Sal, the Roman legate, he repeated over and over in his mind. How can that be?

David looked over at Maggie after she had settled next to him in the car. She was angry. "David," she said, "I know you're very upset. That is understandable. You must try to control your emotions. You must use a part of your mind that you practice law with. It is generally recessive. I somehow feel you are the key to the solution. But you need to concentrate, to think clearly, to forget the usual boundaries. Focus on the issues."

"Okay, Maggie, I'm sorry, but this defies reality. Maybe Sal is psychotic. Maybe he is schizophrenic and has a split personality. If he is, I can't help him. Because of a thirty-minute meeting with an old man who looks like Methuselah, I'm supposed to go to Jerusalem. That not only exceeds the boundaries, but borders on the preposterous."

"David, pull over for a minute. We need to talk this out before we meet with Max and Rabbi Liebman. Do you really think Sal is mentally ill?"

David pulled over to the curb and stopped the car. He studied this woman who had elbowed her way into his life. Or had he stormed into her life? Or was this encounter with her, as he really suspected, meant to happen? At that second, he believed… no, he knew he loved her very much. It transcended desire and any visceral feelings that had marked his initial reaction to her beauty.

"No, no, I don't. I don't think Sal is mentally ill. But, Maggie," he asked, "how did you know the rabbi meant the western wall in Jerusalem? How did you know the Roman legate is Sal? How do you know these things?"

"I'm not sure, David. I just know. I know something else," she shuddered slightly. "But we cannot discuss it now. We better get to Liebman's office."

"I know something, too. Maggie Seiler. I love you very much." He reached over and touched her cheek.

"Do you, David?" She looked straight into his eyes. "Tell me honestly, would you take me home to your mother?"

David hesitated. He thought of Myra's disapproving eyes. The two-thousand-year-old fear of the son marrying a gentile.

"Would you, David? You met my mother. Would you take me home?" She waited for an answer. "Because if you won't or can't, say it now, I'll understand. But if I commit…" She stopped and swallowed her words.

He looked deep into those enigmatic eyes. Who was this woman? A child from the Scottish highlands. Who were her ancestors? The wild tribesman of the clans who roamed the northern mountains of the British Isles. The Romans had once built a wall to lock these fierce people out of the lower lands. The Romans, of course. But from where did her uncanny wisdom come?

"Well, David, if you can't answer."

David interrupted her. "I would be proud and pleased, Miss Seiler, to take you home to my mother. You would add much grace and beauty to my clan."

She kissed him, a lingering kiss that made him want to forget Max, Liebman, the Kabbalist rabbi, Sal, and the whole damn mess.

Ever the responsible person, Maggie said, "We need to get back to Liebman's office." She also reflected silently. He would have to give up those cigars. "Tomorrow is another day," she said. Again that chill. Was tomorrow really another day? She wasn't sure.

Liebman was pacing his office when they arrived. He was patently agitated.

"Took you long enough," muttered Max.

"Sorry," apologized David, "I was a little shook up. Maggie figured I ought to calm down."

"Good thinking, Miss Seiler," commented Liebman.

"Okay!" exclaimed David. "What now, gentlemen? Can we ignore the old prophet? Is this just an old wives' tale or what about it, Rabbi Liebman? Is there anything to the Kabbalist theosophy? Do I call a taxi and go to Jerusalem on a flying carpet?"

"Perhaps," interposed Maggie, "we can examine this matter in a more calm and scientific manner."

"Okay, Maggie," agreed Max. "You start."

"No, Max, you're the doctor, you start. But first, do you believe Sal Dematteo is psychotic and experiencing aberrational delusions? Because if you do, then discussion of the Kabbalist rabbi's solution is academic at best."

"No, I don't," stated Max. "But I can't explain what is happening."

"Good, you three gentlemen discuss it. In the meantime I will call Benson. He should be back from New York. May I use the phone, Rabbi?"

"Certainly, use the phone in the outer office."

"David," Liebman blanched as if embarrassed. "I never believed in Kabbalism. It's medieval. It's illogical. I'm not close enough to this thing. I'm sorry. I'm not sure why I took you there."

The whole experience had disconcerted Liebman. It nagged at his basic belief. You were supposed to believe in a mystic God. To revere and praise him. But actual prophesy, as if you had direct contact with God, that was not in Liebman's realm.

David could see this was going to go nowhere. He thumped the desk in front of him. "I can't afford this odyssey!"

"Halt," said Max. "I'll finance the expedition. But suppose we get you to Jerusalem. How can you get to the area in the east that the Jordanians occupy? Furthermore, you have to be there by sundown on Saturday night."

Both Liebman and David were at a complete loss for an answer.

"It's easy," Maggie reappeared in the door. "Catholics aren't barred. Neither are Protestants. Six will get you a dozen that Father O'Malley has connections that can get you into East Jerusalem. By the way, I just talked to Benson. He said he's nearly certain the Dead Sea Scrolls he found in New York are authentic, though he hopes to carbon date them, too. He wants to talk to David. He claims these scrolls contain conclusive proof that Josephus did not lead the Romans to the secret passages underneath the temple. He mentioned a name: John of Gischala."

"Impossible," exclaimed Liebman. "John of Gischala was a commander of one segment of the Jewish forces in upper Jerusalem during the siege. He was captured by the Romans and never..."

"Never what?" Max chimed in.

Liebman paused, "Never was executed by Titus. He spent the rest of his life in captivity. His co-commander, Simon Ben Gorias, was supposedly crucified. These two actually engaged in an internecine battle for control of Jerusalem. He was also a sworn enemy of Josephus and almost had him murdered when they were in the Galilee together."

Max nodded. "That seems to explain some of the content of the episodes Sal has been experiencing."

"Well, that's all wonderful, but ladies and gentlemen of the jury, what about the verdict? Jerusalem or no Jerusalem? I personally vote no." David plopped down on a nearby chair and commenced studying the floor of the office.

Rabbi Liebman shook his head. Max shrugged. No one was about to render an opinion. For some reason both heads turned to Maggie and waited.

Mary Margaret Seiler, Maggie by nickname, sighed deeply. Why me? she wondered.

Liebman had removed the prayer shawl from the faded velvet pouch that had sheltered it, the prayer shawl that the Kabbalist rabbi had given him for David to carry to the wall. It didn't look any more sacred than a thousand other prayer shawls that a thousand other worshipers wore to temple or synagogue. He placed it on the table. They all focused on it. It was shabby and frayed, with little beauty or distinction. And yet, there was indeed something else, a pacifying quality that caused each one of them to center their conscious thoughts on the issue at hand.

"David," said Maggie suddenly. "I think you should go. So does Benson. He believes we are close to the answers. You know he often perceives events that the rest of us can't see. Why don't you call him back?"

"Maggie! I love Sal like a brother. I would be willing to go half way across the world for him. If it made any sense. But I can't help a person who is sick. I can't restore him to health. Only the proper treatment can help." David looked at Max to fortify his position. Max's response was total silence.

"Maybe not," Maggie continued, "but Benson believes, as does the Kabbalist rabbi, that for some reason, you are the catalyst to bring closure to this whole matter. He was even more convinced after his trip to New York. When I told him about our meeting with the Kabbalist rabbi his words were, 'Yes, that's the answer'."

Joshua Liebman touted himself as a secular rabbi—the conservative leader who preached that the rabbinate had to get closer to the reality of its congregants. That the Jews were losing their younger people because the teachings were too esoteric and the religious hierarchy had lost touch with the generation that in ten years had seen two wars. He felt that as President Truman had once said "the buck stops here" on his desk.

"I am not sure," said Liebman, "why or how I got involved here. But I did. David, I know this. If you are going to go and be there by Yom Kippur eve, the preparations must begin now."

David looked up. His eyes had bored a hole in the floor as he tried to come to some rational decision. "Rabbi," he said incredulously, "you believe I should go?"

Liebman's silence confirmed David's statement. Then the rabbi spoke. "The decision is yours and only yours. If you make the journey, I will assist."

David sighed. It was a sigh of resignation but also of commitment. "Okay, but you will have to fix it with my parents."

"I will," he agreed. Rabbi Liebman now became General Liebman. "Max," he ordered, "use the second phone. Call the airlines and get David a reservation to Tel Aviv. Start with El Al, and if they are booked, try TWA.

"I need to call the Israeli Ambassador. Maggie, please assist Max. You seem to be coolest among us. What else should we do?"

"Call Father Sean O'Malley," she answered. It will take him a day at least to get through to and convince his fellow priests to help. I will talk to him first and explain the situation. But you need to make him understand why David must go to East Jerusalem under the protection of the Catholic Church."

"That's a tough one," Liebman said, "but I'll try."

"But first," Maggie said, "David must talk to Benson."

Max was frustrated. A call to the airlines indicated no available space to the Holy Land either on El Al or TWA that would fit in the required time frame. The Jewish New Year and the Yom Kippur holiday had jammed both airlines' schedules.

Liebman called the Israeli Ambassador. He would not be available for at least two hours.

David then called Benson. He listened and grunted a few times. "I understand," he assured Benson, "but who are you going to call in Beirut and why? I see, say the guy's name again. Him! I'm to advise you if possible before I go to Beirut. If not, I'm to call you when I get there. What makes you think I'm going to go to Beirut? I understand." He didn't understand. He just accepted. "Now, tell me, Benson, who is the Roman legate and what were his duties? He was the chief Roman administrator of the Eastern provinces. Like a judge? He had the complete power of life and death in that entire area of the empire. Thank you. I will need it!"

David hung up. He addressed Max. "Benson says it was this guy, John of Gischala, who was the traitor. It's in the Dead Sea Scrolls. He says I'm going to Beirut. Don't ask me how he knows. He is calling a contact there. He wishes me good luck. He says I will need it. He's going to call you in the morning."

"So what do I do with that?" asked Max. Maybe convince Sal that his brother was not the culprit. He'd have to give it a lot of consideration. It posed some interesting possibilities.

Maggie called the rectory. Mrs. O'Rourke had finished dinner, cleaned up the dishes and was getting ready to leave. "Yes, Miss Seiler," she said, "he's still here."

Father O'Malley came on the phone and boomed cheerily, "Hello, Mary Margaret, how's your dear mother and your Uncle Andy?"

"They're both fine, Father, thank you. Uhh, Father, you know I'm a senior psychiatric nurse at Western State?"

"Yes, I do."

"Father," she hesitated. David had never heard Maggie unsure of herself. She was obviously trying to devise the best approach. How do you ask this serious religious man to assist you in a project that has all the earmarks of nutty fantasy?

She continued. "I have been working with Dr. Max Vogel on the case of Antonio Salvatore Dematteo. I understand it is of some interest to you."

The priest's demeanor instantly changed. "It is of great interest to me."

"I'm in the office here with Mr. Dematteo's partner, David Gold, and Dr. Vogel. You know Mr. Gold, don't you, sir?"

"Yes, I do. David and I had lunch last week."

"Well, Father, there are some very complex medical problems inherent in Mr. Dematteo's case. Dr. Vogel needs to send Mr. Gold to East Jerusalem to get some answers." Her voice trailed off.

She covered the receiver and turned toward David. "God, how do you lie to a priest?" she whispered, before resuming the conversation. "We thought you could help us, Father."

"Mary Margaret!" his voice rose in what was clearly a rebuke. "Is this some sort of a joke? If it is, this is beneath you. Put Mr. Gold on the phone now." She handed the phone to David.

"This is David, Father." David wanted to give the phone to Liebman but he refused it.

"Alright, David, what is going on?"

"Father," David bit the bullet. "Dr. Vogel's research with Sal has deviated into some odd areas. We need some answers on some of the hallucinations that Sal is having. We believe they are in the Dead Sea Scrolls now being studied in St. Marks in East Jerusalem," he lied. "Father, I need to personally make the trip. But I can't get into East Jerusalem. Can you help us?"

Liebman seized the phone. "Father, this Rabbi Joshua Liebman. We met a couple of months ago at an interreligious conference in Philadelphia. Do you recall?"

"I do, Rabbi. How are you?"

"I'm fine, Father. I'm going to ask you to make a leap of faith. I'll understand if you refuse. Do you have any contacts on the West Bank of Palestine or in the old city of Jerusalem?"

Father O'Malley considered the question. He had made a trip to the Holy Land in 1953. He did have some contacts at St. Marks in Bethlehem. But he was concerned. He had heard about Israeli espionage. The lengths they would go to carry out a mission. He hesitated.

"Rabbi, are the Israelis involved here?"

"They are not, Father. I know this has a false ring to it, but this does actually involve Sal Dematteo. Can you place David under the protection of the Catholic Church for twenty-four hours in East Jerusalem?"

Father O'Malley was a principled man who would move heaven and earth, if he could, for someone from his parish. Sal and Catherine were special people, but he felt he had better inform the Bishop. Otherwise, he could receive a severe reprimand. He already knew the Bishop's answer. He was about to say no, that he had to get the Bishop's permission, when something occurred to him. It was an incident that happened a long time ago, in what now seemed like another lifetime. He had no idea what had brought this event back from some deep subconscious crevice in his memory. He recalled a cold, overcast day, when a twenty-four-year-old, newly ordained Catholic Army chaplain had stepped on a grisly beach in France, splattered with debris and bodies. They had named it Utah. Machine guns and rifle bullets sprayed the landing party from vantage points in the hills above, shredding arms and legs and murdering strong men in their tracks. Troops in full battle gear, including the chaplain, had hugged potholes in the sand digging frantically for their lives.

The day had begun with a terrible disaster. A German *Kriegsmarine* patrol boat had gotten past the destroyer screen and crippled the troopship *Susan B. Anthony*. The destroyers had blown the German boat out of the water. But it was too late. The troopship was mortally wounded. The ship was evacuated as it sank, with most of the troops escaping. Many reached the beach but without their gear and their weapons. They were on shore frantically cannibalizing weapons and equipment from the dead and badly injured men. It was a scene from some ghastly nightmare.

Overhead, P-47 fighter aircraft buzzed, angry birds sending fusillades of fifty-caliber destruction against those deadly hills. The chaplain's job was to minister comfort to the wounded and perform last rites for the dying. He couldn't do it lying in a hole. The chaplain anchored his steel helmet tightly to his head, and rose to his full six foot, two inches, a formidable target for German snipers.

"For God's sake Father, crouch and move," insisted a voice. The young chaplain turned and looked at the beckoning figure of

Chaplain Birnbaum. "Let's do this together. But move and stay close to the ground."

And together they did. Though the older man's glasses were caked with mud, they two went everywhere, talking softly in Latin, Hebrew or English over dying men, whatever seemed appropriate. They called for medics, paying little or no attention to the religion of the man they served. Miraculously, for some time neither was struck by the barrage of lead or the salvos of high explosives and shrapnel that blanketed the beach. Then Father O'Malley leaned over one young boy, only a child, from Ardmore, Oklahoma. The boy was shot twice in the stomach. He was about to meet his maker. He was crying. He wanted his mother. For a moment the chaplain forgot and rose to his full height. Crossing himself he prayed for this youngster's soul.

Another man quickly stood up and pulled the priest to the ground. At the same time a chunk of high-powered lead struck the other man in the upper part of his left arm. It was Chaplain Birnbaum. He grimaced in pain but continued his work with a third young man, who was groaning loudly and clawing at his legs. Birnbaum called loudly for a medic. The medic arrived, gave the suffering soldier morphine and turned to Birnbaum. "Nasty wound, sir, better go back to the aid station."

"Too busy, too much to do. Just stop the blood with a bandage and I'll get it fixed later." Birnbaum survived, but his arm was crushed and later had to be amputated. Father O'Malley could still picture Birnbaum, hardly able to see through his filthy glasses, arm soggy with blood and covered by a dirty bandage, saying prayers, talking calmly to frightened boys, a little man with a big mission.

Both O'Malley and Birnbaum received the Silver Star for that day's work. Small reward for an arm. They learned the next day that casualties had been less than expected at Utah and all objectives were met. In the priests' view, if ever there was a reason not to fall from grace, it was that chaotic vision of Hell at Utah Beach on D-Day.

"Father, Father O'Malley, are you there? If you refuse, we understand."

"Rabbi, sorry, I was checking something. What is your time frame?"

"Sometime Saturday afternoon. I can't give you an exact time."

"All right, Rabbi," Father O'Malley said with authority. "David Gold will be met at the Jaffa Gate in East Jerusalem on Saturday afternoon and placed under the protection of the Catholic Church for twenty-four hours."

"Thank you, Father," said a grateful Liebman. "After the holidays I will come and visit and tell you more."

"Please do, Rabbi. I like that idea." Father O'Malley hung up the phone. He wondered if he had committed a sin. He dismissed the thought. What he did was more like several Hail Mary's. He owed Birnbaum one, maybe this would even the score.

CHAPTER 22

THE THIRD WEEK, TUESDAY
GENERAL MARTIN

"May I remind you all that while we have Mr. Gold in Jordan we have not yet devised a way to get him out of the country," Max pointed out. "A visa or a passport takes several days. And if Benson is correct, getting him in and out of Lebanon is a trick that I'm not sure even Houdini could manage."

"We will have to wait for a call back from Abba Eban, the Israeli Ambassador in Washington." Liebman glanced at his watch. "It's almost ten thirty. It's an hour later in Washington. He can help, I'm sure, but we may have to wait till morning."

"Rabbi, he will never make it by Saturday if we wait till morning," said Max, who looked pained. "We are dead in the water."

Maggie looked at David. "Any ideas, David?"

"Yeah, I guess it's my turn now. I have one idea. It's a long shot, but I'll try it." He flipped open a small address book, and dialed.

"Hello, is this General Martin's residence? This is Captain David Gold. I'm sorry to call so late but I have an urgent matter that I need to discuss with the general. Is he there? Thank you. I'll hold on." David paused. He cupped the phone. "I guess I'm going to have a very long career as a captain," he observed.

Maggie clasped his arm. "You can do it, Captain."

Major General George Martin, commander of the First Air Force, Third Air Division, answered the phone. "General Martin here, Captain Gold." His voice rose in a sort of quizzical surprise. "What can I do for you, David?"

"Well, sir, I need a favor. Let me get right to the point. I believe this is possible without a serious breach of regulations. General, I need to get to the Middle East by Saturday. It is extremely urgent. If I could get an administrative temporary duty order, no cost to the unit, to get me somewhere to a MATS station in Europe, I would be very grateful. I believe it's legal, sir. Providing there is no expenditure of appropriated funds. I would be on space-available basis. I need the order to get on an airplane."

General Martin didn't answer. He was mulling over the request. Finally he spoke. "David, how important is this trip? Are you calling in some chips?" Captain Gold had done the unit many favors as its lawyer and had done some personal favors for the general. He was a good officer. Nevertheless, Martin sounded pressured.

"Sir, let me assure you I called as a last resort. This is not a payback, nor do I want any special favors. It is a matter of great urgency or I wouldn't ask."

"All right, David, I believe you. Meet me at the base at 0600 tomorrow. There is a courier plane to Athens by way of Madrid and Naples. It leaves at 1100 from Maguire AFB. If I can get you on it, we'll issue an administrative order with no funds attached. First we have to get you to New Jersey. The order will take you anywhere there's an American installation in the Middle East. The closest one in the Middle East zone is Detachment 91.

"Where is Detachment 91, sir?" David asked.

"Detachment 91 is in the Lebanon International Airport in Beirut, David. See you in the morning." General Martin hung up.

"Well, I'll be damned." David surveyed the room and reported the good news. Liebman's mouth was open in amazement.

Max couldn't believe it. "I can't get you much cash by then," he said.

Maggie had a smile on her face. He was resourceful. She had known that he was smart. He handled the general like a diplomat.

"I won't need much money. Guys, if I'm lucky, by Thursday I'll be in Athens."

Liebman folded the prayer shawl and placed it back into the velvet pouch. He procured a small prayer book from a nearby shelf and earmarked some pages. "Can you read these prayers in Hebrew?" he asked.

"Well, Rabbi, I think my education at least got me that far."

Max went into his wallet and produced six twenty-dollar bills and a ten for a total of one hundred and thirty dollars. "All I have," he said. "We will get you a ticket home from this end."

Liebman added another twenty to the pot and Maggie contributed a ten from her purse. David tried to refuse Maggie's money, but she looked insulted. He backed down and took the bill. His larder now consisted of one hundred and sixty dollars to which he added twenty-five.

One hundred and eighty-five dollars to fly halfway around the world. He felt like Jules Verne's hero, Phineas Fogg, who bet that he could circumnavigate the globe in eighty days. The difference was this: Phineas Fogg had no airplanes or automobiles. However, he did have two advantages—unlimited funds and eighty days.

Rabbi Liebman handed David the prayer shawl. "Guard it," he said. "I believe it is important. Good luck," said Liebman, shaking David's hand. "I will talk to the Israeli Ambassador. I know him well. You will be well taken care of if you can get to Israel safely." The rabbi knocked on wood, a superstition he learned from his mother.

Maggie and David walked slowly to David's car. They held hands. "It's very late," she said. "You need some rest."

"I'm going to drive out to the base tonight, while I'm still awake. We have a small Bachelor Officers Quarters at the facility. At least I'll be there in body at 0600," he said.

When he dropped Maggie off at her door, they embraced again. It was different than the other times. They sensed a certain bond that previously hadn't existed. When David drove away, Maggie wistfully watched the car disappear. They had not really gotten to know each other yet. To explore the hidden feelings and discover the physical pleasures that young people experience in a relationship that had moved beyond a normal male/female encounter. They had never laughed together in a movie, walked quietly in the park, met at an intimate bar or on a corner—just glad to see one another. They had never had a carefree evening where they could just dream the dreams of embryo love. There was always tension, stress, a friend caught in a confusing web of events that nobody could fathom.

The night breeze penetrated her thin cotton sweater and for the third time that night, Maggie shivered.

* * * *

Liebman was about to shut up the office, when the phone jangled. He was irritated. He had already called his wife. What did she want now? "Okay, okay," he said to the phone. "I'll be right home." He was tired but exhilarated. Something had happened which brought excitement into his life. Perhaps he was involved in something important. Could he make a sermon on the subject? Maybe when it was all over. What a story! Yet if he told it the way it was, he would be laughed out of the rabbinical community.

The phone rang again. He picked it up expecting his wife's voice demanding that he come home and relax. She worried. Her father and older brother had died of heart attacks.

"Rabbi Liebman," a voice said. "This the Israeli embassy. Please hold on for Mr. Eban."

"Liebman, what's so important that you call at eleven o'clock at night?"

"Mr. Ambassador, how kind of you to return my call. Abba, we need your help. Let me tell you a quick story. If you say no, I'll understand."

The Israeli Ambassador immediately remembered the liberal support they had always received from this Pittsburgh congregation, including the grocery store owner whose only son had lost his leg in the 1948 battle in Israel. They were all still tireless supporters of the young Jewish state. It was unlikely, he thought to himself, that he would or could say no to any reasonable request.

CHAPTER 23

THE THIRD WEEK, WEDNESDAY
112TH FIGHTER INTERCEPTOR GROUP
GREATER PITTSBURGH AIRPORT

Sergeant Buckholz shoved a steaming mug of coffee into David's grateful outstretched hand. "Here, Captain, this will get your kidney's racing. We talked to OPS at McGuire, and there is room for you on the MATS courier at 1100. General Martin told us to cut orders and he would sign them when he got here. Winecki is mimeographing the orders now. Judge, what's so important?"

"Kind of a confidential mission, Bucky. Sorry, can't talk about it. Thanks for all your help."

Ten minutes later, a well-groomed General Martin, dressed in starched khakis, a jacket adorned with the silver wings of a command pilot and three rows of ribbons, entered the room. "Well, David, you are all set. I spoke to Colonel Fetterman. Fortunately, Wednesday is a slow day for overseas travel. You're on the airplane. Bucky, let me see the orders."

Sergeant Buckholz called the orderly room. "What about the orders, Winecki! The general is waiting. Not tomorrow, now!"

Less than five minutes later, a bedraggled Corporal Winecki, carrying a sheaf of papers, timidly entered the room. It was, he thought to himself, too damn early for this kind of crisis. He nodded at David. "Morning, sir."

"Morning, Winecki." David sipped the burning black wake-up potion. It was working slowly on the mass of cobwebs that dulled his senses.

General Martin examined the orders. He verified there were no finance appropriation numbers. Then he quickly scrawled his name, and handed several copies to David. "Hold on to these. They are your passport."

"Yes, sir," said David. "I can't tell you how grateful I am."

"Jimmy Board will fly you in a T-33. He is in OPS, filing a flight plan. Better get a flight suit, a parachute and a helmet and get going. Good luck."

The two men shook hands. David carefully folded the orders and placed them in a side pocket of a small brown canvas bag. Space in the T-33 would not allow a full-size B4 bag. He had packed two changes of underwear, a khaki rain-resistant jacket, a dob kit with toothbrush and a razor, a pair of civilian cotton pants and a polo shirt. At the bottom of the bag he had lodged the prayer shawl and the prayer book. That much completely filled the bag. The ground crew had rolled out the aircraft, a single jet engine training airplane with a cruising speed of nearly four hundred miles per hour. Lt. Jimmy Board, all five-foot-five of him, in a green cotton flight suit, was doing a visual walk around, searching for flaws or problem areas in the aircraft fuselage. Fueling was complete.

He waved at David. "Hey, Judge. Nice morning for a hop. Get your butt in the airplane, and let's get going."

The two men shook hands and David adjusted the crash helmet and the radio communication headband to the size of his head. He crawled into the back seat and a three striper adjusted the seat straps and the backpack. Jimmy, satisfied with the condition of the aircraft, revved it up and taxied slowly down the ramp toward the runway. He called the tower for takeoff instructions. Clearance came a few moments later and the T-33, impatient to move, whirred up to full throttle, ran one more engine check to test its power and then scrambled down the runway eager to perform the flying mission for which it had been so carefully designed.

It was only after they had reached cruising altitude at 22,000 feet, surrounded by bright sunshine and an almost cloudless sky, that David recalled, with a sinking sensation, that he had left the prayer book in the BOQ. He had taken it out the night before to read it, and in his groggy haste this morning had left it on the little wooden table in the barracks. If this was an indication of how the rest of the trip would go, he was in real trouble. He resigned himself to whatever the future unfolded. He would find a way to fix this minor lapse. The whole trip was insane anyway. But it was a beautiful morning and the jet, a modern mechanical marvel of speed and power, streaked across the sky headed east toward a rendezvous with a four-engine chariot that, God willing, would take him on the second leg of the journey to Europe and the Middle East.

He loved it. The whine of the engine with its inherent message of power and vitality, the world spread out far below, the Allegheny mountains, the green fields and farms of central Pennsylvania, a new adventure. This was a part of him, a facet of his character that clashed with the solid, responsible young man that Myra Gold had carefully raised to always do the right thing. As for the prayer book, well, he'd gone in front of many juries without a script and made out fine. He felt sure when the time came, he would somehow recite the right words.

For assurance, he reached down into his bag and searched for the prayer shawl. It was there, nestled peacefully at the bottom. For some reason, when he had received this token from the Kabbalist rabbi, a heavy burden that had oppressed his spirit from the time Sal first entered his office seemed to lift. He had the sense that he was now being guided toward some predestined rendezvous, and that whatever the future would bring, he would deal with it.

Jimmy Board called him on the interphone. "You want to fly, David?"

"Sure."

"Keep it level at twenty-two thousand and maintain heading ninety-two degrees due east. Call when you're within range of McGuire tower. If I'm sleeping, report in and wake me up. I'll take over." Jimmy had had a long night yesterday. The interphone chatter ceased.

David studied the horizontal indicator, the altimeter and the radio compass. Everything was in perfect trim. He checked the throttle setting and was satisfied it was holding the aircraft steady on a planned cruising speed of 380 MPH. He listened to some commercial traffic for a few minutes. They left the mountains behind and now were heading across the eastern Pennsylvania Piedmont, the flat area that ultimately would lead them to New Jersey and the western edge of the Atlantic Ocean. He spotted a large silver river, glistening in the distance, threading its way nearly due south. He checked the map. It was the Delaware marking the Pennsylvania border. They were getting close to destination.

"They had slipped the bonds of earth and sought refuge in the vast infinity of the heavens." He smiled, pretty corny stuff, but felt a certain personal exhilaration in flying a small jet that brought out the poet even in the most prosaic and unspiritual. This incredible beast, if only for a few minutes, was his to command.

The interphone came to life. "Thanks, David, good job, I'll take it. I'm going to use ground control approach. I need the practice."

"Roger, Captain. The bird is yours."

The aircraft banked quickly to the right. "McGuire Tower, this is Air Guard TF 0 HOTEL - Request permission to land using GCA."

A brief pause and the expected answer. "This is McGuire Tower, Air Guard TF 0 HOTEL. We read you loud and clear. Do a 360-degree once and then use runway three. Descend to two thousand feet and GCA will assume control. You are then cleared to land. Condition is VFR."

"Roger, McGuire Tower, thank you." Jimmy readjusted the throttle and began his gradual descent toward the runway.

To date, it had been an uneventful flight, a reminder that the rest of David's journey was not to be so restful. Were the Fates gathering their challenges?

CHAPTER 24

THE THIRD WEEK, WEDNESDAY
MAGUIRE AIR FORCE BASE

To say that David was despondent would be a gross understatement. The journey, which had begun so full of promise, now threatened to crash and burn.

Jimmy had, following Ground Control Approach instructions, made a perfect three-point landing. They trailed the yellow Follow Me cart to a temporary spot on the parking ramp. Jimmy asked for fuel, made a few notes in the logbook and marched off to Base Operations to file a return flight plan. The two men shook hands and David went to the passenger terminal. In the latrine he slipped off his flight suit, carefully stuffed it into the remaining inch in his carry-on bag, combed his hair, smoothed out his uniform, donned a necktie, and made his way to the Military Air Transportation Passenger Counter. A clean-shaven sergeant, in a pressed khaki uniform, was courteous.

"I'm really sorry, Captain," he said, "but I can't possibly deviate from priority regulations. I know you were on the flight, but a Major Roberts called about twenty minutes ago with a higher priority order. We had to bump you."

"Is Colonel Fetterman available?"

"He's at headquarters, sir. Should be back in about twenty minutes."

"When is the next flight?"

"Tomorrow morning, sir, but it's full right now. I've put you as number one on standby. We have a number of dependent families joining their spouses in Madrid this morning. The base at Terrejón is opening up this week. Why don't you get some coffee and check back in about half an hour. We'll be loading then, and perhaps somebody won't show."

David went to the snack bar. He purchased a cup of coffee and a doughnut. The coffee was powerful, bitter and stale, typical service brew. The doughnut tasted like sawdust, but what the hell, it was food. He sat down in the lounge. The furniture was 1930s modern. Torn green plastic, more damn green. The lounge was populated with noisy, restless kids and their apprehensive mothers, and a few servicemen, some in blue and some in khaki uniforms. In the corner, four officers idly smoked and chatted. He thought about joining them, but he really wasn't in the mood for small talk.

David stared at the floor, a bad habit he indulged in when things were going badly. What the hell was he doing here anyway? The idiocy of this whole mission struck him. Did he imagine himself as some character in a fantasy movie, off on a mystical mission to the Holy Land to save his friend? Reality was all around him. Officers and enlisted men off to new assignments in some duty station where the Cold War was just a little closer. Eager young girls, waiting to join their husbands in Europe. Most had never even heard of the places they were going to live. Complete strangers to cultures in far-off lands where they were being asked to act as representatives for their country. Kids, running around, some crying, some playing tag or punching each other, their mothers trying in vain to referee the ragamuffins. He nodded off for a moment. Fatigue was catching up with him. He was exhausted. All the impossible events of the past two weeks had stretched his nerves to a point where he felt like a taut bowstring ready to launch an arrow.

Why not give up? he thought. Get a taxi, go to the local airport and fly home. Who could criticize him? Who could condemn him? How conceivably in the name of anything within the realm of reason could a trip to say few words in front of a broken down, two-thousand-year-old wall in the old city of Jerusalem help his very sick friend? He should absolutely be home, helping work on Sal's caseload. God, he was tired.

* * * *

"David," his mother insisted, "you must be responsible. You have an obligation. You can't be like your father, always refusing to accept responsibility."

"Mother, dammit, why me all the time? I'm tired. I grew up when I was ten. I don't want any more responsibility. I don't want to get married. I'm quitting law school. I don't care. I'm abandoning this expedition, now!"

Myra said, "Stop staring at the floor."

"David," a small voice interrupted his mother's. "David, David," it kept repeating.

"Maggie, is that you? What is it?"

He awoke with a start. A pair of black shoes suddenly intervened between his line of vision and the floor. He looked up into the face of a man in a blue uniform, a bus driver. Was he in the Greyhound Bus station? He wanted to get to the airport. He hated buses.

"Captain Gold?" It was clearly a question. The fatigue haze cleared. The Greyhound emblem became a silver "U/S" and the bus driver became a lieutenant colonel.

"I'm Jack Fetterman, General Martin called me about you."

"Yes, sir." David started to rise.

"Sit still." The colonel sat down next to him. "Bill Martin and I flew together in Europe during the war. We were young punks then. I have good news for you."

In the background, a loudspeaker was calling the flight. The people in the lounge were making their way slowly toward the gate.

"Damndest thing. This Major Roberts called us at the last minute with a priority order for himself. I was trying to bump someone so we could get you on the flight when I get a call from the base hospital. Roberts is in sickbay with terrible stomach pains. Very sudden they tell me. You got any special connections? Get your butt moving, Captain, you're on the airplane."

"Yes, Sir." David grabbed his bag. He wasn't about to forget it. "Thanks a lot."

Fetterman shrugged. "Good flight, Captain."

The airplane was a Douglas DC-8, a C-54 Skymaster in military lingo. David climbed aboard. He found an aisle seat towards the rear, next to a young mother and her three-year-old daughter and sat down. Well, I'll be damned, he thought. Sudden stomach pains, pretty mysterious, how about that.

The transport, with its full load, kicked its four Pratt and Whitney engines into motion and slowly taxied into position for takeoff.

"Well, I'll be double damned," he muttered. "I'm on my way to Europe."

It was eleven o'clock Wednesday morning. In Jerusalem, it was seven hours later and almost sundown.

CHAPTER 25

THE THIRD WEEK, WEDNESDAY
WESTERN STATE PSYCHIATRIC INSTITUTE

Before he died, Morris Vogel always said, "My Max rarely makes a mistake, but, when he does, it's a whopper." Morris was right, as usual. This morning, Max made two mistakes. They were both whoppers.

At 8:30 A.M. he called a Sergeant Buckholz at the 112th Fighter Interceptor Group and determined that David had left on schedule for New Jersey. The sergeant had no information as to whether or not David had embarked for Europe, but he believed the MATS airplane was slated to leave at 1100 hours. He wanted to know the nature of David's mission. He couldn't understand why a civilian doctor was calling in respect to Captain Gold. Max told him it was a confidential medical matter. The sergeant said he understood and didn't pursue the matter. Max had no idea what 1100 hours meant or what a MATS airplane was, but as long it had wings, engines and flew he didn't care.

At 9:15 A.M. Maggie arrived. She already had an unsettling morning. A violent confrontation had occurred between two patients and before the attendants could intervene, the younger one, a paranoiac truck driver, had badly beaten the other, a nearly catatonic old man. They had subdued the truck driver but the old man was left battered and bleeding. Maggie had a feeling of anxiety that she couldn't shake.

"Max," she said, "I think you should cancel the meeting. I have this odd feeling that things aren't going to go right."

"I can't, Maggie. It's court ordered. Judge Washington wants a report on Sal now. Dr. Adler has insisted we do it today. Marcia Miller, the county psychologist, will be here at 10:30. Adler has to attend, and he's busy the rest of the week.

"You know, Maggie," Max confided, "I have the same damn feeling. I got a call early this morning. Art Dematteo is in Pittsburgh. He flew in last night. He wants to see his brother this morning. I wanted to put him off, but I have to let him come. He has to return to duty by Friday. He is coming at noon."

"I just don't feel good about this session. We can't postpone?"

"We can't postpone," said Max.

"At least delay Art Dematteo until this afternoon. So close to an assessment/eval session might upset Sal and the family."

"You're right. I'll call and put the Dematteo family off until at least two o'clock."

At that point Max committed his second mistake. It was inadvertent and was compounded by intervening events. A serious disturbance in a group session on the third floor had occurred. Max's thought process was interrupted. The hospital could not afford another injured patient. He rushed upstairs to the group meeting room.

The room was in an uproar. Turmoil was everywhere. It was a scene right out of Bedlam. Patients were lying on the floor, some moaning, others crying. One man was beating on the wall. Another older lady with scraggly gray hair kept pointing a skinny finger to a corner of the room and screaming about the anti-Christ. Pete Bernicke, the supervising attendant, had already arrived. Pete, normally the essence of cool, was slightly unnerved. "Doc, the natives are restless today," he said. "Something upset them."

The female therapist, a newly graduated Ph.D., stood against the wall, eyes wide, filled with fear and surprise. The attendants and floor nurses began to gently work with the patients. "Hypos," said Max quietly to Bernicke, "for the violent ones. Calm the rest. What the hell happened?"

"I don't understand. It just erupted," the therapist said. "We were talking quietly when the old lady in the corner began shouting and pointing at something in the corner. I couldn't see anything, but then the others looked and joined in and a crowd psychosis took over. The old lady kept crossing herself and repeating something about the anti-Christ. I tried to calm them, but it only got worse. That's when I called for help."

The young psychologist was petrified. These patients were all categorized as passive, non-violent. The outburst was sudden, as if an outside force had intruded and stirred the room up into frenzy.

Maggie arrived. She kept looking around, studying the room as if she were feeling something in the air. "I don't know, Max, but the whole place is uneasy today. Maybe there's a storm coming in. Sometimes when the pressure drops."

"Maggie, the damn sun is shining. It's a perfect fall day. I don't like it! I just don't like it!"

The loudspeaker was blaring Max's name. "Dr. Vogel, please come to your office or to the nearest interphone."

Max surveyed the room. The patients were quieting down, some still whimpering. He approached a middle-aged man. A meek, generally quiet schizophrenic, once a pharmacist. For the past eight months he communicated only occasionally and then only in very brief sentences. He appeared to have retreated into himself and could barely express himself. The therapists had been unable to stem the tide and had recommended electroconvulsive therapy.

"Mr. Mindheimer," Max asked the former pharmacist, "what exactly did you see?"

"I saw a concentration camp guard." The answer was simple and direct.

"What did he look like? Was he a man?"

"Yes. He was a big man. He carried a whip."

"How was he dressed?"

"He had no pants. I could see his legs. They were hairy."

"He was naked?"

"No, he wore shorts and he had a metal hat on his head."

"A metal hat? Like a helmet?"

"Yes, like a helmet. We were all very frightened."

Max breathed deeply. He turned to the therapist. "Take these people to their rooms. Take Bernicke with you. I don't want you alone with anybody. If you can in a subtle way, and if they are able to describe it, find out independently what they think they saw. I have to get back to my office. Report to me by two o'clock."

"Will do," promised the therapist.

"Mr. Mindheimer, I promise you the terrible man will not be back," said Max. The patient's reaction was easily explained. Mindheimer was a survivor of the Nazi death camps.

The loudspeaker repeated Max's name and this time was more insistent. Max turned to Maggie. "Adler must be here. He hates to wait for anyone." Max headed for the elevator. "Wearing a helmet," he muttered, "and carrying a whip. What next?" In the ensuing confusion he forgot to call the Dematteo family.

* * * *

Marcia Miller was seated in Max's office. She had her legs crossed and a bright smile on her energetic face. Even when she was inert, Marcia looked bouncy. She was wearing a pink blouse and a short beige skirt that accented the contour of her legs. The skirt stopped well above the knees. Yet, in spite of what might appear to many to be an invitation, she had all the characteristics of an efficient, businesslike professional.

"Max, thank you so much for inviting me in on the case."

"A pleasure, Marcia, glad you're available." Max was pleased. He liked Marcia and he constantly looked for reasons to associate her. This was the kind of woman he needed. A psychologist who would be tolerant of his idiosyncrasies and his deep involvement in his work. They had gone out socially twice. Nothing exciting, though. They had discussed case histories and psychiatric theories. But he did have a problem keeping his eyes off her legs, which he considered models of what well-sculpted women's legs should look like. Her children, he conjectured, would never have fat legs like his mother had. For a brief interlude he forgot his gene pool would also be a factor.

"What's happening here, Max? Why does this guy get special court attention?"

"Sal Dematteo is David Gold's law partner. David is a close friend of mine. Sal was a rising star in the criminal law field when he began having these episodes. Judge Washington likes him and is very cooperative with David on working with Sal's problems. Sal assaulted a guard at the museum last Saturday morning. I don't quite understand why. He is now in protective custody. Adler wants to administer shock therapy. Frankly, I don't think now is the time. The judge has deferred binding him over for trial and is looking for guidance."

Marcia showed surprise. "You don't agree with the great Adler?"

"I do not agree with Dr. Adler's recommended course of treatment at this time. Marcia, you have seen the immediate result of shock treatment. The patient is like a zombie, sometimes for months. I want to give every other known method of treatment adequate time to work."

Marcia nodded. Electroconvulsive therapy on patients had produced some positive results but often left the patient incapacitated, an empty shell, devoid of emotion and shorn of the ability to innovate or carry out any complex intellectual tasks.

"By the way," she asked, changing the subject, "is David attending this morning?"

"David is out of town on business." At least Max believed he was out of town, hopefully somewhere over the Atlantic on his way to Europe. However, in the cold light of a turbulent morning, the idea of his best friend chasing off to the Holy Land, on what now seemed like the creative figment of some writer's imagination, angered him. Not because David was doing it, but because he, Dr. Max Vogel, not only let it happen, but helped provide the resources to allow this utterly ridiculous event to occur. He knew if Adler found out, he would probably be laughed out of the profession.

"Are you going to oppose Adler?" Marcia didn't get an answer. The intercom buzzed, loudly announcing the arrival of Dr. Bernard Adler.

Bernie and Max shook hands warmly. Max introduced Marcia and explained her presence. Adler, never a man to mask his likes and dislikes, clearly expressed his approval of the county psychologist.

"Miss Miller," he said, "you must come to my seminar on congenital criminality. It will be at Pitt Medical School on October tenth. As my personal guest, of course."

"Thank you, Dr. Adler, I'd really like that."

"Okay, Max, where is our patient today? I mean in what century?"

Bernie Adler was clearly in a good mood. He didn't often joke about cases. This morning he was just being cute. Max reflected that it must be Marcia's presence on the scene.

"I haven't seen him today. We've had an incident. Kind of a crowd hysteria problem. Occurred during a group session. Left us all a little shook up." Max buzzed his secretary. "Angie, could you please ask Miss Seiler to have Mr. Dematteo brought to the third-floor interview room?"

"Yes, sir, right away, and oh, Dr. Vogel, a Mr. Art Dematteo and his father and the younger Mrs. Dematteo are here. They say they have an appointment with you."

Max brushed his left hand across his forehead. "Shit," was all he could think of to say. "I forgot to call the family."

"Great," exclaimed Adler, "the brother. Perfect time for a reality check. Let's get them all together."

"Bernie, Dr. Adler, I don't know. There's been a lot of unrest here today." Max glanced at Marcia. "I don't think it's a good time."

"Nonsense, it is a perfect time. We need to know if the patient can separate the person he is being commanded to kill from his real brother. We need to advise the court of the nature of this man's illness so a treatment plan can be devised. A confrontation will tell us a lot. Wait a few minutes, and then bring the brother in to talk to him. Max, you might be too emotionally involved in this case, given your friendship with the patient's law partner, David Gold. Can you handle this?"

"Of course I can," Max responded without hesitation. "I assure you I can, Dr. Adler." Max wisely decided this morning's event called for more formal relations with his mentor. He felt conflict brewing and wanted to maintain a formal clinical approach. A serious personal break over the first case in which he and Adler were collaborating would be disastrous to his career and his personal reputation in the psychiatric medical community.

Max went into the outer office. A young, dark haired, strikingly handsome, somewhat younger and smaller, but better built version of Sal was standing there, chatting with Catherine. Frank Dematteo sat flipping through the pages of a magazine without looking at them. Catherine forced a smile when she saw Max.

Max studied the brother. A lean, swarthy man with sharp, intent eyes that had a certain callous penetrating stare. His movements, even the simple act of shaking hands, were catlike and bespoke an athletic grace both guarded and businesslike. Not an easy man to make friends with, Max thought, but implacable as an enemy—a hardened fighter pilot who would give little quarter in battle.

"How's my brother?" he asked.

"He's very ill, Lieutenant. We are in the process of developing a regimen for his treatment. He has periods of complete lucidity and then, for reasons we have not yet determined, experiences dissociative episodes where he believes he is in another time." Catherine was slowly wringing her hands. She was obviously making a strong effort to keep herself in control. "He thinks he is someone else."

"Where is David?" asked Frank.

"He is out of town. On some sort of Air Force business."

"That's odd," said Art, "taking an active duty tour with all the crap that's going on. Doesn't sound like David."

"Something special for General Martin. I'm sorry, I don't know the details." Max felt that if he continued to fudge the truth, his nose would begin to grow and he would be severely chastised by his mother or someone else.

Art shrugged. "Okay, when can we see Sal?"

"Soon, but you and I need to talk a little."

"There's one thing, Doctor," said Frank.

"Yes, sir, Mr. Dematteo. Please feel free to—"

"Dad," interrupted Catherine, "please don't."

"I got to," said Frank gruffly. "His mother insists."

"Go ahead, Mr. Dematteo, please," said Max gently. "What is it?"

"Angela, my wife, who is not feeling well this morning, wants a Catholic doctor to help Sal. I don't care what it costs. Do you know one?" Frank Dematteo was blunt. Catherine was clearly embarrassed. But though Art was silent, his body language indicated he strongly supported his mother. He waited for an answer. It had better not be no.

Max paused. He started to question the request. Then he thought better of it. "Of course, I understand. We will honor Mrs. Dematteo's request. We have a number of excellent Catholic psychiatrists on the staff. I'll talk to my associate, Dr. John Fogarty. I'll talk to him this afternoon. After he studies the case files and interviews Sal I'll have him contact you."

The old prejudices were still evident. Don't trust the Jew. Or maybe it wasn't that at all. Maybe it was just finding a comfort zone. Angela Dematteo needed someone she could talk to, feel more at ease with, someone who could invoke the same saints and comprehend her beliefs. Perhaps it would be best. John Fogarty would be of great value when the tough decisions to come had to be made.

Max next requested that Art come into the office alone. They needed to discuss the upcoming session. Adler was waiting. Max was apprehensive. He feared Adler's attitude of overwhelming superiority would not mix well with the fighter pilot's steely skepticism. He feared the chemistry would clash, even ignite. He was right.

"Tell me, Mr. Dematteo, did you and your brother have a rivalry for your mother's affection?" Adler launched right into the major issue as he perceived it.

"No!!" Art insisted. No explanation followed. No questions or exposition. Art just looked disgusted and glared. Max could read his mind. He was thinking, what kind of bullshit is this?

"Why would he want to kill you?"

"You know, Doctor, I don't think he wants to kill me. I think you shrinks put it into his mind because you're looking for some explanation for his behavior. He's probably got a tumor or something, and you're missing it."

This was going to get nasty. Max quickly intervened. "Art, can I call you Art?"

Art nodded.

"One of the primary issues is Sal's belief, during his episodes, that he has been ordered to kill his brother. I agree with you. I don't believe it's you at all." He glanced at Adler, who appeared miffed. Max didn't give a damn. There was no time for sensitive egos. They only had a few minutes until the interview was scheduled to start. "Still, Art, we have to be sure there are no serious subliminal issues between the two of you. Please try to help us. I'm sure it is painful for you to hear this."

Art sighed. "It's not painful. It's a lot worse. Sal was my idol while I was growing up. He was stability in my life. He helped me all the time. When I got my wings he hugged and kissed me and told me how proud he was of me. Imagine being told your older brother wants to kill you. How would you react?" He looked knowingly at Adler.

"You're right," agreed Max. "Then, there's nothing that you can recall. Your relationship was always good."

"Better than good. I would gladly give my life for my brother. I believe he would give his life for me." Underneath the toughness, Art Dematteo seemed to be an emotional man. His training helped him keep it in check, but he quickly opened up to Max.

Adler was not to be put off. "Surely the two of you had some differences."

"No!!" Art clammed up again. He had answered the question. This time he gave Adler a steely look. He didn't like the older psychiatrist. He had no tolerance for him. He had no knowledge of his worldwide reputation, nor would he much care.

"Art, please try not react too emotionally," Max said. "For the first few minutes you and Catherine and your dad will be in an adjacent room. There is a one-way mirror. Sal will not realize you are there. Just listen and don't interrupt while he's in hypnotherapy unless I request your presence." Max was firm. He made it sound more like a military order; he knew this was something Lieutenant Dematteo could relate to and understand.

The entourage, led by Max, trooped upstairs to the third-floor interview hall. Adler's previous good spirits had dampened. His psyche had been bruised. After the exchange between Art and Bernie Adler, Max's misgivings as to the wisdom of this session had intensified. When he got off the elevator an anxious Bernicke was waiting for him.

"Hey, Doc, got a second? I have something I think you ought to hear." Bernicke took Max off to the side.

"Make it quick," Max snapped. "Where's Sal Dematteo?"

"He's in the interview room with Miss Seiler. But I really think you ought to hear this before you see him."

"All right, Bernicke, what is it?"

"Well, we questioned a number of patients who were in the therapy group. They all saw the same apparition or whatever it was. Described it exactly the same way. Each one just called it something different. Sounded pretty much like what the old pharmacist had described. There is something else." Bernicke sounded truly puzzled.

"Yes, what is it?"

"Well, Mr. Dematteo saw the same thing in his room. He called the guy by name. He said the guy was Trajalinus, chief of gladiators at the Alexandria arena. Pretty spooky stuff."

"My gawd," gasped Max. The whole hospital is in the grip of some sort of a hysterical obsession. Or was it a lot more than crowd hysteria? Another coincidence that couldn't happen.

Bernie Adler nudged him in the back. "Let's do this, Max, I've got to get back to my office."

Max felt a twinge of panic. The hospital's karma had deteriorated and bad things were about to happen.

* * * *

The interview room was austere, painted a soft white. The decor theoretically had a calming effect on the patients. Max had a different view. He wanted paintings of outdoor scenes that involved plenty of trees, blue sky with white fleecy clouds and tall majestic mountains. He disliked the antiseptic, institutional feeling of the room. But he was overruled by the senior medical staff and was stuck with the standard format for interview rooms developed by the hospital's facilities committee. As one ancient member put it, too much color would cause confusion to the patient.

Maggie was chatting with Sal as the trio of Max, Bernie Adler and Marcia Miller entered the room. Max beckoned Sal to have a seat at center of the table. Max called it the hot seat.

"You remember Dr. Adler?"

Sal nodded yes.

"This is Marcia Miller, the county psychologist. She wants to chat with you this morning, too."

Sal nodded again, with no reaction or emotion. The three sat down across from Sal, reminding Max of the three monkeys: see no evil, hear no evil and speak no evil.

"How do you feel, Mr. Dematteo?" Max asked.

"I'm okay except I'm beginning to feel like a guinea pig in a cage. It's awful noisy here at night. I don't sleep well. I have to get out of here. I have cases to work." He looked around. "Where's David?" His anchor wasn't there, which made him uncomfortable. "There's a lot of work at the office to do."

"I understand," said Max, "that you saw Trajalinus this morning."

"You mean the head gladiator of Alexandria. Yeah, another one of those goddamn episodes. I don't know where these people come from."

"Mr. Dematteo, can we hypnotize you this morning?" asked Max.

"You know, Doc, I'm really getting tired of feeling like a lab experiment. When can I get out of here? I miss my family."

"Mr. Dematteo," asked Marcia, "do you think you can function without these episodes interfering with your business and your life?"

"I think so. I don't know. I need to get the dagger. Do you know where it is?"

Oh, oh, thought Max, this is a new wrinkle, the fantasy world confused with the real world. Usually Sal went into an episode first before he became dysfunctional.

Adler scrawled a note and passed it to Max. It read, Get the brother in here now. Max hesitated.

"Now!" growled Adler. "We need to know how badly disassociated he is."

Max gestured to Maggie with a slight affirmative movement of his head. Maggie breathed deeply. She could feel the tension rising in the room.

Dr. Adler was not about to be put off any longer. When Art Dematteo entered the room he looked directly at Sal.

"You goddamn idiots," he said angrily. "You've destroyed my brother." He turned to Adler. "We are getting him the hell out of here today."

Adler ignored Art. "Your brother is here, Sal," he said, more than a hint of anger in his resonant voice.

Sal stared at his brother. Then his eyes lit up with a blaze of terrible resolve. He leaped out of his chair, and before anyone, even Bernicke, could move, he charged across the room, screamed "Traitor!" at the top of his lungs, and went for Art's throat.

It was only Art's split-second reaction time, honed by years of training, that permitted Art Dematteo to sidestep his brother's attack. Bernicke moved quickly. He buzzed for help and followed the attack quickly by interposing himself between Sal and Art.

"Calm down, Mr. Dematteo, please," he said, holding tightly onto Sal's shoulders.

"Easy, Sal," said Max. "This is not Aaron's brother. This is your brother, Art, home from the Air Force."

Sal was breathing heavily. Two attendants entered the room and were quickly cautioned by Bernicke not to overreact.

"Let's go to your room, Mr. Dematteo, and we can relax," said Bernicke quietly. Art started to speak. He was overcome by shock and disbelief. Max halted him in mid-sentence by raising his hands and shaking his head no. Bernicke escorted Sal out of the room. He went without objection, like a wayward child, guilty of serious misconduct.

Max was furious at Adler but contained his anger. He spoke to Art.

"I will bring John Forgarty into the case as soon as I can contact him. I will have him get in touch with you. How long will you be in town?"

"I'll extend my leave another week. I never thought…"

Max reached out to him. "I understand, this is a most difficult situation."

Cathy was crying. Maggie was hugging her trying to console her. When the family left, Adler turned to Max.

"That's it!" he exclaimed. "We meet the hospital board on Friday. I'm recommending electroconvulsive therapy to bring this man back to reality. Please place that in your report to the court."

"Not yet, Dr. Adler. I'm the attending, and I'm not ready for ECT."

"Max, you are exceeding your authority at this hospital. Remember you are only a resident. We will meet the board on—"

Max interrupted. "You'll have to get a court order. The family will never consent. I'll see to that. Furthermore, we need the opinion of a third psychiatrist. At the family's request I'm associating John Fogarty."

"He's a goddamn hack," growled Adler. He turned and stormed out of the room.

Marcia Miller was stunned. This rancorous exchange between these two men, one of whom she liked very much and the other, an icon whom she deeply respected, startled her.

"Max," she began, "why the unbending opposition to ECT? Your career is on the line."

"Well, factor this into your thinking process and try to logically understand it. The apparition that Sal called Trajalinus, a Roman gladiator, was clearly seen by eight other people, who, even though they all called it something different, described it exactly the same way. Does that sound like a candidate ready to be shocked back to reality? Maybe the inmates are in the real world and we need the shock treatment."

Marcia put her hand on Max's shoulder. "It must be crowd hysteria. They all thought they saw it when Sal described it."

"Oh really, well Sal wasn't in the room. He was two hundred feet down the other end of the hall. None of these people talked to Sal or even saw him. I can't explain any of this, but I do not believe Sal Dematteo is psychotic, and I will not let this hospital or even the great Adler turn this bright, lively human being into a walking zombie so that we can incorporate the results into a goddamn case study."

* * * *

At six o'clock that evening, Max was still in his office. When Marcia left she had promised to write in her report that she recommended Dr. Vogel be permitted to continue therapy for at least another month, and that the patient remain in the restraint ward.

Marcia had said, "Keep smiling, things could be a lot worse."

Max remembered his retort from an old joke. "I kept smiling and sure enough things got a lot worse." At 6:05 P.M., Bernicke called. His voice strained and panicky. The chief of security was alarmed.

"Dr. Vogel, I have some very bad news. Two men just abducted Maggie Seiler. One of our maintenance ladies saw it happen. She was walking to the trolley when these guys grabbed Maggie and shoved her into a car. I have already called Oakland police. They are informing downtown and putting out an all-points bulletin. Maggie's uncle is Captain Andy Seiler. He'll get some fast action."

Max was rattled. "Keep me advised will you, Bernicke?" He slammed the phone down and pounded the desk with his fist.

"David," he called out in frustration. "What have you gotten me into? What the hell is happening here?"

CHAPTER 26

THE THIRD WEEK, WEDNESDAY
THE SICARIANS

The 1949 black Ford two-door sedan sped down Fifth Avenue, snaked in and out of traffic and prepared to turn right at Dinwiddie Street hill. Ali had memorized the route. He was not acclimated to driving in this strange country. He detested the red lights and the crawling traffic. He leaned on his horn, standard procedure in Beirut, but nobody moved when the light was red. Now he was first in line and the red light glared silently back at his horn. He ignored the traffic signal, pressed the horn again and careened forward, nearly striking another vehicle. He heard a chorus of horns, screeching brakes and a shrill whistle blow, but continued to move forward. He turned to go up Dinwiddie hill. A man on a motorcycle, in a black uniform, appeared next to the left window of the car. He was obviously a policeman and very angry.

"Pull over, you dumb bastard, what the hell do you think you're doing?"

Ali panicked. Before his companion could stop him he reached down on the seat, pulled out the small handgun Abou Hassan had given him and shot the officer. The officer fell over backwards pulling the motorcycle with him. It probably saved his life. He was pinned down but he reached into his holster and loosed his .38 service revolver. Ali stepped on the gas and sputtered up the steep grade, picking up speed as he drove. Dinwiddie Street was a narrow, decaying residential street lined with once palatial Victorian homes that were now densely occupied, multi-family dwellings. Ali barely missed a youth shooting baskets on the street. It was only the boy's agility that saved his life. Three other kids playing catch scurried for the curb.

The officer fired two shots at the receding vehicle. The first bullet shattered the rear window. The second bullet penetrated the trunk. But miraculously the traffic had cleared, and Ali was able to reach the brow of Centre Avenue and disappear over the crest.

Several bystanders came over to help. The pedestrians pulled the cycle from the officer's body and moved him off the street. The cop was furious. He had been shot in the shoulder. He called central dispatch on his radio, described the vehicle and the occupants and then asked for an ambulance. Minutes later he could hear the approaching sirens. A patrol car screeched to a stop and then an ambulance arrived. Two patrol car cops began questioning eyewitnesses while white-uniformed attendants carefully placed the officer on a stretcher. He was bleeding from his left shoulder but apparently the wound was not serious.

One excited bystander said, "He just shot the cop without a word. I didn't get a good look, but I think he was a foreigner. What a nut! He almost wrecked a couple of cars. What kind of crazies have we got running around in this town!"

"He won't be running around long," said an officer who was taking notes. "Nobody shoots a cop in Andy Seiler's town!"

* * * *

Ali was elated to elude the police and reach a safe house owned by the followers of Ishtar. The house was in the Hill district, an aging ghetto populated almost entirely by blacks, an area Ali was told few white people ever ventured into and those few included policemen. As in Beirut, there were neighborhoods off limits even to the Lebanese Army.

Ali felt safe. All that was required was to get a message to the museum man and demand the dagger of Hammurabi in return for the dark-haired girl. His accomplices moved a bound-and-gagged

Maggie from the trunk of the car into the squalid house and up to a third-floor room. They ignored the blood seeping through her dress on her left side. In their culture a wounded woman was of little consequence.

Ali went to a pay phone in the decrepit, cobwebbed hall and asked the operator to connect him with the Carnegie Museum. While he called, several frightened women and curious children peeped at him from slightly open doors.

* * * *

As in most military plans created by amateurs who don't know the terrain or even begin to understand the culture or strength of their enemy, Ali's scheme was fatally flawed. He and his partner did not figure Detective Sergeant Jerome Becker and Deadeye Ed Bramer into their calculations. Jerome was a six-foot-three, former Pittsburgh Steeler left tackle. He had attended Duquesne University where he played football for three years and received a B.A. in criminology. After a knee injury cut short his professional football career, he joined the Pittsburgh Police as a beat cop. A huge black man, Jerome cut an imposing figure striding down the street in his blue uniform. Andy Seiler met him during a homicide investigation and was impressed not only with Jerome's physical stature, but also with his intellect. Jerome Becker was street smart and Captain Seiler felt it was time to promote a black man. Jerome became the first black plainclothes detective sergeant on the Pittsburgh Police force. He knew every inch of the Hill district, every snitch, lottery runner, pimp, bar owner, religious group—and every petty crook and politician. They all respected, and most of them admired, Jerome.

Jerome's partner, Ed Bramer, was a burly ex-wrestler going to fat in his early middle age. Ed liked to shoot guns. He spent hours on the police firing range. Ed boasted he could shoot the eye out of a gnat. Ed never missed. During the annual police shooting competition, he hit ten bulls-eyes out of twelve shots, and the other two were a hair outside the center of the target.

These two were Andy Seiler's best team. When the call from the Oakland substation indicated that Andy Seiler's niece had been kidnapped and less than fifteen minutes later a traffic cop had been shot by two foreign-looking guys in a green '47 Chevy coupe, Andy ordered his favorite team into the field.

Except for two years in the U.S. Army during the war, Andy Seiler had been a policeman for twenty-two years. He took pride in the fact that, as he put it, he kept the lid on in Pittsburgh. His next promotion, of which he was assured, would be to Deputy Chief. That his favorite niece, whom he had sworn to his dead brother he would always protect, had been kidnapped in his town enraged him. His was a cold, determined fury and he conveyed it forcefully to Jerome and Ed.

"I want these guys caught. I will personally deal with them. This girl is a jewel. She is special, the best my family has ever produced. Do you guys understand?"

They said they did and Jerome, who idolized Andy Seiler, quietly promised that he would not rest until those two snakes were caught, Maggie was returned safe and the kidnappers were fried.

A young clerk knocked and hesitantly came into the room. "Captain, excuse the interruption but there's a guy named Throckmorton on the phone. Claims to be a good friend of your niece. Claims he has some information that might be of help."

Andy took the call. "Yes, Benson, you are a friend of Maggie's. Say that again, we should look where? In the House of what? Ishtar? Are you crazy? What the hell is Ishtar? A sect that worships a Babylonian God? Jesus!"

Andy angrily started to hang up. Then he stopped in mid air. Throckmorton had just told him to call Ed Flaharty in Oakland. Furthermore, he had just talked to the kidnappers. They wanted something he had in the museum. He was prepared to offer it to save Maggie's life. Unfortunately, it wasn't his to give.

Jerome raised a six-inch finger. "I don't know what Ishtar is," he said. "But I think I know someone who will. Don't lose this guy. We may be on to something."

"Where are you, Mr. Throckmorton? Can you meet us in fifteen minutes at headquarters? Okay, you have twenty." Now Andy slammed the phone down. "He works at the Carnegie Museum. Says he and Maggie were working on something together. Thinks he knows who these guys are. Says to call Flaharty. He also knows something about this whole matter."

Andy turned to the clerk. "See if you can locate Flaharty. Get him down here ASAP."

Jerome was already on the other line making a call. "I want him now," he reiterated, "not in an hour, not in five minutes, I don't care if he's at his prayers. NOW!"

In less than ninety seconds, the party that Jerome requested came on the line. His name was Memel Ben Mohammed. He was the chief Muslim holy man, the Imam in the district. "God be with you," he said. "What can this humble servant of Allah do for you?"

"Memel," snapped Jerome, "I want to know what Ishtar is."

The answer came swiftly. "It is an ancient Babylonian God. Its image is shaped like an evil bird. It is an idol, and Allah frowns on its existence."

"Does it exist here?" asked Jerome. "This better be the truth."

The Muslim holy man did not hesitate. "It does. His house is in the district on Wood Street. The last house on the left-hand corner. Their presence here is an abomination."

"Thank you, Memel. And if you warn them, your house will be an abomination."

"The guardian of us all need not fear. Allah has long wanted these interlopers to be gone from our midst."

"They will be gone, Memel, I promise you if they have done what we think they have. If this tip works, I owe you one."

When Jerome hung up the phone, Memel, the holy man, turned to his disciple. "The great Jerome Becker goes after the Ishtarites."

"Shall we warn them?" inquired the disciple.

"Oh no, let the officer have the heretics." Memel winked. "Then the great Becker will owe us. It is always good to be on the plus side of the big ledger. One day we may have to collect our debt."

****

Max was waiting impatiently at the entrance to the hospital. It was nearly dark when Benson pulled up in his rickety, two-door Studebaker coupe. Only ten minutes ago Benson had caught Max just as he was about to leave his office. Benson's message was the ultimate cap to a calamitous day. Maggie, Benson believed, was kidnapped by the same people who had tried to steal the golden dagger. The demand was clear. Turn over the dagger or Maggie would die. Benson was able to stall them for two hours. He agreed to their terms but said he needed permission from the director. Benson was now on his way to Metro Police headquarters. He felt Max might want to come along. He thought they might need a doctor.

The early evening traffic was light. Max sat in the car in glum silence as they drove along the Boulevard of the Allies heading west for downtown Pittsburgh. The Hazelwood blast furnaces churned the sky into a fiery glow of radiant crimson clouds. Max remembered something: A pillar of fire by night had led the Hebrews through the Sinai for forty years to the Promised Land. Was this the pillar of fire? He studied the shimmering reflections in the river and the moving lights of the passing ore boats making their way south to feed the hungry ovens of Cincinnati. His mind was trying to discover some logic to the day's events, which had no more reality than a Grimm's fairy tale. All his life he had scoffed at any suggestion that there existed a dimension other than the body of material knowledge he had accumulated. During his ten years of advanced schooling and countless hours of studying the great scholars of psychiatry, medicine, science and philosophy, he had mastered German, studied French and could read and translate classical Greek and Hebrew. He had excelled in mathematics and physical science. He had what applied psychologists termed a photographic memory. This, coupled with his brilliant left brain deductive reasoning, earmarked him, even in the psychiatric community, as a unique talent. But what had occurred in the past two weeks did not even begin to compute. He was confounded by the implications, disoriented and confused. His intellect begged for answers. There were none.

Benson pulled into a large, mostly empty public parking lot next to Metro Police headquarters. Max got out of the car and breathed deeply. The downtown area seemed unreal at night. Looming above the nearly deserted streets, the huge office buildings were empty leviathans populated only by a tiny cadre of maintenance people. An intangible loneliness pervaded the city, an illusion of a lost world devoid of life. Yet, he wondered, beyond these canyons of steel, glass and concrete, was there another world? If it did exist, was there also a cogent drama, somehow related, unfolding somewhere? And finally, was David a part of this immense theatre? Where was he now? Had he reached Europe? And why at this particular moment did his mind turn to David? Was it because of his now dashed hope that the Kabbalist rabbi was right and David had the key to the puzzle?

Nineteen minutes had elapsed since Benson had received the order to get to the police station. When he and Max were admitted into the inner sanctum they saw a scene of frenzied activity. Andy Seiler was barking orders. "I WANT EVERY STREET SEALED OFF SO THERE IS NO ESCAPE. NO SIRENS! AND NO SHOOTING, UNLESS YOU ARE DIRECTLY ATTACKED!"

A stocky gray-haired police lieutenant was listening closely. "Yes, sir."

Seiler glanced at Max. "Who is this?"

The activity ceased. All stared at Max and waited. Max was uncomfortable. Surrounded by cops, he felt like a kid accused of stealing.

Benson interjected. "I'm Benson Throckmorton. This is Dr. Vogel, Maggie's boss."

The squadron of cops commenced their activity. Andy Seiler nodded.

"Hi, Doctor. You and Benson ride in my car. Jerome, you drive. Let's move it, men, and now."

The group emptied the room. They were a grim, sober-faced platoon. The plainclothesmen patted their upper pockets to assure their pieces were secure. The uniforms touched their holsters.

The special Metro squad, four men, carried shotguns and tear gas. These twenty-two men had a serious mission. There was no force on earth, short of a juggernaut, that could stop them as they left for Wood Street.

CHAPTER 27

THE THIRD WEEK, WEDNESDAY
THE SICARIAN TEMPLE, PITTSBURGH'S HILL DISTRICT

In every well-planned operation, there is always someone who doesn't get the message. In this case it was Ed Flaharty.

The detective had been at home watching Wednesday night wrestling, drinking a beer and relaxing from what had been a hectic day. His wife and her sister had gone to a movie. Ed was luxuriating in a solitude the phone call from downtown interrupted. Andy Seiler wants to see you now. Something about the museum caper and his niece. The message was garbled but one thing was clear: the situation was urgent.

When Ed arrived downtown, the Metro squad had already left for the Wood Street house. Ed was a good soldier. He was concerned that Captain Seiler would be angry. Since he was in an unmarked car, to assure no civilian interference, he placed the portable siren on top of the car and headed for the Hill district. A few minutes from target Ed Flaharty blew the siren.

* * * *

Ali heard the loud screech. Even in Beirut, the populace was no stranger to sirens. He turned to a third man, an occupant of the house who had joined them. "Is it possible, Abou Hassan, we have been found?" He looked at the girl. She was securely tied to a bench. Her dress was now badly stained with a large, round dark red blotch. Her eyes were pleading for help.

"She must die," Ali announced. He had panicked. "Then will the prophecy be fulfilled." His face contorted into a fanatic ecstasy.

Ali's companion objected. "I don't think so. Please, we will never fulfill our mission. The dagger will be lost forever."

Ali drew his assassin's knife. He strode over to a fifteen-inch wooden carving of an ugly, distorted looking bird with venomous eyes. There were fat candles burning on either side. He closed his eyes.

"Oh, Ishtar, ancient spirit and life force of the Babylonian peoples. We give you this young woman. Take her and smile upon the Sicarians. Return to us the once great and magical power possessed by the Sicarian Brotherhood."

Ali's companions were terrified. They heard a loud crash in the room below. There were shouts, the sound of feet on the stairs. Ali turned to stab the woman, but Abou blocked his way. "If she dies, Ali, we will all die!"

"So be it!"

The rotted door splintered. Ed Bramer was the first one in the room. He had drawn his gun. In an instant he observed the drawn knife and the bound girl fastened to the bench. He fired once at Ali. In the closed room the explosion sounded like a cannon. The bullet struck Ali directly above his right eye. He died instantly.

Jerome Becker stood directly behind Ed Bramer. He was followed by Andy Seiler, Max Vogel and Benson Throckmorton. Ali's second accomplice cowered in the corner. Max started for Maggie and Becker reached out to cuff Ali's companion. The smaller man saw Jerome and remembered the second part of the prophecy. "And the giant black man shall destroy forever the last vestige of the Sicarians unless the dark woman is sacrificed." He drew his assassin's knife as he had been trained and lashed out at Jerome Becker. He planned to turn and kill the woman. The thin shiv brushed Jerome's arm, penetrated his coat and drew blood.

Jerome Becker was not a violent man, but once provoked, he took events to what he considered their natural conclusion. He hardly felt the shiv as it sliced through his sleeve. He did see the blood. He seized the man by the arm, threw the knife to the floor and, with one wrenching twist, broke the man's arm. He lifted him and, with a mighty heave, hurled him through the third-floor window. The man's scream was cut short as he struck the sidewalk, head first. He died within seconds.

Across the street, Memel watched with a curious interest. "The Ishtarites join their idol-worshiping ancestors. Allah be praised."

Max was shocked. He gently untied Maggie. She had been bleeding for over two hours, and was obviously very weak. He loosed the gag and tried to examine the wound. The loss of blood was massive. Evidently a bullet had struck her in the spleen.

Andy Seiler ordered an ambulance. He hovered over Max as the doctor called upon his medical skills and worked feverishly to stanch the flow of blood. He fashioned a makeshift tourniquet and slowed the blood flow. He knew Maggie was bleeding internally and had been for some time. Her pulse was so weak he could hardly feel it and her color had drained to nearly pure white. He was losing her, and there was little more he could do.

"Hold on, Maggie, please," he begged.

Her eyelids fluttered. "David," she said. "It's so cold. Please hold me."

Max reached out and cradled her, patting her softly as she spoke her last words, "David" and "I'm sorry, Mom."

"Little friend of all the world," muttered Max, a quote from Rudyard Kipling. The old Kabbalist rabbi had foreseen this death, and that explained his deep sadness when he had looked at Maggie.

Andy Seiler crossed himself as tears welled up in his eyes. "Take her in peace, Lord Jesus. She was the best Seiler the family ever produced."

In a fit of towering rage, he turned and smashed his fist into the wall. The rotten wood cracked and splintered. He then turned to the survivor. "I want this man arrested, all the others detained and this place searched," he said.

He picked up the surviving man and considered strangling him.

Abou pleaded. "I begged him not to kill her."

Ed Bramer restrained Seiler. "It's not worth it, Andy. We need information."

Andy Seiler agreed. He was still a cop. Jerome and Ed Bramer felt they had failed.

Jerome picked up the bird sculpture and asked, "What the hell is this?"

Benson Throckmorton had watched the scene in horrified silence. When he spoke he said, "God Bless you, Maggie. I pray we meet again."

Then he took the wood carving from Jerome's hands and examined it. "This is an image of Ishtar, the Babylonian god. The Sicarians have claimed another victim." He threw the carving angrily against the wall and it, too, shattered into many pieces.

It was not until later, at the inquest, that the questions were posed. "When was Mary Margaret Seiler shot? Why was the bullet lodged in her spleen a Police .38 special?" A traffic officer, who himself had been slightly wounded in a minor altercation during what he thought would be a routine traffic stop, was sadly able to answer the questions.

At the same hearing, they identified the revolver that had shot the policeman and traced it to Abou Hassan. He was bound over for trial, without bail, and under the murder/felony rule charged with kidnapping and second-degree murder. As they led him across the Bridge of Sighs to await his fate, he roundly cursed the day Ali and the Sicarians had come to his house. The newspaper headline read: "Strange Ritual Murder in the Hill District." It sold a lot of papers.

CHAPTER 28

THE THIRD WEEK, THURSDAY
NAPLES AIR STATION

A heavy storm was brewing over the eastern Mediterranean. A mere squall when it was born over the Caspian Sea, the storm now swirled over Georgia and the Black Sea, drenched eastern Turkey and was headed for Athens and the Balkans. It had picked up considerable force and was now of hurricane proportions. All flights east were canceled.

"Sorry, Captain." The amiable tech sergeant was apologetic. "I'm sure your mission is important, but nothin's movin'. We'll be glad to send a telex to advise your destination of the problem."

"How long do you estimate?"

The sergeant shrugged. "Hard to say. Could be days."

David was exhausted. He had slept only fitfully on the trip over. They had a three-hour stop in Madrid for fuel and a maintenance check. The U.S. was building a huge logistics base at Terrejón. Most of the dependents got off and were joined by their sponsors. A few troops heading for Italy had boarded. At the flight line PX, David had spent two dollars for a larger tote bag and a dollar for another change of underwear and an extra pair of socks. He changed ten dollars into American scrip he could spend in Europe. He bought some orange juice and a bacon and egg sandwich in the snack shop, drank two cups of coffee, shaved in the latrine and doused his face again and again in cold water. He was still exhausted.

He reached into the new tote bag just to make sure he had repacked the prayer shawl. The old tote bag smelled of sweat and gym trunks. He had thrown it away. The prayer shawl, somewhat to his surprise, remained in pristine condition. His repeated actions to preserve the shawl had become obsessive. Losing it, he believed, would be nothing less than a disaster. Each time he touched the prayer shawl, he experienced renewed energy. This strange garment had, he felt, taken on a life of its own.

Just a few hours before, at 6:00 A.M., as the first hints of dawn filled the eastern sky, the Douglas Skymaster, half empty, had climbed into the airspace above the storied city of Madrid and circled once, heading due east for Italy. He could see the Plaza De Toro and, in the early mist, many buildings being constructed.

Only twenty years ago this nation had been torn by a bloody civil war, the prelude to the devastating conflagration that was World War II. The Fascists had won that round, but the free world had rallied and the next round went to the Western Allies. When Hitler and Mussolini were defeated, their nations literally destroyed, Spanish fascism had tempered its attitude and philosophy and now fully supported the North Atlantic Treaty Organization. The dictator Franco not only allowed but also encouraged American bases to be built on Spanish soil.

David resolved that someday he would return with Maggie. They would eat paella, drink in tapas bars, listen to Spanish music, see the many historical sites, stay in the most luxurious hotel and maybe even attend a bullfight. The thought warmed his fatigued brain and yet somehow, on some level, he knew it was never to be. He dozed several times on the next leg of the journey. He slept restlessly, waking up, thrashing about, as if somebody kept calling his name. Once, the flight attendant, a young airman, came over and asked him if he was all right.

"You were talkin' in your sleep, kind of loud, sir."

"I'm okay, just over-tired," he had answered.

Now he leaned against the transit passenger counter with the depressing realization that this distant way station outside of

Naples, on what seemed like the road to nowhere, might well be the ignominious end to an impossible errand.

"Why don't you get a shower and take a nap in our visiting officer quarters upstairs, Captain," the sergeant had suggested. "I'll wake you if anything is stirring."

It was a good idea. He stood under the shower for many minutes, thoroughly enjoying the healing powers of steaming hot water. He closed his eyes and let it splash liberally on his neck and back. Still feeling numb and tired but at least clean, he dried himself and sat down on the edge of an uncomfortable cot complete with a khaki blanket that smelled of chlorine.

He surveyed the surroundings, a dismal shack that might have harbored condemned souls on the way to purgatory. There was that sickening green paint, chipped in several places, and the deathless bare walls. He resumed his habit of staring at the floor. At some point he leaned back and slipped into a restless sleep. Seconds later someone was shaking him. It must be my mother waking me up to go to school, he thought. Responsibility was her religion. "Okay, okay, Mother, I'm getting up, but I sure could use more sleep. Can't I have another five minutes?"

He opened his eyes. His mother was the friendly tech sergeant. "Captain Gold, I got a hop for you if you're interested." The sergeant was smiling.

"You're kiddin', how long have I been sleeping?"

"About two hours."

"Boy, it seems like two minutes. What's the deal?"

"Two officers in a C-47 heading for Athens. Landed an hour ago. They have been advised of the weather, but they want to chance it. Apparently need to be in Athens. They are eating lunch in the snack bar. The aircraft is getting refueled and will be ready to jump off in about an hour. They are willing to carry you. Shall I put you on the manifest?"

"You bet. I'll be dressed and ready to go."

David splashed icy water on his face and slipped into his flight suit. He changed his socks and then carefully checked the tote bag. Everything was intact. He had a dull headache, and his stomach was sour. He needed an aspirin, but he disregarded his physical discomfort. More coffee might help. Maybe a glass of milk would be better. He yawned, grabbed his bag and headed downstairs to the snack bar.

****

Joe Stepanian was a fighter pilot relegated from time to time to flying cargo from Châteauroux Depot in France to points east in the Mediterranean chain of bases. Today they had spare parts for Naples and Athens. Nothing of great urgency in the cargo except Joe had a date in Athens. He didn't want to miss the lovely Greek lady waiting for him at his favorite Athens bar. The rendezvous was for early evening and Joe felt the mission merited trying to beat the hurricane, now boiling over the Dardanelle straits heading directly toward the Aegean Sea and southern Greece.

"Screw the storm," he said. "If we get out of here now, we can get under it before it hits Athens. He had two hot items waiting for him in Athens, a body and a bed, and he wasn't going to miss either one of them.

Fred Hernandez, his co-pilot, wasn't so sure. He didn't like the odds. But he knew better than to argue with the aircraft commander, especially when it was Joe Stepanian in the left seat.

When David entered the snack bar he spied a lone officer in the corner, dressed in a flight suit, sipping a cup of coffee and chewing on a sandwich. David approached.

"Hi, I'm David Gold. Understand you may be going to Athens. I sure need a ride."

"Sit down, Captain, have a martini, better yet the coffee in this *tienda* is *muy bueno*. The spam is also a real delicacy."

He offered his hand to David. "I'm Fred Hernandez. We'll be happy to act as a conveyance for you. But let me warn you now, the ride could be very bumpy. There is one hell of a storm out there."

"If you guys will chance it, I'm with you, Lieutenant Hernandez."

"*Por favor*, please just call me Fred. By the way you haven't lived until you've flown with brother Joe. You are so lucky." He rolled his eyes. "Joe wasn't scheduled for this trip, but he has a hot one in Athens so he volunteered at the last minute this morning. Joe thinks our old clunker is a fighter plane. He flew F-86s in Korea. Still want to come along?"

"Hell, yes."

"Good, *amigo*, we will be glad for the company. Can you work a radio or a Direction Finder?"

"I think so."

"Well, we may need the help. Come on, grab something, and we will head over to operations."

David wolfed down a slice of stale sweet roll and gulped down a glass of milk. The milk sat in his stomach like a leaden weight. He didn't care. The mission was moving forward again. Once again fate had intervened in the form of Captain Joe Stepanian, who wouldn't allow a small event like a hurricane to interfere with his social life.

CHAPTER 29

THE THIRD WEEK, THURSDAY
THE LAST TRAIN TO ATHENS

David stood on the tarmac looking at the battered C-47. Designed and built by Douglas Aircraft of Long Beach, California, in the middle 1930s, it was also called a DC-3. It had two Pratt and Whitney HP engines and passenger space at absolute maximum for about twenty. Still, American Airlines and TWA used it for the first transcontinental passenger flights. It had a cruising speed of 170 knots, and an operational ceiling of fourteen thousand feet without portable oxygen. During World War II the C-47 became a workhorse for the Air Force. It flew the Himalayas and delivered supplies to the beleaguered armies in China. It carried paratroopers to Europe and dropped them over France to fight the last great battle of the European theatre. Its hundreds of cargo and passenger missions during the Berlin airlift and the Korean War were too numerous to catalogue. Its exploits gave the airplane almost legendary status.

Pilots who flew the C-47 had a true love-hate relationship with the airplane. It was incredibly reliable. It usually got where it was going. It was also damnably slow. It took what seemed like forever to get there. With a headwind of forty knots, increasing by the minute, Lieutenant Fred Hernandez was duly concerned. On the ramp, prior to takeoff, he sniffed the air. It was fresh and contained more than a hint of the sea. The best they could hope for would be about 130 knots in this headwind.

Joe was in the cockpit completing a last-minute instrument check. Both engines were whining and beginning to rev up. Fred had completed the walk around assuring the flaps and ailerons were free and in working order and all the red choc blocks that secured the airplane were removed.

David stood outside near the hatchway of the airplane. The breeze was fresh, except it wasn't a breeze. It was a whirlwind. Fred was clutching his hat and trying to make himself heard over the din.

"You can abort, Captain," he hollered. "It's not too late. This is gonna be a white knuckler."

"I'm with you, Hernandez. This might be the last train to Athens. I have to be on it."

"Okay, *amigo*, suit yourself. Climb aboard and buckle your seat belt tight. Hot shot Joe Stepanian will give you a ride that will do more than tickle your digestion."

Securing his overnight bag tightly to one hand and keeping the other anchored to his overseas cap, David carefully hoisted himself through the open door.

"Sit up front. We're not carrying a radio operator," said Hernandez. "He was on sick call this morning."

David made his way through the stacks of cargo to the cockpit. Joe Stepanian was chatting with the tower. They were trying without success to dissuade him from launching. He was also carefully studying the instrument panel. He seemed satisfied.

He turned to David. "Hey, Captain. You know the DF?"

"Direction Finder? Sure, no sweat."

"How about the radio?"

"I think I can handle it."

"Good, you got a job. We're in for some tricky navigation. When I ask you to get me a heading on the DF, it has to be exactly right. A degree or two could cause us a real problem."

"I understand."

"Great. As soon as Fred gets in place, we are out of here. I figure roughly 220 nautical miles. At an average true speed of 120 to 130 knots, we ought to make Athens in a couple of hours. But with this weather, I don't know. We head due east and then swing south when we're over the Aegean Sea and then head north by northeast." He handed David a pad. "Here are the headings."

Fred Hernandez lifted himself into the now vibrating airplane. With some effort he swung the hatchway shut and made his way to the cockpit. On the way he examined the ropes securing the cargo netting. "All secure," he said as he plopped down in the right seat, donned the radio headphones, pulled out the checklist and prepared to obtain permission for takeoff.

"Let's get the hell out a here," said Joe.

Fred called the tower and requested clearance for C-47 AF WC3NW.

"All runways clear, AF WC3NW," responded the tower. "Use runway three, take off to the east. Nothing else is moving. Good luck!"

David crossed the fingers on his left hand. It was a habit he learned from Colonel Dennis Shock, who had flown thirty-two missions in a B-24 over Europe in 1943 and 1944. "Takeoff is critical," old Shocky would say. "Always cross your fingers when you're in a takeoff mode. It is a sure sign to God that you are now in His hands."

The first thirty minutes were turbulent but uneventful. Then the buffeting started. Per instruction from Fred, David buckled himself more tightly to his seat and stayed buckled. He located Athens radio and zeroed in on the frequency. At twelve thousand feet they were in heavy clouds. An ominous gray world where the sky appeared to close in on them, stifling their visibility and creating a sense that they were lost in eddying mists of bleak desolation.

Occasionally they would fly into a clear patch and the Mediterranean Sea would appear like magic. Then a gust of heavy wind would strike the plane and shake it violently. But like an old faithful horse, the airplane moved doggedly forward. Somehow Joe, the wizard, kept it at altitude and on course. He lit a cigarette, puffed deeply on it, kept his left hand on the stick and from time to time would adjust the trim tabs. Fred seemed a lot less relaxed.

He would look at the map, run some calculations and shake his head.

Athens was forecasting hurricane force winds but not for another couple of hours. The plane would run into intermittent sheets of rain that would beat on the fuselage, a merciless waterfall that would lower visibility to nearly zero.

"When we turn to south 180 degrees we're going to run into a serious crosswind that could really blow us off course," Fred said. He looked really worried. "We should be over land. Two minutes to a right turn to south 178 degrees. I hope this crate holds together."

"Amen," muttered David.

Fred Hernandez had been correct. David's stomach rose to his throat, and his eyeballs were at the top his head. He felt like his Maker was out there somewhere in the gloom, and he would probably meet him any minute. It was too late to consider that maybe he had made a bad decision.

A tremendous gust pitched the airplane upward. It lost power. It had been pushed by the force into a stall attitude. Even Joe was startled. He quickly manipulated the trim tabs and the engines, temporarily starved for air, immediately picked up their normal beat and resumed their drum song. They all breathed an inward sigh of relief. Joe glanced at his watch.

A few minutes later Joe said, "Captain, get a DF fix on Athens beam. Let me know when you get the heading. Athens DF is ATH."

"Roger," acknowledged David. Now came the test. Let's see, he couldn't remember the Morse code letters. Let's see, A is dit dah, T is dah and H is, shit, what was H?

"How you comin'?" shouted Joe. "I need that heading."

"Almost there," he shouted back. My God what is H? he asked himself. It came to him like a message. During the war he had learned international Morse, but that was a long time ago. The H crawled out from somewhere in his brain and said I am four dots. Dit dit dit dit.

He slowly moved the finder straining to hear the right set of sounds. There was nothing but static and more atmospheric noise.

He felt a rising panic. It had only been four minutes, but he was sure it had been four hours. He was failing.

The responsibility was his, and he was failing. Myra was really angry. "David! you must find that frequency now."

"I'll find it, Mother. There it is, dammit to hell. There it is."

ATH...he scrutinized the radio compass and homed in on the call letters.

"What about it, Captain?" Joe was getting irritated.

"Roger," he said calmly. "ATH course is 43 degrees, north by northeast."

"Roger, acknowledge 43 degrees north by northeast. Thank you, Captain."

The lumbering beast turned from its southern heading and pointed east again. David glanced at the heading list. They were on the final leg. Once again they were pointed directly into the wind. While the airplane slowed considerably, the ride was a little smoother.

"Captain, raise Athens tower and get an on-the-ground weather report."

"Athens tower, Athens tower, this is C-47 AF WC3NW. Do you read me?

"Athens tower, Athens tower this is—" David was interrupted by a crackling voice.

"Roger AF WC3NW, we read you. Where are you? You are not on radar screen."

"We are about fifty miles out. Please report on ground weather."

"Better get in here, WC3NW. Field minimums are almost reached. We may have to close down."

Joe interceded. "We are coming in, tower. We have no GCA. We are low on fuel and cannot be diverted."

"Roger WC3NW. Land east-west runway 4 at 110 degrees. We have you on radar now."

"Roger, thank you. See you soon." Joe pushed the throttle slightly forward. The aircraft bucked and straightened out. Then it started a slow descent.

Fred quickly studied the airport map. "There are hills to the immediate north. We should be coming in over the bay. I can't see a damn thing."

At the lower altitude, the storm picked up in intensity. The tempest was fierce, and verbal communication became impossible without shouting. Joe Stepanian was concentrating entirely on driving the airplane. David noticed even Joe appeared a bit flustered.

They kept descending and still no visible landmarks. The storm slashed at the airplane, furious that a foreign object had dared to invade its domain. David glanced over Fred's shoulder at the altimeter. It was so close to zero he expected to feel impact at any moment. Well, I guess this is it, he thought. But he knew it wasn't. He still had a mission in Jerusalem and he had to complete it.

They broke out of the mist. There was the bay so close he was sure he could touch it. The C-47 was literally skimming the waves. Joe kept the wings at a perfect level attitude. With pelting rain and a sixty-knot blow pounding at the nose of their aircraft, Captain Joseph Stepanian had somehow amazingly maneuvered the C-47 on a true course for the east-west runway. A few minutes later the aircraft touched down and skimmed furtively along the runway. A beat-up, groaning, but intact airplane carried a crew of three souls, two of whom silently gave thanks to the third, who, like an air knight of old, flew by the seat of his pants and with unerring, innate skill had brought them safely to earth. Hernandez crossed himself.

"Christ, Joe, I thought it was all over," he said.

"Not yet, Fred," Joe shot back. "I'll let you know when it is all over."

When they came to a full stop, Joe shut down the engines and for a few seconds sat frozen in the cockpit. "I had the damndest feeling," he said softly, "like somebody else was driving the airplane."

Three minutes after they had landed, Athens air base dipped below minimum visibility and the facility shut down. The last train to Athens had arrived.

CHAPTER 30

THIRD WEEK, THURSDAY
ATHENS AIR STATION

To say the rain poured down in relentless sheets would be an understatement. To describe the storm as a downpour that dumped continuous vats of water on the airfield reducing visibility to zero and nearly drowning everything in a veritable avalanche of liquid—that would be accurate.

After the airplane was lashed down by a crew of four drenched ground personnel, the three officers got into the Follow Me jeep and, under the protection of some yellow foul-weather slickers loaned to them by the troops, made it to base operations, wet to the skin but relatively unscathed.

David studied the huge area wall map posted behind the OPS counter. There he spotted, a couple of hundred miles southeast, Detachment 91 in Beirut, big as life. So near and yet so far. He read the weather report. It was completely discouraging: winds reaching one hundred knots and heavy rain. No letup in sight. Tomorrow was Thursday and the chances of reaching Beirut were almost nil.

The three men decided to get rooms, take showers and meet in the small mess hall next door, in the Visiting Officers Quarters. The transient passenger lounge was in the same building as base operations. David decided to check in there before he got a room.

He knew it was a fruitless gesture. There was a lone airman 2nd class seated behind the counter, absorbed in a Mickey Spillane novel. He looked up as David entered. The lounge was empty. He nodded as David strode up to the desk.

"Hi, Captain. Crappy weather, huh? What can I do for you?"

"Look, I have to get to Beirut. It is very urgent."

"I'm afraid it would take a miracle, Captain. As you can see, ain't nothin' movin'." The kid had a pleasant southern drawl, freckles, red hair and a sleepy look in his eyes.

"I understand," said David, "but if, by some miracle, something does move in the next twenty-four hours, could you make sure I get on the airplane? Here's five bucks for a beer. Take my name and make sure I get called. I'll be nearby in the VOQ. If I get a hop, there's ten more bucks in it for you."

"Yes sir, Captain." He studied the name, Gold. "But the odds are pretty heavy against you. Sorry, I think you're stuck here for a couple of days."

The airman took the five dollars, pocketed it and went back to the blood and gore of Mickey Spillane. Mickey's main character, Mike Hammer, was about to be shot by a woman who had double-crossed him. The youth had no more time for lost causes when his buddy Mike was in peril.

David left and crossed to the adjacent Quonset hut in a few seconds. Not five minutes after he departed, a second lieutenant barged out of the back office at Base OPS and showed a telex to the major in charge. "Look at this, sir, Priority One from Det 91. There's a VIP C-47 AOCP in Beirut. They are requesting the part just as soon as the weather allows. There are three generals on their way to an important assistance pact conference in Wiesbaden. They're stuck in Beirut."

"Well, that is tough shit. This weather isn't going to clear till Saturday. They'll just have to enjoy the climate in Beirut." The major began working on some reports. Anyway, he mused, the only pilot I have available is Uncle Al.

To send Uncle Al on an important mission always worried him. Captain Al "Dutch" Dortch was a real problem child. He was a genuine screwball. They called him Uncle Al, the kiddies' pal. He loved to do acrobatics. In fact stunt flying was like a religious ritual to him. He had been a fighter pilot, but the command had yanked him from the assignment for some irresponsible behavior. He was now attached to base operations where he flew short missions to various out-of-the way destinations in their lone T-28 when the C-47 was not available. Al also had a grand penchant for women. Young, old, fat, skinny, wrinkled, smooth, all shapes and sizes. It didn't much matter to Al, as long there was sex at the end of the rainbow. Everyone felt sure he would be shot someday by an irate father, an angry husband or a befuddled grandfather.

David got a room from a sleepy Greek civilian employee. He took a quick shower, grateful for the hot water. He noticed a leak in the corner where the driving rain had penetrated the roof. The room was painted a dull green. What a surprise. He changed underwear. In the waterproof tote bag the undergarments had remained reasonably dry. He checked the prayer shawl. It was not only intact but to his surprise it exuded warmth. His spare pants and shirt were also dry. He placed his soaked khaki uniform on a hanger near the potbellied stove that supplied the room's only heat. The clothes might be wrinkled but at least, perhaps, they would finish drying. He decided to eat a light dinner and get some much-needed rest. No sense brooding over the weather. Nothing he could do would change the forces of nature. Who would have figured on a damn hurricane?

Joe Stepanian and Fred Hernandez were already seated in the nearly deserted mess hall when he arrived. There was a third man at their table. The three were laughing loudly at some joke or story.

David did a double take when he saw the newly arrived officer more closely. He was a thin, wiry man with great pop eyes and a face that wore a frozen quizzical expression. He reminded David of a cartoon character named Barney Google; his eyes did all the talking.

"Meet Captain Al Dortch. I used to fly F-86s with him in Korea. Al is exiled here in Athens. He was a bad boy. He buzzed a general's quarters at Langley. The general happened to have a twenty-year-old daughter that Dutch was trying to impress. The general was unimpressed. Al is now an OPS pilot here at the end of the world."

Dortch chuckled. "I think the general was screwing his wife or someone else at the time. I disturbed him. Lousy timing." The two men shook hands. "I understand you need a hop to Beirut."

"I sure do."

"Well, if this crap clears a little, maybe we can arrange it."

A young Greek waiter came over to take their orders. "Our specialty tonight is Moussaka. It comes with rice, lemon soup and stuffed grape leaves. Otherwise, we got sandwiches with everything on it."

Everybody except Dutch ordered Moussaka. He asked for a hamburger with everything and French fries.

"Say, Gold," inquired Dutch, "what the hell you doin' out here at the end of the known world? We're only a stone's throw from the Communists."

David swallowed hard. "Kind of a classified mission. Sorry, Dutch, I can't discuss it. But I sure need to get to Beirut."

Dutch nodded knowingly. "I understand."

It was interesting, thought David, how dropping the word "classified" immediately brought an end to questions. In a Cold War military environment, "classified" was a common expression. Even a spaghetti recipe could probably be protected by classifying it as confidential.

When they finished eating, David excused himself. He needed sleep so bad, he said, that his fatigue was fatigued. He ached all over, had a headache and could hardly keep his eyes open.

Dutch was on duty and had to hang around.

Joe said that if the rain calmed down, he was going to try to get a base taxi to town. It was only a ten-mile trip. There was someone waiting.

Fred, Joe and Dutch lit cigarettes and went into the small adjacent bar to have a beer and tell war stories. It was a favorite pastime of old fighter pilots, to relive their exploits. Once more to dive on the enemy Migs, Fockwolfes, Messerschmitts, Zeroes, whatever, adrenalin rushing, guns blazing, fight the kill-or-be-killed battle. Their bell was tolling. With new weapons and new tactics the sun was setting on the lone air warriors of yore. But to fight that battle once more, over a beer with their comrades, was worth the price of admission.

With only clean underwear to sleep in, David vowed to hit the PX in the morning and purchase another change. He literally fell onto the small cot and within less than five minutes was snoring loudly. Mercifully, his demons temporarily deserted him. He fell into a deep, untroubled sleep. But toward early morning, they returned with a vengeance!

* * * *

He was in a charnel house. The stench of death was so strong he gagged. The old caretaker sat inert in the corner, his hoary face frozen, his eyes unseeing, oblivious to the unspeakable horrors that surrounded him.

Outside, he could hear screams as the Roman soldiers chased those that still lived, slaying the aged and infirm with spears and broadswords. The young, they captured to be sold as slaves or trained as gladiators for the arena. An hour before dawn a picked team of shock troops had entered the city through the underground cisterns. They were led by the directions the traitor had revealed to them to save his own miserable life.

The Jaffa Gate had been attacked from within, the guards all killed by trained assassins. The massive gates were thrown open to the horde of legionnaires who waited beneath the walls. They streamed into the city, mad for revenge. Initially, the soldiers were repelled by the sight of starved bloated corpses and thousands of diseased people, sick with fever and plague. But their blood thirst was not to be denied. For months they had besieged the city and the stubborn defenders had repelled assault after assault. Pleas for surrender and promises of mercy had failed to sway any of the three major factions that defended the city. Those few that did heed the call and were able to leave were treated well. However, many Romans had died horribly beneath the walls, destroyed by burning oil or crushed by Hebrew missiles. The army wanted revenge, a thirst that could only be quenched by looting, fire and rivers of Jewish blood.

The Jerusalem fortifications had consisted of three walls. Of necessity, an invading army had to attack from the north or northwest. Thus, to prevail all three walls had to be breached. The second wall was the highest and strongest. Some Roman commanders had counseled Titus to surround the city, shut off all food supplies and starve the Hebrews into submission rather than suffer the losses they knew the taking of the inner wall would cost. But a more warlike view prevailed: the Jews will find ways to smuggle food into the city, keep up the pressure.

ATTACK! ATTACK! ATTACK!

The second wall had been reduced at a fearful cost. Siege engines, missiles, fire, every weapon at Roman command had been used. Now the Romans were in the lower and middle city. The fifth, tenth, twelfth, Vespasian's old legion and the fifteenth all camped beneath the Temple Mount where, to the northwest, towered the formidable fortress of Antonia. One hundred regiments were primed and waiting for the order to storm the upper city, the last remaining bastion of resistance. Behind the wall was Simon Ben Gorias, his son Eleazar, and a few thousand exhausted zealots determined to resist to the last man.

Titus had given Ben Gorias a safe conduct pass and four handpicked Greek guards to assist him. He was permitted to conduct a search for his family, his mother and brothers. His father had been imprisoned by John of Gischala after he had, from outside the walls, entreated the Jews to lay down their arms, promising them both safety and food. He had foreseen the devastation and ruin that would be the legacy of the final assault. But the Pharisees would not relent. Gischala had hated him since they had clashed at Tiberias during his tenure as Commander in the Galilee. At the time Gischala had gathered a small group of dissidents and threatened his life. But he had, by trick, quelled the uprising and allowed the mutineer to return to his home, sparing his life, a mistake he now regretted.

He had gone to several charnel houses and then to the main prison seeking his family, but his search had been futile. He carefully made his way down the narrow streets of the bazaar. All the shops were closed or looted. Everywhere there were corpses. Those that still lived stared at him with hollow, veiled eyes, their bodies wasted by famine and their expressions blank and devoid of humanity. He was sick of heart and beset with nausea.

He remembered the terrible words of the Nazarene uttered the day before he was crucified: "When ye see Jerusalem compassed with armies, then know that her desolation is at hand. Then let them that are in Judea flee unto the mountains; and let them that are in the midst of her depart out; and let not them that are in the country enter therein. For these are the days of vengeance."

He turned a corner onto a wider street and was met with a startling sight. An entourage of six men had surrounded a cart being carried by two servants and guarded by two soldiers. The covered cart had been turned over. One servant lay bleeding next to the cart. The other looked about in fear, seeking an escape route. He could find none. The two soldiers had drawn their short swords and, though outnumbered, prepared for battle.

The six men wore dark cloaks. One leaped on the back of the servant and stabbed him in the neck with a long, thin knife. The servant gurgled and died. The two soldiers waited for the onslaught.

A dark-haired young woman, her dress and long flowing cloak pure white, had left the security of the covered cart and stood angrily facing them. A quick sweep of the scene told the story. "My God," Ben Gorias muttered, "they are Sicarians, the most merciless of killers. Carrions of evil, they now freely roam the streets."

A Sicarian turned, saw him and advanced toward him extending a thin stiletto. Ben Gorias drew his sword and shouted for his soldiers. Unseen around the corner, they were a few paces behind him, brandishing spears and swords.

The first to arrive was Hurculanus, an agile young Greek expert in spear throwing. Soundlessly, he hurled his spear at the onrushing Sicarian and watched him drop with a loud scream as the missile pierced his chest and exited his back. He then rushed to guard the woman. One of her guards, already dead, was stabbed many times by three Sicarians. The other guard sliced off a Sicarian's arm, and the man ran shrieking in pain down the street. A Sicarian reached for the woman, but by this time Ben Gorias was beside her and his ready sword thrust skillfully upward into the Sicarian's abdomen. Three more spears were thrown by the Greeks, and two of them found their mark in Sicarian bodies. This was, Ben Gorias observed, indeed an elite troop as Titus had ordered. The last Sicarian, no longer comfortable with the odds, vanished into a nearby alley. The Greeks were ordered not to pursue.

He surveyed the battle scene. Two servants and one soldier dead, four Sicarians dead and a fifth maimed, armless and out of the struggle. Two very lucky people, a woman and a soldier, survivors only because his small troop had happened upon them.

"Why, Madam, are you here in this ravaged city that Jehovah has surely forsaken? You have only two servants and two guards? Who are you?"

"I am Miriam." She paused and studied him. How honest could she be with this man? He had certainly saved her life. But who was he? Could she trust him?

He was immediately struck by her beauty. It was less sensual than elegant. A stream of dark hair and deep, searching eyes spoke of wisdom far beyond her years. A slight woman, light brown in complexion, not voluptuous, but not frail. She was patrician, with proud features, delicate yet strong, but from what kind? Roman, Hebrew, Sumerian, or Egyptian? A descendant of Ptolemy, perhaps.

She had faced the Sicarians, more angry than afraid, with dignity and courage. They would have destroyed her or perhaps taken her for ransom. She made a decision. "I am Miriam," she repeated, "wife to Sylvanus, the Roman legate. I seek my mother who is a Jew and was here in the city."

"Madam, you must return to your tent in the cradle of the army. This city is a graveyard. Tomorrow the legions of Titus will take the Temple Mount. The end will be awful to behold. Only the scavengers, brothers to the scum that attacked you, remain in the city. Stay with us. We will see you safely to your tent."

She agreed. Three of her guardians were dead and a fourth badly shaken. Further search for her mother would be folly.

"Why is the wife of Sylvanus here with such a small retinue?"

"My husband has been in Rome for close to a year. He seeks an assignment closer to the emperor. I thought the city was safe."

He shook his head. "You are in grave danger here. Even the Romans are unrestrained in their blood lust." He pointed, "We go this way."

He knew the city well. He placed three guards toward the rear of the sedan chair. Then with Herculanus and the surviving soldier that had accompanied Miriam, he positioned himself in front. They proceeded to carefully make their way through the narrow lanes toward the Jaffa gate and the lower city. Numerous corpses were strewn randomly everywhere. Buildings had begun to burn, victims of Roman and bandit torches. Columns of stifling black smoke and flame rose on all sides, obscuring their vision and, at times, blocking their very ability to breathe. It was clear. They had to get out of there and fast, else they would be trapped and incinerated.

To the extent possible, their eyes continually swept the rooftops and alleyways looking for pillaging bands or Sicarian assassins. He glanced at Herculanus. The Greek was like an animal, seeking prey, alert, poised to do battle, fully concentrating on his assignment to protect this little band. Two other soldiers strained mightily to carry the sedan chair and maintain the speed. These Greeks, descendants of Philip of Macedon and Alexander the Conqueror, had learned their soldiering skills from their fathers and grandfathers. They served well.

The woman signaled for them to stop. The sedan chair was an impediment to movement. She knew it. She stepped out and shouted. "I will continue on foot. Throw away the chair else we all burn."

Without the additional burden their pace quickened. Ben Gorias was amazed at her strength and endurance. Never wavering, she kept pace with the soldiers, a truly remarkable woman.

He sighed audibly, with undisguised relief, after coughing, choking and rubbing their eyes from the acrid smoke, they finally emerged from the alleyways into bright sunshine. They had reached David's road. The Jaffa Gate was in sight. A Roman captain and several soldiers had set up a road block. They examined his pass, with the seal of Titus. It signaled a person of importance.

The captain waved Ben Gorias and Miriam's retinue through the gate into the main encampment. A vast array of tents spread out before them. An air of intense excitement prevailed among the Roman legions. They sensed victory. The end was near.

Ben Gorias was seized by an overwhelming sadness. This Jerusalem, the city built and beloved by David and Solomon that had known so much joy for their people since its birth long ago, was being reduced to ashes. It was now the ruined skeleton of a once-great metropolis. Its destroyed soul was about to be dispersed to the four winds.

The little group reached the tent of Miriam and paused to rest, the soldiers around them glistening with sweat. Soot and ashes soiled their clothes and blackened their faces.

"You must all remain at my tent. There is fresh water and food. There are women to bathe you. Stay, you have done me great service. I owe my life to you."

In the evening, bathed clean and fragrant with perfume and oil, she came to Ben Gorias and beckoned him to her bed. "I am much alone. I crave the company of a good man. I am much taken with you. You are a gallant and honorable man."

He lay next to her and studied her body. A sheer white gown revealed all. Her breasts were small but her thighs were strong and her legs were slim and well curved. Her skin was a smooth light brown, of a Middle Eastern race. Her most compelling feature were her dark eyes. They were an indefinable mix of wisdom and passion with a hint of wild, primitive ancestors who once roamed trackless mountains and survived in a wilderness of forests and streams. Who was this woman? A Jewish mother, but not a Jewish father, and certainly not a pure descendent of the tribes.

"Who are you?" she asked, a bit ashamed that she had allowed this man into her bed, though she hardly knew him. But he had saved her life and guided her to safety. Surely she would have perished in the fallen city. She trusted him.

"I am the son of Mattathias. We are of the priests. My father was jailed because I pleaded for my people to surrender, to save them from this awful ending. It was foreseen. Roman power is at this time omnipotent. My mother is dead, and I fear my brothers have joined her. And you, Madam, why has the legate left his wife in Judea while he politics in Rome?"

"The legate is angry with me." She looked discouraged as if she had been assigned an important task and failed. "I have not yet given him a son and heir. My father is an officer in the Ptolemy army. He is a descendent of a soldier who was captured in the far off island of Britain and whose skills were so great that he became an important general for Augustus, the great Caesar. I have not conceived for the legate."

That was it. The Scot tribe, that was the characteristic he detected in the woman's eyes—the image of unbridled forces, a sense of great distances and unrestrained energy. A part of her came from the world beyond the Brits where tribes of savage warriors roamed free, unconquered by the mighty legions of Rome.

"You indeed possess wondrous beauty," he said, then he leaned over and kissed her full on the lips. She responded and placed her left arm about his neck. With gentleness and patience, only unfettering her passion in gradual bursts, they began those tender touches and merging movements that led to sexual union. Their lovemaking came naturally as if they had known each other many times. His lips moved down her body and stopped at her breasts and went further to her hips and legs. She was not inexperienced. She raised his body to a heat but not enough to end the encounter. She then caressed his genitals but stopped before his orgasm. He became more passive, he groaned, saying little. They made love only with sounds, no speech. He finally penetrated her and together, she first, they experienced the deep feeling of mutual satisfaction. He thought, as he moaned in ecstasy, perhaps I made a baby. He didn't care. He would love this woman forever.

They slept for several hours. Then he awoke with a start. Something was wrong. He heard muted sounds. There were shadows outside the tent and in the tent. Where were the guards? He slipped naked out of the bed to retrieve his sword. "Alarm," he shouted. There was no response.

Two guards lay dead, throats slit, silenced by Sicarian daggers. A third was too drunk to react, but the slave girls were screaming and Herculanus, at rest with a young house slave, heard and, ever vigilant, seized his sword and rushed to his aid. A cloaked Sicarian, moving like an animal, attacked Ben Gorias who was now fully awake. Long ago he had learned of their tactics and how to counter them. He moved swiftly and as the Sicarian's arm descended he sliced it off at the forearm. He turned, in time to see Herculanus burst into the tent. Two Sicarians surrounded him but he backed into a corner so they could not assault him from the rear. He quickly hacked one to death with a powerful blow to the neck. The second one was proving more difficult.

Out of the corner of his eye, he saw another assassin heading for the bed. This was not a random attack, but a well-planned plot to murder this woman. The Sicarian's arm was raised over Miriam and with a rapid movement descended onto the bed where Miriam, now awake, cowered.

"NO!" Ben Gorias shouted. He pitched his sword, like a javelin at the man. It struck him full in the chest. The camp watch, aroused by the shouts and noise, burst into the tent. They found him, holding her, a body doused in blood, in his arms.

****

"Captain!" the lead guard shouted. "Captain Gold, wake up! You're having a nightmare. Wake the hell up."

David found himself staring into the huge pop eyes of a Roman guard. But it wasn't a Roman guard, it was Barney Google, the cartoon character. Barney was smiling. "Hey, buddy, you were making noise like a possessed banshee. Wake up! You want to go to Beirut? We got a window but we gotta move now."

It wasn't Barney Google at all. It was Al Dortch. He was wearing a flight suit. "What about it, Gold? Time's a wasting."

David suddenly became conscious that the rain had slowed down to a light patter. "What's the deal?" he asked.

"We got a VIP airplane down in Beirut that needs a part. We got the part, and I'm going to Beirut with or without you. We are in the eye of the storm. We'll have to break through a cloud wall south of the eye. The weather in Beirut is clear and sunny. If we fly due south, we might make it. Are you game?"

"Hell, yes! David was out of the sack and on his way to the bathroom. "I'll be dressed in five minutes. What time is it?"

"It's Thursday, 0600. Move your ass. Our window is only good for an hour at the most and the airplane is being fueled."

"I'm moving, Captain Dortch." Well, I'll be damned, flying into the eye of a hurricane, David thought. Well, this was going to be one for the grandkids. That is, if he and Dortch made it. If not, he'd be just another statistic, lost at sea while on a fool's errand. In that case, there would never be any grandkids or kids for that matter.

When David arrived at operations shack, Dortch and the OPS officer were engaged in a violent argument.

"Dammit, Al!" exploded the major, "I tell you it's too risky."

"Bull, Mac, the cloud wall south of here is paper thin. We can make it, slam dunk."

Dortch's face was beet red and his abnormally large eyes were now bulging. He was hopping mad. They had apparently been debating for some time. David listened, and he knew the major was right. Someone tugged at his elbow. He turned slowly. To his surprise, it was Hernandez.

"Listen *amigo*, Major's got a point. I like you. You are a good troop. Don't put your life on the line. I don't care how important this mission is. It ain't worth your life. This is just a job."

"If he goes, Fred, I have to go."

"David, these fighter pilots are all crazy. They read *Smiling Jack*, and they think they're Hot Shot Charlie. They don't give a damn. They like to roll the dice. It makes them feel like heroes. Every flight is a dog fight. They have a death wish. Stick around till Monday. The weather will clear and the courier will go to Beirut. Why sacrifice yourself so Al Dortch can have another shot at committing suicide?"

David was surprised at Fred's dogged veto of the flight. "That bad, huh?"

"Worse! Those winds will rip that airplane apart."

David paused and considered the ramifications. Death in an airplane crash in the middle of a raging sea was not a pleasant possibility to consider.

Dortch suddenly turned to David. "Gold, if you're going, get a damn helmet and parachute now. If you are chickening out, well, that's fine. But decision time is now. We have to go or you rot here till at least Monday."

Hernandez became more intense. He grasped David's arm and took him off to the side, out of Dortch's earshot. "*Amigo*, this guy doesn't care. He died a long time ago, maybe over Europe in World War II or over the Yalu in Korea. Too many buddies lost. Too many burning planes and broken bodies. Look at him, the storm is waiting, the impossible challenge and he loves it. He doesn't care about you. This guy has a death wish. He has nobody, and he wants you to join him in the eternal void. He wants company because he is afraid to die alone. He's *loco*! Look at him."

David glanced at Dortch. His skinny body was shaking with anger. His eyes were still bulging and his blood pressure, reflected by the scarlet color of his complexion, looked close to a convulsive level.

David stared at the floor. Hernandez was right. Why was he throwing his life away with some ghost from a bygone war who felt guilty because he survived? It was not his responsibility. His left hand tingled. It was like a wake up call. He was clutching his tote bag tightly. He felt like something had stung him.

"Fred," he replied, "I really appreciate your concern. But I have to make that flight. I have a mission I must complete or . . ."

Hernandez shrugged his shoulders in disgust. He finished the sentence. "Or die trying. What a waste."

The two men shook hands. "*Vaya con dios, amigo.*" Lieutenant Fred Hernandez ambled off shaking his head in disbelief. "*Loco hombres,*" he kept muttering.

The freckle-faced kid who had been reading the Mike Hammer mystery story the day before arrived with a helmet and backpack parachute. He presented them to David. "Good luck, sir."

"Listen, corporal, you want to make another fifteen bucks?"

"Sure, anything, sir, as long as I don't have to fly with you guys."

David grabbed a notepad and a pencil and scrawled a short message. "Can you get through to Detachment 91?"

"Sure, no sweat by telex."

The kid scanned the message. "What's this guy's name, Ibrahim Rasheed?"

"Correct, at the American University."

The kid read it aloud: "Imperative you contact Professor Ibrahim Rasheed and advise David Gold arriving USAF Detachment 91 /about 1400 hours."

David peeled off fifteen more dollars from his meager supply. "Don't spend it all in one place."

The kid smiled. He wondered how they would describe this captain in his obituary.

"Let's go!" shouted Dortch.

He burst through the door with the major following, still arguing in righteous anger.

"I am not taking responsibility, Al, I order you not to fly! Okay, if you do any stunt flying this trip, you'll meet a flying evaluation board, I promise you."

"Blow it out your ass. I'll call you from Beirut. Hey, the whole flight is stunt flying. It's a warm and sunny day there. I'll be on the beach with a Lebanese broad."

The T-28, a single-engine training plane, was standing at the end of the parking ramp. In the early morning drizzle it was a fragile and solitary statue framed against a lonely gray sky.

A silver-haired tech sergeant in a plastic foul-weather slicker was finishing the visual inspection. "Looks and sounds okay, Captain Dortch." His face, etched with deep lines and tired eyes glanced upward. "No friendly skies today."

He helped the two men get into their cockpit seats. He watched as the aircraft kicked into life and left the ramp for the runway. He was a sober, laconic man who many years before had launched B-17s into English skies and sent them with their crews to the carnage of Schweinfurt, Hamburg and Berlin. He had seen them return with gaping holes in the fuselage and mangled bodies. Many never returned at all, flaming wrecks shot down. In Korea the faces and airplanes were different. They were fighter pilots in F-51s and F-86s. Some laughed and played at bravado. Others, retreads, World War II veterans, were sad and tired of war. They had envisioned a world of peace where they could live out their days without the gnawing fear that tonight might be their last. They, too, died, or lost arms and legs and sight. All of that, the sergeant could accept and almost understand. But why in the hell and by what crazy logic was Al Dortch flying into the eye of a hurricane on a Thursday morning when he could have stayed in his sack, or sipped coffee or, better yet, Scotch in a warm, dry Officers Club?

CHAPTER 31

THE THIRD WEEK, THURSDAY
"UNCLE AL, THE KIDDIES' PAL"

The North American T-28 is a training airplane built in the early 1950s as the next generation successor to the T-6. It had a limited range of a few hundred miles. Its engine was more powerful than the T-6, the old World War II workhorse, but like all training aircraft, it had severe limitations. The airplane had a maximum operating ceiling of 35,000 feet, with portable oxygen. The max speed was three-hundred-forty-three nautical miles per hour. The aircraft was fairly reliable but had a tendency to stall at certain attitudes. It was almost impossible to restart the airplane in mid air. It was only a primary trainer and not designed for serious cross-country flying, let alone cross-water travel. That meant instrumentation was limited, no radar. It was not designed to fly in serious bad weather and certainly not in a storm of hurricane force.

It did have several redeeming features. It was unusually durable and stable and contained some anti-spin characteristics. It had a range of over a thousand miles and a Wright cyclone engine that generated 1424 HP. It was built to withstand the abuse of young, inexperienced student pilots who often believed the airplane was like their favorite toy wagon. They could bang it around to their heart's content without seriously damaging it.

None of that mattered to Al Dortch. The kiddies' pal would fly a snow sled or an electric train if he could. His motto: "If I want the airplane to do something like a loop or some other more difficult stunt, it will do it because I want it to. The airplane obeys me because I am Al Dortch."

A hurricane is an out-of-control phenomenon of nature. It is a whirling, destructive vortex of rain and winds starting at seventy-five miles per hour, and it's usually two to three hundred miles in diameter. The storm spins counter-clockwise around an eye, a calm area usually about twenty miles in diameter. The eye itself moves at about twenty miles per hour. The strongest and heaviest winds are in a wall of clouds that surround the eye. Hurricane force dissipates in one of two ways. It can be slowed by friction generated by passing over a land mass, or weakened by contact with cool oceans. Hurricanes, typhoons and monsoons rarely occur in the Mediterranean. Violent windstorms in the Middle East are called mistrals. The last storm of daunting proportions occurring in this part of the world was described in the Bible. A Hebrew prophet named Jonah, sailing in a ship off the Phoenician coast, was cast into the sea by the crew to abate a raging storm. He was swallowed whole by a whale. The storm ceased and Jonah was later saved by the Lord's miracle to fulfill a mission he had been assigned, like David.

As Dortch's T-28 fought to gain altitude in the eye before it plunged into the tumbling chaos of the southern cloud wall, the story of Jonah occurred to David. He peered into the awesome gloom of nature's fury and speculated on their chances of survival. If there was a Jonah on this ship, it was he. If this puny mode of transportation was ripped apart at twenty thousand feet or even five thousand feet, they were lost. Not the Lord or any heavenly force could save them. David was sure that the odds were so stacked against them that perhaps he had better make his peace now.

He questioned himself. What curious quirks of fate had brought him to this place where he was contemplating his own demise? He had been a relatively good person, whatever that meant, or was this personal evaluation only the figment of his own self-serving judgment? Was there really a book of judgment with an omnipotent jurist possessing the power to make a final decision as to whether your life continued or was terminated? What would Myra's reaction be if he died? Would Maggie, whom he had barely gotten to know, cry or even feel sad? What would his friends say? "Good old David Gold, what a nut? Just what the hell was he really doing floating in that damn cauldron four miles up over the Mediterranean Sea?" If this was the bottom line on taking responsibility, then no wonder he had fought accepting it all his life. He should be in his office now, dictating an agreement or researching a legal issue. Not here, where it appeared nothing could prevent his inevitable descent into oblivion. He was accompanying a living corpse whose soul had already died in a forgotten battle. Dutch wanted to join his lost friends and assuage his guilt. Fred Hernandez had warned him. He had called it a death wish. But misguided valor…no, actually, responsibility had overcome discretion.

The airplane had penetrated the south cloud wall and now faced the full force of the storm. The winds seemed determined to end their journey, to send this diminutive craft reeling into the sea. Huge raindrops beat on the canopy, like monsters trying to reach their hapless prey. David felt hopelessness. It wasn't really fear, just sadness. He was sure this was the end for him. And there was so much more he wanted to do.

Dortch's intercom had been completely silent since takeoff. Probably frozen with fear. Can't even communicate. What a phony hero. David could not have been more wrong. Captain Al Dortch was having one hell of a good time. He loved the challenge. All ten thousand hours of his flying experience, garnered since he had entered air cadets in 1943, were being utilized. The fact was, Dutch Dortch was a crack pilot. He had gotten out of many tough scrapes, shot down enemy airplanes over Germany and Korea, flown the Berlin Airlift and even walked away from a couple of smoking wrecks. He was lucky. The true burning question was, would his luck hold? People, so-called daredevils who push the envelope, generally survive for two reasons. Their number is not yet up and they are good at what they do. Al Dortch was good at what he did. That was to fly airplanes. Where exactly Dortch's number was currently positioned in the big book was the unknown factor in the whole equation. As for David's number, he figured it was up.

The aircraft held together. The engine snorted and puffed but never ceased its rhythmic pounding. The rain lightened up, the buffeting ceased and the air currents were still and silent. The airplane seemed to be floating in kind of a quiet vacuum. David was startled by a beam of radiant light that flashed into the cockpit and for a moment obscured his vision. Was this the light that near-death people claimed they saw when the Grim Reaper approached? The bleak, dreary world around him had suddenly taken on a brilliant blue aspect. If this was death, he was confused. He did not remember crashing or even falling into the sea. He could also still hear the engine. Death was certainly a strange experience.

Now the intercom was alive with a bellowing laugh. "Sonofabitch, I was right, Gold! Look at that beautiful sight! Down there. Have you ever seen anything more bitchin? I just won fifty bucks from the major. I said one hour and ten minutes and it only took sixty-five minutes to get out of the soup."

David's vision cleared. There, spread out before him as far as the eye could see, were the sparkling blue waters of the Mediterranean, alive and shimmering in the bright sunshine. "Dutch, you're a wizard. How did you know?"

"I cheated. I studied the storm pattern and knew it turned north over the Anatolian highlands. This end of the cloud wall had passed over the mountains and nothing takes the teeth out of a storm like high mountains. The storm had turned. We were in the outer south reaches. When I checked, the weather in Beirut was fair and warmer. The rest was a piece of cake."

Therein lay the difference. This guy wasn't some kind of a clown who flew by the seat of his pants. Dortch was a skilled pilot who took calculated risks based on data that his trained mind and natural instinct could process in a very rapid manner.

Twenty-eight minutes later, a city like Sinbad the Sailor's from *The Arabian Nights* loomed on the horizon, a wondrous gleaming mirage with huge mosques, towering minarets from which the

Muezzins called the faithful to prayer five times a day. Its fortress castle, teeming bazaars and ten-story office buildings were all set against the brown bare highlands of the Bekka Valley Mountains.

This was Beirut, the Paris of the East, where Saudi and Iraqi financiers and French and British businessmen and bankers met to transact business and play in the nightclubs and casinos. An unlikely blend peopled the city: Shiite and Sunni Muslims, Druze Tribesman and Christian descendants of invading Crusaders who had arrived a thousand years before and stayed on as permanent residents. The tiny country balanced precariously between Syria and Israel and, in spite of its prosperity, was teetering dangerously on the edge of a disastrous civil war.

Dortch was exhilarated. He shoved the throttle forward and the airplane went into a steep dive. He pulled back on the throttle and began an even steeper climb. He flipped the aircraft over and went into a loop. He banked the airplane to the left and then spun around in a circle. He had gone into his acrobatics mode. He was now Uncle Al, the irresponsible kiddies' pal. He was totally oblivious of his passenger whose lack of decent food and serious sleep deprivation was culminating in a violent inner gut rebellion. David was getting very dizzy, too. He tried to shout into the intercom but he was forced to swallow instead. On the fourth loop, as the aircraft straightened out, the usually grinding, roaring vociferous engine coughed and became quiet. He heard Al say, "Shit, we lost our engine!"

David's relief was fleeting. He quickly realized they were in trouble. The aircraft floated in the air currents for a few seconds and then began a slow, downward descent.

"David, tighten your parachute and abort when I blow the canopy." Dortch tried to keep his voice restrained but he was shouting. "Have you ever jumped?"

"Hell no!"

"Remember, count to ten so you clear the airplane and then yank the ripcord across your chest. Pull hard!"

David grabbed the tote bag. It was hot, almost burning. He was determined not to lose it. He clutched it in his left hand and secured it to his wrist. His right hand was free to handle the ripcord. He tightened the straps on his parachute and prepared to close his eyes and jump. He was too sick to be scared and too scared to be sick.

The airplane was now in a steeper dive and Dutch was feverishly working to level it out. He began once more to repeat the checklist in the futile hope that he could restart the engine. It was, he knew, an impossible gesture, but it was standard emergency procedure. He coolly called Det 91 and reported a mayday condition. It was quickly acknowledged. At least there would be a boat out searching for them.

"David, in a second I'm going to blow."

He pulled the choke and pulled it again. The engine coughed feebly. It was starving for fuel. He pulled it a third time. He was concerned about flooding and choking off the fuel line. The engine coughed again as if begging to be fed. It spit, made a loud noise and gunned itself twice as if catching its breath. Then, haltingly, it sprang to life. He trimmed the airplane, nursed the throttle gently backward and at three thousand feet, corrected to a perfect straight and level tack heading directly for Detachment 91 and Beirut International Airport.

CHAPTER 32

THE THIRD WEEK, THURSDAY
METRO POLICE HEADQUARTERS, CAPTAIN ANDY SEILER'S OFFICE

Captain Seiler was adamant. "I tell you guys, somebody else had to be involved. How could two fugitives from a Lebanese nut house get into this country, and find out the dagger was here? Then they come to Pittsburgh, stake out the museum and then find a safe house. They operate from the Hill district and use local contacts."

Captain Seiler turned to Jerome. "What about it, Jerome? We got some kind of a murder cult operating in this town?"

Jerome's expression was impassive. He drummed fingers on the desk. "Could be. I'm not sure. But I think Abou Hassan has the answers. He is, for some reason, too scared to talk. That tells me there are other people out there. I need to have another heart-to-heart talk with him. Remind him of who and what he really should be scared of. I asked the D.A.'s office if we could negotiate for some answers, but Assistant D.A. Marx says absolutely not. The crime is much too serious. No promises. No plea bargain."

Captain Seiler turned to Ed Flaharty. "What about the guards at the museum? Nothing new on the two murders; motive, reasons, suspects, nothing?"

Both men shook their heads and signaled an emphatic no.

Benson had been invited to the meeting. Seiler turned to him next. "What about it, Throckmorton?" asked the captain. "Got any hot ideas?"

"I completely agree with you. We're not through yet, Captain. There are others involved. The dagger was only on exhibit for two weeks when the Sicarians showed up. Some person or some group recognized it and imported these knife-toting cutthroats. Their purpose was to steal the dagger. It has a strong religious connotation for their brotherhood."

"Religious? How so?"

"Let me explain. Ishtar was a female fertility goddess. She had a warlike male sidekick name of Humbaba. Her shrine was thought to be at Agade, near Babylon. The evil bird, like the one we found, is a winged harpy and represents her principal male servant. I was thinking about who…" He stopped in mid-sentence. "My God, Rasheed. He was here the night the aborted theft occurred. You remember him, don't you, Flaharty?"

"Sure, the big guy." He was about to say "black" but Flaharty was sensitive to Jerome Becker's feelings. "I questioned him. I wanted to get back to him, but he was leaving the country the next day."

"If it was Rasheed, then…" Benson put his palms to this forehead. "Then I have put David in great danger."

"David," snapped Andy Seiler. "Who the hell is David?"

Benson swallowed his next words. Benson knew that to tell Andy Seiler the whole story would destroy his own credibility, perhaps buy him a ticket to the cell next to Sal Dematteo. "David," he said, improvising an explanation, "is working with our team at the museum, tracking some issues involving the Mesopotamian exhibit. He is on his way to Jerusalem. I told him to stop and contact Rasheed in Beirut. Oh, God. What have I done? It all fits. First Rasheed refuses our invitation to the conference. Then he reverses his decision and decides to attend. He inspects the dagger the night before he leaves. While he's with us, he relates the story of the Sicarians and their connection with the dagger. I just couldn't see it. My God! This man has a worldwide reputation in the archaeological community. He must be their high priest!"

Becker was impatient. He rose to his full height and stretched his injured knee, which had begun to pain him. He had dimmed out. All this talk about ancient gods was garbage. "The hell with Rasheed or whoever this guy is. There are others here in this town who are accomplices. Abou knows who they are, and by this afternoon I will have the same information or Abou will be one sorry ass."

"Be careful," warned Seiler. "He's represented by Bernie Kalb. That turkey could cause us a lot of problems in the papers."

"No sweat, Captain. We are not looking for admissible evidence. Just answers. I'm certain our friend in the pokey will be more than delighted to supply them."

The captain agreed. "We need some answers and soon. Tomorrow morning we are burying my niece Maggie. Yet the chief is about to have a nervous breakdown. The mayor is on rampage, and the papers are scaring the hell out of the community. This murder cult thing is serious. People are buying guns and locking their doors." His eyes narrowed. "I want every bastard who had a hand in this thing. If I have my way, there'll be no trials, only executions. Everyone understand?" The room went silent, everyone understood. The judge and jury had just pronounced sentence.

Benson watched Becker's huge frame vanish through the door. He felt a sharp twinge in his gut. David was walking into a trap. There was nothing he could do to warn him. Even worse, he had sent him there. First Maggie. Now David.

The phone jangled. The sound tore into the silence like a dropped hammer in a steel mill. It rang again. Seiler picked it up with a disgusted gesture. "I said no calls. Don't you guys understand English, NO CALLS!"

The voice at the other end was clearly in a panic. It was the jailhouse.

"When? Ten minutes ago. Sergeant Becker is on his way there. No one leaves that jail. Lock the place down. No one! Guards, visitors, lawyers. No one leaves. I want statements from everyone. I'll be right over."

He slammed the phone down. "Dammit! They just found Abou Hassan hanging in his cell by his own belt. I thought Muslims don't commit suicide!"

"They don't normally," said Benson, "unless they are on a holy mission. Then it's a ticket to paradise. But remember, Hassan wasn't a Muslim. He was an Ishtarite. Hassan was another sacrifice to the evil bird."

The second phone call, four minutes later, was even more startling. It was for Flaharty. They had just discovered a body in the basement of the Carnegie Museum. The cop making the call quickly described the scene. The corpse was one of the new guards, found in the furnace room, on his back, arms folded, one wound in the back of his neck. Flaharty closed his eyes. He groaned. He was sure the dead man was Harry Abrams, Metro's undercover man.

CHAPTER 33

THE THIRD WEEK, THURSDAY
BEIRUT INTERNATIONAL AIRPORT

The T-28, moaning but unbowed, pulled to a stop close to the front of a small Quonset hut identified by a shabby wooden sign. Large white letters on a blue background read USAF. BASE OPERATIONS, DETACHMENT 91, BEIRUT LEBANON. The sign was a simple reminder that American power now stretched across the rim of Africa and was perched on the borders of the Middle East, the very cradle of western civilization and the outer perimeter of the Soviet empire.

Locals, hired by the Air Force to staff the small detachment, quickly placed wooden blocks under the wheels. With great effort, David lifted himself out of the cramped back cockpit. He groaned as he lowered himself to the ground. Blinking in the bright sunlight, he noticed a C-47, a Goony bird, parked a few yards to the left. Save for this plane, the T-28 was the only United States Air Force aircraft in sight. The warm sun and the solid turf, minus the noise and the interminable movement, felt good. He put on sunglasses, grabbed the tote bag and started for the Base OPS hut.

Dortch was making some notes in the logbook. He carefully avoided eye contact with David. David paused. He couldn't let it go without a comment. "Thanks for the ride, Dutch. Don't think it hasn't been fun." His tone was dry. He couldn't mask his anger.

"Hey, look, David, I'm sorry. You won't report this to the major, will you? If you do, I'm finished. McCloud is looking for a reason to bust me."

"Look, I'm grateful. I know without you I would be sitting on my fanny in Athens. You're one hell of a pilot. But Christ, you might have killed us. Just to get two minutes of an adrenalin rush."

"It's worse than that, kid. We were dead. I've never known a T-28 to restart after it lost an engine in mid air. We experienced a once-in-a-blue-moon miracle. I quit. It'll never happen again, kid."

David stared deep into those saucer-like eyes; they were contrite. Bullshit, he thought. You'll do it again. You're about as sincere as Hitler at Munich. Dortch was a dinosaur. A restless child-warrior, who perennially sought a battle and could no longer find it. Take away his toy airplane and he's dead.

"Okay, Dutch, I won't be your funeral director. You're off the hook this time. Happy flying. Thanks again for the buggy ride. See you around the campus."

The two men shook hands and saluted. Both were grateful. David, just to be in Beirut. And Dutch, secure David would keep his promise, that at least this time his report card would be clean.

David went into the OPS shack. He checked in at the desk and discovered they had received the telex message from Athens. They had contacted the party as requested. The party would meet him outside the terminal gate in the main parking lot. He thanked the sleepy tech sergeant who advised him that civilian clothes were required in Beirut, no uniforms permitted. Also, he winked, ten bucks at customs goes a long way.

David found the latrine. He spent twenty minutes shaving, changing into civilian clothes and trying to whip his abused body into functioning. The sergeant also directed him to a snack bar in the terminal where David bought a small cup of coffee that resembled a few ounces of mud but actually, when laced with hot milk and sugar, tasted pretty good. He got a sandwich that was presented as slices of roast lamb with tomatoes and mushrooms, on something that looked like unleavened bread. This also tasted surprisingly good. Feeling refreshed enough, he prepared to make his way through customs.

Two uniformed soldiers—one carrying some kind of automatic weapon, the other looking very official and bureaucratic—were seated at a small, high-top wooden desk. The official one brandished a pencil; with his armed buddy they formed an imposing gauntlet.

The bureaucrat looked him over and spoke in French. "*Votre passport, s'il vous plait.*"

"*Anglais, s'il vous plait,*" David replied, "American." He presented his orders and an ID card. The second soldier woke up at the sound of English. Maybe some bribe money. He didn't look like the typical rich American. But you never knew.

"Your business in our country, Captain?"

Lebanon's guardian at the gate was very stiff and proper. David hadn't thought to concoct a cover story. How dumb can you get? His mind moved slowly. "I'm here to attend a meeting on some Roman artifacts at the American University."

"On military orders?" The guard wasn't stupid. "You are not carrying much luggage."

"These are permissive travel orders." His thought process rapidly improved. "I understand there is a small fee." He folded two ten dollar bills and handed them to the customs officer. "My contact at the university is Professor Ibrahim Rasheed. I'm only here for a couple of days. My luggage is in Athens."

At Rasheed's name, David sensed a marked change in the man's demeanor. The guard stamped his orders without another word. "You have a three-day visa. Today is Thursday. You must leave by Monday." He placed the money in an upper left hand pocket. "Enjoy your stay, Captain Gold."

David left the terminal building. Outside he surveyed the scene. He had stepped through a time-warp. What lay before him was the colorful tapestry of a cosmopolitan Middle Eastern city. People everywhere: beggars, taxi drivers in ancient pre-World War II taxis, street vendors hawking their goods, some leading donkeys and others carrying baskets, still others lounging idly in front of their small stalls. Numerous travelers wore rich Arab regalia with flowing gowns and keffiyahs guarding their heads. Others wore traditional western dress. All seemed to carry briefcases. In a minority, but still readily apparent, were the western businessmen in their well-tailored London suits and bowler hats. They walked briskly, purposefully, as if each had a mission. The women were adorned in an array of colorful costumes, some in full-length jellabas or full Islamic mufti, others in the latest chic Parisian styles. The effect of this teeming spectacle was overpowering. David hesitated, unsure how to proceed.

A beggar, spying his confusion, started toward him but then fearfully walked away when he was interrupted by two large men in coal-black suits. Both had mustaches and hard, expressionless faces. He didn't like their looks, but he had to know the next move. The larger of the two approached him.

"Mr. Gold?"

"Yes." David was reluctant to say more, trying to be careful.

"Rasheed sent us. Please accompany us."

David noticed the other man kept glancing around as if he was concerned about being spotted. He distrusted these two men immediately. But what choice did he have? They mentioned Rasheed's name and knew David's name. If he refused, he would be left standing in front of the Beirut terminal with no plan for how to proceed. He concluded that they must be legitimate. He followed the larger man into the back seat of a vintage, unmarked Mercedes. The smaller man drove. Their conversation skills didn't improve. They drove off in silence.

David sensed danger. But he was helpless. He could see no other option than to go along with the program.

"Where exactly is the American University?" he asked. There was no answer. After driving for what seemed an interminable time, he repeated the question. Still no answer. They had entered a neighborhood of narrow streets. There were few cars and many small shops. The streets were overflowing with pedestrians, all in local dress. The pungent smell of charcoal cooking permeated the air.

"Where is the American University?" His voice rose. He was reaching the limit of his patience.

The man in the passenger seat turned. He had a sizeable German luger in his hand. "If you make another sound, Mr. Gold," he said calmly, "I will shoot you."

David suddenly felt an overpowering sense of weariness. With virtually no sleep, two harrowing rides through a hurricane, one with a cartoon pilot who had a death wish and a failed engine, with little decent food for two days, his nerves were now stretched far beyond any reasonable limit. He began to giggle as the utter absurdity of the whole situation struck him. He goes for a ride with two comic-opera villains, one big and one small, both with ridiculous bushy mustaches. One guy pulls a gun on him in the middle of strange city six thousand miles from home. He is on some kind of journey to Jerusalem. He has no real idea why or what is supposed to happen except he needs to be on the Arab side of Jerusalem by Saturday evening. It is now Thursday afternoon and, for some reason, the two guys sent to pick him up at the airport decide to hold him captive or, even worse, kill him.

"You guys can't be serious! Who the hell are you? What do you want?"

"We are serious, Mr. Gold, and you will shortly find out what we want. In the meantime shut up or this gun will silence you, for good!"

About ten minutes after the Mercedes left the terminal a very official looking Army jeep, carrying three uniformed soldiers, one an officer, drove up and parked at the front of the terminal. They were admitted through an access gate by an armed guard and drove immediately to the U.S. Air Force Quonset hut. There they were informed by the sergeant on duty that Captain Gold had gone to the main terminal more than forty-five minutes ago. Inquiries at the main customs office indicated Captain Gold had passed through the gate as well. Outside the terminal the three men stood baffled until a beggar with sharp eyes and the need for alms advised them that the English-looking man, dressed in brown and carrying a small bag, had driven off with two men in a black Mercedes touring sedan.

CHAPTER 34

THE THIRD WEEK, THURSDAY
THE CARNEGIE MUSEUM

When Benson arrived at the museum, there were six police cars parked in the front. All entrances were blocked. Patrons were being questioned and IDs were being checked. The museum, normally a tranquil refuge for scholars or people seeking a quiet afternoon, was a sea of activity.

Benson immediately went to his office and breathed a sigh of relief. The door was still closed and locked. But when he opened the door he saw a scene of muddled disorder. Files were scattered everywhere. Drawers had been searched and the contents scattered on the floor. Floorboards had been ripped up. His desk had been emptied down to the last piece of paper. Someone had been searching for the dagger. But only he knew where it was hidden. He was about to ask a policeman to get Flaharty, when he paused. He had a thought. He carefully closed the door and glanced at his watch. It was 2:00 P.M. in New York. He picked up the phone, his hand quivering. This latest violation had completely unnerved him.

He dialed the operator. "I'd like to call New York, the Columbia University History Department. This is person to person, to Professor Boris Gurevich." He gave the operator the main number of the university.

It took nearly ten minutes but finally a deep, hearty voice came on the line. "Gurevich here."

"Boris, it's Benson Throckmorton. I need your help."

"Tovarich, you sound upset. Calm down. Speak to Uncle Boris."

"Well, you may think I'm crazy, but I believe there is a team of Sicarian assassins operating here. On Wednesday they murdered my friend, Maggie Seiler. We found a wooden statue of the Humbaba harpy at the crime scene. Three museum guards have already been killed. All by sacrificial piercing in the back of the neck. This morning somebody ransacked my office."

"Good God, Benson, what are they after?"

"I believe, in fact I know, they want Hammurabi's dagger."

"Isn't it on display?"

"I removed it from the exhibit. I secured it after the first attempt at stealing the dagger failed. It's in a safe place. Only I know where it is hidden. Boris, what do you think I should do?"

Boris Gurevich didn't hesitate. His former KGB hat was already on.

"If it's a Sicarian cell, there are six members. One is their high priest. Remember the text of the Ebla Tablets? The Sicarians murder to create terror. But they always have a design. They kill around the victim—friends, wife, children, whoever, to accomplish their objective."

Benson felt true panic. He had hidden the dagger at home. He and his mother lived alone in a large house on a quiet residential street in Mt. Lebanon. "Boris, my mother is home alone during the day. She could be next."

Boris Gurevich spoke, again without hesitation, for in 1950 Benson's family had come to his aid when he needed to validate his asylum claim with the U.S. government.

"Listen carefully, Tovarich, and follow my instructions exactly. Get your mother out of the house and put her somewhere safe. Preferably out of town. Move into a hotel tonight. Go to the William Penn. I will get an airplane either tonight or first thing tomorrow morning. Wait for me at the hotel. I will join you. Be very careful. Do not open the door of your room unless you are absolutely sure it is me. Follow my directions—move fast, do it now. Do you understand?"

Benson hung up. He felt relieved. He would send his mother to her sister's downriver in Ambridge. Tomorrow Boris would be here. The old Russian fox would be more than a match for the Sicarians.

What Benson didn't know was that the Sicarians were about to change their base of operations. They had two objectives. Number one was to reclaim Hammurabi's dagger, and the other was the elimination of the Roman legate.

As he sifted through the mess of papers on the desk, a crumpled-up, dirty envelope with his last name scrawled on the cover caught his eye. It was an odd piece, one that he didn't recognize. He opened it and found a message. To his surprise, to decipher the contents would take several hours. The note, message, warning or whatever its purpose, was couched in ancient Babylonian Cuneiform—a language that had been defunct for nearly twenty-five hundred years.

CHAPTER 35

THE THIRD WEEK, FRIDAY
SOMEWHERE IN BEIRUT

They kept slapping him. Rather than beat captives, especially Americans, with a truncheon or fists, they subjected them to a regimen of asking questions and then slapping the prisoner if they didn't like the answer. This was a technique designed to humiliate and terrorize, instead of injuring or maiming the captive so badly that he could not carry out their bidding.

On a few occasions when David would try to answer honestly, they would not strike him. At other times, using an open palm, they would pummel his face even if he was trying to be honest. There was no pattern. No rhyme nor reason to their actions. The questioning and the battering continued. David was bound and blindfolded, an additional tactic to demoralize. For what felt like hours, he was given no food or water. His throat felt dry and parched, as if a sand dune had been stuffed down his mouth. His head resounded like an empty cavern. His ears were ringing. Blood trickled out the left side of his mouth.

"What do you guys want? Who are you?" He kept asking questions, pleading at times, begging. The only response was further stinging blows to the head and cheek.

"You only speak when we ask you a question. Do you understand?"

David was disoriented, close to delirium. At one point, he thought they had left the room. Then he could hear them whispering in a strange guttural language. The whispering sounded like two chippies arguing. It melded with a stream of dissonant voices and sounds that had begun to resonate in his brain. He was reciting a poem.

I shan't forget the night
when I was fell behind the fight
with a bullet where my belt plate
should have been.

I was chokin' mad with thirst
and the man that spied me first
was that good old grinnin', gruntin',
Gunga Din.

Where was Gunga Din now? Just a swallow of water away, that's all, just one swallow. Where the hell was he?

He heard other voices.

* * * *

"David! It's important to be a professional man. You don't like blood so you can't be a doctor or dentist. You will have to be a lawyer."

David's mind ran round and round, voices from the past chasing one another and what was left of his reason.

"David, you were a good boy today. You practiced your violin and didn't get dirty. You are a responsible boy."

"I am not. I don't want to be responsible. I want to play ball. ...half a league, half a league, half a league onward, into the valley of death rode the six hundred, forward the light brigade, charge for the guns, he said; into the valley of death rode the six hundred. They thundered past him all six hundred riding bravely into the teeth of the Russian guns and certain destruction."

"David! It's important to be a professional man. You don't like blood so you can't be a doctor or dentist. You will have to be a lawyer."

"I can't. Lawyers have too damn much responsibility."

"You must learn to handle it. That was your father's problem, hated responsibility. But he assumed it. He is now a success in the clothing business."

"I hate the clothing business!"

Where the hell is the cavalry? John Wayne ought to be here by now. I can hear the trumpets but where are they?

Somebody was screaming!

"Do you hear me? I want you to assume responsibility. You will write that letter now!"

"Okay, I'll write the letter but where is Gunga Din? Just a little water, please!"

"No water till you write the letter. Do you understand?"

* * * *

Someone ripped off his blindfold. He blanched. He blinked, a bright light was shining in his eyes. His vision gradually adjusted and he saw a fat man with several chins, a large rounded belly, a flat nose buried in his face giving him a freakish disfigured look. The man was standing before him, wearing small round glasses and a turban, or what David thought was a turban. Fatty was holding David's tote bag. The two men who had escorted him in the Mercedes were also there, impassive, the larger one smoking a cigarette. A fourth man, hairy, with a simian face and a squat powerful torso to match, sat at a table drinking water, sloshing it on the table and the floor. He kept laughing. Not a pleasant group to have over for Sunday dinner. The room was small. No windows, no furnishings except a cot, a wooden table, two or three wooden chairs, and two bare light bulbs suspended from the ceiling, creating grotesque shadows.

"You write a letter to Throckmorton," said the fat man. "You tell him that unless he turns the dagger over, at once, both you and the girl will die."

"Girl," David was puzzled. "What girl?"

Wham! A stinging slap on the right side of his face and the bridge of his nose. It brought tears to his eyes.

"We ask the questions! We have the dark girl. Our people in Pittsburgh have her in custody. Now only you can save her life. You write the letter?"

Oh, shit, they got Maggie, he thought. "Mister, your guys better look out. Her uncle the police captain won't like that."

Wham! Another slap, this one even harder. It opened the cut in his mouth. The blood flowed more freely. His head was reeling, the room spinning in a wide circle. Now there were two fatties holding the tote bag and six men, two sets of twins and two apes, in the crowded room.

"Okay," he muttered. "Stop hitting me. I'll write your goddamn letter."

What did it matter? They wouldn't give these jokers the dagger. But for some water he would agree to write the five books of the Old Testament and recite the Lord's Prayer. It was worth it. Anything to stop his body from being a smacking bag.

The fat man dug into David's tote bag and with a triumphant smile pulled out the prayer shawl. "What is this? Your weapon? Your protective shield?"

"It's nothing," David started to explain. But he stopped mid-sentence.

The prayer shawl was emitting smoke as if being consumed by an unseen fire. The fat man's eyes opened wide in surprise. "Yi" he said, followed by several expletives in a strange tongue. "It burns!"

He threw it on the floor where the shawl curled up and continued to emit some kind of black vapor. At that point another man burst into the room and quickly surveyed the situation. He was tall, wiry, light-skinned, with dark wavy hair, a polished man dressed in western clothes with an air of authority. He wore a large, menacing gold ring. David's eyes had difficulty focusing. But he could feel the sudden change in the air, the man's presence a signal for conversation and activity to halt. He was obviously the boss.

"Mr. Gold," he said in a soothing tone. "Let me apologize for the conduct of these buffoons. I realize we have inconvenienced you. Perhaps even injured you. I am truly sorry."

To halt the rotation of the spinning room, David peered through the left side of his face. He blinked several times. Good Cop, Bad Cop—an old trick.

"Some water, please." The blood had leaked onto his shirt and now slowly trickled onto his pants.

"Certainly," the new arrival turned to the grinning fossil with the water. "Idiot, a cup of water for Mr. Gold."

The water was warm and brackish but it restored life. He drank slowly, in small gulps. He remembered this trick from a desert movie. These foreign legionaries dying from thirst got to an oasis and were warned by the main character, Ronald Coleman or Burt Lancaster or somebody, to sip the water slowly or they would get sick.

"You know, Mr. Gold," explained Good Cop, "we are merely humble worshippers of another God. The dagger is a sacred symbol to us, much like your Torah or the Christian cross. Or," he gestured, "the shawl on the floor. Too bad it is burning up."

The man did a double take. The prayer shawl while still smoking actually was not destroying itself. It was undamaged.

"Remarkable item," he said. "I must examine it when we are through here. We merely want the dagger returned to its rightful owners. It was lost to us when Titus burned Herod's temple. We would have preferred to get the dagger directly from Throckmorton. We had him trapped in New York. We lured him there with the Dead Sea Scrolls, which I might add were authentic. Unfortunately, I only had two men and he had the Russian with him. The odds were too great. The Russian is a formidable opponent.

"Now, Mr. Gold, I will loosen your bonds, and you will write the letter as I dictate it. I would not advise anything heroic. You are in the middle of the old city of Beirut, the Medina. You have no place to go. My men are well trained. They will snuff you out in a minute. So just write the letter and perhaps you will get another cup of water."

David continued to peer at the man through a dazed cloud. You're not a good cop at all, he thought to himself. You're just a talk-nicer.

"Okay, I'll write your damn letter. Then I get another cup of water?"

"We will see." Good Cop gestured to the Missing Link.

"Omar, kindly untie Mr. Gold. If he tries to escape, break his neck."

Omar, the tentmaker, or was it Abou Ben Abou? May his tribe increase; God forbid. David still couldn't collect his thoughts.

Two powerful arms grabbed him, cut off the ropes with a thin knife, grazing the palm of his left hand and drawing blood. He was quickly moved to a chair next to the small wooden table. A pen was thrust into his hands, a piece of paper shoved in front of him.

"My English is perfect, Mr. Gold. Write exactly what I tell you or this time your face will look like applesauce."

The fat man roared with laughter. The other two men never cracked a smile or changed expression. The fourth man, or whatever he was, grinned through crooked teeth and shook his head in gleeful agreement.

Jesus, this has to be a nightmare, David thought. Any minute I'll wake up. This can't be a for-real group. This is evil. It's too much of a stereotype, a scene out of a horror movie.

"Benson," the well-dressed man began to rapidly dictate, "I have been taken by group of Sicarians. They will kill me, unless…"

"Please slow down. I can't think or write that fast."

"Sorry, Mr. Gold, I'm sure your mind is a little confused."

Confused! I can't remember my mother's name. Myra, that's it. He felt better.

David began to write. "Benson, I have been taken by…" It was starting to flow. A loud staccato sound blasted into his ears. What the hell was that?" He stopped writing.

The Bad Cop's attention turned toward the door. "Who is on guard?"

"Samir," answered the fat man.

The staccato sound had stopped. There were noises, voices, pounding, banging on the walls. Then came the unmistakable thump of heavy footsteps on the stairs. The big man with the German luger threw open the door and plunged into the hallway.

Revolver shots came one after another in quick succession. More staccato sounds. Then sudden silence.

"Strangle the Jew with his own prayer shawl," growled the leader.

The ape man leaped for the prayer shawl and seized it in both hands with great relish. The Jew would be dead in seconds. He screamed in pain. His hands were on fire. They were actually engulfed in flames. He continued to scream.

The leader stared in disbelief. What manner of weapon was this cursed scarf? The din continued until the first intruder leveled his sub-machine gun at the screamer and fired a long burst. The ape collapsed in a bloody heap. The fire extinguished itself, as the shawl lay inert on the floor. A huge black man in a khaki uniform entered next, glowering in rage and carrying an Uzi machine pistol. Three other uniformed men joined him, all carrying submachine guns.

David gaped in surprise. The guy didn't look much like John Wayne. He wasn't riding a horse, didn't blow a bugle or carry a Winchester 73 carbine. But the Calvary was right behind him.

"Mr. Gold," said the man with the Uzi, "I am sorry we took so long to get here. I hope you were not injured too severely."

He handed David a towel to wipe the blood from his face. "It took us a couple of hours to squeeze the location of this house from the toad in my office. He spied for this man."

He gestured toward Bad Cop. "Bring the son of sheep dung in and let him face his heroic leader for the last time."

Two soldiers dragging a third, tightly bound soldier by a rope entered the room and forced the third soldier to lie prostrate on the floor.

David stared at the imposing figure who, apparently, was his savior. He blinked his eyes. This huge specter of a man looked like an opaque Biblical vision. Somewhere, someplace he had seen or perhaps met this man. "Do I know you?" David asked.

"I am Dr. Rasheed. We met at the museum. You sent me a message about your arrival. I am Benson's friend. This donkey worked in my office and intercepted the phone call from your people. He waited an hour and then informed us of your arrival."

David surveyed the man, their leader, this huge black man, and Benson's friend. He remembered his words. "We spring from the same loins, you from Sarah and I from Hagar. This time we are on the same side." But he wore a uniform and led a troop of soldiers. He was a professor of archaeology, or so David had believed.

"You are puzzled, Mr. Gold. In the Middle East nothing is as it seems. We wear many hats here."

Rasheed gestured to one of his men. "Momar, take Mr. Gold, or is it Captain Gold...?"

"Mr. Gold will do just fine."

"Escort Mr. Gold to the border checkpoint at Sidon." Rasheed lowered his voice. "He will be delivered safely to an Israeli patrol that is waiting for him. I repeat 'safely' or your ancestors will weep in shame."

The soldier did not reply. But his eyes spoke of complete understanding.

Rasheed turned back to David. He handed him a canteen of fresh water. David drank gratefully in shallow gulps.

"Well, Mr. Gold, permit me one indulgence. This son of a sardine, who worships a false god named Ishtar, purports to be the leader of a sect of assassins called the Sicarai. He made a promise to me that he would regain the golden dagger of Hammurabi without shedding any blood or hurting any Americans. His name is Katoubian. He lied. Already several have died, including the beautiful dark-haired girl. To tell a falsehood, so the Koran says, is a terrible sin. Do you have a message for Mr. Katoubian before he joins his ancestors?"

Suddenly David knew that the dark-haired girl was Maggie. Through his overwhelming fatigue, the swirling paralysis that engulfed and dulled his senses, he felt a rising sensation of intense rage. He stood in front of Katoubian and stared into his eyes. He saw the dark reality of centuries of relentless cruelty. With every ounce of strength he could muster, he lashed out at the man. His right fist connected with Katoubian's nose. He felt it crunch under the blow. Katoubian fell, a lifeless rock. David felt faint. He swayed from the exertion.

Rasheed's strong hand steadied him. "Thank you, Captain Gold. Permit me in respect to call you Captain. Take your prayer shawl and your bag and go with the blessing of Allah. We are about to execute an age-old custom called Hamas. It is a cleansing ritual. No need for you to witness it."

David gestured toward the fat man. He lay in the corner, a heap of terrified blubber. "Is he," asked David, "included in Hamas?"

"Oh, yes, Captain, be assured this heretic is included. His sins carry much weight with Hamas."

David smiled weakly. "Many thanks, Dr. Rasheed."

Rasheed nodded. "May your mission be blessed with success."

As David was led down the stairs to a waiting jeep he heard the same chattering sound in the desert that he had heard earlier in the evening. There were several bursts, sleet bouncing rhythmically off a slate roof, then complete silence. Katoubian and his minions had been consigned to the dustbin of history, their bodies to ashes and their souls sent to meet the great Satan.

CHAPTER 36

THE THIRD WEEK, FRIDAY
SACRED HEART CEMETERY, NORTHSIDE PITTSBURGH

Maggie was buried on a crisp fall day. The air was fresh and the sky almost a cloudless blue. The weather was a true anomaly for the smoggy city of Pittsburgh. It was as if nature paid homage to the gentle beauty of this girl and called a truce with the approaching winter.

The service was being conducted graveside. Max Vogel led a contingent of nurses, doctors and hospital orderlies. Max surveyed the crowd. The diversity was a testament to the respect and affection accorded Maggie Seiler. There were many uniformed policeman, for out of deference to Andy Seiler the entire Metro squad was present. There were, of course, many family and friends. Mrs. Seiler, numb with grief, clung to her son Bart. He held her firmly lest she collapse. Catherine Dematteo, anchored tightly to her brother Stan, was bewildered. Her eyes were red with tears. In one short week she had gained a wonderful friend and lost her to an act of savage cruelty.

Presiding over this hushed group was a deeply saddened Father O'Malley.

Jerome Becker and Ed Bramer hovered on the edge of the crowd. They were searching for a strange face. They knew that murderers often return to burials to witness their handiwork. In this instance, the chance of such a return was next to impossible. Ed did notice what he considered an odd man but that was just Benson Throckmorton. Ed Bramer nudged Jerome Becker and with his eyes pointed out the man to him. To Jerome's surprise, Throckmorton was crying.

The coffin was in the center of the grave covered by a white shroud. Father O'Malley stood over it and, in a calm but reverent voice, intoned the mass. "Hail Mary, Mother of God, take this child to your bosom." When he finished, the crowd, almost in unison, crossed themselves and recited several Hail Mary's. He called upon Andy Seiler to say a few words.

When he rose to speak, Andy Seiler's anger was apparent. With great effort he kept it in check.

"She was universally loved. A child who freely gave of herself. Her greatest satisfaction came when she could relieve pain or alleviate suffering. Maggie's compassion for others was unlimited. Now we lay her to eternal rest next to my brother Jack, her father, who asked me on his deathbed to guard her. I failed, Jack, and I can only say I am deeply sorry—please forgive me."

He could go no further. Andy Seiler's voice broke. The tough cop who had seen three years of war and witnessed almost on a daily basis the extent of man's inhumanity to his fellow man could go no further.

Father O'Malley grasped him about the shoulders and comforted him. To complete the service, Father O'Malley called upon Dr. Max Vogel, Maggie's friend and supervisor at the hospital. In a soothing tone, reminiscent of his counseling sessions, Max talked of the inner beauty and incredible wisdom of this remarkable woman. He spoke of her great empathy for those unfortunate people whose sick minds caused them so much internal torment. "She was," he said, "like an angel as she moved among us. We will all miss her." He completed his eulogy with a poem which he read in a subdued voice.

Do not stand by my grave and weep.
I am not there, I do not sleep.

I am a thousand winds that blow.
I am the diamond glints on snow.
I am the sunlight on ripened grain.
I am the gentle autumn rain.

When you awake in morning's hush,
I am the swift uplifting rush
Of quiet birds in circling flight.
I am the soft starshine at night.

Do not stand by my grave and cry.
I am not there. I did not die.

Benson now lost it completely, literally hit bottom. Maggie had been a pillar for the time detective. She had encouraged him when he was sure he would never get his thesis written. She made him feel as if his obsession with the ancient past was not the meandering of some oddball egghead but something meaningful and important. Secretly, Benson Throckmorton loved Maggie Seiler, but he had never dared to express himself. When Max Vogel read that touching poem as part of the eulogy, Benson tried to find comfort, but instead, he then realized he would never see Maggie again. He would never sit with her in a coffee shop and watch her dark eyes flash as she described how she had helped a patient that day, or how Dr. Vogel had complimented her on her insight and empathy when dealing with an inmate whose mind had been ravaged by some unknown thief. Only Maggie had been interested when Benson excitedly explained in detail an incident from some lost civilization that had both flourished and died in the dim, forgotten past.

His anger, his hurt, his deprivation, was deep. But he knew it wasn't over. David Gold was in Israel and the last chapter was yet to be written.

He stared at the metal coffin as they lowered it into the dark, gaping hole. Father O'Malley sprinkled dirt on the lid. "Ashes to ashes." He crossed himself. "Rest in peace, my child."

"Until we meet again," muttered Benson. When the service ended a startling thought occurred to him. "They will go after Catherine, the legate's family. I must warn her."

A tear-stained Catherine was on the other side of the grave. Her brother Stan shielded her with his left arm. Benson moved around the grave to a position beside them.

"Don't leave her alone," he said bluntly.

Stan was perplexed. "Who the hell are you?"

"It isn't important. Do not leave your sister alone, especially for the next two nights. She must be protected."

Stan surveyed the short figure, the ridiculous spectacles, the green sweater and the rumpled pants.

"Who the hell are you?" he repeated the question.

"Stan," explained Catherine, "that's Professor Throckmorton. He's a curator at the museum. He was a friend of Maggie's."

The hushed group of mourners had now moved quietly away from the grave. They headed toward their cars. Stan started to turn without further conversation. This strange man gave him the creeps. Then he thought better of it. "What exactly are you suggesting? Why don't we tell the cops? They are all over the place here."

"I have no proof, but if the pattern is followed, they will make an attempt on the life of Catherine."

Stan Kowalczyk was a simple man. Sports was his life. Insurance was his bread and butter. Murder, conspiracy, cloak and dagger crap he left for the movies and pulp magazines. There were those who claimed Stan had thick skull and a brain that functioned only when the whistle blew, signaling the kick off. But something about this quirky character's demeanor ignited his concern.

"Okay," he agreed, "I'll call my brother. We'll stay with Catherine and the baby tonight."

Benson nodded his approval. "Be careful," he cautioned.

Stan also decided to call his brother-in-law Art. He didn't mention this to Benson. There were a lot of unanswered questions. He thought perhaps the two of them could begin to sort out this bizarre scenario. Nobody knew Sal better than his brother.

Benson knew Stan had listened and would act. He repeated to himself the final lines of the poem Max had read: Do not stand by my grave and cry. I am not there. I did not die.

* * * *

Thus, at age twenty-seven, was Mary Margaret Seiler laid to rest in a grass-studded cemetery, on a balmy Friday, in late September, 1955.

CHAPTER 37

THE THIRD WEEK, FRIDAY
WESTERN STATE PSYCHIATRIC INSTITUTE

Max knew the outcome of the Psychiatric Treatment Board before he heard their finding. There were few in the medical community who had the temerity to oppose the recommendations of Dr. Bernard Adler.

Max and the Catholic colleague the Dematteos requested, Dr. Tom Fogarty, had met for several hours trying to develop a position opposing or at least delaying the use of electroshock treatment on Antonio "Sal" Dematteo. Initially, Fogarty had been skeptical. He read several times the record Max had compiled. He conducted three therapy sessions with the patient. He compared the notes of Benson Throckmorton, the local archaeologist, with the stories the patient told while under hypnosis. He interviewed the family, including the patient's wife. The sum total was a truly baffling case. A most unique and confusing puzzle that did not square with any case history then on the books. After two days of nonstop work, Tom Fogarty concluded that in spite of the diagnosis by the renowned medic Bernard Adler, he reluctantly agreed with Max Vogel. Electroshock therapy (ECT) should be delayed until additional data could be gathered and the case better understood.

However, the board, consisting of five gray-haired or balding senior members of the profession, with an experience level averaging twenty-three years, would not be swayed. They unanimously recommended the use of electroconvulsive therapy, commencing at the order of Dr. Adler and in whatever frequency Dr. Adler prescribed.

Max wondered what other disasters could occur. He felt as if some malignant force had interposed itself in his life and nothing could counter its evil disposition. He stopped a determined Bernie Adler in the hall and made one more plea to halt the procedure.

"Bernie, Dr. Adler, I am begging you to delay the use of ECT, at least until the end of next week."

"Max, you are too emotionally involved in this case. You should default to Tom Fogarty."

"But he agrees with me. The case is too complicated to prescribe any drastic treatment at this time."

"He was unduly influenced by you. By next week he will see it my way. ALL RIGHT! How much time do you want, Max?"

"Give me a week. Please, I have something in mind."

"A week! What difference can a week make?"

"You're right. So give me the week."

Adler knew that in a week he might convince Tom Fogarty to reverse his opinion. "All right, Max, you have a week. If the patient's condition shows no improvement by next Friday morning, we commence ECT."

The great Adler strode off in a huff. "A week," he muttered. "He should have asked me for a year. That would have made sense. With acute schizophrenic delusions, a week wouldn't even dent the trauma." He was grievously disappointed in his prodigy. Max was failing the vital real-world test of logically supporting his own conclusions.

Max, dejected and physically tired, shook hands with Tom Fogarty. They agreed to meet first thing Monday afternoon. Tom had some other cases that needed attention. He would spend Saturday working, but first he would call the Dematteos. The two doctors discussed getting a court order to halt the treatment recommended by Adler, but they agreed to revisit the subject on Monday. Obtaining a court order in this instance would be equivalent to high treason—and professional suicide. They needed to talk more.

When he returned to his office there was a message from Benson. My God, Max wondered, what's happened now? He dialed Benson's number and caught the time detective as he was leaving the office. He listened and received the first bit of good news that he had heard since this whole drama had begun. Benson had gotten a message from his friend in Lebanon.

Late last night, Pittsburgh time, David Gold had crossed the Lebanese border and had been delivered into the custody of an Israeli Army patrol. David was now on his way to Jerusalem. The major issues as to how he would enter Jordan and get back out again, safely, and what he would do when he got there, still remained to be solved. Rasheed, Benson was happy to report, was an ally after all.

CHAPTER 38

THE THIRD WEEK, FRIDAY
NEAR THE LEBANESE BORDER

The biting predawn chill penetrated his thin outer garments. Shivering, his body ached each time the jeep slammed a pothole and bounced several inches into the air. For hours they had edged their way along a narrow mountain road, two soldiers continually haranguing each other. Obviously, as David interpreted their arguments, they were lost.

A heavy mist engulfed the jeep, a shimmering blanket of gray haze that reduced visibility to a few yards. Visions of hot boiling coffee alternating with Myra's chicken soup appeared in the fog.

In his confused reverie, David's father kept offering him a large bowl of something, but, when he reached for it, he was denied. The reason had something to do with an unsubstantiated allegation that he had forgotten to sweep the floor, the usual complaint that the boy was irresponsible. On some level, David knew he was semi-delirious. He knew he was in a pitching vehicle on a bumpy road in Lebanon, but the bowl of vaporous soup, a yellow steaming mirage, was there in front of him. His father wouldn't let him have it. It just didn't make any sense. He was sure he had swept the floor.

A voice interceded. It was his buddy, Irving. Good old Irving, always there with a wisecrack when you needed him. "Halt," Irving said. "What's the password?" That's a real kick. Irving wanted to know the password.

The jeep driver muttered something back in Arabic.

"Irving, is that you?" David was sure it was Irving except that Irving answered the driver in Arabic. When the hell did Irving learn Arabic?

"It's not Irving," answered the voice out of the fog. "It's Herschel."

Herschel, who the hell was Herschel? The conversation continued for a few more minutes. The second soldier then prodded David with the rifle butt. He gestured with his head toward the voice in the fog.

David gathered he was supposed to join Herschel. He climbed out of the jeep and started to walk slowly toward the hidden voice. He was still sure it had to be Irving. He knew that voice anywhere. He blinked his eyes, trying to clear his obscured vision.

As he approached the voice, the gray pea soup slightly cleared. He saw several ghosts. They all had rifles pointed at him. He stopped.

"Don't shoot," he said. "I'll marry your daughter." Now why did he say that? He shook his head. His mind was clearing. There was no chicken soup, no coffee, no Myra, and certainly no Irving, just an Israeli army patrol. He was on the border. He turned toward the jeep. He had forgotten his tote bag. "Wait," he hollered. He ran back.

"Halt," he heard someone behind him shout. "Or I'll shoot."

It was a tense moment. The two Lebanese soldiers were frozen. They both gripped their rifles, ready to return fire. Another calmer voice intervened.

"Hold your fire, Herschel."

David wasn't sure, but he thought it was a woman's voice. He retrieved the tote bag and gripped it tightly. "Why don't you boys take off," he told the soldiers. "Thanks very much for your help." He shook their hands, pressing two ten dollar bills into each palm. They agreed, smiling. In a few seconds they had revved up the jeep and headed north back to Beirut.

This time David made it across the line. The ghosts mutated into Israeli soldiers. They lowered their M-1s and followed David with puzzled looks. The officer with the high voice eyed him.

"You are Captain David Gold?"

"Yes, I am. How did you know my name?"

"Listen, Boychik, you must be some important guy. Orders to escort you to Jerusalem came straight from the top."

"I'm not important, just tired. What day is it?"

"It's Friday morning. I'm Lieutenant Elkind. You can call me Sarah since you outrank me. Are you Army intelligence or CIA? You must be some kind of a hero."

"I'm neither." As he spoke, David began to feel nauseous.

"You know, I'm really sorry but I think I'm going to throw up." He walked to the side of the road, leaned over and vomited.

"Some hero," said Herschel. "He's so scared he's sick."

"Corporal Jacobs, shut up or I'll let Major Steinbaum know you almost shot the American. You'll be washing toilets for a month."

"Big deal, we risk our lives on this mountain road for some guy who gets sick when he meets some real soldiers."

The rest of the company remained prudently mute. Sarah Elkind walked slowly up to Corporal Jacobs, looked him in the eye, then removed his helmet and with the flat of her hand banged him loudly on the top of the head.

"You know, Herschel, you got a big mouth. If you don't shut it now, you will be a private no class for the rest of your military career. You will rotate from toilets to garbage."

Herschel started to answer, but this time discretion took hold. He retreated into a sullen silence.

David, thoroughly embarrassed by his vomiting, shakily lurched over to the jeep and leaned against it for support. He wiped his face with his sleeve. "I'm better," he muttered.

Sarah retrieved a large kerchief from a rucksack in the rear of the vehicle. "Wipe yourself off," she said curtly. "I think you need some rest. We're going to a camp in Tiberias. You can get some soup, clean clothes and some sleep. We can still get you to Jerusalem by Saturday evening."

"I'd be most grateful."

Sarah Elkind looked into the eyes and surveyed the battered face of this unlikely piece of human freight she had picked up at the border. She liked what she saw. "Come on, Captain Gold," she said softly. "Hop in. Elijah says we must give succor to the weary traveler. You look pretty weary to me."

As they drove rapidly along the mountain road, the curtain of mist began to rise and David noted they were on a barren, rocky hill overlooking a lush, well-cultivated valley. In the distance he could see what looked like a body of water.

"The Galilee," explained Sarah. "The land of milk and honey. The land of Canaan that the Lord forbade Moses to look upon."

David reached into his tote bag and felt for the prayer shawl. It was intact. It radiated surprising warmth, giving him renewed strength. He dozed, much comforted. He was in the hands of friends. As for the prayer shawl, it was home.

The Israeli military had constructed a base near Tiberias on the eastern shore of the Sea of Galilee. It consisted of the usual Quonset huts and a permanent headquarters building built of wood and sandstone. A rough plywood sign adorned the building, announcing both in Hebrew and English the home of the 2nd Israeli Infantry and Armored Division.

Sarah Elkind led David into the building to a back office. The door was closed and marked in small English letters Captain Avrom Basinger. Sara didn't bother to knock. She barged into the room.

A mustached, sunburned young man, wearing what passed for captain's bars on a rumpled khaki uniform, glanced up in annoyance. He was reading papers and seemed angry at being disturbed. His look changed to a smile when he saw Sarah. He rose and quickly scrutinized David.

"So this is the VIP." He offered his hand. "Captain Avrom Basinger."

He spoke in what David assumed to be a clipped English accent. In fact, with his handle bar mustache and military crew cut, he was a character right out of Her Majesty's horse marines.

"David Gold, I'm certainly glad to be here. My thanks to your people for picking me up. It's been a long trip."

"Well, why the hell are you here, Captain?"

"Avrom," interrupted Sarah. "He's had a tough time. He needs some food and rest. Why don't you let me get him fed and into a bunk. We can question him later."

Captain Basinger quickly agreed. It was obvious that the woman's word carried great weight with Avrom Basinger. He patted her affectionately on the cheek. "Take him to the mess hall and get him a room at the BOQ. I'll see you this evening."

He turned to David. "We will talk later, Captain Gold. I'm very interested in your mission."

So am I, thought David. I wish I knew what it was. David nodded with a tired half smile. "Thanks much for your hospitality."

Sarah led him briskly across what appeared to be a parade ground. Groups of men and women were precision drilling with both M-1 assault weapons and British Enfield rifles.

"We are out of the range of Syrian artillery here," explained Sarah. "They like to drop a few rounds on the valley every once in a while. From up there on the Golan." She gestured toward a range of mountains to the west. "It's annoying but not dangerous."

"Avrom," asked David, "is he your boyfriend?"

"We spend time together. He has a wife in Tel Aviv. Does that shock you?"

"Not really, Sarah. It's your business."

"It gets lonely out here. Avrom is a decent man. He was eighteen when he joined the British Army. He's been fighting ever since. Why did you ask that question?"

"I'm not sure." He inspected her more closely. This was not one of the pampered Jewish girls he had grown up with and dated. There was strength in her demeanor. More like his grandmother, the diminutive yet spunky, gray-haired lady who, before the turn of the century, had crossed the Atlantic Ocean. The journey had been in the noisy, smelly hold of a crowded ship, with four little kids, to join her husband in a strange world called Pittsburgh.

"I must be awfully tired. I'm sorry. I'm usually not that indiscreet."

Sarah shrugged. "I don't mind. We Israeli's are pretty blunt. We don't have time for small talk."

They entered a long, open-aired wooden building, guarded from the elements only by screens. It was pin clean. There were long rows of shiny tables. "Sit down over there." She pointed at a corner with smaller tables. "That is the officer's area. I'll bring you a tray."

He started to protest. "I can—"

"Sit," she ordered brusquely. "I don't have time to argue." It wasn't Myra talking. It was Grandma and there was no argument.

In a few minutes Sarah returned with a tray of food. There was steaming soup, some cold chicken and a Middle Eastern grain dish called tabuli, along with sliced tomatoes, pickled beets and fresh oranges.

Sarah watched him like a mother hen supervising her brood. "Eat, you need the nourishment."

He obeyed. The soup tasted like nectar of the gods. He ate slowly, a symptom of his utter fatigue.

"You Israelis," David said, "it must be difficult. Always on guard, waiting for the next incident to happen. Where do you get the energy? The faith to keep going? Often I feel guilty that I didn't help in 1948."

"Many Americans say that. They help with money and support. You are Jewish, but you are not an Israeli. I am a Sabra. I was born here in Haifa. We will survive because this is our land. We have no choice. This sacred land was given to us by God more than three thousand years ago. Before we give it up, we will die defending it. Where else can we go? Where else can the remnants of the death camps go? David, you live in a rich country. You wear the uniform of a great nation that can raise millions of men to fight tyranny. Only the American Jews were saved. Do you realize how lucky you are? For what should you feel guilty?"

"For being so lucky, I guess."

A hot breeze suddenly blew through the mess hall windows. It flapped the cardboard blinds and rattled the dishes. It caught David on his left cheek. Instinctively, he raised his left hand and rubbed his face. He felt a slight burning sensation. He was about to reply further to Sarah but paused instead. Without a word he rose and strode to the entrance of the building. He stepped outside onto the porch. Sarah followed him, puzzled but curious.

"David, what is it? Are you okay?"

He surveyed the large, flat, dusty field that stretched out in front of him. The green grass and trees had vanished. The soldiers were still drilling with their weapons, or were they? They were no longer in neat disciplined ranks. They had traded their khaki uniforms for robes and their boots for sandals. They were milling around in groups, some apparently shouting at each other. They carried spears and swords and some carried shields.

"Sarah," he muttered. "What is this place?"

He turned to her, but Sarah was gone and so were the mess hall and all the buildings. The field, now a barren brown plane, seemed bathed in a strange mist. Yet he could see the people clearly.

* * * *

Three men spied him and shouted, "Hail, Josephus!" They moved toward him. They were led by Gorion, his oldest son.

"The men fear for their families, Commander. With the Roman legions approaching they want to return and defend their towns."

"Gorion, in the name of God, piecemeal, we will be quickly destroyed. It's what Vespasian wants."

"So I have argued, Father, but to no avail. The mutineers persist. They should be put to death."

Briskly, he made his way across the field to the center of the large gathering. As he approached, their strident voices ceased. He held up his right hand. "Cease this destructive bickering! If we divide ourselves now, the Romans will surely crush us town by town."

The spokesman for the mutineers was, as he suspected, John of Gischala. "Tell us all, Josephus. What will you do when this army is destroyed and our women and children are at the mercy of Nero? How will you prevent the young from being sold as slaves, the women from being concubines for the Roman soldiers and the men from being crucified? We cannot meet the Romans in open field. We must defend from fortifications. Only then can we protect and save our families. If you stand in our way, we shall surely kill you."

"As I recall, Gischala, you were a principal agitator to start this war with the Romans. Now you default. I tell you we can meet and defeat the Romans. I have trained you all in their tactics. Together we are an army. But divided and separated, we are nothing but a rabble."

But the grumbling mass of men began to shake their fists at Josephus. Their protests became louder. A huge, bearded man in the front rank, who towered above the crowd, cried out in a shrill voice. "I go to my town, to Bethmaus. Men of Bethmaus, do you follow your leader?" He turned and made his way through the crowd followed by a large contingent.

It was the break in the dam. In sizeable numbers the men filed off the field and continued their respective journeys in different directions, toward their towns, their homes and families. Nothing Josephus could do or say would discourage them from their course. The army he had painstakingly trained, his well-laid plans to ambush the enemy and fight a hit-and-run war, his vision of defeating the Romans with innovative tactics all vanished. He turned to Gischala who watched with apparent approval.

"Execute Gischala," shouted Gorion. He unleashed his sword.

"Sheathe your weapon, Gorion. Jews cannot kill Jews. In a short time there will be plenty of Jewish corpses to go around."

"Well then, Gischala, where do you go to fight the war?"

"I go to the only fortified city that will withstand the Romans. I go to Jerusalem. The Romans will never reduce the fortress of Antonia."

"Jerusalem is dead, Gischala. You have sealed its fate. The city of David shall suffer great tragedy. The Jewish race shall be scattered to the ends of the earth."

"Nonsense! The Romans will never breach the walls of Jerusalem!" Gischala, bristling with anger shouted. "Who follows Gischala to Jerusalem?"

Several more men deserted the group and followed John of Gischala to the South Road. Josephus watched them depart in anguished silence.

"Father, what do we do now? Can this handful of men fight the mighty Roman legions?"

"No, impossible. It appears Vespasian has God on his side," Gorion said.

Josephus pondered a moment, then decided. The few men left were from the city of Jotapata. This was a city, strategically placed on high ground, that could be fortified and perhaps held against the Roman legions.

"We go to Jotapata. We can build strong defenses there. You go to Jerusalem. Bid your mother and brothers to leave and go to Masada. I will meet you in Masada. Our chances are slim but perhaps we can devise some means of blunting the Roman juggernaut." Secretly, he was convinced all was lost and the sorely divided Jews would be cut to pieces.

* * * *

"David! David! What's wrong? Talk to me. Are you all right?"

David Gold closed his eyes and blinked. The Israeli Sarah was back. The mess hall reappeared. The khaki-clad soldiers were marching smartly on the field, calling cadence. The blue and white Israeli banner flapped in the wind on a flagpole in the center of the well-manicured drill field.

"David, your eyes were strange. They were vacant and far away. What is it? What's going on? Are you ill?"

"I'm okay. I'm very tired. I need to sleep. What was this place?"

"It was always an army camp. Even in Biblical times."

"That's what I suspected, Sarah. I have been here before. A long time ago I stood out there, on a hot, dusty plain and watched the Jewish armies melt like wax. It was the beginning of the end for the Jewish state. As the prophet Samuel said to Saul, 'The battle is not yours but God's. Do you not know the end will be bitter.' I knew it and I couldn't stop them."

Lieutenant Sarah Elkind placed her arm affectionately around David's shoulder. "David, you are far more tired than I thought. You are having delusions. Let's get you to a shower, then a bunk and some sleep now—or your mission will surely fail."

CHAPTER 39

THE THIRD WEEK, FRIDAY
BORIS GUREVICH

When Boris Gurevich departed the Soviet Union in October 1950, he was in a hurry. In fact, he left some of his most precious possessions in Moscow. Chief among them were his wife, Irina, and his son, Nikolai. He had sewn American greenbacks into his coat. He had gathered the dollars during his assignment as a KGB agent in Budapest. This had given him ample funds. He had developed many contacts in the Western intelligence community. As an archaeologist with a modest reputation, and aided by his friends in the CIA, he was able to get across the line into Austria.

One of those American agents instrumental in his escape was a Professor Harold Throckmorton, a noted professor of antiquities who had been excavating Roman ruins in Budapest and other Balkan countries. The professor was arrested later during a failed coup in a small South American country. He was shot before the agency could rescue him, leaving behind his grieving widow and their oldest child, Benson, who followed his father's footsteps into the archaeological field.

Not one day passed without Boris consciously plotting his wife and son's escape. To date, he had been singularly unsuccessful. Boris's defection was a serious thorn in the side of the KGB. Irina was closely watched, her phone tapped and her movements tracked. She was not arrested. Boris was able to get a few coded messages to her, but such contacts were brief, and few and far between.

One hour before Benson had called with his own dilemma about Maggie's death, the Sicarians and the cursed dagger, Boris had received another message through a Bulgarian house painter who assured him the offer was valid. It was a simple statement: "Put fifty thousand dollars into a numbered bank account in Switzerland within two weeks, and your wife and son will be delivered, in good health, to checkpoint H on the Austrian Hungarian border."

Boris was no novice to the intricate byways of the Communist underground. He knew it could be a trap, an extortion plot or an elaborate conspiracy hatched by some of his old enemies seeking retribution. Yet, he felt compelled to explore the remote possibility that the offer was legitimate. He called a former contact at the agency in Washington. The man was out of town for two days and could not be reached. If the offer was real, there was a second barrier to success. With his meager resources, fifty thousand dollars was a small fortune. Raising it legally within the short time frame would be a real problem. The agency might help but could he afford to wait for the ponderous bureaucracy to act?

When Benson Throckmorton called for help and Boris determined that Benson had personal possession of the golden dagger of Hammurabi, the germ of a plan began to grow inside him. Boris Gurevich was not a treacherous man. He was, however, a pragmatist. Benson's father had been a good friend. He had helped Boris get out of Hungary and later, obtain a position at Columbia where he was now a respected member of the faculty. He would always support and protect Harold Throckmorton's son. But to miss an opportunity to rescue his beloved Irina was unthinkable.

In Russian culture, convoluted conspiracy is the common mindset. Since the days of Ivan the Terrible, Russian czars and their Communist successors betrayed and murdered each other with regularity. Boris had no thought of murdering Benson. But there were two strong points in favor of his plan. One, Hammurabi's dagger would bring an excellent price and a quick monetary return on the antiquities black market. Two, no one knew that he was going to Pittsburgh. He could slip into town, obtain the dagger and be out in a few hours. No one would be the wiser. It might take a week to get the appropriate buyer. With luck he would have the cash in ten days—plenty of time to meet the deadline. He was sure he could convince Benson to turn over the dagger. Certainly Benson would understand. Benson could claim the dagger was stolen. Later, Boris knew he could devise a way to get it back. They would both be heroes. But above all, his wife would be in the West and his son could grow up in a country where he was free, not oppressed and stifled by government control. A country where he could sleep in peace, could attend any school he desired and be anything he wanted.

Boris arrived at Greater Pittsburgh airport at 12:10 P.M. One hour later, a yellow taxicab deposited him in front of the William Penn Hotel. By this time Boris Gurevich was an agitated and desperate man. While still rational, he was single-mindedly focused on his purpose: he must obtain the dagger and then check out the alleged rescue plan. He would not take no for an answer. He called Benson in Room 1110, and soon vigorously knocked on the door.

When Benson heard Boris Gurevich's voice he heaved a deep sigh of relief. He opened the door carefully and Boris stepped into the room. To Benson, the presence of this huge bear of a man, with his assured calm and broad smile, brought him a sense of safety and security. The marines had arrived. "Damn, Boris," he said, "I sure am glad to see you."

"I'm glad to see you, Tovarich. We will get an action plan going. We will get these so-called Sicarians and eliminate them."

Boris Gurevich had a serious problem. Americans did not understand the art of intrigue. Russians understood that in a plan, only the end result was important. You could break your word, double-cross a friend or an enemy, lie, cheat or scheme, even make a deal with the devil, but you had to have a legitimate objective. To Boris, no objective was more legitimate than the rescue of his wife and son. But he understood that Benson, while sympathetic to his plight, would never relinquish the dagger if there was only a remote possibility that they could at some time in the distant future find a way to steal it back. He needed a more devious plan. He needed to create a situation where the dagger was stolen and Benson believed what occurred was a bona fide robbery. Then when Boris retrieved the dagger, he would be a hero.

And if he didn't get it back? That would be, as his American friends often said, "The way the cookie crumbles."

"Your mother is safe?" Boris needed small talk to distract Benson while his plan took shape.

"She is at her sister's in Ambridge. They have no reason to harm her."

"True, their next victim has to be related to the legate. That's why I believe Sal's wife Catherine will either be taken hostage or murdered."

Benson brightened up. "Of course, they need a hostage and the legatee's wife is the obvious choice. Why kill her? She is of no use to them dead."

"Exactly. So Tovarich, we position ourselves outside Catherine's house tonight, and we wait for them. Perhaps we can intercept them and finish this matter once and for all."

"I hope so. I must go to my bank now and secure the dagger from my safety deposit box."

"Not a good idea, Benson. All they will need is the key."

"But what can I do? The museum isn't safe. I can't leave it at home. I can't carry it around. I must find somewhere to hide it."

"Tovarich, tonight I feel we can resolve this matter. I have to stop at my hotel to get something from my suitcase. Then we will have a meal. I am hungry as a bear."

"But how can we resolve it tonight? How?"

"During lunch I will explain. After lunch we will go back to your office. I need to make some long distance calls. Then we wait for dark."

"We call the police?"

"No police. My revolver will be the police. This will be a KGB-style operation."

****

The mild weather had turned cool, the first signs of winter already apparent. Periodically, the full moon, a pale lantern in the night, would burst from behind a heavy cloud cover revealing the world and its hidden secrets, only to retreat quickly behind another cloud bank that hovered over the city. The ancients had worshipped the full moon. First the Druids, then other cults were mesmerized by its place in the heavens. It brought on madness in certain beings, stifling inhibition and feeding an impulse that could result in rampaging violence and murder. Benson thought of the werewolf legends and the human sacrifices of the Aztecs.

Sitting in a parked, darkened car, Benson shivered. He was sorry he had not brought a warmer jacket. He glanced at Boris. The Russian, a veteran of many freezing winters on the steppes outside Kharkov, didn't seem to notice the chill. Boris had been nipping out of a small metal flask. Benson could smell the alcohol. In the confines of the closed car, the pungent, sour odor caused him to feel slightly ill.

They had been parked for over an hour watching Catherine's house. The street was deserted save for parked cars. Earlier, a crowd of rowdy boys had been hanging around, laughing, shouting and smoking cigarettes, but they had long since departed for somewhere warmer.

"Do you think they will come?" Benson was anxious. This whole operation seemed fruitless. Yet, he trusted the old spy's instincts. Boris Gurevich was a pro.

"Patience, they will come," assured Boris. "Once in Warsaw I waited seven hours in a truck for a German general to leave a prostitute's apartment. It was snowing."

"What happened?"

"When he came out we blew him up him with seven sticks of dynamite. He and his driver and his Mercedes. They went out with a glorious bang. Don't worry, they will come!"

It had been a deeply confusing day for Benson. The museum had reported the dagger as stolen. Benson confided to the head curator that he had the dagger safely hidden. Then before Benson could stop him, the curator broadcast the news over the intercom to the guards. He felt they had a right to know. In the meantime, Boris had made a number of mysterious long distance calls on the museum phone. Add Maggie's funeral to the events of the last twelve hours and Benson knew he was living the worst day of his life.

"Boris, I need to get some air. Can we open the window?"

"Just open it slightly. An open window is a sign of habitation. We must be absolutely quiet."

Benson sighed. He didn't understand. Why didn't they just alert the police? Surely Captain Seiler would have assigned some officers.

Two men came up the street singing. Friday night revelers coming back from the local bar. Or were they? Weaving unsteadily up the street, they paused in front of Catherine's house. They were singing in raucous, off-key voices, a chorus of "My Wild Irish Rose." They were loud, maybe too loud. They were drunk, maybe too drunk. Boris slipped his Beretta from under his greatcoat and checked the safety. His arm gently pushed down on the door handle so he could exit quickly. But the men moved on and when they passed under the streetlight, Boris relaxed. A false alarm.

Benson checked his watch. Another two hours had passed. It was close to midnight. Benson began to yawn. An overwhelming weariness engulfed him. Boris had been silent for more than an hour. This was becoming a useless exercise. Why not give up and go back to the hotel? Benson needed sleep so badly. He was just plain out of gas. He started to tell Boris of his exhausted state when Boris nudged him into silence.

"One of them just went around back. I almost missed him. Let's go. They move fast. Stay behind me."

For a large man, Boris moved like a nimble panther, an ancient warrior stalking his prey. He stopped behind a tree directly in front of the house. The lights had remained on. Inside, they heard a loud crash, shouts. Then two shots. The door was thrown open and a figure, dressed entirely in black, darted out the front door.

On the first shout, Benson had broken cover and run for the house. Boris could not restrain him. "No, Benson!" he shouted.

The two figures collided, like two blind freight trains on the same track. Benson was thrown against a tree and lay stretched on the ground. The fleeing figure stopped momentarily. He stumbled, but recovered his balance and resumed his flight.

Boris shot him four times in rapid succession. The intruder was dead on the second shot. The third shot tore into his throat, the fourth into the top of his head.

Boris Gurevich had seen death many times. But nothing unnerved him more than the sight of Professor Throckmorton's son lying prostrate on the ground. He feared that one of his shots had struck his friend. He crouched over Benson and felt his pulse. It was beating. He was alive. There was no blood. Perhaps he was only unconscious. He glanced around. No one had yet come out of the house. The door was open. In the distance he could hear a siren. He reached under Benson's sweater, into an inner pocket and retrieved a foot-long leather case. He slipped it into his greatcoat, rose and started toward the house. His plan had worked. Benson would believe the dagger was stolen. Irina would be saved.

A man stepped out of the shadows of a nearby tree and shot Boris Gurevich twice in the back with a silencer. When Boris fell, the man, moving with lightening speed, rolled him over, threw open the greatcoat and took the leather case. He vanished, swallowed by the darkness, a phantom, a specter in the night, seen and heard by no one.

* * * *

Stanley Arnold Kowalczyk was not known for his mental acuity. The oldest in a tribe of five, all boys save one, he earned and paid for a bachelor's degree in business by spending Saturdays every September to January, for three years, as varsity left tackle for the University of Pittsburgh. He was well-known for his relentless skill, for diagnosing a play and viciously chopping down an opposing ball carrier. In his senior year he was nominated for All-American and missed the honor by two votes. One of Frank Leahy's Notre Dame boys made the cut.

Stanley, or Stush as his friends called him, was also, as his sister Catherine insisted, a pussycat off the gridiron. He was good humored. He did not engage in barroom brawls as his three brothers often did. He was slow to anger. He was conscientious in his work and protective of his mother and younger sister. He was gentle with babies and kind to old ladies and pets.

When Benson Throckmorton warned him of an impending danger to his sister, all he could think was what crap, especially coming from this silly looking character in the Mr. Magoo eyeglasses. Then he reconsidered. A lot of funny stuff had been happening. Especially since his brother-in-law Sal had been placed in the restraint ward of the psychiatric hospital.

After the funeral he had a lunch of sausage and fried potatoes at his mother's house. He then phoned Sal's brother.

Art Dematteo had just returned from a frustrating session with Tom Fogarty, Sal's new doctor. He had been told they could find nothing organically wrong with Sal. They had suspected a possible brain tumor but skull X-rays and other neurological tests showed no sign of one. A true man of action, Art wanted answers, fast. To date, there were none. That his brother was mentally ill was just not a possibility.

So when Art answered Stan's call, he was already agitated. "What the hell do you mean Catherine might be in danger? From who?"

"I'm not sure, Art, but this goofball Benson says we should keep our eye on her for the next couple of days."

"Okay, I'll be over around five. Don't leave her side. We'll talk some more. I'll bring some backup."

Art went upstairs to his dresser, opened the bottom drawer, dug through a mound of shirts, sweat pants and socks and extracted a .38 police special that had belonged to his uncle. Uncle Louie had taught him to shoot when he was twelve years old. "Art," he used to say, "you are a natural cowboy. You have the reaction and instincts of a killer. You either have to be a hit man or a cop." Art settled for a career as a fighter pilot. The pay was better, and the Air Force furnished a free, faster-than-sound toy that brought an adrenalin rush far superior to anything the mob or law enforcement could offer.

He checked the weapon carefully, loaded six bullets into the chamber, set the safety and pocketed the revolver. He hoped some sonofabitch would try to hurt Catherine. It would be his pleasure to welcome the bastard to perdition.

* * * *

When Art arrived at Catherine's house it was well past six o'clock. Stan, his younger brother Andrew, Catherine and the baby were eating dinner. Stan was on his first beer and Joe was on his second.

Big Joe, as his friends called him, was the antithesis of his older brother. An intolerant, humorless man, he was quick to anger and merciless in a fight. However, as a rival for Stan on the football field, he failed. Fortunately, he did have a talent that gained him a four-year scholarship at Pitt's eternal rival, Penn State. His accuracy as a kicker was amazing. He rarely missed an extra point. He could straddle the goal posts from forty yards out when the team needed a field goal. As linebacker or a guard he was a failure. One hard scramble during a play and Andy was in a fight. He had so many personal fouls by the second game of the season that he was banned, except as the team kicker.

"Hey, Art." Stan welcomed his brother-in-law with a broad smile. "Have you eaten?"

"More spaghetti than I needed."

"Well, have a beer. You remember Joe?"

"Sure, at Sal's wedding he got into a fight. Almost started a riot with the Northside mob." Art extended his hand.

"How are you, Joe?"

"Can't complain; still playing soldier, are you?"

"Regular paycheck and my own toy F-86 for play time."

Art leaned over and kissed Catherine on the cheek. "Hey, beautiful, you okay?"

Catherine forced a smile. "I'm trying, Art."

Art sat down, spent a moment tickling the baby's hand and then said in a gruff voice "Where the hell is Sal's Jewish partner? Why isn't the big shot here?"

"I'm not sure," answered Catherine. "But he's on some kind of a mission for the Air Force."

"Mission! For the Air Force, Jesus, at a time like this. I think he's yellow. Skipped town to get away. Scared, abandoned my brother. Damn it!"

"I don't think so, Artie." Catherine's response was meek and unsure. "His trip has something to do with Sal's illness. He cares a lot about Sal."

"What? What can he possibly do somewhere else? It's all happening here!"

"I don't know, Artie." Catherine began to sob quietly.

"I'm sorry, kid. I'm so damn mixed up. None of this makes any sense."

"Have a beer," muttered Joe. "You'll feel better."

Stan popped a Fort Pitt and shoved it toward Art. "Stay cool, buddy. It's gonna be a long night."

By 11:00 P.M. Stan had had six beers, Joe had consumed seven and been to the bathroom three times. Ever the circumspect warrior, Art had downed three. So far there had been no incidents, and the three men were beginning to relax. They sat in the front room arguing for hours on the merits of Knute Rockne and Jock Sutherland, legendary coaches in the football world. At 11:25 Andy headed upstairs for his fourth bathroom break. After nine beers, his kidneys cried out in protest.

Stan had been eyeing a fishbowl all evening. He was hypnotized by the lone goldfish that kept swimming in the same circle for several hours. Art noticed Stan's fascination with the fish. "Like a Polish fighter pilot, hey, Stan, flying in circles."

Stan chuckled. "Now, you tell an Italian joke and then it's my turn again."

"How about this one. What does it say on one end of a Polish beer bottle?"

"Artie, that's not fair. You tell Italian jokes. I get to tell Polish jokes. Okay, one more for you. What does it say?"

"Open other end."

Stan's chuckle abruptly ceased. His eyes opened wide in surprise, and his relaxed mood changed quickly to fourth down and a yard to go. A figure in black had rounded the corner from the kitchen and paused like a stealthy cat. The figure had a long, thin knife in his right hand and was heading for Art.

"Artie! Look out!"

Art turned, saw the attacker, rolled over the back of the sofa and landed on his feet.

Stan seized the fishbowl and hurled it at the oncoming figure. It caught the assailant full in the face and splattered. The force stopped the intruder and sent him reeling backwards. Art's .38, which he had concealed in his jacket, was now in his hand. It barked twice. The figure dropped like a lead weight and struck the floor with a resounding thud.

A second assailant had started upstairs, secure in the notion that only a woman and a baby were awaiting him. Earlier, his leader assured him there would be no resistance. He was to kidnap the woman, not harm the baby and quickly exit. About a third of the way up the stairs, he met a giant. The giant barred his way. He lashed out with his knife, which should have struck the man in the stomach. For his size the giant moved quickly. The knife hit a left ankle and drew blood, which enraged the huge man who lashed out with his right foot and caught the assailant in the middle of his groin. The assailant screamed. The pain was excruciating. He reeled back down the stairs, smashing against a nearby wall.

He had been trained to resist pain and somehow recovered from the powerful kick. But fear now trumped pain and the mission. He headed for the front door.

Out of the corner of his eye he saw his partner sprawled on the floor in a pool of blood. Throwing open the front door, he dashed down onto the walk leading from the house. He crashed headlong into another form that went flying against a nearby tree. Now terror stricken, he managed to recover again and continue his flight. Then he was struck twice by what felt like the hoof of an elephant, Boris Gurevich's first two shots. At that point he gave up. He didn't feel the second two bullets. He was dead before he hit the sidewalk.

CHAPTER 40

THIRD WEEK, SATURDAY
ED FLAHARTY

When Flaharty arrived he was greeted by a scene out of the St. Valentine's Day massacre. It was either a mob fracas or a battle scene. What else could have resulted in this mayhem?

Outside were two bodies, both shot dead. One on his back and the other one lying on his face. An additional dead body, also shot twice, lay still bleeding inside the house. That figure had numerous cuts and wounds, as well as a dark pool of blood underneath his head. Shattered glass and water were splattered everywhere on the floor of living room, as well as sixteen empty beer bottles on the floor, on the tables and various other spots around the area.

Inside, Ed also found a terrified Catherine Dematteo, clutching her baby and circled by her two brothers. A dazed young man sat on the couch, holding his head, while another young man carefully ministered first aid to him.

Ever patient, Flaharty, the consummate cop, began to give orders.

"Don't," he said. "Don't touch or move anything until forensic has made their examination of the scene. Officer Randall will bring you one by one into the dining room and take statements. I must warn all of you that you have the right to remain silent and that anything you say may be used..."

He paused and did a double take on Benson. "Hey, don't I know you? You're the guy from the Carnegie Museum. What was this, some kind of a drunken brawl?"

He glanced at the two brothers, both bleary-eyed and exhausted. "Aren't you guys ashamed, with a little baby here?"

"Detective Flaharty," stammered Benson, still dizzy from the collision, "look at the clothes on two of the dead guys. They were professional assassins."

Flaharty studied the body of the dead man. He was dressed from head to foot in black. He wore black pants, dark, dingy leather boots, a charcoal shirt partially covered by a black vest. The most puzzling item of all was a black ski mask that, save for two slits for eyes, a small breathing hole and a horizontal gap for the mouth, covered his face. There was a small dead goldfish in the middle of the mask.

Flaharty reached down and yanked the covering off the dead guy's face. The guy was young. He had knotted dark hair and swarthy skin. Didn't look much like a soldier in any Mafia family.

"What the hell is goin' on here?" He turned to a nearby uniform. "Call downtown. Get hold of Captain Seiler. If Becker is on duty, get him out here."

Benson, holding his forehead where a large red lump had now appeared, rose gingerly and studied the dead man out of his left eye. His right eye had almost completely closed.

A medic had arrived. One glance at Benson convinced him that the guy needed treatment. "Mister, if you can walk, you better come with me. Better yet, why don't we get a stretcher. You might have a concussion."

"Wait." Benson continued to examine the man's face. "Let's go look at the other guy."

Benson started to walk. He grimaced. His left leg and lower back were howling in protest. Benson tried to ignore the pain as he made his way outside followed by the medic, a uniformed cop and Ed Flaharty.

Thick clouds had obscured the full moon and masked this violent scene. Suddenly, bright moonlight made one of its appearances.

It bathed the two dead bodies in a ghostly pallor that emphasized their tormented, next-world state.

Sick with guilt and remorse at seeing Boris's corpse, Benson felt a wave of nausea. Then he saw the face of the second assailant. "My God," he said turning to Flaharty. "I know these men. They are the two guards we hired at the museum after the murders two weeks ago."

Then the full tragic impact of the event became apparent. Somebody had taken the leather case containing the ancient artifact from his inner pocket. It wasn't Boris, so there must have been a third assailant. This unknown had killed Boris and escaped without a trace. He had stolen Hammurabi's dagger. All of their collective efforts, Maggie's death, involving Boris in the matter, sending David to Jerusalem, all in vain. The Sicarians had won. Or so Benson thought.

CHAPTER 41

THE THIRD WEEK, SATURDAY
WESTERN STATE PSYCHIATRIC INSTITUTE

The hospital was like a graveyard. A sanitized mausoleum, complete with shiny metal doors and ornate numbers that catalogued the tombs of the living ghosts. The halls were devoid of furniture, pictures or decoration. Most of the light was artificial, a pale florescence that colored the few early Saturday inhabitants with gray, shapeless features and created the illusion of zombies wandering without destination or purpose.

Max hated Saturdays. This particular Saturday was a day he would never forget. He kept expecting Maggie to round the corner, sound off with a cheerful, early-morning greeting and ask if he had his coffee yet. He could not yet fathom that there was no Maggie and there would be no Maggie from this time forward. The mere thought raised waves of anxiety inside him.

Max hurried to his office. Perhaps the more familiar surroundings would calm him down. With its easterly exposure, the office was awash with bright sunlight. He sank into his chair and wanted to ring for a nurse. There was no nurse and no Maggie. He needed to hire a behavioral psychologist. But not today.

On an impulse he dialed Marcia Miller's number. A Mrs. Miller answered. Who the hell was Mrs. Miller? Marcia wasn't married.

"Sorry," said a refined voice, "Marcia is still sleeping."

Marcia's mother, dumb head. Max apologized. He would call back in an hour. He rubbed his hands together, agitated. He needed to talk to someone. A human who could empathize with the aching melancholy he felt.

He stared at the seascape. He focused on the sailing ship caught in the foaming whirlpool. In the swirl of churning violence, he could feel the final agony of this ship as it headed toward certain destruction. Perhaps there was peace inside this agitated mass of water. That was what he wanted most, some escape from the reality of a world where he spent his days dealing with disturbed minds who continually cried out for help. Frustrated, he heard their wrenching tales and knew there were so many sick minds he really couldn't help. Max was drowning. The waters were closing over him. One random shot at a fleeing car and an important human being was lost forever. There was no reason for him to live. Take some pills; seek serenity.

The phone jangled. He ignored it. It jangled again, an insistent, determined ring that would not go away.

He reluctantly answered. "Dr. Vogel here." It was Bernicke.

"Say that again, Bernicke. I don't understand. There is something funny going on. What exactly is happening? Somebody has given orders to fill up the ice tub and prepare someone for electroshock therapy. Prepare whom? Talk slowly, Bernicke. No, you won't get fired for calling me. Sal Dematteo! Who gave those orders? Oh my God, no. Drag your feet. Don't commence any treatment. I'll be right there."

Electroshock therapy or electroconvulsive therapy (ECT) was conducted in the basement of the hospital. The theory was that electronic impulses induced to the brain by low-voltage alternating current would result in harmless convulsions and a coma, which, while usually lasting only five minutes, would produce a therapeutic response, especially in cases of acute schizophrenia. Unfortunately, in many cases ECT also resulted in a post-confusional state sometimes lasting hours, and memory impairment often lasting for weeks. Other side effects such as some loss of intellectual capacity were also known to occur.

The elevator took forever. Max knew that pressing the button several times was futile. But he leaned on the button anyway in the faint hope that the continuous signal of the buzzer would somehow deter what was about to happen in the basement. He could hear creaking machinery in the distance, but the elevator never seemed to arrive. He thought about the stairs, but they were at the other end of the building.

At last, with an audible sigh, the vessel groaned to a stop. The door, timed to move slowly so that no unsuspecting patients would have their arms or legs pinned during transport, finally opened. An empty elevator loomed in front of Max. He quickly entered and once again the steel carriage began its journey, this time downward, hopefully the next stop being the basement. It wasn't. He had pressed the lobby button in his haste. The elevator paused two floors down, the door went through its perennial struggle and finally opened, once again to a scene of vacant desolation. Max wondered if aliens had attacked the hospital and all human life had been destroyed. He frantically pressed the down button. But the elevator had a mind of its own and would not be rushed. While it crawled to its destination, Max had visions of bolts of electricity tearing into Sal Dematteo's brain, attacking the nervous system, baking the cranium and severing ganglia and nerves.

Max reached the basement just in time to see two white-coated attendants wheeling a cart with a supine figure through the door into the therapy room.

The so-called therapy or treatment room was a white-tiled, large cubicle inhabited by several hot and cold tubs. Wires lay strewn everywhere, and obsolete equipment gathered dust in the corners. It resembled, as Max had often observed, a medieval torture chamber.

Max charged into the room prepared for battle. He was met with a spirited argument between Bernicke and the two attendants who had definite marching orders from a very senior official to prepare the patient for electroconvulsive therapy.

Bernicke had firmly planted his rather portly figure between a metal tub packed with ice and the cart where Sal Dematteo reclined, his eyes open, but clearly confused. Max sensed that he had already been given a shot of succinylcholine, a powerful muscle relaxant given to patients prior to administering ECT.

"No fuckin' way you guys are putting this patient in that tub," he said adamantly.

The two men hesitated. Bernicke was another authority figure and neither had stomach for a clash with him.

Max surveyed the scene. Sal was lying completely at rest on the cart.

"Take Mr. Dematteo back to his room, now."

Once again the pair hesitated. The door behind Max was filled with an imperious figure, a furious Dr. Bernard Adler, whose anger at finding Max in the room sent him into a rage.

"Dr. Vogel," he said. "This procedure is being administered at my orders. Do you dare—"

"Fine, this man is my patient, and I am countermanding your order. You just can't wait to prove your point can you, Bernie? You can't wait to tout your theory at the convention in New York. You promised me a week. I've two more days. You broke your word. That is unethical and reprehensible. Not like you at all, Dr. Adler."

"Two days," shouted Adler. "You can't do anything in two days. It's a useless delay. This man is critical. He needs treatment now!"

"Your diagnosis, not mine. Both Tom Fogarty and I agreed to two more days. If you persist, I'll bring a lawsuit through the family. It may destroy both our careers but I don't care."

For what seemed like an eternity, the two men glared at each other in a standoff. Max, his eyes wide in a mixture of fear and defiance, and Adler, his left cheek pulsating and his face a deep red. Only the drip drip of the water in the ice tub punctured the stunning silence.

Bernicke and the two orderlies were petrified. They were about to watch two medical titans come to blows. Who, if anybody, should they support? Bernicke's allegiance was clear. To him, Max Vogel had been a benevolent prince. Never in his fifteen-year career in working with mental patients had a doctor treated him with more respect and consideration. To Bernicke, only Maggie Seiler was a greater person, and she had been a goddess. He might lose his job, his pension and his seniority, but he was firm in his commitment.

"I'm sorry, Dr. Adler," he said quietly, "but there is no way I can permit you to override Dr. Vogel."

Instead of infuriating Bernie Adler more, Bernicke's calm pronouncement caused him to pause. For the first time, he seemed to realize that there were others present and the enormity of his personal actions became apparent. His anger fizzled. His fuse flickered and sputtered out.

He sighed. "You are right, Max, I promised you a week. I broke my word." He turned to the orderlies. "Please take Mr. Dematteo back to his room and make him comfortable. Max, let's get a cup of coffee and talk this over."

The crisis had ended. At least for now.

On the way to the cafeteria Bernie Adler put his arm around Max's shoulder.

"I'm sorry, sometimes we allow science to overrule what is ethical and the duty to our patients. I would have given you six months. But a week, of what conceivable consequence is a week? I was angered by your stupid decision."

Max considered the question. "Bernie, as impossible as the premise sounds, I believe that a week is all the time I will need." As he spoke he wondered where David was and what he was doing.

* * * *

In Jerusalem it was 3:00 P.M. and as dusk approached Jews everywhere prepared for the holiest evening of the year: the Kol Nidre, the prelude to the fasting and prayer of the Day of Atonement. It was the time when the righteous chanted in Aramaic to ask forgiveness for all their sins. Soon, Jews the world over would lift their voices, begging absolution from the Lord for their many trespasses, the confession of a whole people.

For Max Vogel, the day was only beginning. But for David Gold, who was travelling to the Jaffa Gate outside the ancient stone walls of the three-thousand-year-old city of Jerusalem, a long and terrifying night awaited.

CHAPTER 42

THE THIRD WEEK, SATURDAY
THE ROAD TO JERUSALEM

If the Middle East were a huge pancake and the Mediterranean Sea a great, rectangular pot of water, the Holy Land would be less than a tiny fingertip on the eastern end of the pot.

For four millennia, the armies of the world had fought over this virtually barren strip of land. Untold tribes of people had left their footprints in the desert sands of the Negev and the Sinai, the rugged desolate hills of Qumran and the fertile breadbasket of the Galilee. From this postage stamp on the map, three major religions sprang, survived and flourished.

The secular western world and the eastern world, from Morocco across Africa and the vast continent of Asia to the islands of Indonesia, had been shaped by those religions' teachings, myths and realities. At the heart of this ancient land is the city of Jerusalem, the city where David ruled in Judea and Solomon built the first temple as a place of worship for the Jews. During its long and venerable history, first chronicled by the Holy Bible, it had seen some joy, but also much sorrow, blood and hatred. The Hebrews, the Canaanites, the Philistines and later the Hittites, the Assyrians, and the Babylonians, followed by the Egyptians and the Romans, all shed their blood over this patch of land. In the Middle Ages the Muslims, led by Saladin, and the Christian knights of the Crusades clashed in two hundred years of combat. Finally, the Christians, their zeal abated, their ranks decimated by the Black Death in Europe, retreated. For five hundred years, Palestine was left to the Ottoman Turks, only to be invaded by the English and the French when the Ottoman Empire, rife with corruption, decayed and fell after World War I. All of these nations left mounds of dead to sanctify the soil of the Holy Land. Soldiers killed in a thousand forgotten battles. Now it was left to the Arabs and the Jews to settle the ownership question in a trial by combat.

Mohammed Ben Raffir entered the dimly lit cave. His movements were catlike, soundless. Not even a rustle of his garment disturbed the man who surveyed a large map of Palestine, illumined only by a solitary flickering oil lantern.

The shabby wood sign on the cave wall read Arabic Operations Central. The Israelis called it Terror Central. This was one of the many nerve centers the Syrians had built and hidden to confuse the Israelis and keep them guessing as to when and from where the next guerilla attack would take place.

"Major Wahid," Raffir said. "We have a problem. The American escaped from Beirut. Katoubian and five of his men are dead. The bastard Rasheed wiped them out."

The other man raised his head slowly, as if the statement made no outward impression. For a fleeting second his dark eyes flashed a message of passionate hatred. Then he was back to business.

"We will deal with Rasheed another time. Do you know where the Jews have hidden the American?"

"They do not hide him. He is in full view in Tiberias. Our source believes he will be transported to Jerusalem this afternoon. The Great One has ordered our cell to destroy him at all costs."

Major Mohammed Wahid was a careful man. He did not appreciate risking his precious resources on risky ventures.

"Assad has ordered this operation?" he asked

"No, our leader in Lebanon," Raffir said.

"I will ask Assad for permission to set an ambush. We will be in Hashemite territory."

For several minutes he studied the map. His finger traced the main road from Tiberias to Jerusalem. He pointed to a spot about two-thirds of the way between the Israeli army camp and the city of Jerusalem.

"Here, we will ambush them. This is where the road dips down into a steep gully. We can block the road on both sides, trap the convoy and destroy them. We will need four men. I also want a Muslim truck driver who yearns for paradise. I want the truck loaded with plenty of plastic explosives. We must know exactly when the convoy leaves Tiberias."

"It shall be done. Ishtar wills it."

"Quiet, fool," the major said. "If the Muslims hear you, we will join Katoubian."

He tapped the spot on the map with his middle finger. "Here, we will capture the American. We will make him sorry he ever set foot in this land." He paused, then asked, "Why, Raffir, is he here?"

"We think he carries a message from the CIA to a contact in Jerusalem."

"What kind of message?"

"We are not sure. But he flew into Beirut in an American warplane and contacted Rasheed. I believe he carries orders to an American agent in the old city."

Wahid looked puzzled. "It doesn't make any sense. Why send a message by such a roundabout route?"

"I don't know," shrugged Raffir. "But what does it matter? Tomorrow he will be dead."

Major Wahid allowed only a faint smile to disturb his stoic composure. "Yes, he will be dead. But why not wait so we can identify the American agent in Jerusalem?"

"Then we must involve the Hashemites. I say the hell with them. They and their British masters question every operation we undertake. There is no time."

Wahid stroked his beard. "I don't like it. I don't see the military significance. Who is this American? This doesn't sound like a CIA operation." He sighed, "More useless killing."

All of his adult life he had been fighting. His father, his brothers, his friends, all dead, all in the cause, but at what cost? And for what victory?

"We cannot question this order. It comes from the high priest of the Brotherhood."

"But I'm being asked to risk half my cell. We kill this American officer and the Israelis get fifty more F-4s."

"Wahid, Humbaba requires retribution. I will lead the operation myself. The American must die."

Major Wahid fell silent. Fanatics, he thought. They are brave but stupid. They kill women and children and sacrifice themselves for nothing. We will not win this round. Maybe the next. Someday perhaps we will trust each other and see the big picture. How ridiculous to think that the CIA would send an agent, in uniform, to Lebanon with a secret message to an important agent in Jerusalem.

"All right, Raffir," he agreed reluctantly. "You will lead the operation."

CHAPTER 43

THE THIRD WEEK, SATURDAY
BETWEEN TIBERIAS AND JERUSALEM

The road south from Tiberias to Jerusalem was a well-paved two-lane highway. Two thousand years earlier, the Roman legions of Vespasian and Titus drove their chariots on the stone roads, their foot soldiers marching in long, unbroken lines of burnished armor. Thirsty, dirty men, yet an awesome sight to chill the very soul of those tribesman who dared to stand and watch as this seemingly endless horde wended its way toward the capitol city. Titus had destroyed any cities in his path that had resisted and, after two years of sustained fighting, had subdued the Galilee. The fortress of Jotapata, defended by crack troops trained by General Josephus, had fallen after forty-seven days of brutal siege. Josephus himself was a captive of the Romans. It seemed that no force could stop this juggernaut.

Only Jerusalem stood, its walls a daunting challenge to the might of the Roman Empire. The forces defending the sacred city were small but determined. There would be no surrender. There had been several internecine battles between the Jewish factions in Jerusalem. The defenders were weakened but determined. The zealots who now controlled the capitol would fight to the death.

Sarah's jeep rattled along the uneven stone road, its worn-out shock absorbers protesting every foot of the way. David watched her in admiration. Sarah was a skillful driver. She missed potholes, circumvented rock barriers and sped along without missing a beat. She was, he silently observed, a remarkable woman. They had reached a stretch of highway that the British had failed to repave. Not believing it to be of strategic value, they had allowed it to deteriorate. Not a good decision since it was the last extended link on the main south road to the capitol city. The Israelis planned to improve it when the war ended—if, as Sarah observed, the war would ever end.

They were approaching an area where the road dipped into a deep gully. Sarah nervously scanned the surrounding hills. She nudged Herschel, her armed companion. "Keep your weapon ready. This is a perfect place for an ambush." Herschel clicked off the safety and moved the M-1 rifle from the floor mount to his lap.

They were almost to the bottom of the gully, ready to climb the upside out of the pocket, when the first shot rang out. It struck the front body of the jeep. Sarah careened the jeep to the opposite side of the road, heading for a nearby ditch. The shot was followed by a staccato burst of machine gun fire. Fortunately, most of the bullets fell short, spattering on the nearby road. One shot cracked the windshield.

"Keep your head down," she shouted, adding, "hit the ditch!"

Herschel exited the right side. A rifle bullet slammed into his shoulder. Bleeding and in obvious pain, he managed to crawl around the jeep. His M-1 lay in plain sight on the other side and the machine gun zeroed in on the rifle in an attempt to destroy it.

Sarah had unsheathed her Uzi. Given the distance, she knew the Uzi was useless but she also knew if their assailants came closer, it would prove deadly. Sarah noticed the attackers had parked a truck at the pinnacle of the hill. She felt a cold chill creep down her back. The enemy was known to pack explosives in a truck and send a suicide bomber crashing into Israeli ranks. "I'd give my right arm for a bazooka," she muttered to David. She frantically worked her pocket radio in the hope she could raise someone. The radio was silent, its signals obviously blocked by the hills.

As she bandaged Herschel she thought, it's hopeless and my fault for not bringing an extra rifle. Three helpless souls lying in a ditch carpeted by machine gun fire. Miraculously, no one else had been mortally hit yet, but she knew it was only a matter of time. It was all over. Any minute the truck would come crashing down and blow them all to the arms of Jehovah.

Helicopters have a unique sound—similar to the whop, whop, whop of the continuous beating of a massive drum. They let you know they are coming. The machine gun grew quiet. Sarah peeked over the side of the ditch. There was frenzied activity around the truck. The copter leaped over a nearby hill and headed directly at the truck, launching a rocket as it flew. Suddenly, the truck erupted into a sheet of flame followed by a massive explosion. But for the faint crackling of the fire set by the explosion, when the smoke began to clear the top of the hill was graveyard silent.

The helicopter's observer, radio operator, gunner and crew chief shouted, "I think we hit it!"

The pilot, a former U.S. Navy helicopter jockey, smiled to himself. "Yeah," he said quietly. "I think we hit it."

CHAPTER 44

THIRD WEEK, SATURDAY
THE WAILING WALL

"Do you require further assistance?" asked the helicopter pilot.

"I think we can handle it," Sarah said. "Many thanks. You guys performed a real mitzvah."

The helicopter, an ancient Sikorsky rescued from the trash heap by a sharp Israeli arms dealer, wagged its tail, gunned its throttle in a friendly gesture and flew off, rapidly disappearing into the distant clouds.

Somehow Sarah, the miracle lady, got the jeep started. It coughed, sneezed, cleared its pipes and moved reluctantly forward, struggling out of the ditch. She had also checked and bandaged Herschel's wound, judging it minor.

A few minutes after three, the tired trio arrived on the outskirts of Jerusalem. By 3:50 P.M. the jeep was parked less than a hundred yards from the Jaffa Gate, the doorway to the old city. Jaffa currently served as the dividing line between Jordanian and Israeli Jerusalem. It was guarded on the Israeli side by several soldiers and presented a formidable border between the two countries.

Sarah's instructions were to deliver David to the Israeli side of the gate exactly at four.

The two sat in the jeep awaiting the drop-dead moment. David was still nervous, though he had cleaned up as best he could in a nearby public restroom. He could not shake the feeling of dread that gnawed at his stomach. He was about to venture into an unknown world, a world of ruthless treachery peopled with vicious enemies.

While a truce existed, it only took one shot or one single knife-wielding Jordanian, acting alone, to break the fragile peace. He would be helpless and, worst of all, he had no idea what he was supposed to do or what, if any, prayers he was supposed to recite. This whole scenario pitched him into the rabbit hole of *Alice in Wonderland* where the busy bunny kept repeating "I'm late, I'm late" but never said for what. Then there was the glass that turned the world upside down. All of this made no sense, yet here he was in a jeep at the edge of the western world about to be transported into an eastern world where his people were not only unwelcome but, apparently, mortal enemies of the inhabitants.

"David! It's time. Are you okay?" The voice cut into his train of thought. In a second it heightened his fear and brought reality to his consciousness.

"Sarah, I am scared shitless. Why in the hell am I here?"

Sarah smiled, leaned over and kissed him tenderly on the cheek. "Boychik, there is a reason you are here. Of that, I am sure. My orders are to pick you up at the Jaffa Gate at midnight. I will be there." Sarah paused for a second and looked full into David's eyes. "And so will you," she said quietly.

CHAPTER 45

THIRD WEEK, SATURDAY
JAFFA GATE

At exactly 4:00 P.M., a neat young Jordanian officer armed only with a Webley automatic and a white flag, yet followed by six others with submachine guns, appeared at the Jaffa Gate.

"Is there a Captain Gold here?" he asked.

"There is," replied the Israeli soldier posted at the gate. He opened the gate carefully and smartly saluted the Jordanian officer. "Sir, Captain Gold is here and this is Lieutenant Sarah Elkind, his escorting officer." Sarah saluted smartly. A salute with equal courtesy was returned.

David, feeling shaky, with great trepidation, slowly got out of the jeep. He had the presence of mind to salute the Jordanian officer. He noticed there were at least six soldiers behind the Jordanian, all poised with submachine guns. David knew that once he crossed the line and the gate closed behind him, his life wasn't worth a rubber nickel. He felt naked, completely exposed.

Suddenly the Israeli sentry shouted, "Mustafa, is that you?"

"Yes, Sheldon," came the immediate answer.

The gate stopped closing and there was a single moment of extreme tension. David could see himself cut in half by a half dozen machine guns. The soldier called Mustafa stepped forward. Everyone gripped his weapon.

The Israeli sentry tossed a small package to the Jordanian. "I got you Chesterfields," he said.

"Great," replied Mustafa. "My mother thanks you, Sheldon."

Sarah watched until David disappeared behind the huge medieval gate. Corporal Sheldon Birnbaum smiled at Sarah "We have made our own peace agreement here at the Jaffa Gate, Lieutenant. Captain Gold will be fine."

Mustafa drove slowly toward another jeep parked in front of a huge stone wall. The wall looked to be part of an ancient fortification and was composed of hundreds of large black rocks. David noticed they were in a massive courtyard which, but for a few soldiers lounging about, was completely empty. The sun glinting off the surrounding buildings created a distorted, hazy picture at the top of the wall, as if the structures were part of a desert mirage.

As they approached the second jeep, David could make out a figure in a black suit. He wore a white collar and appeared to be waiting patiently for Mustafa to drive alongside. Mustafa pulled to a stop a few feet from the jeep. "I have your cargo, Father." He turned to David. "This is where you get off, Captain. Good luck."

Visibly reluctant to abandon the safety of the jeep, David carefully got out and approached the second vehicle. To his surprise, he was greeted by a red face and a jolly smile that, unspoken, proclaimed its Celtic origin. "Father McNalley's friend, Chaplain Shea," the face said, as the body extended its hand.

"Captain Gold," replied David, shaking the hand. Okay, he thought, what the hell happens now?"

"Captain Gold, I am supposed to leave you here until midnight so you can perform your mission. Good luck. I'll be back for you a few minutes before twelve."

With that, the Catholic priest saluted good-bye and drove off. David stared at the jeep until it lost itself in the sun's shadow. Then alone, surrounded by three thousand years of history and the ghosts of the multitudes of the many races and religions who died within these walls, David Gold lifted the colored shawl, that he had guarded and had protected him well, from his tote bag and placed it around his neck. He raised his eyes toward the heavens and cried, "O Lord, give this humble servant some guidance. What the hell should I do now?"

It felt like a thunderbolt. Lightning flashed. A great force struck David between his shoulder blades and drove him to his knees. For a split second the radiance blinded him. He lost touch with reality. The force kept him in a kneeling position. He could not lift his head.

Then the load lightened. The intense pressure ceased. He lifted his eyes and stood up.

* * * *

He was in a strange world, a large, tall room ringed by many stone pillars where men were dressed in cloaks and carried lighted torches. There were no women. There were many guards who carried spears and swords and shields and wore polished armor. They hung out in busy groups. One of the guards' officers noticed him and cried out in a commanding voice. "Hail, Flavius Josephus!"

David saluted back by thumping a fist to his chest. Apparently, he was mistaken for someone named Josephus. Toward the back of the gathering David noticed several circles of men. He distinguished them from the other soldiers by their dress. They wore black cloaks instead of the white traditional dress of the guards. He was puzzled. They looked familiar but the uniform was strange.

"Who are they?" He addressed the question to the back of the muscled guard who stood in front of him. The guard turned to reveal the hard faced grimace of Herculanus, the captain of the guard. He had led the small contingent of troops that had provided the escort during his recent incursion into the city.

"Has General Josephus forgotten our recent skirmish? These men are Sicarians. The scourge of the empire. They are here to murder Sylvanus when he renders his decision on the Jewish East Bank School."

David glanced around. The theatre area was rapidly filling. Evidently the so-called East Bank School decision was considered a vital issue. Many attendees were from the civil sector. But most were members of an occupying Roman legion. One chilling fact was clear. The Sicarians, with their raven black capes, constituted by far the majority of warriors. The Roman guard would be overwhelmed and massacred.

Herculanus patted his sword. "They will not succeed. I have ten of my best men here."

Almost at that moment a loud cheer arose at the theatre gate. Mounting a large black horse at the head of nearly two hundred Jewish guardsmen was Josephus' younger brother Aaron. A soldier by trade, Aaron surveyed the battlefield and quickly grasped the situation. "Follow me," he waved his broadsword. "Death to the Sicarians!"

At that moment, Gischala turned to ward off the blow from Josephus. He turned in the opposite direction and the thrust from Josephus tore into Gischala's chest. Josephus had put all his frustration and anger into the thrust. And so Gischala died, and with him the secret of who had guided the Romans through the underground cisterns that allowed them to take the fortress Antonia.

Sylvanus, unscathed, stood behind Herculanus. Now he turned to the Jew who had saved his life. "My eternal thanks, Josephus," he said. "You shall have your school."

****

The bolt of lightning that struck David felt like a drop hammer on his neck. He fell to his knees. When he regained his senses he saw Chaplain Shea, who led him outside the Jaffa Gate. Not twenty feet away, Sarah sat in her jeep with Herschel, who hugged his M-1 carbine as if it were his long-lost girlfriend. David was exhausted. Had the mission been accomplished? But what he really wanted to know was whether his girlfriend Maggie, the dark-haired girl, was actually dead.

****

At Western State Psychiatric Institute, Catherine Dematteo sat at her husband's bedside holding his hand. She prayed for a cure to his illness, begged God to end the nightmare besieging her family. Suddenly Sal released her hand. As if struck by the same bolt of lightning that dropped David to his knees, Sal sat straight up and said, "It's gone. This curse has lifted. I'm free!"

CHAPTER 46

LATE NOVEMBER 1955
PITTSBURGH

After those three mysterious weeks, winter came early to Pittsburgh, bringing snow flurries, wet pavements and a chill that sent shivers through a populace that could only dream of sultry Florida breezes and warm tropical sunshine.

The jury had been out for several hours. For the first two hours, Sal paced the floor of his office. He was joined by his partner, David, and a visibly nervous Father O'Malley. David, on the other hand, felt relaxed. Sal had done a terrific job at raising the defense of reasonable doubt. David had feared Sal would have a relapse, but not only had he performed admirably, he had clearly illustrated how anyone of a hundred or more people could have thrown the beer bottle that severely wounded the victim.

When he cross-examined the only witness who alleged he saw Tom Feeney hurl the bottle, the guy admitted on cross he'd had five boilermakers that evening. Sal countered with an expert witness, a Ph.D., who testified on direct examination that he had studied the effect of alcohol on the senses of human beings and that with well over a hundred drunken people present, given the witness's position at the bar and adding the five boilermakers he had admitted to, it was highly unlikely that he could have seen Tom Feeney or anyone else throw a beer bottle into the crowd.

The jury apparently agreed, and when they returned from their six-hour ordeal, they had voted eight to four in favor of acquittal. The judge dismissed the charges with an admonition that he didn't want to see any more drunken brawls, or next time they would all go to jail, and he would personally throw the key away.

Less than a week later, a six-man SWAT team, led by Jerome Becker, entered an upstairs room. They were members of an elite team carefully trained to conduct urban missions where the brass suspected that a firefight could occur and a lethal response might be required. Jerome seethed with a cold anger. His boss's niece had been murdered and he felt responsible. He would exact payment, but the first order of business was to find the dagger. Andy Seiler had ordered the early morning mission but he had miscalculated.

The suspect had spent the night elsewhere. The warrant emphasized a search of the premises was permitted. After two hours of searching, the cops found a wall safe behind a picture of a naked woman. Experts cracked it in ten minutes. Inside they found a wrinkled brown leather pouch that at first glance appeared worthless. When Jerome Becker reached inside the pouch he quickly removed his hand. The pouch felt hot, as if a bonfire raged inside. Jerome quickly doused the pouch and his hand in water. He used a drenched cold towel to attempt to extract the contents of the pouch again. This time he was successful. A metallic object wrapped in tissue paper fell to the floor with a loud clang. Becker carefully brushed aside the paper and found himself staring at a beautiful jeweled dagger.

"Well, my friend," he said, "you certainly caused a lot of trouble."

****

The combined law enforcement council met on schedule the following Monday. Everyone came to hear Andy Seiler's explanation of the brutal museum murders. His story was bolstered by statements from several guests including the archaeologist and curator Benson Throckmorton and an eminent guest psychiatrist who explained the difference between hallucinations and visions. Dr. Bernie Adler made no mention of time travel except to indicate that the entire mystery had been unraveled by a brilliant young doctor named Max Vogel.

Attorney Marvin Marx had a question. "What about the dagger and the first murders?"

"Glad you asked, Mr. Marx." Andy's face took on a stern look. "We have evidence that two members of the Sicerian cell murdered guards Harry Abrams and Willard Sockel at the Carnegie Mellon Museum, the same two who attempted to kidnap Catherine Dematteo. Sal has been cleared. You needn't concern yourself with this case any longer."

Then Captain Andy Seiler motioned to David. "Will you finish the story please, Mr. Gold." And to a rapt audience, he did.

* * * *

The next morning David went alone to the Sacred Heart cemetery. He stood over Maggie's grave.

"I am sorry, little Irish, that Max and I got you mixed up in this. You are a beautiful person, and I shall never forget you. I will love you, always love you." He wept. "Somewhere, somehow," he said. "I know you can hear me."

HISTORICAL AFTERWORD

In 70 C.E., the Roman legions of Titus, son of Emperor Vespasian, sacked and destroyed the Temple of Jerusalem. It is estimated that over 600,000 men, women and children were massacred in this first genocide of the Jews. A Jewish historian named Flavius Josephus accompanied the Romans. The city had been taken and the temple destroyed, but only after four years of sustained bloody fighting.

Josephus had been the commander of the Jewish forces in Galilee. He had been captured and taken before Vespasian where, for reasons still unclear, he was not only granted amnesty but also given permission to join the Romans. He chronicled the events of the siege and the subsequent devastation of Jerusalem. Josephus, later renamed Flavius Josephus, died circa 100 C.E., a respected historian who to this day is reputed to have written the most comprehensive and credible eyewitness account of those violent times, when a divided Jewish nation valiantly battled the might of Imperial Rome.

The times also nurtured the birth of a messianic warlike religion that emanated from the gentle teachings of the Carpenter of Nazareth. This religion ultimately spread across half the world. It was called Christianity.

To many Jewish scholars and teachers, Josephus was the worst kind of rebel and traitor: a Jew who sold out his people for personal survival. His infamy dwarfed the sin of Cain and his name was cursed through the ages.

ABOUT THE AUTHOR

Currently in his 86th year, Jay Cooper has had an extensive background in military service, law, education and the aerospace industry. This experience, along with a life-long passion for history, became the basis for *Hammurabi's Dagger*, his first novel. A native of Pittsburgh, Pennsylvania, Mr. Cooper was a World War II Merchant Marine radio operator, traversing the Pacific on an oil tanker that brought supplies to the troops. After graduating the University of Pittsburgh law school, he spent a few years in private practice, then signed on as a U.S. Air Force Assistant Judge Advocate working with the Strategic Air Command and Air Force Logistics Command. While stationed in Morocco, he served as liaison to the International Court in Tangiers where he negotiated international agreements in Europe and Africa.

Mr. Cooper remained in the Air Force JAG as a reservist, eventually retiring after 31 years as a full colonel. During this time his legal career continued, first as a civilian Chief of Procurement Law for McClellan Air Force Base, followed by Division Legal Counsel for Litton Industries, then Legal Counsel for Ford Aerospace and finally 17 years as a Corporate Director of Small and Minority Business for Northrop Grumman. While at Northrop he developed training courses on TQM and Negotiation Tactics and served as liaison to the U.S. Congress, testifying before the House Armed Services Committee, Senate Small Business Committee and White House Committee on Minority Business.

His extensive teaching career includes graduate and undergrad-level courses in international law, business and legal ethics, and government contracts at Stanford, UCLA, Webster University, and a number of community colleges. He has been a guest lecturer at the U.S. Department of Commerce and, during his retirement years, has led seminars for Osher Lifelong Learning through the UCI extension on topics including World War II and Famous Trials in History. In addition to his JD law degree and BA in history and political science, Mr. Cooper is a member of the State Bar in Pennsylvania, Ohio and California and is a cum laude graduate of National Defense University Industrial War College. He and his wife, Judy, have been married 49 years and live in Corona del Mar, California. They have two grown children, Beth and Bryan.